the Ghost who wouldn't give up

Will Lorimer

**INKISTAN
.COM**

ISBN 978-1-536902-31-0

Typeset for print by Electric Reads
www.electricreads.com

I would like to thank my friends in Mexico who gave me such a warm welcome, and kept me safe, and made my time there so memorable. You know who you are.

For their support, I also thank: Deirdre Nolan, Ron Smith, Magic Gordon, Bernard Shir-Cliff, Dougie Barnett, Sheila Brook; Will Beaton, my sister May, the team at Electric Reads, Emma Westwater at Source Design, Judy and Julio at Viva Mexico, and all the friends who have helped me along the way.

PROLOGUE

R ain was falling in sheets, the college campus dark and deserted. The hazy outlines of its postmodern buildings could have been the towers of a long-abandoned city, lost in gloom but for a haloed light spearing from the farthest block.

Behind the steamed-up glass of that one unboarded ground-floor window, two men, obviously arguing. The nearest, broader in the beam than he stood. Yea, not to put too fine a point on it, borderline midget, back turned, fists bunched at his sides. His mustard jacket and flaming red hair, fluorescent in the harsh neon light. The other, by his white shirt, black tie and rigid demeanour, clearly an official, sat behind a desk, empty but for a phone.

Though unseen in the darkness, my arrival outside the window had heralded an impasse of sorts, but then the official seemed to relent, reached into a drawer of his desk and, after a pause, passed something thin over. The stocky wee man hastily pocketed whatever it was and turned around, presenting a face I had never seen before.

But at least I had his name right. It seemed to fit his angry glare as he stepped out into the rain, and, though he did not have a droopy moustache to match his red hair, to me he was still the mad Mexican of the *Loony Tunes cartoons* I so loved as a child.

As I introduced myself, Wee Donald's beady eyes glinted dangerously, but then he flashed a broken-toothed smile and punched me in the ribs.

As I rubbed my bruised side, he growled in a thick accent of the old country, 'Ach, I remember ye now! Y'er a fuckin' prayer answered, an' just when I need ye's. Yesterday my brother was swept away in a flood in fuckin' Can-ad-a!' He spat each syllable. 'D'ye ken whit tha' means? It's Spanish, *ca nada*, eh! Meaning there's nothin' there. The wurds o' a Spanish sailor, looking oot tae the fogbanks o' Labrador, frae the furst galleon passin'. *Ca nada*,' he repeated, in a climaxing dirge. 'Well noo,'

1

he sighed. 'That's true. An' today I learned,' he grinned, a characteristic of hard men of the old country imparting bad news, 'I wuz sacked six months ago from this dump.' He gave me a new look of approbation, implying I'd earned at least a quantum of respect. 'You're fuckin' lucky tae catch me, I wuz only here tae collect the outstanding.' He brandished a thin envelope. 'This, my wife says, is all that's stonding between wir family an' destitution.' His jaw jutted. 'But I say it's beer money,' he said, extending broad hands, 'And you're my first foot from hame in mair than twen'y years.' He wiped a tear from an eye as he embraced me. 'I love you brother,' he sobbed, resting his red head against my chest as I wondered how the fuck I had gotten there.

In the small hours of the day my lease on the Greenwich Village apartment was up, I was awoken by the phone ringing off the hook, and with a name tipping my tongue. Yea, I knew that imperious caller hanging on the line. Ignoring her insistent clamour, I thumbed the dog-eared pages of my address book, until my finger stopped on the name of a professor of Meso-American studies, under a college address in Mexico City. I couldn't fix the face, but as I closed the apartment door, leaving the phone to ring on, I remembered our chance meeting on an ancient mound in the middle of a desolate moor, Macbeth country.

On the summit loomed three standing stones known as the 'little sisters', huddled over the 'cauldron', a truncated black stone cupping the sky in a pool of rainwater. Mist coiled, the clouds were low and the wind biting. I was there with a party of friends, but had drifted away, when we struck up conversation, while watching a small police car approaching slowly along a long straight track, from where the distant hills blurred into the sky, making the moorland seem a desolation that went on forever. We heard the car stop out of sight below, before two red-faced policemen clambered panting over the brow of the mound. Yes, even in that remoteness, there was no escape from the long arm of the law. I'd heard the news item on the radio that morning, and now two police constables were delivering it to a friend in my party. It seemed that the elderly couple who drove their BMW into a dry dock in Blackpool had been his parents. I didn't know whether to be happy or sad they weren't mine, but I did get that college address.

2

Despite or because of all the threats and insults, the driver of the taxi I'd hired at the airport, depleting what remained from my cards, emptied at the ATMs of la Guardia, refused to drive to Wee Donald's locale, and instead set us down in pouring rain at a deserted street corner, some distance away.

'Pussy,' Wee Donald called after the departing cab, its one tail light blurring in the rain before it disappeared, a red streak into a maze of back streets.

'What's the problem?' I asked, looking down at my bags and the crate of beer Wee Donald had just bought at a 24-hour *cerveceria*.

'Och,' Wee Donald shrugged, 'A few mair murders and kidnappings than usual these past months.'

'Really?' I said, more alarmed by his nonchalance.

'Ach dae fuss ye'rself. You're wi' me. Perrrfectly safe! I'll show ye's.' Wee Donald cupped his hands about his mouth. 'Fuck yuz cunts!' he bellowed at the shuttered windows of tenements on all sides. 'Come and get us, assholes.'

'That just proves you're mental,' I laughed, as his challenge boomed back, echoing empty city streets.

'Aye,' Wee Donald nodded, 'But mental means too much fuckin' bother tae the murder gangs round here. Besides,' he grinned, 'They're a' boys, no real men like uz. C'mon,' he said, heaving the beer crate onto a broad shoulder, 'We've a wake tae get oan wi'.'

The block where Wee Donald lived appeared archaic and semi-derelict, sandwiched as it was between a sports arena and the glass tower block of a TV corporation. At street level the block held some small shops, all shuttered, while above the windows were oddly juxtaposed, suggesting the old building had been rebuilt, and more than once.

'Bonny, eh?' Wee Donald said, nodding at a pinched face that had appeared in a lighted first floor window above a fizzing neon sign, which featured a cherry and a lime in a cocktail glass, blinking red and green, at the corner of the block.

'If you say so,' I shrugged, wondering if the woman was his wife.

'No' her,' Wee Donald grinned, '*Her.*' he waved his free hand, taking in the whole building. 'Look at thae lines mon. Dae they no' remind ye o' a ship o' state, magnificent eh? Originally that was whaur Prince Falling Eagle hung out. Yes, it was Cuhuatomec's fuckin' palace. The last Aztec building left stonding in Mexico shitty,' he laughed, with a sweep of his hand including the whole city, 'Though o' course it's much broken doon noo. Dates back tae 'afore the Conquest.' He pointed to the lower facade. 'See whaur that plaister's fallen awa', yon stane's the pink o' auld Tenochitlán.'

'Pay any nae heed tae the missus,' Wee Donald cautioned over a heavy Latin beat from somewhere below, leading the way up worn wooden steps. 'She cannae abide me drinkin',' he chortled, 'But that's her fuckin' problem, no' mine.' Throwing open the front door, he waved me in.

In a small dingy kitchen, Wee Donald's wife was on her knees, polishing pairs of kiddies' shoes. By the tears stains on her sallow cheeks and her bleary red eyes, she had been weeping a week. Hung on the back of a chair were school uniforms, a girl's and a boy's, neatly pressed.

'Oh god, not more beer,' she bleated in an accent redolent of Pimms, cucumber sandwiches and croquet on green summer lawns. Flicking a couple of strands of hair from her eyes she noticed me over the crate on Wee Donald's broad shoulder. 'And who's this?' her thin lips twisted. 'Another stray from the street?'

'A freend a' the wi' frae the auld country, so you be mindin' yer manners, hen,' Wee Donald's glowered.

'Welcome, I'm sure,' the English wife muttered, resuming polishing shoes, which, in the dingy kitchen, already shone with a brilliance that was almost supernatural. 'Your other *friends* are in the back,' she added, as under her knees the floor rafters began to shake, and the Latin music below increased in volume.

'How do you put up with that racket? I said, following Wee Donald's dancing zigzag course, hefting his beer crate with surprising agility to avoid the various tins that had been strategically positioned to catch the steady dripping of water from gaping holes in the plaster ceiling. Twisting around, he raised a finger to his mouth. 'Ssh,' he cautioned, swaying uncertainly, 'Dinnae want tae wake them.' He pointed through the glass door of a bedroom where two children lay sleeping. Just their small faces above bunched covers, blinking pink, white, green, and back again, as the neon sign below their window fizzed and sparked in the heavy rain.

'Aye, I ken what ye'r thinking, son.' Wee Donald grinned like a fiend in the lurid light. 'Yon's Mexico's national colours! C'mon.' He turned, resuming his balancing act, like a footballer jinxing the opposition, dodging tackles – only they were tins – on into the gloom of the dingy passage, throbbing with the sound of Santana from below.

'That's wir resident DJ doon stairs in the... heh... heh transvestite brothel,' he called back.

'A transvestite brothel? You're putting me on,' I laughed.

'See for yourself,' Wee Donald said, stopping, his florid face under-lit by a roseate glow as, swaying, he pointed to a crack in the bare boards by his feet. Enough of a gap to make out a giant pink puff ball and the bouffant hairstyle of an Elvis wannabe in a sequin suit on a stage directly below.

'That's the tosser at his decks,' Wee Donald sniggered. 'Thinks he's the king o' fuckin' Graceland. I only wish he'd play something apart frae fuckin' "Black Magic Wumman".'

At the end of the passage a door opened into a lounge furnished in contemporary, if conventional, style, hung with large lithographs of Mayan temples. It was uninhabitable, however, since a large section of the ceiling had fallen onto the sofa and carpet with the start of the seasonal rains a few days before.

Behind a door, six bearded anthropologists in worsted jackets were crammed into a narrow, smoke-filled study, done up like a train carriage, its walls decorated with railway memorabilia from the old country, and black and white photographs of Wee Donald's school days. The general familiarity of the images, together with the rusting enamel signs from the Age of Steam, made me feel I was trapped in a time tunnel as I sat on the edge of a chaise longue beside two Mexican men – obviously *caballeros*, since both wore tweed jackets swapping insults and turns as they played backgammon for high stakes that, with every few rolls of the dice, kept doubling. A stack of dollars beside the board on the table staked against a set of keys for a Cherokee 4x4 and a kilo bag of smelly grass buds.

It was a fine wake and, as the night wore on, talk turned to a recent find by one of the group in a Mayan pyramid threatened by a new highway being cut through the jungle. If the artefacts in the unopened chamber weren't removed soon, the precious hoard would be looted by the *jefé* of the road gang. A rescue mission was proposed, and I was invited to join what could be a rewarding adventure.

But I had other, potentially more lucrative plans in mind, and so, my head swimming from booze and dope, I left the claustrophobic study and wearily climbed some steep wooden stairs to a flat roof, hemmed in by the giant satellite dishes of a TV relay station on one side and the curving roof of the sports arena on the other. It was when I saw the blue flashes of electric plasma, rimming the big satellite dishes and striking upwards in a column of rising sparks from the dome of the sports arena, that my head exploded. Through slashing rain, outlined in a luminous interplay of banded colours, soaring out of a purple backdrop of cumulus cloud, the shadow play of the three puppeteers of my existence. Gods or demons, I didn't know, though the thought did intrude that my life was hanging in the balance; in an abyssal realm higher powers were dickering, my fate being decided, as I stood transfixed.

BOOK I

THE SON

1. THE SUN OF DEATH

I was looking out a bus window, half-blinded from staring at a red eye spiked on black peaks. Silhouetted *sierras*, tricorn witches' hats in a huddle, casting inky shadows and spilling a scratchy desert of tarbrush and thorn, lit like the set of a Mexican snuff flick. And the sun? Going down to do battle with the astral armies of night. To return? No say. Once, that depended on the valour of the vanquished - thousands of hearts at a time, ripped out on Aztec pyramids, cascading sacrificial blood. A tide that, by the evidence of my eyes, still lapped the high chaparral hereabouts ...

'*Mira! El sol del muerte!*' Cutting off my mental drift, the hairy smoker from the seat behind, blowing smoke in my ear, leaning heavily on my shoulder, jabbing his burning *cigarro* at an angry face glaring in a bus window.

'The sun of death,' I recycled, peering through dirty glass, between the tall telegraph poles, sentinels by the desert road, strobing past my window. Do re mi, the wires carrying messages I didn't want to hear. This joker with the shaggy black dog moustache, breathing brimstone and beer, giving the local weather lore. Wanting me to believe that the *sombrero* of a corona brimming the sun indicated bad weather on the road ahead. Considering that high cirrus, I supposed he was probably right. But those wisps of an advancing weather front, might just as well have been racked seaweed, seen from the deck of the doomed ship of my drowned hopes, spiralling down to Davey Jones' locker room, in the stygian depths of the Sargasso Sea.

'*Es muy mallow para gringo!*' he insisted in guttural Spanish even worse than mine, suggesting that Nauatl, the ancient language of these remote parts, was his mother tongue.

But when I shrugged, wondering what was so bad for this *gringo* in particular, he seemed to take the hump and sat back down, raising a squawk from his prize cockerel in a crate on the seat beside him. Bemused, I turned away and got the picture. Glaring through the bus window, not the sun king in a *sombrero*, his valour guard trailing sparks over the *sierras*, but the grinning skull of a ghostly bandit chief – Pancho Villa, or some such masked desperado, holed up since the revolution. Every night, come hail, thunder and lightning, going down on the three sisters, riding out on the broomstick of the tarbrush horizon, flying over bandit badlands, thorned as a flagellant's cloak.

Mexico, more than a pilgrimage, *mucho mas*.

And now, cupped by a black caldera, pinioned by three purple-robed eminences, a shimmering egg, shrinking as it descended into a snake of gold cracking the world, coursing vitrine peaks. Then, as it flashed out, captured in an eidetic blink, a burning nest high in a tree, hatching a baby snake that changed into a yellow oriole bird and flew away chirping into the blue.

Was that from the never-neverland land of lost childhood or a long-forgotten dream? How could I ever know; my memory was so porous. And no, it wasn't the drugs. The cause in a mire that needed examining like my head. If I survived the next leg, there would be time, I supposed, turning to look out the window again, as a fleeting shadow crossed the bus and I caught a glimpse of wing tips as a large black bird swept low above.

Another sign as the little bus banded red and green, the colours of *Líneas Fronteras*, the only bus company serving these parts, lurched from uncertain asphalt to certain cobbles, paused, gathering energy before the long assault on bandit foothills. There, at the turn, a crude sign with the words '*Trópico de Cancer*' grooved on bleached wood, marking the crossing of a boundary and another journey begun.

Behind me now routes *norté* and the junk of my past. Was that phone still ringing, in my old apartment? I could still hear it. No matter, what glittered but baubles and trinkets. Slow lanes on a fast track, jumping saddle to saddle. Haymaking in the fields of my youth sheaved with golden stacks blowing chaff in the wind, but now, entering my thirties, all I had was a fistful of corn slipping my grasp.

I was here, too, sheltering in a geological book so vast I couldn't make out the pages. There, high on the haunch of some antediluvian beast, my name in looping copperplate on cinnamon-banded scree, proving I had made it - if not hereafter, then *sic gloria transit*, as a bishop might have opined. Quinton, after my paternal grandfather; Eric, from a Laplander great-uncle on my mother's side, no doubt a tall straw-haired numbskull like myself; Diogenes, from when I slept in a bathtub in a flat shared by three girls who took pity on my homeless condition and nicknamed me after the cynic philosopher. I loved them so much I adopted the moniker by deed poll, and signed QED with a flourish on a bouncing cheque at the restaurant where we dined, after I flunked out of university without a degree, but with sad parting kisses from all three, who might have been sisters they were so similar in looks, though not nature. In the plain words of a dead language, *quo erat demonstrandum*, meaning thus proved the proposition. An absent father's pronouncement, I imagined, upon receiving the news of my latest failure from Mr Crook. Not that the well-worn Latin phrase would have meant anything to the other passengers - all *mestizos*, Native American genes predominating. All moustachioed, *machos and muchachas*, bumping two and three to a seat, like this was the love bus to Cancun, hanging on, hanging in, even the goggle-eyed turkey, dangling over the back of that portacabin squaw blocking the aisle, joining in the fun. I was alone, a stranger in the midst of one big happy family.

We had reached a way station in a gloomy gully, the most level gradient thus far. Even so, all that stopped the little bus from rolling back the way we had come was a boulder wedging a bald front wheel, parked perilously close to the sagging roofs of some shacks shedding tiles – telescoping terracotta dammed by the roadside ridge. A whole tribe lived down there. At the head of a steep path, by the open bus door, three, four generations. Gaunt, pale, pubescents; tots saddled on hips. More barefoot children clutching the torn skirts of bent-backed crones, who might yet be in only their thirties, I guessed, watching them passing back cracked containers filled with water, careful not to spill a precious drop. Out front, *el comandante* bus driver doing much the same. Just the shiny brim of his cap and gold star, lost in a rush of steam as he refilled the radiator. Ahead, cresting the long spine of the canyon, a pair of lofty pines, black against the electric *sierra* twilight, marking a gateway, and a couple of stars pirouetting in the azure - astral outriders from the netherworld.

I was jolted back to the now by a young girl standing outside at the bus window, staring out of my mirror image on darkening glass. Under the brim of my black hat, which we both shared in the window, my pale foreign face, her Toltec eyes, my Castilian chin, her chapped cheeks, my mercenary jowl, her tribe's pain, absolved in a new world trigonometry, proving that victim and oppressor can be one and the same. Of course I was a *gringo*, with my green eyes and white skin, no one could mistake me for anything else. But she was safe with me, and could keep her virtue intact, the only treasure she had left. No, not I. Not a drop of red conquistador blood in these blue veins. Well, none that I knew of.

'... neh ... neh ... neh ... 1,' the nasal sound issuing the barrel-chested *hombre* sitting next to me, snoring since Chihuahua with his *sombrero* over his face. Now the brim was pushed back on glittering black eyes focused on the Super Lights in my denim breast pocket – Yankee cigarettes, another form of currency in out-of-the-way places south of the Rio Grandé. Good for petty bribes and breaking the ice.

'... neh ... neh ... neh ...' the sniggers continued as I split the soft pack and, with a practiced slap to the base, raised a couple of butts to order. Slyly he took one, tucked that behind an ear, winked and reached out again.

'Go on,' I said, staring at his fingernails, 'They're only dirty frees.' Of course I meant to say 'duty'. Same difference, sometimes.

'... neh-neh-neh ... *gracias señor*,' he somehow managed between nasal snickers, grinning hugely, revealing a mouth full of gum boils pegged down by a few decayed stumps, like the remnants of an old sea pier washed by black tides.

'*De nada*,' I shrugged, flicking a flame on my old brass zippo, thinking of neurotics I had known who would have simply expired at such a sight. Yet he seemed hale and hearty. Perhaps those pustules actually kept him healthy.

After cogitating on nicotine, recycling smoke via stained moustaches and flaring nostrils – an economy measure born of hard times? – his black fingernail prodded in my direction again ...

'Ahem ...' he coughed. Perhaps he thought I was *alto Anglo* and that this was the correct manner of address for such a *caballero* – *I was* dressed in the best of British worsted gear; in Mexico, apparently, such apparel denoted a gentleman of worth. '*Tieñes niños, señor?*'

'*Si* ...' I replied, feeling pressure as termite eyes bored in.

'*Hijos o hijas?*' He was asking if I had sons or daughters.

Thinking that Toltec girl last seen through a bus window, '*Ninas,*' I sighed. '*Ey tu?*'

'*Hijos!*' he snapped, raising a fist – a hard-on for the universe, the bus and me.

I smiled thinly.

'*Quantas niñas tieñes, señor?*' He grinned, eyes like he was hypnotising a snake. That snake was me. Perhaps he was after my cigarettes or wallet, or both? The Third World over, card-carrying *gringos* are excluded from age-old laws of hospitality. I guessed, given half a chance, those mountain natives would rob you of all you owned, but – since they were mountain natives – if they found you hungry and alone, they would snatch the *tortillas* from *bambino* mouths to feed you. Probably put you up in the only bed, if they had one ...

Thinking of a couple of the strangers put up in my bed, I held up two fingers. Perhaps it was the *mescal?* That inner fire glittering his dark eyes reminding me of distant flares – the Pémex refinery passed in the desert – just gas burning off; in his case, I supposed cactus spirits. Probably home-brewed *mescal*. I wondered if he was carrying any. Sure would relieve the tedium.

A question seemed expected. After all, we were discussing the relative merits of our respective, in my case fictional, families, even if we were both doing so in broken Spanish, which for him, being a native of these mountains, I supposed was a second language.

'*Ey tu?*' I blinked.

'*Diez!*' again *el borracho* shot up a fist, this time twice fanning and retracting his fingers, in the manner of mental defectives, and dealers in futures markets.

'Ten! And *hijos* too,' I exclaimed, entering the number in the notebook open on my knee, adding, for his benefit, 'You old *macho* son of a gun, you.' I winked, knowing in such conversations language is not a barrier. It was obvious, the sperm count rose with elevation. Clearly, it was the altitude that counted, not the attitude. We were still climbing. The desert plains, now miles below, those Pémex flares still burning, way off in the west. A world away now, on this cobbled old road winding the three sisters towards a glittering Horus eye, the shining capstone of an icy peak reflecting the last rays of the sun, heading towards a tunnel leading to the other side of this untoward Mexican reality.

Another question seemed imminent as, with a lurch of the bus, he shouldered in, boss-eyed with determination to get whatever it was off his barrel chest.

'Cigarettes?' I ventured, wondering how I was supposed to reach my breast pocket when we were virtually chin to chin.

'*Qué es?*' I demanded, returning his blind stare.

'*Señor,*' he smiled, '*Tu tieñes ochos la mismo que la bruja de la norté.*'

'You're saying I have eyes the same as the *bruja* of the north?' I recycled hoarsely.

'*Si,*' he nodded. Clearly satisfied he'd sussed me out, he settled back in his seat.

More than I had at that moment, I reflected. But the last detail suggested I was on the right track, and that somewhere up in the mountains were the answers I needed to penetrate the fogs of an amnesia my New York analyst, a practitioner of the Now School of Therapy, failed to dispel, connected to an early trauma, haunting my dreams as a child, reoccurring in nightmares ever since, reaching across the years like the left hand of darkness.

2. THE TUNNEL

We had reached Capstone Canyon. Sheer ice walls ascending to Asgard via haberdasheries and a black void. Dead ahead, the way through to Valhalla, where Woden and Votan were waiting. Mixing my mythic metaphors again, but then in the Nordic and Central American legends both were travelling tricksters who 'measured the world' and wore black hats with big brims and matching cloaks: a dress code that Cortez adopted on the advice of the witch Malinché, who had him delay landfall in the Americas to coincide with the prophesied day of Votan's return. Like myself, I reflected, cloaked in darkness, hiding my pale face below a black brim. Ahead, the gaping tunnel; at first glance, less an entrance and more a mouth, stalactites of ice spectral in the beam of a lone headlight, so many fangs of a canine bite. Cerberus perhaps, or just the hound of the Baskervilles – different cultures, same myth. Closer, a rustic cabin set-down on the icy ground as if it had been helicoptered up from the Tyrol. The shingle roof dusted by snow, wide eaves sheltering a billy goat, bearded as Satan at a sabbat, yellow eyes turning luminescent in the glare of our bus' headlight, tethered to wooden boards banded familiar red and green, suggesting a far-flung outpost of empire. A supposition confirmed when, straight out of an old comic book, goose-stepped a major-domo buttoned up to his chin in the livery of *líneas fronteras*. A hat to cap our bus driver's; bigger, grander, more gold braiding. Seven-pointed stars like on the Australian flag, suggesting that the story of the Ozzie explosives experts, once employed in the mines hereabouts, might be true. An impressive sight, certainly, as he marched across the frozen ground to the driver's window and tore a ticket out of a little book, receiving a dirty ten peso note in exchange, then saluting smartly, stepping back, and we were moving once more, heading for an icy black hole.

Mary, Mother of God. Jesus, blessed redeemer, protect us from the *malo gnómos* that dwell under the earth ... well, something like that. Then, more gabbled prayers from the passengers, as we entered a rough-hewn passage, its walls riddled with voids that I supposed were old mines. But that wasn't all. After about five minutes, the little bus stopped at a branching of the passageway, prompting another mad session of furtive crossing and native mumbo-jumbo. Not because of our driver's uncertainty over directions, as I had assumed, but a candlelit grotto to the right side. Bus exhausts fanning an avenue of wavering flames, leading to an altar cleaved out of living rock, below a gnarled white Christ impaled on stellate silver pickaxes and shovels, the polished metal of the implements gleaming in the gloom.

'Neh neh neh,' a familiar nasal snicker sounded in my right ear. '*Es una MADERA!*'

'Yea, yea, I can see that,' I smiled, glad to see my companion back at his *borracho* best. 'It's made out of wood.'

'*No, no, señor.*' Pointing with a stubby finger, he leaned heavily across me. '*Estas Christos es nacio en la madera.*'

'Born in the wood,' I repeated, peering through dirty window glass. 'Yes, I can see now the statue's naturally formed,' I said, noticing the pale bark was stippled like that of white oak. 'How odd.'

'*Es un milagroso,*' he insisted slyly.

'Sure,' I smiled, reminded of the frequency of miracles in Mexico, wondering how much more ubiquitous, then, in the last unmapped range in Central America. Unmapped? Because, as Wee Donald went on to explain, invariably the three sisters were blanketed in cloud, while magnetic anomalies and the frequent storms made aerial reconnaissance simply too dangerous.

'*De hacé mucho tiempo.*'

'From the old days, uh-huh,' I nodded.

'*Cuando lás Trés Hermanitás cubiertas del arboles.*' He went on, confirming at least I'd guessed right the local name of the mountains.

'When trees covered the three little sisters?' I exclaimed, forgetting in my excitement a pair of lofty pines, last seen from the bus stop, silhouetted on the *sierra* skyline. 'I don't believe you.'

'*Si, señor, antes el conqustadores, lás sierras es un jardín mas sagrado.*'

'A sacred garden, my god, yes, I can see that.' I muttered, the lost pieces of a scattered jigsaw that baffled scholars down the ages reforming, as I pictured the fabled garden, which in the legends was guarded by the three daughters of night. 'Then, after the Conquest,' I continued excitedly, 'All the trees were cut-down for pit props. Yea, all the locals converted at the point of a sword, and indentured in the new mines. Their only solace, Jesus, the living spirit of the garden, pointing the way through to the ...'

Fortunately, before I could turn even more pedantic, movement, blessed movement. Up front, our steersman, outlined against the moving picture projected on a windscreen by the bus' wayward eye. The headlight illuminating incoming ... rough-cut, choppy waves, the tunnel walls flashing silver as if shoals of swordtails were passing through. Once a phantom party shouldering picks and shovels, shielding their eyes as we shaved past. Miners I supposed, heading to the Chapel of the Lost Christ, to kneel before starting the back shift, in one of the many shafts leading off the tunnel.

3. IN TOWN, LOOKING ABOUT ...

Last off and last in, everyone else scattered to the four corners, not
even echoing footsteps to guide me, stumbling over the rutted
cobbles that served for a street; a Mexican stand-off of slab-
sided buildings, outlined in a lightning flash, vaulted stone aspiring
to crow steps and turrets. Did I say Mexico? More like a stage set for
Don Giovanni. Bring on the kettle drums. Now the lightning forking
on fifteenth-century Pamplona, minus the frills. A medieval slum town
after the plague, following the footsteps of the Grim Reaper. All the
population, with the exception of the town doctor and a black cat, in
mass graves or long since rotted behind boarded doors. Wee Donald had
been right. This ghost town was the best preserved, most authentic and
least-known *pueblo fantasmos fabulosa* in all of the Americas, the Town
With No Name. Surpassing strange, yet so eerily familiar, as if I had been
here before. An impossibility, but then so was this medieval town and
those three sisters above, their jagged peaks, vivid in a lightning strike. As
if all were coexisting in a Möbius present, that would have been doubly
perfect, had not I recalled my secret purpose, born out of a past that
was nothing if not imperfect – and questions, so many questions, about
missing chapters in my palimpsest, scattered life.

One more thing to do, but first I had overcome this overwhelming
desire to turn and run, all the way back to my old brownstone apartment.
Shutting my eyes, I could almost hear that phone still ringing as I raced
up the stairs and flung open the door. But, I reminded myself, that
was then and this was now. And, as my analyst might have said, the
eternal NOW is always moving on. The past? *No existé nada*; only the
present. Who knows what might transpire? I must forget my dragon
Chinese landlady and lately hard-to-please lover, and our metro-life
that never was in her refurbed duplex on 5th. My analyst was right, this
was something I had to face on my own.

23

I opened my eyes. The ringing stopped. Before me was an heavy looking door, its blackened stone lintel, carved with sheaves of corn and the Roman numerals MCDXXXII – if my prep-school Latin served me correctly – dating the building to sixty years before Columbus landed in the Americas, just as I had been assured. And, above that, a rusting sign painted with the faded legend, '*La Castilla de la Dinero*', swaying slightly in the gusting wind. Its slow creaking, I realised, translating in my head, as the ringing of a phone. There was nothing else to do, but take courage in both my hands, along with that door knocker.

Just audible, shuffling steps, then high on the door a small panel sliding back on a metal grill and, behind that, a suspicious eye, green as the ice on Scapa Flow, ringed with mascara.

'Go away!' Heavily accented. Resonating halls of memory I'd thought a closed chapter. Even shouting the same message as before, but with the addendum, 'We are closed for the season.'

'But I'm a friend of … ah, Anon's,' I improvised woodenly, reasoning Wee Donald had enough woes without a curse from the *bruja de la norté* adding to his troubles.

'Anon? Who is this Anon? I do not know any Anon!'

'Let me in!' I spat back, a familiar blood rage taking hold. 'All the way from Chihuahua. Three hundred crappy miles on a wooden bus seat, with the black laptop of Mictlán on my knees,' I snarled, mixing my metaphors yet again. 'My name's Pilgrim, Peter to my friends, and bus-buggered is not the word!'

'That is so much better Peter, I love lap-dogs too.

'Specially Chihuahuas. Such long tongues,' she chuckled, drawing a collection of long bolts.

I had only a photograph to remember her by – arm in arm with my father, entering a society fancy dress ball – a pouting Amazon, stacked in matching silver Stetson and stilettos, looming over a Roman proconsul in toga and circlet of laurel. Unchanged as far as I could gather, except she was now clad in a plaid dressing gown instead of burlesque Scythian chariot gear. Still, looking down, in her right hand a candle, in her left anodised metal. A pistol, small but no doubt deadly. Given her former position, could it be anything else? Palmed into a pocket as she pulled open the heavy creaking door. Some things don't change. Helga, straw-haired troll of my childhood nightmares. The hand that rocked my cradle. There are mothers and there are *mothers*. Mine was a crocodile, crawled out of a primordial swamp; such was my fate. But I deserved her, and fool that I was I'd actually searched her out. Now *that* I couldn't believe. If I pretended strength perhaps I would be. But strong enough? One thing and one thing only in my favour: she could have no inkling who I was. Let it remain so. Mummy, alien womb that bore me.

4. MOTHER - AN INSIDE VIEW

S oon as I put a foot over the threshold, like I'd tripped a switch, the lobby light flashed on. Then, as the heavy door slammed shut behind me, a more distant clap of thunder announced the storm was passing.

'My *gott*, Peter!' Helga trilled, pinching the candle flame. 'You bring luck to the house. The first time the electricity is on for a week.' She frowned. 'Look at that,' she tutted at hot wax dripping gloss red talons, held upto the light. 'How I hates the *borrachos* down at the *éstacion*, always drunk out their *pocito* skulls.'

'That bad, is it?' I said, glad of small talk and distraction from the assault of first impressions, in which her cute looks were at odds with her height, giving me the feeling she was increasing or diminishing in size whenever she scowled or smiled – though admittedly she *was* tall. Now I knew why I like women that way. I was programmed from when she claimed to be twenty and signed a birth certificate, Helga Johnsdottr. But that Hega was never anyone's daughter. One source confided that, in the course of official duties, on secondment from a Swedish government department, my mother procured twenty prostitutes, all perfect specimens, for the Shit Eater's Club of Brussels, a shadowy group of *cognoscente*, who no one ever admits to knowing. All men, sharing a dirty secret, eating shit from gold plates in a lodge as old as the hills. Anyone who's anyone at the pinnacle of global power is a member, and you've got to eat shit to get in.

That's the rule, the nail crapitalism is hung on, there wouldn't be any point otherwise. So it's got to be golden shit in this club, where apricots is all the flaxen haired girls get to eat for thirty days in purdah, locked in a luxurious country house in Belgium, supervised by a nursing sister from the Swedish Ministry of Defence; very nice work if you can get it, for a witch. Helga, of course. So that's it with the intro: Helga with capital H. And that sorry son who had to have that bitch for amother,

27

was me. A startling fact of my existence, which might have stayed put under amnesiac slabs, had not my well-informed Austrian analyst set me digging, with his tip about the Brussels connection to my old man, the day he told me to get a notebook and write it all down ...

'You think that is bad?' she said, bolting the door.

'I don't know,' I shrugged, wondering what the hell we were talking about.

'Let me tell you,' she cast back over her shoulder, mincing past a dusty suit of armour I had taken to be a drunk old night watchman, slumped against the lobby wall. 'Here in the mountains, you get used to shortages. One week the water is frozen tight. Then rock slides block the road. Sometimes the lightning strikes peoples down in the street.' She chuckled, leading the way along a dimly lit corridor.

'Can you believe that?' she went on, her voice resounding in distant rooms. 'Once, I even loose a burro from the hail stones, big as snooker balls zey are, always firing out of the blue. Never you know when.'

Despite my hoarded resentments, I was warming to her. She was my mother after all. Genes of my genes communicating at a sub-cellular level. Maybe everything would be OK? Sucker thought.

Get it straight.

'... *crocodile emotions with the bite of an asp* ...'

My father's exact words, the day he came down to my boarding school – Elias Ashmole's, an elite institution for the wayward sons of journeymen – in his chauffeur-driven green Bentley of the long running boards, a car, which, looking back, I loved far more than him. In the years since, I have wondered what happened to the old shithead. At the time, all that came across was cold indifference. Not one question. As if I didn't exist. My mother was a mistake he regretted, ergo so was I. He had done his duty and hoped I would do the same by him. Not many boys had my educational opportunities, and he expected my best. Just half an hour out of his life and, even so, he did not bother to wave goodbye. Sitting very upright in the back seat of the Bentley, the brim of his black fedora shadowing his solemn brown eyes. All I knew, he was somebody important in the world, but I never found out exactly who. What did I then know about a lodge as old as the hills? I was eleven, minding my Ps and Qs, prepared by matron for the big day, in pressed shorts and blazer. A right pair, my parents. All my life like the swamp fever. Penumbra, impossible to shake off, except with strong medicine, obsessive work and hard drugs.

The devil was high-tailing-it to *las hermanitas*, taking the electricity and my luck. Just as Helga pushed open the swing door and we stepped into the kitchen, all the lights crashed. 'Damn!' she swore into the dark room, the sound absorbed by bare stone walls like spilled ink on blotting paper.

Boobty ... boom ... Squeezed in the doorway, half in and half out of the room, her heart beat beating time next to mine. O god, pneumatic boobs, pointed and hard.

'One day I shoots them down at the station, *mescal* madmen.'

Boobty ... boom... Hips and thighs, hers or mine?

'They drink anything when it runs out, even the diesel for the generator.'

Boobty ... boom ... Too much body heat, not enough fucking action.

'Always it is this way. The light goes on. The light goes off. Maybe in an hour it comes on.'

Boobty ... boom ... Not with my mother. Fuck.

'Maybe never!'

Suddenly her hand shot out. Boobty ... boom ... *Madre de Deus.* Those were crocodile claws.

Boobty ... boom ... getting louder ...

'Wait here, and stand where you are.'

Stand in the dark? Hard for dyslexics muddling their lefts from rights. In this case, my horizontal from vertical, or maybe just the altitude getting on top of me? No heartbeat, only the scratchy sound of a croc crossing bone shingle. Africa? No. Just Mother in the next tomb, searching for candles, gloss-red claws scrabbling stone shelves. Mother? I had to stop thinking of her that way. Only one reptile in my family. She was a brood mare, used and abused and put out to pasture. Between us the vast, teeming stockyard of life. The mare who suckled me, seen through a clash of horns, a stranger now and always. Just treat her with consideration, that's all I hadto do. She was flesh and blood and bruised easily. A complicated kind of mother who needed tender loving care, just like me.

Yea, sure, carry on trying to warm the iceberg that sank the Titanic. And if, against the odds, I melted that heart, she'd drown me in her sorrows. She was sad, I knew that, a recluse, more walled in than Rapunzel braiding golden locks, shut in this hotel. But she made her choices. I was only five when she left. Why, I might never know. Perhaps she didn't even know. Maybe she didn't care. Well, if she didn't, I didn't. No way would I put up with shit from that harpy. Harpy Helga, I liked that. My mother a harpy in the garden and, like me, after the treasure. But there was no garden any more, the fabled treasure, if it ever existed, was lost, and this wasn't Mexico, it was bloody Norway. My mind so far gone, I didn't even know which fucking country. A bad place, this town overlooked by the three sisters. For fuck's sake, I should never have come.

Light, sudden and awesome, banishing spooks to the far corners. That flaming wick, sustenance more vital than food.

'Here you take this, and mind no spills. I have no need for seeing in the dark, not here anyways,' she breathed, her face spectral, cheeks under-lit by a dancing green flame, shining like poisoned apples in candlelight.

'I have to put on something ... shall we say ... .more coming. So long since I have a real man for company. You are a real man I hope?'

A real man? How, when all my life I felt swamped by circumstances, so isolated and alone. All the women I had known, no substitute for ... Helga.

Stone me, it was cold in the dark kitchen. The only cooking facilities I could make out were a primitive griddle and a blackened hearth, sitting numb bum on black basalt, feet siphoning frost from the stone slabs. When the chill reached my heart, I would be an ice statue in Nifliem, back in the cold kitchen of the old presbytery. Forced to sit still on my special stool, and keep my dancing feet unmoving on the stone floor. Worried Jack Frost might bite off my numb toes, wishing I was a blue bottle fly, with nothing better to do all that long summer afternoon than buzz between the hanging bunches of drying herbs, strung out on sagging lines, where on 'wash Mondays' the housekeeper pegged her ballooning knickers over the old cooking range in the dark, cobwebbed alcove.

Was that a memory? So opaque with the passage of time, the fly was now petrified in Baltic amber? Or an old nursery story about the little boy who ran away, returning to find his mother a troll and his father resting under stone slabs?

Father, are you down there? In your make-do sarcophagus, rigid as ever, laid out with hands clasped to your chest? Keeping close your secrets, fucker.

Nothing else to do but count distractions. Steel in serried ranks, ascending points and milled edges, shining in the gloom. Pestles and mortars, *pequeño* to *más grande*, reminding me of Rivera murals with large native women pounding the yellow corn.

Pot noodle black now that my candle stub was exhausted and the flame guttered out. Mother, where are you? Beyond my ken, changing skins, for all I knew. Stone, I was stone. Stone cold and unable to think.

Sounds from the netherworld: ragged breathing, reminding I was alive ... and from cavernous sinks, a continent away, it seemed, an incontinent drip ... and through the window shutters, retching, that might have been a donkey tethered outside ... then a church bell, tolling the hour.

'... *nueve, diez, once, doce* ...' I spoke out loud, for company, my heart tripping a beat as I counted thirteen. How could that be? Clocks only struck twelve at Midnight, even in Norway, I supposed. But this was the *bruja* of the north's lair, right? Nothing normal around here. These were the fucking tropics, for fuck's sake; my nuts were frozen, and this town was getting stranger by the minute. The way I felt, a little bus was still labouring bandit foothills towards a glittering eye on a shining capstone, putting me in mind of dollar bills and treasure, so much treasure, it was piled up to heaven ...

A dream, yes, and so much more vivid than a mere nightmare. I was living it, lost in it, as a high-kicking *bruja* entered, spinning a cocoon of candlelight out of a black void.

'Da-ra-rum-da-ra!' Scheherazade of the *sierras*, back to her *bruja* best, pirouetting purple silks, her powdered face spectral, pouting lips crimson. Geisha break. Yep, that mother just materialised. Scary, I'll say. Jezebel could not have looked better – to a mouse.

5. BEDOUIN FOR THE NIGHT

Woah ... My head in a spin ... Perhaps my drink was spiked. Locally brewed *mescal* with a bitter almond aftertaste; Helga wouldn't, would she? I guessed not, sinking back into soft silk cushions of a low white sofa at odds with the stone surroundings, watching her heaping cactus onto leaping flames.

'Another drink?' she said over the snap and crackle of nopal cactus popping in the grate. Dancing flames, casting a carousel of death, in a shadow play of prickly heads flickering across four stone walls, reminding me of a double suicide that now seemed like a sacrifice, the day my life changed forever, my marriage so abruptly ended, and my journey begun.

'Oh yes, to the brim please.'

'Oh my *gött*! Peter, look at that,' she whooped.

'Ésa *es* muy grandé!'

The worm. Bobbing belly-up, pink, in my glass, just the way I felt. I'd dragged my slime round the world and up a mountain, only to haemorrhage from the effort.

'You have to drink it up in one gulp,' Helga breathed. Pressing close, her eyes blurred, turning pyrotechnic green in firelight. 'Is good for the manhood they say.'

'That's your game, huh?' I snapped, upping it in one. 'So, I'm to be the worm that catches the bird. Or maybe you have in mind another pecking order?'

'How can a worm catch a bird?' Helga frowned, the sinews of her neck standing out like a cat on a hot tin roof.

'I'm sorry, it's just I find you so damned attractive. It's, um, painful.' I sighed, making a show of crossing my legs. 'I suppose I should explain, or you'll never understand.'

'Explain then!' Helga said, ice eyes hard on mine.

'It's not what you think. No woman could know what I have gone through,' I said, feeling a familiar tightening of my chest.

'You sure 'bout that?' Helga hissed.

'No way to put it but straight,' I nodded, grateful I had been prepared for this moment by my analyst with his handy metafiction of what he insisted was an embedded narrative brought on by the trauma of a messy divorce, manifesting as castration anxiety, but in the process giving me a lasting phobia of pinking scissors.

'A woman I knew once,' I sighed. 'A week after we married, she started on patchwork quilt of our lives. She said we were going to be together forever and a day. Boy she was obsessed. Always snipping away with pinking scissors, I don't know how many hexagonals, but it ran into thousands. Our first night under Amish covers, she came at me with those same scissors. That's how the axe was wielded. The bitch even shouted timber as she did it.' I glanced down – anywhere but at Betty Davis eyes – noticing a small needlework box open on a table to the side, and inside ... damn it, a pair of pinking scissors. Resolute, I ploughed on. 'I woke up and it was a bleeding stump. Funny, huh?' I laughed, wondering at the persistence of the implanted suggestion, which was clearly increasing in power, for how else had the pinking scissors appeared just like that, and in such close proximity to *mother*. Clearly if I couldn't be rid of the phobia, and soon, I'd have to create another to replace it. But then what would materialise – a demon? Involuntarily I groaned, holding my head.

'No!' Helga gasped, jerking upright. 'That it is terrible!' she said, a broad hand covering massive breasts, somehow magnetic and repellent at the same time. She drew a deep breath. 'Allow me to say I am disappointing.' 'Tell me about it,' I snarled.

'I mean, look at you.'

I shook my head. 'A gorgeous woman. And now I'm bare-arsed with embarrassment.'

'My dear, don't be!' said Helga, arsenic morphing to lace in a trice. 'This may sound not nice, but do you never consider surgery?'

'What man wouldn't?' I shot back, knowing, to pre-empt further questions, I had to end with a flourish. 'Seven specialists in as many countries, all my money, double-stitching bastards.' I shrugged, feeling my much-maligned Peter-man retracting into my groin. 'But even though

I had the presence of mind to put my phobia,' I stumbled, 'I mean the glans, in the freezer, it turned out no use. My rebuilt soldier won't stand and deliver, no matter what the attention.' I grinned at the finale. 'So, you've heard my story, now it's your turn.' 'Oh no.' Helga's eyes narrowed, her Slavic features now bleak and harsh as tundra wastes. 'You do not trick me like that. One titbit and you thinks that is worth a whole life.' Pausing, she eyed me intently, breathing slowly. 'If we are to become friends, you must understand one thing: personal information is just that.

I do not ask to share your pain, and I do not expect you rhaps, I tell you a few things.'

'Fair enough,' I snorted. 'But why don't you let me guess?'

'A game,' she grinned, getting appreciatively smaller – a trick of the firelight, I guessed. 'I likes that, but no fishing. Either you hit the nail on the hat, or nothing.'

'You were born on an island.'

'You are fishing.' Helga swelled ominously.

'No,' I shook my head. 'Not a guess.'

'How you know then?'

'That would be telling,' I smiled.

'You are making me angry now.' She glowered, and I hoped she wasn't about to pop. But she wasn't a balloon. Not with that face of rock.

'If you really want to know,' I dissembled, 'It's all to do with semantics. The world over, island people phrase their words in a different order than mainlanders.'

'Why do you not tell me this in the first place?'
she said suspiciously.

'Maybe I didn't want to bore you,' I shrugged. 'I can get quite pedantic on the subject. My dissertation at university was on word order in colloquial dialects, but most people don't find the general area interesting.'

'Hmm, you are right,' she nodded. 'Too much study makes Jack a dull book, I always say.'

'That is because you are an islander. I bet when you were young you were always out of the house exploring.'

'How you know that?'

'Because on a small island, kids are that much are easier to find. I take it the island was small?'

'Not when I am young, it is a universe then.'

'A very small universe,' I laughed, finally at my ease with this big busty blonde, who, for a moment at least, I had forgotten was my mother.

'It is exactly on the Arctic Circle, or was when I left.'

Pausing almost imperceptibly, she raised an eyebrow. A cue, I knew, but I merely nodded.

'Just like this town is on the tropic,' she continued.

'Is that not strange?' She smiled, reflectively. 'On the shortest day, from top of the Blodsdfell mountain we can see the sun over the horizon. There are cows in the fields below and many, many trees.'

'Really?'

'Yes,' she nodded, 'We have mountain ash, hawthorn, spruce.'

'So far north? I find that surprising.'

'We have the Gulf Stream to thank. It is no colder than here. We even have apple trees with beautiful golden apples.'

'Sounds like a mythical garden.' I lofted an eyebrow. 'Only in the wrong place.'

'That is true, but in summer the sea is not so cold,' she smiled, diminishing again, 'And sometimes on the beach we find Malacca beans.'

'From the Yucatan, I suppose,' I chuckled.

'Why not?' she frowned, inflating slightly. 'The Gulf Stream starts there.'

'So it does.'

'Everything on the island is so beautiful.'

'I am sure,' I nodded. 'Whereabouts exactly?'

'That is personal,' she glowered, swelling.

'Sorry,' I said, already informed that the island was one of a chain of three, some three hundred nautical miles due south of Spitsbergen.

'So many questions,' she pouted, stabilising.

'Just one more.' I implored. 'Please.'

'If you must, you must,' she sighed. 'I suppose.'

'How's about this then?' I said, playing my ace in the hole. 'Once, you worked in a circus.'

'Why you say that?' Iceberg eyes flashed a warning.

'Call it a hunch.'

'Always you must guess so close?' Helga's eyelids narrowed to slits.

'My, ah, Now therapist suggested it was sexual energy re-channelled after my injury. However I prefer to think intuition is a higher form of intellect. Logic is just too slow.'

'But a circus?' She slapped her knee. 'Come on!'

'Oh there are clues. Your height for one,' I grinned, glad it wasn't my knee, 'Kind of restricts employment prospects. Your sureness in the dark, even if you do know this, ah ... house back to back. Your strength, I guess, the crazy dance when you came back, those high kicks, definitely trained. So it was a toss-up between a dance company and something a little less disciplined but just as demanding.'

'So you do use logic?'

'Not when I'm employing my intuition.' I paused.

'Soon as you opened the front door, I had this image in my head. You're all in glittery white, clamped to a spinning target, and I'm the one throwing the scissors.' I laughed. 'Of course, I mean knives.'

'Tra la la!' Helga, back to default size, clapped gaily. 'My *gött*, Peter, you are better than Professor McMental; he read minds too. What a team we make!'

Beddy-byes, back in the cradle, tucked in by a circus giantess of uncertain size. I liked that, so I rewarded her goodnight peck with a warm hug. Helga, what nightmares I had of you. The witch ever in my wardrobe. Counting my jackets, picking my pockets – always somewhere about as I drifted to sleep. Casting a shadow that only got longer after you left. Mummy, ever absent, always omnipresent. We were friends, I knew that now. Fair-weather friends for the moment. But how long would that hold? Until a change in weather. A tornado twisting down from Texas, spinning a vortex over the high *sierras*.

'You want I should blow out your candle?'

'That would be a relief.'

'Goodnight, Peter.'

'Goodnight, er, Helga.'

Coffin-lid darkness as, with a click, she closed the door. Faintly the sound of slippers shuffling into oblivion. As I drifted into sleep my last thought directed to the spinner of dreams, no more nightmares, please, Sister.

At first I was sure the persistent tapping was knocking on the door. But no, the source was closer. The wardrobe then? No, not that Napoleonic nineteenth-century walnut-burr monstrosity, relic of Emperor Maximilian's ill-fated campaigns in Mexico, with a wooden eagle and a chamber pot on top. How come I missed details like that? Drunk, I supposed, I couldn't even remember getting to bed, but not now. Senses on alert, the sound fading as I struck another match and lit the candle, holding it high, peering into the vaulted gloom.

Nothing, it was nothing. The only spooks in the room were cast by the wavering light of a flame. Even so, I left the candle to consume the darkness till morning and fell instantly into the catacombs of night.

6. GRIPPED ...

Something in the room. Before I opened my eyes, I knew. All the claustrophobic nightmares I had ever known, compressed into one monolithic, tottering tombstone, incised '*Diogenes, a cynic unknown*', an epitaph that was none at all. Crushing pressure, bearing down, compacting the grey matter in my skull into an ingot of incapacitating dread. Fear was all I knew, and fear was all I had, contemplating mortality in a descending coffin lid, sliding back into a bottomless grave and a yawning invitation to a dank, green, sulphurous realm. Back-lit, standing in the opening, a figure I recognised – I even remembered his teeth-chipping name – Mictlán-te-cuh-tli, that same evil god on display during my one visit to the National Museum in Mexico City. Only this wasn't a life-size clay sculpture, but the skeletal lord of death himself, reaching out with a scything embrace. As if that wasn't enough, a crowding of gaunt shoulders stuck out like gantries over his rib cage, where a rookery of crows picked at hanging strips of flesh.

And more ghouls, too ghastly and too many to describe; some I knew from personal experience: Back Stabber, Brussels Shit-Eater, Fork Tongue, Black Dog, Fist Fucker, Blood Blister, Pus Prick, Rubbishin-the-Cor- ner, Wolf Bane, Crocodile Cunt, Hedge Fund Owl, Paedo Priest, Politician Big Cheese, Bad Apple Banker, Hag-in-Daz-Nappies, Demented Dick, Huggy Hepatitis, Lizard Lawyer, Bin-Gone-on-Jihad, Born Again Crusader, Black Cap Judge, Persistent Arse-Licker, Miserable Presbyterian Minister, Curious Cop on my case, Wanton Bed-Wetter, of course Pinking Scissor Sisters holding up bloody sheets, Shared HIV Needles, Phantom Brother, Bat Boy, Nosforatu ... The fucking list went on forever. It reminded me how much I hated lists.

My reaction? Reach for my notebook and scribble blindly under covers. Ridiculous I know, but note taking always calms me, and besides, in extremis, the ostrich manoeuver is sometimes all there is. A warning, I knew, but signalling what? Then a picture filling my mind – a treasure chest overflowing black gore ... a rising blood tide losing my moorings, my bed now a chariot, harnessed to thirteen skulls, leading me down ... down into the catacombs where, in pitch blackness, native sons toiled with pickaxes and shovels. Another detail I scribbled down as the chariot steadied on its hurtling descent. Maybe I had died, I thought, as an echoing answer came back from dripping labyrinth walls. 'Not dead yet, but soon will be ...'

My father, sure to god that was my father's voice. *Darth Vader.* Wasn't that German for 'dark father'?

So the old shit eater *was* dead and buried, somewhere about, perhaps under the floor of this very room. This town was built on silver mines. Perhaps he was buried in one. He might even have been the owner. An ironic twist going towards explaining his wealth – never mind what he must have shelled out for my boarding school and university before I flunked my degree course and my allowance was stopped. Ten years later I was the only guest in a deranged Mexican hotel run by my mother, wondering if the treasure chest was a figment of my imagination? Those sons of the soil, toiling with picks and shovels, symbolising the mass travail of indentured Indians living out their short lives in the mines below, generations upon generations, all the way back to the fucking Conquest, and possibly before, if that date above the door of the hotel was right. A hideous prospect. Because, if correct, I *was* connected; guilt, I guessed, even if only by patrilineal association to the shit-eating elite of the world. For, as it says in the Bible, the sins of the father will be returned unto the seventh generation. Far as I knew, I was the last of the line, successor not just to my mysterious father, but to his before him, and so on, into the mists of time. Whatever treasure was contained in that chest – bars of gold, Spanish doubloons, title deeds to the mines or even just my father's bones – was mine by right of inheritance, and that meant I had to take whatever came with it, including all that accumulated guilt.

Only one thing to do when faced with a vastly overweening opponent ... dicker ... parlay for terms ... negotiate a moratorium on heritable dues outstanding. In this case, discover exactly what this demon-god Mictlán-te-cuh-tli wanted of me. As surety, offering up my immortal soul, in case I reneged on the deal. For the record, I even jotted the salient details of our contract in my notebook, just in case. When I woke in the morning, I couldn't make out a single word.

7. THE MEXICAN BREAKFAST

Resurrection? After my all-night travail, I awoke with a banging bedpan for a head. It was still screwed on the right way, though made of inferior brass. Nothing to do but grope towards bumping shutters, weathered wood sieving stars through hairline splits, it was that dried out.

Retinal overload when I threw the catch. The shutters banging back, no window glass against a piercing blast. God-awful Mexico, arid and barren, blowing a gale in my face – painterly slopes, scrub splattered and scree stroked, bisected by a *barranca* – the ragged ravine, from my perspective, more a fault than a chasm, zagging up to where a grey, oversized raptor was perched, feasting on the red fruiting heads of a large cactus. Its pose reminded me of Huitzilopochtli, the Aztec god of war, his double depicted on the Mexican national flag as an eagle atop a cactus bush, eating a snake. Sacrifices on stepped pyramids running blood and *chupacabras* that, in Chicano urban legend, are doppelgangers of an Aztec god, whose unpronounceable name translates as 'smoking mirror of the sun', revisiting the present through a time slip opened up by atom bomb tests in the Mojave Desert. This, of course, unverifiable, unless the monster bird had migrated south from the *barrios* of LA and Watts. Still there, perched on the many-headed bush, preening now, big, whatever it was, proving there was no escape, not even in bandit badlands. Yea, wherever I went in Mexico, God, in some guise or other, was staring down from smoking mirror heights. In this case on red tiles in abundance, threatening landslides onto narrow streets; on one flat roof, a heart-warming sight, proving there was life hereabouts, pot plants all in a line, disguised with plastic roses, but still unmistakably Mary Jane. On another, double-pegged washing, horizontal in the wind. Did I say no escape? There he was again – this time Jesus *mix-Mex* Christ – taking it full frontal for mortal sinners, showing the way, embracing the cosmos from the limestone cupola of the cathedral gleaming white and pristine under the savage *sierra* sun.

God! Jehovah! Quetzalcoatl! I needed breakfast. I moaned, mesmerised by His glare, feeling insubstantial with nothing but a worm for sustenance since Chihuahua bus station the day before. Taking stock, I looked around, intense white light, highlighting the bare masonry of the room, and the dust where stone walls met old floor tiles. Then I saw it, partly hidden by a leg of the bed, scratched on a tile: a hobo sign. Zigzag lines enclosed by an arch, suggesting flowing water in a mine, and below that a box etched with six lines. Could that indicate the treasure chest? Plenty to think about as, drawn by the aroma of frying bacon, I headed for the salon.

'*Chorisos pequeños, huevos rancheros, tortillas y café, por los dos.*' Helga ordering for us both, addressing a hatchet-faced maid, who gave me a glare as she leaned around the door of the kitchen.

'*Chorisos pequeños?*'

Weeny sausages, for my delectation, Helga said. Commentary on my performance the night before, I guessed.

Just the two of us in the old salon, furnished colonial style, window shutters wide to the world. Just wrought fancy Spanish scrollwork and iron bars between us and the hole-in-the-wall *cantina* across the way, where a big man with a red apron over his beer gut was swilling last night's slop into the gutter.

'And how do you sleep?'

The civilities of the morning, I considered sourly, wondering if it had been a dream. What had the lord of death granted me? I couldn't think. Oh yea. Six 'intimations', which I pictured as get-out-of-jail-free cards in a game where the aim was to survive to the end.

'I asks you a question,' she glowered, swelling slightly. 'And you just sit there not answering.'

'I slept terrible! Not a bloody wink, for my sins.'

'Hmm ...' Helga murmured, her attention straying back to her paperback novel, open on the table; the title, I noticed, *The Eagle Has Landed*.

'You want to know why?'

'If you must,' she scowled, without looking up from page one hundred and three.

'A surprise visitation. A ghost, actually.'

The effect was instantaneous. Helga jerked upright, just as the kitchen door pushed open and the native maid – bottom half knobbly and knitted, above sultry *salsa* – clacked in on clumpy clogs, bearing a heavy tray.

'Ah, Malinché,' Helga said shakily, lifting her book, making space for the plates as, under the table, an insistent pressure of her toe on my foot, bid me silent.

When the swing door finally ceased creaking on its hinges and shut, Helga leaned closer across the small table, staying within her size range as proximity allowed, unlike the previous evening when she had fluctuated on a range between XXXL and monster. 'You have to be careful,' she whispered, 'Or the girls they hear everything.'

'The girls?' I exclaimed, reaching for the red enamel coffee pot. 'I thought there was only one maid.'

'The Malinchés are identical twins.'

'Malinchés?' I reiterated, recalling the maid's sullen look. She'd only been named after the mother of Mexico, who gave Cortez, her lover, the inside track on the Aztecs and sold out her country.

'*Las Double Equis*, I call them. XX and always looking for a Y. So be warned,' she said, watching for spills on the mantilla lace tablecloth as I refilled her cup.

'Even I have problems to tell them apart.'

'So how do you do it?' I asked, spearing the sausages. Seven on the fork, and one more; I opened my mouth wide.

Glancing away, Helga sighed, 'There is one that is sweet, one that is sour. What you think, Mr Clever Dick?' She clicked fingers. 'Now tell me what it is you see?'

'Like a flag,' I said, improvising between chews,

'Fluttering, floating and for all I know farting 'til dawn. Fucking evil black shroud.'

'My *gott*.' Helga massaged the vex lines etching her brow. 'Just the same as I see on my first night.' Slumping in her seat, she stared at a point over my shoulder. 'A lifetime ago it seems now.'

'So does every guest get a visitation?' I blinked.

'Or is this an exclusive service?'

'No!' Helga snapped, her prodigious bosom swelling like the boobs of a giant pneumatic Barbie inflating on an airline. 'It is a warning,' she hissed, venting pressure. 'Death, that is the *massage!*'

'Shit,' I choked. 'That sort of massage I do not care for.'

'Just one of the tests if you are to succeed.'

'Succeed?' I frowned. 'How do you mean?'

'I know what it is you seek. You and me, we are one of a kind. Not like the others,' she smiled darkly, flicking fluff that only she could see from the sleeve of her cashmere cardigan.

Now I knew where I stood in her world. Her son, a thing that cried and sucked and then had to be weaned the only way she knew how. Yea, by walking away. Thereafter, a riddle to myself, left alone in the wide universe for reasons I still couldn't comprehend. But I supposed I should be grateful, given what I knew of her past. Even if she recognised me, in her eyes I would still be inconsequential fluff.

Helga stood up. 'We talk more later, when we are sure we are alone.'

She bent close, hissing in my ear, 'And remember not to trust anyone. Most of all that *cabrón.*' She extended a muscular arm about level with my eyes. 'There, you see him?' she whispered, pointing through the window at the hole-in-the-wall across the street. 'Like the black crow he is, looking out from the *cantina*. My *gott*, how I hates him!'

Inflating with indignation, she straightened up.

'That Guzman,' she snarled, 'Always he is spying.'

I was confused. A *cabrón* meant male goat, yet in the next breath she compared him to a crow. Such insistence, such vehemence. Nothing else to do but ponder the matter while exploring the town. I guessed I would have to start in the *cantina*.

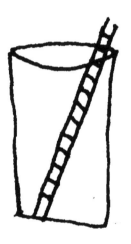

8. ALCOHOLICOS ANONYMOUS

'Cantina Joe.' That's what he said his name was. But the name by the saloon's half-doors was Don José Genaro. Was he not the proprietor?

'Of course!' Joe laughed through yellowing teeth, waving a hand to no one in particular, along four walls of bullfighting memorabilia and posters. A riot of red and black, the blood vital and always on a beige background. Vaguely I wondered, why such uniformity? Sandpit life, I supposed, reduced to its bare elements – a scarlet cape, a sword, hooves and horns.

'Es how everyone around here knows me.' Joe, the universal barman, reeling me in – not at all goat- or crow-like at close quarters, more a greying turkey buzzard, lumps and bumps all over his boozy hooter.

'But Helga said you're called "Guzman",' I said, thumbing towards the hotel, grim and foreboding across the street. Why were the dining room shutters now closed? Did that signal disapproval? Did she see me slip into the *cantina*. Did this conversation rate as betrayal?

'She did?' Joe chuckled. 'A strange woman, my friend.' He winked slyly. 'Who but the north wind can understand her?'

'Yea.' I shrugged, staring into my empty beer glass, scrying strange tales in the thumb prints and froth remaining. 'I suppose that's right. We are all mysteries,' I offered dully, preparing to go, setting the glass back on the table. 'Even to ourselves.'

'Why the long face my mysterious friend?' Joe slapped my back with a spade hand. 'I feel good today,' he grinned. 'Have another beer, *es* on the *casa!*'

Another beer and another beer. And then overhead the cathedral bell tolled thirteen. Midday? You couldn't be too sure of anything round here, I considered, rising from my stool, regarding my boots shrinking into the middle distance as knees ratcheted unsteadily. Drinking in the morning was definitely not my speciality, hair of the *chihuaha* notwithstanding. Perhaps I just needed another.

Behind the bar, head and shoulders over the *sombrero*-ed clientele, the three 'mouseketeers' so presented, backs turned, the appliquéd denim of their jackets, chalk stitched and silver studded. A gun, a cactus, a rose. What else? Joe, waving me over, all patent smiles and polished bonhomie.

'But my friend, you only just arrive. In Mexico midday *es* for *mescal*.'

'Oh no,' I pushed out a palm, 'Not that worm, not at any hour of the clock. *Hasta la* ... I'll see you later.' I shrugged "*Mañana?*"

'Of course,' Joe beamed broadly. '*Es* no other *cantina* in town. But before you go, *señor, una pequeña, por favor*. Only one *mescal* – on the *casa*, naturally.' He reached for an unlabelled bottle. 'And I promise you no worm. *Es* bad to swallow the local ones, *los gusano del diablo*, the worm of the devil, you know they are called that? The fattest are the worst, especially the pink ones. Always watch out for those. Once you swallow you never lose the craving, they grow huge in the stomach, and always it is crying out, more, more, more.'

'What the hell, I'm persuaded,' I smiled grimly, reminded of the fat pink worm downed the night before.

'But aren't you going to introduce your friends?'

'Of course!' *cantina* Joe gestured as three identical faces, motioned around. 'I am proud to present: Señor Rose, Señor Revólver and Señor Cactus. Already you know their cousins, *lás Trés Equis Malinché*.'

'But I thought there were only two maids in the hotel?' I said, turning to shake the hand of Señor Cactus, smiling amiably, and not at all prickly, as I discovered.

'No, you have it wrong my friend,' *cantina* Joe said, pouring me four knuckles of *mescal, sans* worm. 'I should know, for I am their *oncle*. The strangest thing, maybe a world first if it gets into the newspapers.' He shrugged. 'But that is never news in Mexico. Only what is normal in every other country. Double triplets, and both sets identical. A medical triumph only possible by the combined efforts of the United Nations.' *cantina* Joe pointed proudly to the UN logos on a plaque above the doors.

'The Canadian doctor in charge says the odds are maybe four billion to one.' He winked slyly. 'I think more, what you say?'

My sort of town, where one and one makes three, and clocks strike thirteen. So many questions. I didn't know where to start.

'Start at the beginning,' *cantina* Joe said. '*Es* always the place.'

'Really?' I replied, unawares I had asked a question. *Mescal* madness obviously. But at least I was feeling better. Fire satiating the worm? I guess.

'So why does the town have no name?'

'Shh.' Leaning across the bar, *cantina* Joe sealed his sun-cracked lips with a finger. '*Es* unlucky to say, only outside and well away. You have to wait for that story.'

'I see,' I said, unaccountably nervous. 'Well then, can you explain why so much of it is rubble?'

'You don't know?' His eyebrows, bushy enough to nest birds in, shot up. 'Ever since the *revolución*, from the four corners, *hombres* packing picks, dynamite and spades. All convinced there *es* just such a treasure.'

'And?'

'Sure *es*,' *cantina* Joe laughed lazily, 'The whole world knows of the treasure of the *Sierra Madré*. But no one ever finds it, for it belongs here, like the *tzitzimime*.'

'*Tz-it-zi-mime*?' I repeated slowly.

'Yes, my friend,' *cantina* Joe beamed, 'Like the Condor, only the *tzitzimime* they fly higher. You never get close, except with a spy satellite.'

'Perhaps they're just large vultures.'

'*Zopilotes*, no.' Joe waved airily. '*Mucho* bigger,' he grinned toothily. 'But that was a good try, my friend.'

'The birds are native to Mexico?'

'Oh yes, but only to these mountains. Is the double of an Aztec god.'

'God of what?'

'Thunder, they say.'

'Something new every day,' I said, standing up,

'And that's it.' I smiled, proffering a hand.

'You are most welcome my friend,' gravely *cantina* Joe nodded, maintaining an even grip as we shook hands. 'Any questions, you know where to come.'

'That's quite enough answers for the moment,' I said, turning unsteadily towards the swing doors.

9. OEDIPUS REX

Two choices. Left, right and straight ahead. Another instance of numbers not adding up. Even at siesta time the shuttered hotel was a definite no-no. Left then? Towards blackness, an avenue of ruins leading to a sheer face of rock, boss-eyed in the sun, shadows near the summit, caves, I supposed, bordered by two stone lions below, reminding me of Babylon and captivity, guarding the entrance to the tunnel and the world beyond.

With my assumed name, only one choice: follow the pilgrim's way to the staircase wending a conical mound, squared at the base, and topped by the cathedral squatting sphinx-like above the plaza, the white-washed basilica and cupola tucked in between two bell towers. A head and shoulders guarding secrets, secure between giant haunches.

A question came to mind. 'What goes on four feet, two feet and three? But the more feet, the weaker it be?' The Sphinx's riddle demanded of travellers who ended as bleached bones strewn in Sakkara sands. Solved by Oedipus, mother fucker and father killer, blinded for his sins, who still became king, no eyes better than one in that cruel land. The answer? Man. Child, boy and *borracho*. That was me, stumbling worn steps, about to regress to a centipede crawl. Yes! Drunk on *mescal* in the midday Sun. Father, are you watching?

'Yes, my son,' a voice answered, *'Within and without you, always. In the smoking mirror guarding the gold of the sun. Wherever you look, there I shall be. Waiting for the weary pilgrim on his way to Thebes.'*

Thebes? I considered, rationalising the voice as the result of too much study in dusty libraries and not enough fun in the field.

Now the voice was me, tallying up in a book I keep in my head. How many steps, and each one a hurdle? Near enough a god damn year's worth, I considered, counting three hundred and sixty four. One more to go. Enough to put anyone off religion permanently, I reflected, reminded of the Sphinx and his stupid riddles, staring down at the town;

from that perspective like another planet, alien and odd. Impossible to think it was inhabited. So desolate and abandoned, where a scything shadow was sweeping red tile rooftops. That bird again, same as before, just a fleeting glimpse of black feathers, swooping down behind one of five rock pinnacles, like the fingers of a raised hand, jutting the cliff wall that enclosed the town on three sides.

Heat on my back, then cold, that cloud a smoking mirror guarding the gate to the sun, reducing my choices to zero. Before me, the truth, the way and everything else Catholicism stands for. A door within a door, and a handle on that door, like the ring pull of a hatch on an ancient hull.

Noah's Ark maybe? The copper bottom barnacled, marooned in stone impedimenta, bordered by sins; pride taking a fall, gluttony sleeping on the job, the head of avarice swapping places with his arse, a green snake of envy winding up the thigh of a wanton woman – or perhaps that was lust, I didn't know. All I could see was lust for life in the rutting skeletons breeding serpents. Or were they just *mescal* worms? And fuck it, those concentric carvings, obviously modelled on the circles of Mictlán, meaning that this cathedral was also a pagan temple, which reminded me of long evenings in the New York Public Library, boning up on Meso-American burial practices.

Nothing else to do but take that penultimate step; plunging into darkness, feeling my way round the screen like the *borracho* I was, secretly ashamed but going ahead anyway, crossing myself dyslexically and again, reversed – just to make sure – waiting in the gilded gloom, waiting for dancing noughts and crosses to add up.

Clue one to two hundred and twenty. An anagram for suffering: wounds gory, a bloody pincushion, except those were arrows and that was wood. Now I got it. Martyrdom, glorious to behold, St Sebastian on a plinth, staring sullenly. One saint down. How many more to go? They were all round the basilica, snug in niches, imminent and transcendent on wires as performers in a circus – the congregation of the saints according to papal edict. Or maybe not, I thought, noticing Gregor, the saint of drink, and his famous St Bernard; neither recognised by the Vatican for seven hundred years. There were even some fallen from grace elsewhere, St Boniface, the protector of children, leaning on his broom; St Christopher shouldering a lamb; St George, twisting his spear into a life-like worm, a saint dismissed as a myth by the Vatican council of 1910, but still believed in these mountains. Mad Catholicism, at its most perverse in gold leaf. I loved it, and I hadn't even penetrated the inner sanctums – confessional boxes, screened by frayed red curtains.

'How long has it been?' my confessor asked, after I got down on my knees, unable to resist baring my soul. An Irish brogue, cosy as Spanish fleece, Paddy-whatever, Einstein hair silhouetted in a grill, like they were doubles.

'Father, I can't remember, it's been that long.'

'If you take a moment for reflection. There's no hurry, my son.'

'My son ...' What I'd come to hear, trust the Irish to provide honeyed words.

'Father, I have to confess, I'm not even a Catholic.'

'T'at's a new one on me, I must say, but the Church is as wide as the world, wider if you need, my son. There is room for all.' He paused, and I felt such a fluttering – my heart a fledgling bird. I was a Catholic. So much of my early past a locked box, anything could be true.

'Somet'ing you need to get off your chest?' he asked helpfully.

'Yes. No. I'm a dyslexic fool and liar for one. Or is that two? I'm so confused, Father. For all I know of my early life, I might even be a Catholic. And yes I've had lustful thoughts. You see my mother is a very attractive woman. We've only just met after many years and she doesn't yet know who I am. I think we're in danger of forming an incestuous relationship, Father.'

'The devil comes in many disguises. Are you absolutely sure she is your mother?'

'I am.'

'Well don't you tempt her with the worm, it could be her downfall. And being a loving son, you wouldn't want t'at?'

'No, most definitely not, Father. And yes, I do love her.'

'Love sometimes comes all too easy, my son. It's separating the flesh from the bones, t'at's the t'ing. T'is old cathedral sits on a pyramid of bones. Did you know t'at? Not just any bones, my son, the bones I'm talking about are the bones of Indians sacrificed on the old pyramid on which this blessed cathedral stands, dedicated to Tláloc, a name which means 'the germinator'. Each one a martyr to that pagan deity. What do you t'ink they cry out for? Justice? Revenge? Absolution, more like! Bones is your inner core, my son. Bones is your forefathers, all the way back to Noah. And the ink that joins them? Sin! Incest! Fornication! Patricide! You name it, they did it. It's all in there, my son. Reflect on bones and you'll realise the transience of life. All else is vanity, my son. Vanity!'

'I see,' I said, thinking about the portrait of my hard-to-please Manhattan landlady, haunting my nights in an oppressive New York apartment, spreading perfect legs, in the buff as when I got to know her. 'So that's what I've got to do when I get the, ah, urges. Think about bones?'

'As a matterphorically speaking, yes. It's a hard one, I know, but t'at's the way.'

'Any special sort of bones I should think of, Father?'

'Thigh bones, hip bones, they're all much of a muchness, my son. It's the marrow you've got to get to, the core of the core. The pip of the pip, so to speak. Only the other day I was reading in *Scientific American*, you know, the ah ... scientific magazine, all you are is encoded in your marrow. Now isn't that a wonder! Genes, that's the vital substance, you must understand. Even in the bones of ancient Egyptian mummies, they're finding it, and some of those mummies are soon to be regrown from the marrow out. Proving there is hope, even for the worst cases. To t'ink that Ramses, the pharaoh who had a run-in with Moses, could soon be as alive as you and me, walking, shopping, doing ordinary t'ings like that, makes me t'ink that the last days are close at hand. Remember the scriptures my son, at the last trumpet all the dead since the beginning of the world, six t'ousand, six hundred and seventy-five years ago, to be exact, shall be raised. Now wouldn't that be a sight worth crossing the Liffey for.'

The Liffey? I was in Mexico, not in a snug in a pub in Dublin. I'd come to confess, and now this garrulous Irish priest had taken over my starting stall and was off and running. Geneticists? Moses?

'But Father,' I protested, a vast oppression coming on, 'What do I do about all these sins?'

'What sins was that?' He really sounded like he'd forgotten.

'I guess all the way back to the garden,' I said, succumbing to temptation. 'My forefather monkey believing his sibling's heads were apples.'

'Now t'at's a most interesting theory, my son. Would you care to expand?'

'I didn't come here to talk about *Scientific American*, or genetics or Genesis, I just need to confess, Father.' I paused, becoming aware I was wringing my hands. 'But what ... I don't recall.'

'When you do,' he soothed, 'Just come back to the cathedral. You will always be welcome, my son. You have my word on that, and I don't give it lightly. If I'm not here, one of the Black Friars will hear you.'

Black Friars? Now I knew I was in trouble. Unwittingly I'd poured out my heart to a Black Friar

'Shemite', a renegade sect of priests, accused of double heresy – denying Jesus Christ and assimilating Native American beliefs into the Catholic liturgy – who were now the subject of a secret Vatican commission, as covered in a recent edition of the Notional Enquirer, my favourite tabloid. That 'certain somewhere' in the Sierra Madre was here. In a place that, by not having a name, had one, as the capitalised letters of the Town With No Name, demonstrated, in the article. As if its existence was tantamount to nonexistence, and both states were interchangeable and confused one for the other.

New meaning on old bones then. That priest laid a lot of stress on old bones. And I hadn't seen a single crucifix in the cathedral. More to this than meets the eye, I thought, returning to the hotel in a pensive mood.

The Notional Enquirer, *Issue No. 12633. pp. 12*

POPE ORDERS CRACKDOWN ON NASTY HABITS AS MAD MONKS GO NATIVE

By our special religious affairs correspondent, Poop-a Snooper

Rome. Tuesday 23rd July 2013. New Pope Sixtus V has convened a secret Vatican commission to look into the habits of the 'Shemites', a breakaway sect

of Black Friars who deny virtually the whole Catholic liturgy, Jesus Christ, the entire New Testament and indeed all the books of the Old Testament after the Book of Noah, with the exception of the Epistle of St John the Divine. Claiming that ancient Native American texts uncovered in the sacristy of an unnamed Mexican cathedral have revealed we are merely mutinous survivors cast adrift on a glutinous lump of dark matter, acting on our thoughts as a magnet does to iron filings, orbiting a smoking mirror otherwise known as the ' fifth sun', which is positioned between man and God. The Shemite brethren, or 'eagles', as they address each other, are preparing for the 'second coming' in a remote fastness in the Mexican Sierra Madre, where the 'pilot', Shem, son of Noah, apparently known to the Aztecs as 'Tláloc the thunderer' will arrive in a space ark, to return the self-appointed 'elect' to their home the planet Æden, which lies beyond the solar system in the constellation of Pegasus. Vatican sources attribute these heresies to 'vitamin deficiency caused by a meagre diet through a lack of funds down to the parsimoniousness of their congregation, prolonged altitude sickness and an excess of religious zeal, particularly self-mutilation'.

10. THE VOICE

'So, the wonderer returns.' Helga, posed in the doorway, busting the buttons of her designer dungarees, barring my way.

'You want chapter and verse; where I've been, what I've done? Really, Helga,' I sneered, 'You sound like my ex-wife.'

'Do you humiliate her like this also?'

'Yes,' I winced, 'I mean no. What do you mean?'

'You can ask me that? When I sees you falling out of the *cantina*, crawling like a cockroach up the cathedral steps.' She scowled, towering over me. 'You stink of *mescal*!'

'And what if I do?'

Helga arched a plucked eyebrow. 'I ask you to stay away from the *cantina*. Do not I deserve a little respect?'

'Not if you nag me like this,' I said, observing that the pencilled lines of her freshly denuded eyebrows followed precisely the contours of the previous incumbents, making me wonder why she had plucked them in the first place. Women, I thought, you never really know them.

'I only nag you because I care for you, and I know the dangers of this town,' she said, checking the empty street in both directions. 'Come!' she gestured. 'We needs to talk, but first you must change your clothes and scrub up. Your trousers, they are filthy; there is dirt on your hands.' Her lips curled. 'My *gott*, so disgusting you are!'

A night and a day, not even twenty-four hours, if the cathedral bells were anything to go by, and already we had arrived at this station. Clearly there was no other direction but down. My poor father, who could blame him for casting her out? At least he had come see me, even if only once; Helga never had. I felt abandoned, watching her stride up the corridor, out of sight but not out of mind, round the corner at the far end. No one to share my thoughts but the 'old retainer' – the dusty suit of armour – back against the lobby wall, stiff and unyielding, impervious to the insults of women, his privates protected against manic scissor attacks, enigmatic under his helmet that demanded to be set straight.

'There,' I said, taking engraved Toledo steel, in need of a good polishing, between my hands and easing the dusty helmet into a more upright position. 'That's better, isn't it?'

'*Much better.*' The voice was back, now resounding the confines of the lobby.

Jolted, I looked behind, and then checked the corridor, but it was empty.

'Father?' I said, peering under the helmet at the black void within, wondering if the voice heralded the onset of a new phobia. 'Is that you?'

No answer. Just eyeless hollows staring back. Under the helmet a mummified, toothy corpse, cheekbones protruding bitumen skin.

'You like him?' Helga said, suddenly appearing over my shoulder. 'My favourite man in the whole world,' she pouted. 'Never he gets drunk. Never he talks back. Always doing his duty guarding the front door.'

'But, who is he?'

Helga shrugged. 'What does it matter? I buy him from the Black Friars. Plenty more under the cathedral. Nothing rots in these mountains, something to do with the dry *sierra* air, they say.' She smiled winsomely. 'The armour suit,' she sniffed, 'It comes with the house. Spanish, five hundred years old.'

I was back in my room, but no escape there.

'*You ask me if I am your father.*'

'Now I suppose you're going to tell me?' I groaned, rolling over on my bed and staring at the wall.

'*Yes, I acknowledge your claim. Forefathers, how many generations? Seven to the power of seven? At least that – numeracy never a strong point, plenty of scribes around for that – the house of Inkenhaton, a many-branched tree, rooted in the rich mulch of patricide and incest.*'

'Just what I needed to know.' I moaned, pulling the pillow over my head.

'*A noble lineage of how many twists and turnings, all the way back to the deluge and before,*' the voice droned, oblivious to sarcasm. '*A fine boy, one any father could be proud of, but the cause of much current concern. My former consort is the problem.'*

'You mean Helga?' I interjected. Throwing off the pillow, I noticed in a corner of the ceiling a large spider in his web, motionless above the window.

'She has many names, is always making forbidden ends meet. Her way of avoiding the cut, self-renewal and all that. Incest, supping from the smoking mirror ...'

'Smoking mirror?' I said, wondering if a sudden buzzing in my head signalled the imminent reappearance of the demon, before realising it was only a large blue bottle fly tangled in the spider's web.

'The steaming liver of her unredeemable double ...'

'How can a double have a liver?' I demanded, as, up by the window, the fly's struggles weakened.

'Oh, they do, most certainly, my son, they are used in augury at the sacrifice. White lead of the sky in that cup, self-love and eternal gratification, all the way down the line.'

'And what line is that?' I said. Like a tightrope artiste, the spider scuttled a gossamer thread over the dark canyon that was my room.

'My line, my son,' he said, as the spider reached the end of a line, and a paralysed fly gave up the ghost. *'Like a predatory nuthatch she is burrowed into my wood, always emerging to nip-off the best buds soon as they reappear. She, knows, of course, who and what I am, that's why she keeps me captive in this armour, so blisteringly hot in summer, so perishingly cold in winter, but I never blister and I never perish, would that I could – a prisoner at the gate, my manhood cut off at the root and kept in its sarcophagus, held by a cord, the knot secured by an unbreakable spell given her by the Witch of Endor, another fiend. Always a stickler for detail my ex-consort. Presentation and paying close attention her special talents.'*

11. FOOTIE IN THE NIGHT

'We needs to talk.' Her words still ringing in my ears, but, even so, I was putting off the moment, stretched out on my bed, holding a hand up to a candle flame, staring at four fingers glowing red in the gloom. Just like I used to, I realised, with a jolt. Unbidden a memory surfaced of that never-never land of lost childhood: hiding out in my den under the eaves at one end of the attic in that rambling old house. The cisterns gurgling, every time a tap ran or a toilet flushed. A jackdaw scuttling the slates above. A crow cawing from the chimney pots, another answering from the canopy of the whispering trees. A bishop pacing the boards of his study below, the same old board creaking every time he circuited the Bukhara carpet. The housekeeper at her chopping block by the coup in the courtyard at the back of the scullery, where the concrete was stained around the drain. The squawking of a chicken, held in the tight grip of a giant hand, its neck on the block. Its pitiful squawks cut off by sharp sound, an axe striking through to the block. Over the high wall of the front garden, where I wasn't allowed to play football, in the cobbled street beyond, the knife sharpener, come round again, this being Thursday. Whirling the mysterious gears of his barrel, already busy sharpening Mrs P's shears next door. There was so much treasure at the bottom of this well, below where a pale snake circled turgid black waters. My first step back into the fold then – self-realised Shemite, Catholic, whatever I was – just as a confessor abjured me, meditating on bones, pip of this pipsqueak and all that. But I would grow withered before I penetrated those secrets, I thought wearily, far better put trust in Helga to suck them out.

Think of the devil and the devil appears in some guise of other. No chance to work out exactly who or what, when my door was flung wide, the air shock banishing my little flame out of existence. That apparition backlit in the opening? Hullabaloo Helga, hot to trot, legs spread in a subterranean up draught, the grande madama of bordellos, flouncing in flamenco finery, red lace over starched black underskirts, exposed by a high kick. Was I

71

dreaming again? The same blue of the camiknickers that hung between the bunches of herbs on the clothes pulley in the presbytery kitchen – one theme not explained by my New York analyst's metafiction. But, back to a button-popping bodice and the 'v' of her plunging décolletage, drawing my gaze like a gannet diving for silver fish where thermal geysers gush into the icy black deeps of *la mer*. My mother, for pity's sake, clacking castanets and snapping jezebel fingers. Blood of my veins, that was *piquanté*. *Mamamia*, fuck you! No gainsaying a worm's blind impulse.

'Peter, we must to talk. Have I to stand here all the night?'

'No. Yes. Of course. Come in,' I flustered, wondering if I was dreaming, looking wildly around for the chair that wasn't there.

The devil never enters unless invited. A saying I should have remembered. Rules to play by. Too late to tango now, as a *bruja* took command, heel toeing stone slabs, clicking castanets over bouffant hair, reminding me of a rattlesnake about to strike. Lightning more like, I thought, smelling ozone.

'Um, you'd better ... sit here,' I said, patting the bed, giving up for lost what was already gone.

'So dark in here,' she said, sliding close on seersucker sheets. 'Tell me, do you always sit in the dark when you are alone?'

'No. The candle blew out,' I croaked. 'When you opened the door actually.'

'Just as well, for I likes the dark,' she soothed, her hand staying mine as I reached for my lighter on the bed side table. 'So much the better for seeing you by,' she breathed, the polyester ringlets of her copper-tone wig a torment, resting her hot head on my bare chest, looking up with pupils grown huge in the half-light.

Black pools to drown a world in. My world, for Chris' sake! Even my memories are false – my past a construction, implanted my mad Austrian analyst. His metafiction branded forever a bloody pair of pinking scissors, intruding between our tête-à-tête and our little party of two, as, with the strength of desperation, I shoved Helga off and leapt to my feet.

A dead giveaway, I thought, looking down at a tent pole bulging in my trousers. Dead was right; I would be dead on the cockcrow if I let Helga have her way. Fuck's sake, I'd sworn off women anyway, and Helga was my mother, what was I thinking?

'Peter,' she grinned, pretty as a goshawk, pulling on my waist band. 'What it is wrong?' she said, hands like land crabs fumbling with my flies. 'I only wants to talk.'

'Yea right! Well, so do I,' I said as the zip popped.

'Hey, what the hell is that?' I blurted, breaking free as, from the hall beyond, came a calamitous clatter of ... cymbals? One engorged member swinging wildly in the cold air, I sprang for the door.

Rounding the corner at the end of the long corridor, I found the tin soldier fallen across the lobby, his prune head, minus its helmet, resting upside down against the door, vestigial vertebrae vertically inclining – the black hollows of bitumen eye sockets gaping sightlessly upwards. I knew him then. Don't ask me how. Just that that the old mummy fitted into my genetic jigsaw somehow.

Pip of my pip, marrow of my marrow. Not a phobic stress reaction, but new-found knowledge best kept to myself, I thought, hunkering down in a corner, strangely comforted by the leathery feel of the mummified head cradled in my lap. But then I tensed again as Helga, hustling her bustle, hurtled past a turn of the corridor in the direction of her room. Strange behaviour from the *grande madama* of disguises in this bordello with only one client, me, temporarily released from a basting. It was clear I needed some advice.

'What the fuck is going on?' I demanded of no one in particular.

'My ex is making sure my most vital organ is secure in its sarcophagus, while you are holding my second most vital organ, namely my dehydrated brain. There simply is no time to waste. Open the front door now, throw this old head across the street to where cantina Joe waits. Any delay and both our heads could be on the line, son.'

Son, he said son. I had to know. 'Is this my father talking?' I demanded.

'Only in the sense I founded the Inketaton line of which you are the most miserable example.'

'You are the founding father?'

'Yes.'

'You are not the demon?'

73

'*No my son. My demon is … *'

'Your demon?' I interjected, incredulous.

'*You may know it as the ka.*'

'Then what are you?'

'*The Ba of the Ka. But there is no time for discussion. We are in extreme danger. Now open the fucking door and do as I say!*'

It was in my mind. My research. This conversation. This hotel and the treasure below. My troll mother intent on adding adding my penis to her collection in her room. The *cantina*, Joe and all the mad *borrachos* across the street. The heretical Black Friars up at the cathedral. This Möbius Mexican reality where everything ended up before it began, here in the town at the end of the tunnel. Yes, obviously this was just a primal scream therapy session gone wrong and I was back on my analyst's couch having a nervous breakdown - that was all. However, when I looked down, there was no lip-sync on the puckered prune in my lap. Not a flicker of life in the dear old biltong. Obviously, this was a classic case of projection. My analyst had morphed into another father figure, and this mummified head on my knee was it. Since mydivorce I projected onto every strong male personality I came across, including Wee Donald. For Chris' sake, now I was suckered by this prune. It was obvious, the fears my analyst had dredged from my unconscious were the thwarted desires of my beastly inner child. One day I'd find the key to unlock his cage and let him out to vent his rage and spleen against everything unfair that had happened since he was first locked up. And stop blaming my parents, who had their own reasons for abandoning me. Helga wasn't the *bruja* of the north, she was my mother and my new friend. I was just having trouble with the extreme nature of our mutual attraction. Considered rationally, such a planetary pull was not uncommon between mother and child reunited after a separation of many years; otherwise everything was quite normal.

'*I said, open the fucking front door and do as I say.*' The imperious command blasted like a broadside from a cannon, blowing all doubt from my mind - no second thought as I leapt to my feet and threw open the front door.

'*Stop!*'

Now they were both at me, I thought resentfully. From the ends of the universe. Father and Mother, closing nut-cracker jaws. I felt like throwing down the fucking head and stamping it to dust. I was having a nervous breakdown. I hadn't been this way since I was thrown off a bucking kangaroo, one blue day at a funfair when the carrousel shredded its gears, the sky turned to mud and I landed baby face down in the dirt. Bone knowledge that shook me to my core.

'*You young fool. Why did you not do as I say? Blood of my blood, I ... I ... disown you.*' Words frothing my brain as

Helga seized the prune relic.

'Ah, not too undamaged,' she announced, rolling it over between her hands. 'With a bit of glue, we can stick him back together, then with sand paper and filler he is as good as new!' She looked up, her ready smile exchanged for a scowl. 'My *gött*, Peter, what you think you are doing, half out in the street, with your shirt hanging out, you catch you death! And look you,' she pointed, 'Guzman is watching, spying as usual, curse him. Close the door now, we need a nice cup of tea after all this communion.' She took my arm. 'That is the right weird, no?'

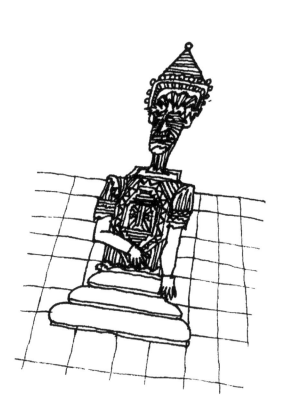

12. BISHOP DOWN

Commotion in the salon before a big fire of nopal cactus. Helga toasting marshmallows on a stick. High on the mantelpiece, a withered old prune gazing down, his expression sad, all the fight gone out of him.

'My *gött*, Peter, you are a difficult customer, but I likes you,' she said. 'Here,' she withdrew the marshmallows, sizzling from the flames, 'Take one and careful now, or you burn fingers!'

So much concern. She really sounded as if she cared. My only living relative - not including the dubious case of a prune - had to have a place in my life. Even if she was a *bruja*, and a troll to boot. Size was important, though I wasn't used to women looking down on me, especially my mother; a word that both thrilled and terrified. Lightning shorting out my mind, leaving me captive and prey ... I was gyring a witch's whirlpool, the pull getting stronger with every turn, but I had to go on, discover the rules of engagement. That was the way, I knew with sudden certainty.

'More mooshmallows, my dear?'

'No, thank you.' I shook my head, politely.

'*Manners maketh man and shields him from enemies.*' Unbidden, a Biblical admonition, springing to mind. Perhaps from my days in the old presbytery. Sage words to remember, I thought, taking a napkin and wiping granules of sugar from my lips.

We both spoke at once, uttering each other's names - her given and my assumed - in the same moment.

'Please,' I smiled, giving her the floor.

'No,' she smiled, 'After you.'

This smiling back and forth was turning the worm in my gut. And there she was again, no word adequate to describe the effect of pouting lips, paired on shining teeth, divided right up to the gummy clit. A come on, those twinkling ivories.

'I insist,' I said, behind a steady smile, grindingteeth.

'I do not know if this is the best time, Peter.' She frowned.

'There never is a best time, Helga, you know that.'

'You are right,' she sighed. 'If I have to spill the whole pan of beans, that is what I must do.'

I nodded, finding her quaint English amusing. Pan of beans indeed. Couldn't even get that right, my kooky mother; she was lovely really.

'All my life Peter, men trying to make me. Maybe because I am tall, they feel they must to. You know, I get in some hell of a scrapes. I even marry once. But the good times in the old church house do not last. Soon we are fighting over the names he calls me from his Bible. Jezebel. Delilah.' She paused, hang dog. 'Harlot, always harlot.' She looked up. 'Do you know what this means? Always I am wanting to find out!'

'You really don't know?'

'Why do you think I asks?'

'Prostitute,' I sighed, wondering how much more I could take.

Her green eyes gleamed. 'My next job in Hamburg, always with sailors making spurt from every port.' She shook her head. 'Always they are telling me this.'

'But what happened to the bishop?'

'I never say anything about a bishop,' Helga growled.

'But you did say he was always reading the Bible,' I soothed. 'Perhaps I assumed he was a bishop because you mentioned a church house.'

'Did I?'

'Yes, you lived there, remember?'

'You are right', she nodded slowly. 'Yes I did say that.'

'Why so suspicious, Helga?'

'Because I kill him!'

'What?'

'An accident,' she shrugged.

'How so?'

'It is so long ago,' she sighed. 'Maybe is better I tell.'

'Well, you can't stop there.'

'I had to survive.' Her pout changed to a scowl.

'Sooner or later one of us was going to do it. I take no shit, you know. Better him than me. And now he can complain to the god he prays to.' She eyed me intently.

'Do you think me a bad woman, Peter?'

'Not for me to say,' I offered woodenly. 'Everyone has to answer to themselves.'

'Exactly! That is why I like you!' Helga nodded.

'You makes up your mind. No one can make it for you,' she sighed benignly, her mood change prompting a proportionate reduction in size, making her seem cute and homey.

'You know, it is strange.' She settled back on soft sofa cushions with a languid cast of a hand, conjuring a face. 'In a way you remind me of him.' She sighed.

'Nothing physical, you understand. He was, how you say, sallow and short, where you are fair and tall.' Frowning, she looked away. 'Maybe it is how you move.'

So it *was* confirmed, this bishop was my father. I had almost given the game away with that slip, never mind all the questions. But there were so many things I needed to know, like had I been baptised a Catholic; why she'd given me up; where the bishop was buried; the manner of his death; source of his fortune; what was the Belgium connection – did he just go along with the shit-eating or was he really a coprophiliac? And how did he end up owning mines in the town? But a voice in my head said no – there will be another opportunity.

'Ok, so that was the bishop.' I smiled grimly, condemning her not so much for the murder but more for being casual about it. 'And then there were sailors?'

'Oh yes,' Helga grinned. 'So many sailors. I likes that work!'

'Spurting over the waves, eh?' I winked.

'Ooh la la!' Helga laughed.

'And then?'

'Whips, sawdust, clowns and,' she pouted, 'Tricks.'

'The circus?' I cocked an eyebrow.

'Yes and my ringmaster.' Helga blushed. 'What a man. So strong. So, how you say, big. For the first time in my life I am happy.' Her cheeks darkened. 'But of course that does not last.'

'What happened?'

Helga looked up at the ceiling. 'He dies!'

'Another accident?'

'No.' She shook her head. 'Not me this time, I swear, even so I get the blame. Is High Wire Serena. Never I trust her. A Ruski, a bitch always on heat. After he leaves me for her, one day I look through the window of her trailer and see him without any clothes, tied to a chair with a sword stuck in his collar bone, and the point out his tummy button. Right through. Blood is everywhere. So shocking I am. Because it is my sword, you understand, the one I swallow every night in the ring,' she said, miming her circus act, upping her chin, exposing a throat, pellucid and pink in the glow of embers banked in the hearth. 'But I get my revenge. Before I leave, Serena takes a fall, breaks her pretty little neck ...'

'And?' I prompted.

Helga shrugged. 'She dies, but not before she knows, it is I who cuts the high wire. So that is why I come to Mexico.'

'Hold on a minute,' I cut in, 'All this happened in the old, um, I mean another country?'

'I am not so stupid as to tell you everything.' She swelled back to J-cup bra size. 'What sort of fool you take me for?'

'I was only asking, no harm intended.'

'Ok. But remember,' Helga raised a finger, 'Too many questions, makes me ask questions.'

'Sure.' I said. 'Ask away.'

'I have no need. You are like an open book. Already I check you out,' she smiled darkly, 'Cover to cover. And you know what I read?'

'No,' I gulped.

'A nice man, kind and thoughtful, who I can trust to keep his mouth shut.' She winked. 'Clever too. Just the man I need for a partner.'

'A partner?' I sat up straight. 'What the hell for?'

'Never play the fool with me. Always that is a mistake!' she scowled. 'For the treasure of the Sierra Madré, here in this house.'

'So,' I said heavily, 'If it really is here, what do you need me for? You are in charge.'

'Yes,' Helga hissed, deflating as her sudden fury abated, 'But I am a woman alone. Even if I find it, that is only the beginning. I still have to get out of the town alive. So many dangers,' she thumbed over her shoulder,

'Guzman for one, always spying. The girls in the kitchen for another. And now we have a new problem.' She sighed, her face crumpling. 'I get a message today. Gomez, the owner, he wants to sell up. Not enough business, he says.'

Another dark chapter, in an unwritten book. *Pride and Prejudice and Gomez.* Her first lover in Mexico, a man of the mestizo under-class, climbed the greasy pole of ambition in the only profession then open to mixed bloods, becoming the police chief of the region, before taking up a senior position with the federal police in the state capital. Hated in the town on account of his ten-year reign of torture and terror, and the fortune he had made from the drug trade, facing certain death if he returned. That was the reason I had to go see him and, posing as a potential buyer, find out how advanced were his plans to sell the hotel.

13. DON'T LOOK BACK …

Good to get away, boarding the little bus with Helga's money zipped tight in my belt. We were partners. But Helga was the stakeholder. I had a lot to think about as I set off into the tunnel, treasure mostly, and our Q&A session over breakfast.

'Liss'en,' she hissed, 'As they say around here, gold is shit, it attract a lot of flies.'

Yea, I liked that. So we were the flies. But where was the ointment?

'Shit is like gold, it make a bad smell. And I can smell it.' She tapped her nose. 'Is close, somewhere in the house.'

Nice one, Helga. I could hardly contain my *huevos rancheros* – double yolkers, golden apples of the sun. Was she sure it wasn't the drains?

'No, is true! Big drains under the hotel. Like the catacombs of Rome down there. Mine-es for miles.'

'Surely not?'

'Oh yes! All the short-life miners down on their knees, get born, fuck and die!'

'How many over the time?'

'A million?' She frowned. 'More I think. Here were the richest min-es in Mexico. So many bones for the priests. Men, women, children, only those that convert, allowed to see the light on *Domingo* after Mass. Each carrying as much ore as they can balance in the palm of one hand. All their wages to build the cathedral.'

'How long did that go on?'

'Since just after the fall of Tenochitlán.'

'Not sixty years before?' I said, thinking of the date carved on the door lintel.

'No.' She shook her head. 'Three years after, not before. Thirteen *conquistadores*, hunting the last Aztec eagle knights in the mountain forests, camp down for the night. In the morning, silver in the ashes. Where they make fire is the mother hole.'

'Mother hole?' Laughingly I interjected, 'Don't you mean mother lode?'

'Hole?' she snapped. 'Load? For some mothers is the same. Soon all the trees are cut down cut down for pit props, and the land turns to desert. Three hundred years later they are still mining, so much silver there is, the street outside is cobbled with ingots, their descendants still ruling the show. But then comes Pancho Villa and *la revolución*, the silver cobbles on the street outside from the cathedral to the tunnel are dug up, and the Spanish patrons pay for the bullet, taking to their graves the secret of where they hides their fortunes.'

'Ah, the treasure,' I grinned. 'Everything leads back to that.'

'Of course.' She nodded slowly.

'And you think it's hidden somewhere here.'

'I am sure.' Her eyes wandered. 'Why else do you think this house is called *la Castillo de la Dinero?*'

'Any idea where?'

'You see how thick the walls are.' She looked around. 'Three, four meters.'

'No.' I shook my head. 'There'd be signs of disturbance in the bare masonry. I think it's deeper. Perhaps in a sealed-up mine?'

'Why you say that?' she scowled.

'Just a hunch,' I dissembled, careful not to breach the terms of a deal struck with a diabolical ally, who I was counting on coming good in the future with get-out-of-jail cards, or whatever the six intimations were.

'Maybe you are right,' she sighed, looking away.

'Why the sad face,' I said, wondering if she had just thought of my dead father.

'Sad?' she pouted. 'Not me. I am just remembering a story Gomez tells me about skulls blocking the drains when he is changing the house into a hotel.'

'How many?' I demanded, a sudden tingling on the nape of my neck, suggesting the demon phobia had just manifested and was scrutinising the proceedings. Was there ever any escape from my fears? I guessed not, at least within the confines of the hotel.

'Thirteen,' she shrugged. 'Miners, he said, from the old days before la *revolución*.'

'How did he make that out?'

'From the style of the tools his builders find close by.'

'Pickaxes and shovels?'

'No,' she scowled, her mood downshifting and her size swelling accordingly. 'Adzes and shovels, the same as the miners use up to the eighteenth century.'

'But why just their skulls?'

She smiled, 'An old belief, separate your enemy's head from his body and he cannot return to haunt you.'

'There could be another reason. Like they knew where the treasure was. They might even have buried it and that's why they were killed.'

'Of course that is possible,' she inclined her head,

'But I do not think so.'

'Why you say that?' I demanded, sure she was lying.

'The treasure was hidden when the town was under siege by Pancho Villa, and not before, when those skulls were buried.'

'But thirteen skulls, in this building? Come on, there's got to be a fucking connection – and I don't mean Belgium!'

'Around here,' she shrugged, 'Thirteen is not many. Why, only a few months back, they are finding maybe forty skeletons under the bandstand Gomez has built in the plaza, before he left.'

'From revolution times?'

'No,' she smiled, 'Much more recent. Ten years ago Gomez is brought in as chief of police.'

'Why?'

'To stop the drug traffic.'

'Is there much round here?' I said, wondering if she knew where I could score some grass.

'Do you not yet understand there is no money in anything else in this country?'

'Yes, of course,' I nodded, knowing this was not the right time. 'So what was his problem?'

'A tribe of albino Indians. Five hundred years after the Conquest, still hiding out from the conquistadores,' she laughed. 'Yes, Gomez really believes a white tribe is growing marijuana in a secret canyon up in the mountains. Then in a storm the fool crashes the special helicopter the governor gives him into a stupid thunder bird.'

'Thunder bird?'

'Yes, yes, sometimes in thunderstorms, you see them, close by lightning, high up in the mountains. As I say, they are just stupid birds. Gomez never finds the canyon, because it is a story in a book he read by an idiot Belgian, and so he makes an example of a village, where the people are selling the marijuana. But then he goes too far, even for the state governor, who had turned a blind eye. There is even a report of the massacre in a national newspaper, and calls for an inquiry, though of course nothing happens. That is why he can never return to town and wants to sell up,' she laughed. 'Too many relatives out for blood.'

'He sounds a right cunny funt,' I muttered dyslexically, jolted by a roseate glow pulsing her midriff. But then with another jolt, my viewpoint again shifted and the glow was all around. I was in a veined red cavern of living flesh, pulsing boompty-boom, the glowing walls creeping with pestilential black ferns.

Equally abruptly, my viewpoint shifted again, and I was back staring at Helga across the table and wondering whether I had just experienced a womb memory.

'There is nothing to worry for,' she smiled, to my considerable relief, back to her default size. 'You are my friend, and Gomez will respect that.'

'I hope so,' I said, realising that I had just received the first of my six intimations from the lord of death. This one was a shift in perception, the black creeping tendrils revealing, in graphic detail, that she was eaten up with cancer, brought on by greed for treasure. Helga was a dead woman then, just a matter of time, but still my mother, the only one I had. Whatever she had planned would go awry, I knew that now. For myself, I had undertaken to go and see Gomez, which is what I intended to do, come hell or high water – the freedom of the road would rid me of my new demon phobia, at least temporarily.

14. CRAZEE VILLA

So that was the conversation, and now for the view. The bus belching out of the tunnel, black fumes clearing on cactus-buttoned mesas, cross stitched by tracks and snaking with roads, freightliners grinding down on donkey carts and Cadillacs – the high plains bisected by atlas biceps – *cordilleras*, ranging north to south, corded knots knuckling a map, mounting as far as the eye could see. The top of the world from a Mexican perspective. A strange feeling, as if I'd entered a different dimension – not the last time I'd experience that sensation – the Town With No Name, a ghost in more than one sense, misting up in memory, making me wonder if I'd ever existed back there.

But this was my world. A world of colour instead of the monochrome of the mountains, where it was warm instead of freezing and you could buy newspapers, and pass the time waiting for your connection drinking coffee at the bus station kiosk.

A hell of a kick, that newspaper picture. Real life out there. Gangsters and cops battling it out. Mexico *arriva!* The punchy headline, '*Cazereria de Hombre*'; in plain English, 'man hunt'. Man hunts man hunts man ... was ever it not so? At least that wasn't me. '*El número uno narcó tráficante*' – even I had heard of Jaime Everrárdez de Léon – 'Robin Hood' to his pals, on the run after blowing away a US DOA agent, I thought, in dyslexic mode again. Or was he a DEA agent? My eyes had gone funny in the half-light, same difference either way, the world had moved on and another soldier bitten the dust. Nice one, I thought. I never liked the feds and their rule book anyway. With every new entry, in closed the walls of the world.

But this was Mexico, where but one law applies – all depending on who you know, what you know and a poker face – comedians and *gringos* excepted of course. The foreigner was easy meat for any Mexican pointing the finger. Under Mexico's Napoleonic code of law, a simple j'accuse is enough to get you extradited or indicted.

Another of Helga's cautions: don't try to bluff out cops. Especially high-ranking federal cops like Gomez.

Plenty to ponder as, in falling twilight, I made my way to the bus stance, to the head of ... what queue? A novel experience in Mexico where the masses go by bus. Pulling in now, a *Primera Clase* space liner, royal blue curtains tied back on vacant portholes, sleek and burnished excepting the tarmac-bitten tyres and scrapes attesting to donkey carts pushed off the road. No conductor for once, only a highway bandit for a driver, grinning as he opened the door, jacking *zapata* eyebrows as I announced my destination.

'*En serio señor?*' Like he really meant it. But then, when I asked if there was a problem, he shrugged with the coded message, 'What did he care about *chinga gringos* anyway?' He'd take my money anyhow. Even more to ponder then, as we set off into the real blue yonder.

Plenty of scheduled stops to mark time by; after five lay-bys and still no takers *el capitán* abandoned the three-lane highway – about as good as I'd experienced in Mexico – raising plumes over the chaparral, taking a dirt track short cut, cross stitching the barbed wires of cactus plantations, agave stretching to sandbagged desert defences. A no-man's-land now consumed in dust, as we climbed into the stronghold of night; sentinel pines guarding the passes, timber-tops cresting the high ridges of finger-lickin' sugar-frosted stars gone patchy with mist; the bus defying all known laws of gravity as we descended, shuttling switchbacks, the driver intent over illumined dials, his face console-green, *el extraterrestrial capitán* flying by the seat of his *Star Trek* pants.

Even the atomics of the seat I was gripping, with a tenacity born of vertigo, seemed in doubt, careening in a bus out of time and out of this world. Brought back to earth by the jewelled splendour of the city blazing into view below, a firefight of topaz dragons and peridot boulevards locked in immortal combat, all the way to the glittering prize – *el céntro* – high-rises and hoardings, a tiara garnished with emeralds, sapphires and rubies, competing with the stars. Let there be light! Man in abundance, banishing night with his flares.

Did I say abundant? A gross error. The bus' broad windshield, a panorama onto desolation. Where were all the *mariachi* bands? This the best hour to be plying their trade, serenading *borrachos* stumbling *cantina* doorways, all closed now, as were the shuttered shops. Perhaps a national hero had died? But that would mean firecrackers and fusillades, a funeral was never a dull affair in Mexico. What then? Mass pestilence to explain the absence of tamale vendors at street corners? Hardly. Food poisoning not an issue south of the Rio Grandé – for many dysentery was a way of life. And where were all the squeegee monkeys, prosthetic clowns and brain-dead fire eaters parading backed-up traffic at intersections? All gone ... along with the courting couples, the promenaders, legless skateboard beggars, the dispossessed and befuddled huddled in doorways ... unfathomable mystery, as the bus jumped the red lights, the driver as good as blindfolded, all the way to *el céntro*.

Perhaps we'd crashed back in the mountains – this bejewelled city a necropolis of the dead, waiting at the bus station Aztec morticians with obsidian knives separating the incorporeal from the weights of tiresome flesh. A long queue back there, given the poltergeist population.

No one, just no one. No taxis and no payphones, but plenty of morticians skulking the crumbling concrete halls, sliding into slatted shadows whenever I turned. Nothing else to do, but start walking; one direction as good as another, I supposed, faced with threading underpasses to nowhere, or climbing buckled barriers onto spaghetti flyovers – and that no use, all the roadside signs plucked for roofs in the nearest *barrio*, misdirecting crows and low-flying aircraft. Nothing makes sense under harsh neon, everything a metaphor and all ultimately untranslatable; those close-grouped electricity pylons screened by high wire, Angor Watt in quarantine transported from the jungles of another Siam, that corrugated assemblage framed by scarified scaffolding, a slice of Black Forest gateaux fit for a hobgoblin king straight out of Brothers Grimm, and what about that stepped square of gravel by a city block-wide excavation? The pyramid of the moon, where nightly flayed bodies were consigned to the pit, stone chips settling, spooking me out as I walked by.

A car! One of those cruising sedans I'd spied, but only at a distance, either at the next intersection, or slotted between tall, earthquake-cracked buildings. How come they were all two-tone black-tops of the same *marqué*. Fleet cars, I suppose, confirmed as one neared me. Police pheromones I can smell at a hundred paces. I needed no sensor to realise here were heavy cops.

Gomez was a cop wasn't he? Nothing else to do but hitch a ride. I know how to brass the case when all else fails – and wasn't the car stopping anyway?

'*De dondé eres?*' My heart beating faster, rasped words, drawing a bow across over-strung sensibilities.

'*No hablár Español, señor.*'

True, my Spanish deserting me at that moment.

'Ah!' In the darkness of the car his grin was a glint of gold on an otherwise blank page. 'You Eeenglish tourist?'

'Yes. No.' I nodded then shook my head, hoping that way to confuse them. 'Not exactly. Just visiting. My uncle actually.' Randomly I pointed to the Grecian colonnades of a large mansion, partially obscured by cypress trees set out like traffic cones, gracing a nearby hill. 'He lives somewhere in that direction, I think.'

'*Es Méxicano*, this oncle of yours?'

'*Si, señor*,' I said into the open car window, giving the script to the four blank pages arranged about the seats. 'Maybe you know him, for he is an important man in the federal police.'

The name Gomez: a magic carpet to satellite dish summit, where I found myself before the ornate but stout panelled door of a rococo pink villa, columned in the Doric style, at my back canine heads on pillars, commanding a sweep of rosy marble steps, leading down to a driveway that artfully snaked parking cone cypress trees and Greek statuary to a big black hedge and no-nonsense high-security gates, behind which the police in their car were watching as I pulled on a repro antique bell chain, drawing a chorus of celestial chimes. Verdi on tap, the 'Rite of Spring', drowned out by barking, as the front door flew open on a stick man, all angles and interstices in tow to a black brute of a Neapolitan mastiff – a breed of dog I recalled was favoured by the Camorra.

'*Señor* Gomez? I'm a friend of Helga's', I said, wondering if he was a cappo of the Camorra in on the Belgian connection, looking askance at the dog's drooling jowl, paddling paws and straining lead, which was chewed in the middle and fraying to snap the clasp where it linked to a spiked metal collar. 'The name's Quinton,' I said, so rattled I forgot Helga knew me as Peter. 'All the way from the bloody Serengeti,' I added, recovering.

'Serengeti?' he frowned, then Sat Nav references seemed to slot in place. 'You better come in then,' Gomez said, clearly impressed I had come all the way from Kenya.

'Bruno,' he mouthed, kneeling to earwig the brute, pointing a long finger, as his bloodless lips nuzzling black velvet. '*Es amigo.* Friend of the family. No biting now.'

So I was now included with the 'family'. Could it be that Helga's stories of a bishop were a smokescreen, and her Mexican lover was my real father? I would still have been born a Catholic. But no, I thought, checking out daddy-long-leg genetics, I came from a higher order of life, and besides, no father of mine could be a cop – particularly not an Indian-murdering cop like him.

'You come at a bad time.' Gomez cast back over a dandruff shoulder, his blue blazer flapping, gold buttons glinting, a shirt tail hanging. Bruno padding happily ahead, leading the way along the flock pink hall decorated Versailles-style, between cut-crystal etched glass mirrors reflecting uncertain futures, and gold cherubs aiming arrows from porphyry plinths inset in the gilded frames.

'A very bad time,' he said again, flinging open a tall mahogany door.

There goes a man of action, I thought sourly, watching him eat up the carpets in attenuated spider-like strides, his heels clicking on parquet along bay windows draped with a makeshift assortment of brocade, sheets and blankets quite out of character with the designer look of the room. He headed for a ghastly monument to bad taste that occupied a good portion of the far wall: Tutankhamen's cocktail cabinet in diamond dust lacquer, striped gold and black, complete with horns and wings, the boy pharaoh looking down on a splendid selection of drinks. Gomez refilled a glass with Napoleon brandy, drenching it in ginger, before remembering to ask what I'd like.

'Johnnie Walker Black Label,' I replied crisply, settling into one of several sofas, deciding against Chivas Regal, the only other blend available. I was reminded that, when it comes to whisky, the rich know next to nothing about malts the world over – in Scotland the preferred choice of courtiers and paupers. No bar without a selection, and most smaller than that effete faux-Egyptian cabinet.

Johnnie Walker it was. Another man with long legs and alcohol for innards, I thought sourly, watching Gomez reach for the awkwardly placed bottle, a ladder and a crane for anyone else, strain showing on his pasty long face as he turned. He handed me the bottle and a glass, telling me to please myself, loosening his tie and sighing loudly as slumped in the opposite sofa.

'*Chinga su madré*,' he swore to no one in particular.

'What, my mother?' I snapped.

'No!' he replied hotly. 'Just chinga every mother except your mother, if that's the way you want it. What the fuck do I care? All *putás*, always shopping and making men pay for restaurant bills, and babies always more babies filling up the world. I hate this life, you know. Hey!' he sat up, not caring that he had just slopped drink on his Armani slacks. 'I forget you name. So sorry. You must be wanting to show me the brochures.' He clutched his head. 'A lot on my mind right now.'

I smiled, confused by his mention of brochures, then, recovering my aplomb, jumped up and bowed in the Prussian manner, which I hoped would impress him. Holding a hand to my heart, I announced, 'Peter Quinton, at your service.'

'Peter Quinton?' His eyes widened. 'You are not from the travel company? You are the Peter from the hotel, the joker Helga tells me about?'

'She did?' I said, somehow pleased.

'Sure,' Gomez said, breathing easier, 'She text me every day on the mobile.'

'Really?' I interrupted, 'I thought there was no signal in the mountains?'

'There are base stations for military communications.' He shrugged, 'You know Helga and her connections.' He unbuttoned his shirt collar. 'But yesterday I tell her, no more.' He shook his head, looking like a mop on a pole as his lank hair showered fresh dandruff on his blazer. 'Not now they have the number.'

'Who has the number? I said, quick as a shot.

Gomez tensed. 'What does it matter, who? Cops for cops,' he choked, wiping spittled lips with he back of a hand. 'Worse,' he continued, '*Gringo* cops for *Mexicano* cops.' He gestured wildly towards the heavily draped window. 'One thousand in the city tonight! *Con permission* of the *pinché* NAFTA agreement. They can go anywhere with all the back-up they want. Mexico is a country no more,' he wailed, pressing spider fingers to his temples.

'The *gringos* can do as they like with us.'

'Is this about drugs?'

'*Comó no?*' Gomez said. 'When that is seventy per cent of the trade with the States. Everything else is alfalfa,' he sneered. 'All the players, north and south, have a piece. Ever since Reagan, when the US budget deficit starts a pile of hundred dollar bills now well past the moons of Jupiter. Operations those Congress fat asses, pretend never happen, paid by what we bring over. As my confessor at the cathedral called it, "*el izquierda mano del obscurio*" – the left hand of darkness wiping the shit in secret places. A sad fact of this shitty life, my friend. That is why I cannot understand this disaster!' Hands deep in trouser pockets, he stood, perhaps seeking confirmation of his continuing existence in the black shine of Italian foot leather. 'Maybe is because of the exchange rate,' he muttered.

'Come again?' I said, wondering if his confessor was a secret shit-eater. Father O'Flattery, I was sure. Could he really be a member of the most exclusive club of all? If so, it was an ass overhead underworld.

Stepping over to the sofa, Gomez sat down beside me. 'In my country, you must understand,' he said, 'All serious *négocio* is in dollars. And for that you have to pay the black market rate. Is like a tax on the people, eight maybe ten cents above the official rate. But recently that changes. The same *narco tráfico* who ices the sacrifice, like kills the *gringo* agent,' he shrugged, 'Starts the war when he sells cartel dollars for pesos, and undercuts the official price. His trade is so many billions it drops the dollar ten cents worldwide. Now the Chinese are panicked and jumping

95

out of US treasury bonds, which are propping up that Jupiter-high junk pile of bills, meaning that *mañana* the dollar could be confetti.'

'Bad fucking scene,' I said, connecting all this to the newspaper report. 'That is fucking heavy.'

'You are right my friend.' Gomez clapped my shoulder. 'And this is the wrong place.' He stood up. 'Is a bad time, a very bad time. You must leave, now.'

I was about to protest this was not at all a good time, what with all the heat about, when came a thunderous banging of the front door – hideous barking too. Bruno sprinting from behind the sofa, the lead snagging his master, towing him by the heels, drink arcing as Gomez skidded to the floor, taking a rug with him, out of the room and down the hall, ploughing a furrow in the marble tiles.

'Gomez, you *pinché* fok!' said a man's voice, pitched to make himself heard above the din of bells, barking and banging. 'For the love of God,' he cried in a falsetto. 'Let me in!'

15. TRAFICO

Call it instinct, second sight, whatever you want, but I knew who was banging on the door. As the paper said, '*El número uno narcó tráficante*'. Forget Sid Vicious of the Sex Pistols, Elvis Presley, Eminem or any impostor. This was the man himself. My ultimate hero.

And here he was, Jaime Everrárdez de Léon, ably assisted by a palpitating Gomez. And what a prince of the Tulullan blood – Moctezúma's line of course – of the order of valour. Well, I'd give anyone an award dressed like that in body-hugging Lycra, bar-coded black and gold, diamonds studding playboy shoulders, more on his fingers; his sallow pencil moustachioed face was just as I imagined d'Artagnan of the Three Musketeers, small but perfectly formed – only more handsome, if that was possible, saturnine with flaring nostrils, quirky bushy eyebrows juxtaposed at angles, and below … such danger in burning black opals, staring directly into mine. It came to me then: I would die for this *hombre*.

'Who the *fok* ees that?' Jaime shrieked. My all-time hero fingering me? *J'accuse*, in an out-thrust hand, impugning me of unnameable crimes, innocence personified on the sofa, supping my whisky, any residual coolness down to my state of shock. That just could not be.

And then I realised, Jaime wasn't pointing a finger or any such extension, in his steady hand, aimed at my pounding heart, was a small revolver. Pearl handled, from this low angle.

Wait a minute now, I ain't no *gringo* foker. I'm a friend … your best friend if you'd only believe me. Words I wanted to say, dying on my lips. The divide of the Conquest between us, as I met Aztec obsidian eyes, and all that happened since.

'Gomez tell him I am OK. For fuck's sake man! Before it's too late!' I pleaded, momentarily ensnared by panic. The red-hot tableau forever branded – Gomez stranded high and dry, his mouth opening and shutting like a pike out of water, Jaime exuding deadly force, his finger curled on the trigger.

Time for a diversion, I thought. 'Hey Gomez,' I grinned, 'Why don't you tell Jaime that joke about the pie, the cook and the sticky fingers?'

'What the fok you saying man?' Jaime frowned.

'It's really funny,' I insisted. 'Go on Gomez! Don't be a party pooper.'

'What is this foking joke?' Jaime hissed.

'I forget!' Gomez tore his hair. 'I don't know any such joke.'

'Make up yo' mind!' Jaime's eyes bulged.

'Put the gun down,' Gomez snapped, back in control. 'Peter is family. *Un hombre de honor*. You can trust heem, even as you trust me.'

What a recommendation. Something to write up in my CV. Jesus, I didn't even know who I was, only that I wouldn't play the sacrificial victim. No one could lay that penance on me. Not this pilgrim. I'd see them in hell first. Well, maybe.

Jaime had múchas próblemas muy grandé. Número uno, the ring of steel, corralling the city. Número dos, the night curfew. Número tres, his image flashing on TV news bulletins on the hour. Número qué? I just lost count, his pistoleros either shot dead or getting the third degree, gonads wired, sweating gigawatts under bright lights. Most of all the five million peso reward. Who could he trust with such a price on his head. Who indeed? I wondered for the umpteenth time, checking out Gomez, on a marathon, wearing a circuit round the carpet, calling up associates on his mobile, hand clamped to his ear, speaking *urgente* gangster euphemise.

'*Chingone!* Turn the sound down, I cannot hear!' Gomez swore, pointing towards the plasma TV and Jaime on his knees, chain snorting from a beaded nose bag, channel hopping, entranced by his fuzzy YouTube image repeating on news bulletins. His face red, Gomez slammed the phone on the smoked-glass top of a gilded coffee table. 'Is no use. The whole town shut tighter than Porfiro Diaz's sphincter! Every way out blocked!'

'No,' I said, swaying slightly, over by the bar pouring my third Chivas Regal, down to my second choice after drinking steadily through the night. 'Not every way?'

'Fok! What you say?' Jaime, for the first time in hours showing a different side than a bobbing Lycra ass, as he turned away from the TV.

Whisky, ambrosia of the gods! Accept no imitations or adulterations, stay on the amber trail, and you'll always return full circle. The rule applying even with blends. That third Chivas had quite cleared my head, all the clouds rolled back off the heather.

Jaime was small, even petite, I pointed out, no insult intended. If we plucked his eyebrows, shaved his moustache, dressed him in a blouse and skirt, and applied lipstick and mascara, anyone would take him for a woman. No curfew had been announced for daylight hours, and who would suspect a *gringo* and his *muchacha*. Of course he would have to practice the hula, swinging his hips, but I had been coached by the best, so that would be no problemá. For delivering Jaime through the ring of steel, best achieved by mingling with the masses - a dreadful prospect for someone so refined, I knew, but of limited duration - it being my certain experience from travelling round the world, buses are only cursorily checked at roadblocks. As for a refuge, both Gomez and I knew somewhere that, to all intents and purposes, was out of the world, so fucking obscure, it didn't even have a name.

I had almost forgotten my purpose, why I had come to *casa* Gomez in the first place; to plead for a stay of execution and leave off selling the hotel. At least wait 'till we found the treasure. No, I didn't mention that, but I thought of it, watching Jaime smacking lips - in love with his reflection, Scarlet O'Hara posing in the bevelled hall mirror, hands on hips, winking at me. What a sweetie. I was entranced.

'Is too late,' Gomez replied, button eyes hard on mine. 'Helga sold it to me in the first place, and did not exercise her option to buy it back, so I do not understand why you have to come. However, only last week, after *mucho negocio*, I exchange it with a small contribution towards my pension, lock stock and wine cellar for a *pequeño* castle in the Pyrenees,' he smiled disingenuously,

'Or somewhere like that.' He rotated pasty hands, reassembling castles in the clouds. 'Even harder to find than the hotel.' Flaky eyebrows emphasising the point.

'All through intermediaries. But I can tell you, he is a high-ranking diplomat and a member of the very best clubs. Belgian?' Fingers taking a walk, scratching his scaly scalp. 'I forget!'

Shit-houses, I thought, at this latest reminder of a connection best forgotten. Not another colonialist on the make.

Gomez approved my plan, but only after he had proposed a couple of '*poco*' alterations. The last stage of the journey, as outlined, was simply too dangerous.

'Mountain Indians' were not like city folk, too self-preoccupied to see beyond their noses, they possessed a sixth sense, he insisted over Jaime's loud guffaws; in the close confines of the little bus, his disguise surely would be penetrated. Some stupid *borracho* would start feeling him up and that would be that. But there was another way. An old *burro* trail fallen into disuse, the only option long before the tunnel.

So it was to a bus and a train, and then ... but I was getting ahead of myself. Probably the most dangerous stage of our journey before us. The long walk to the bus station.

'Wok? You out you mind, man? Never, in my whole life!' That was Jaime's one protest before we started. But then Gomez pointed out taxi drivers all were radio connected via cab-central to police headquarters and, like the mountain Indians, possessed an acuity that stripped bare all pretence. Quite a thought that, I considered, a sense of power and possession taking a grip, as I took Jaime's delicate little hand into mine.

16. HEADS OR …

By bus and by train into the night. Standing-room only in the unlighted third-class carriage, shuffling with menacing moustaches, as matches flared in the sullen crowd – *clandestinos* heading *norté*, glad not to be with their *compañeros*, clinging to the carriage roof, gathered in silent contemplation. New prince of Bel Air or a prison cell and the bum rush back? My thoughts were mostly directed through the open but barred windows, however, wafting sweet scents of … jasmine? Boletus cactus? I didn't know. The only certain thing the knotty outlines of the shadowy *sierras* tracking our clanking progress, the eye of the hunter Orion, winking balefully where jagged peaks scratched the stars. At last the familiar outlines of the three sisters and our stop, a lonely estación in a bleached vastness. No platform, just a great drop onto drifting white sands that silted a shot-out sign pointing towards the mountains – and the town, I hoped. A string of bullet holes rendering the legend all but unreadable, only one word legible, '*Catorces*', in faded letters, the paint cracked and peeling.

Another nameless mystery to ponder as we set off.

Easy enough following Gomez's crudely drawn map, navigating the desert by starlight, following a trail of.

Of rotting carcasses and the gusting stink of shit to a vast and deserted pig farm, marked on the map, at the foot of the mountains. Skull and cross bone signs warning of the dangers of swine fever on its high perimeter fence, which was busted outwards as if by a stampeding herd; we skirted it to where the path divided before a low mound covered with the gnarled roots of a most singular tree. Closer at hand, a stone stele, about a meter high. On the nearside, a bas-relief of a bearded wayfarer with his staff, pointing to a weatherworn inscription that might just have been cuneiforms, though it was hard to be sure in the shade of the looming canopy above. The huge half-dead oak, last survivor of the great forests once swaddling now naked slopes, forked by countless lightning strikes. Old? Bloody ancient. Ancestor spirits, congregating twig thickets, rustling the great girth of the trunk, which, on closer inspection, I saw was hollow and charred at the base, as though burnt out by a hobo's fire.

'Which way, man?' Jaime demanded in a grating – now all too familiar – whine.

And again, when I didn't answer, he just turned and stared sullenly starwards, petulantly stamping his heel, be-Jesus, casting down his bags – black plastic bin liners I had insisted on, so much less suss than svelte pigskin valises.

Perhaps, I suggested acidly, he might consult the oracle? Often the best remedy in such situations.

Jaime tossed his coin, snatching only darkness on the way down, stumbling onto hands and knees, truffling knuckled tree roots, before he found it. That cast he declared to be 'foked up,' so he tossed again, and then again, since he didn't trust that decision. I knew the feeling well, but wasn't letting on, secretly amused by the sight of Jaime in a head scarf. Hermes, of course, raising between skirted knees, mascara staining sibylline cheeks.

'Come on,' I said, grasping his hand, 'We'll take the right path.'

'But how you know it is not the other way, man?' I smiled encouragingly, 'Whatever you like, sweetie. We'll take the left then.'

'But you just say is the other way? This is not like the city!' He stabbed a finger at three icy peaks above.

'These are the mountains of the foking giganté zipolotes.

You get lost up there, you foking die. Not even you foking bones to find.'

'Fok off!' That was me, dragging him to the right side, strength so much easier when responding to abject weakness. Giant birds indeed. Legends of the mountains, mere skeins of shifting cloud and shadow, baseless fabrications like that wooden imperial eagle on the wardrobe ... well, maybe not entirely baseless, sticky lies always carry a grain of truth, *'Like the condor, only they fly higher. So high you need a satellite to catch them.'* Yea, right, Joe! Nothing better to do all day I suppose than tell tall tales. What had he called them? The *tzitzimime.* A ridiculous name. And then I remembered, the first morning, that huge raptor perched on a cactus.

No doubt it was a trick of the light and the bird closer than it looked. Probably a large peregrine falcon, if they had them in Mexico.

Fifty yards up the steep path, I was brought up short by odd rumbles underfoot.

'Look!' That was Jaime, pointing back in the direction we'd just come.

Perplexed, I followed the line of his trembling finger, gasping as I made out a shaft of ethereal green light spilling from the hollow tree by the fork in the trail.

'Quick! This is not a good place,' Jaime said, hurriedly gathering his bags.

'But I need to see this!'

'You foking *loco*, man?' Jaime rasped, throwing off my hand. 'That is the death light of Mictlán-te-cuh-tli!'

'Mick who?' I dissembled, even as I realised the baleful light was my second intimation from the lord of death. The hollow trunk was the entrance of an ancient labyrinth that extended below the mountains, under the town and far beyond. There were lost cities down there, long since abandoned by troglodyte tribes, like the Hopi, who claimed to have ascended from a cavernous realm and never lost the habit of living underground. If ever I had a chance for everlasting fame and fortune, this was it. All I had to do was enter by the trunk ... but I couldn't overcome my fear of what waited in that hidden realm, so I turned away, regretting my decision even as I ran after Jaime, scrambling up the precipitous path ahead.

17. FIRE ON THE MOUNTAIN

How long is an hour measured in footfalls? By the luminous dial of my watch, just that, but by any subjective measure, so much longer. Check the desert down there, all that sand, an eternity of pounding *sierra* rock, climbing this fucking mountain, and now that boxy barrier to surmount, grim adobe tacked to a black precipice, the shuttered village a haunt of '*ladrones*' – robbers and worse, according to Jaime.

'But there's no alternative. We have to go past the village,' I insisted, my voice sounding monstrously loud in the neck of the canyon where we were standing. 'Are you blind?' I rasped.'

'Yes, but do not you see?' Jaime said, hitting on Xochipilli and his nose bag – coke and plenty of it.

'There, by the big rocks, *ladronés* in the foking shadows.'

'Fok off!' Yea, that was me, playing the hard man when all I felt was fear. For all I knew, he might be right about bandits. Those gargoyle shadows, weird. But one of us had to play the role. 'Jaime,' I hissed, 'When you're paranoid, you see what you want to see.' I shook my head.

'How you survived so long in your line of work is beyond me, Mr *Narcó Tráfficante.*'

'I foking survive because I always check the ground ahead.' Jaime lifted his skirt, revealing the antique pearl-handled silver pistol, tucked into black suspenders. 'Is lucky I bring this,' he grinned saucily, giving me the eye.

'Oh yea?' I nodded. 'One shot and you'll only wake the whole village.'

Jaime brandished the pistol. 'And what is the alternative?' He scowled. 'I do not think you know anything, Mr Foking Expert.'

According to Gomez, the mountain Indians possessed a sixth sense, but they were also a superstitious lot, easily impressed by mendicant charlatans. Six senses be damned. We'd give them seven, with these plastic bags full of designer clothes, make like black, turbaned, giant ancestor spirits – how we'd scare the shit out of them. Did I really believe that? Not really, but neither did I believe Jaime and what only he saw. Coke madness, that's all it was. Yea, I was infected too. I should never have taken that snort.

Walk tall, that was the way, the settling contents of drooping black plastic obscuring my vision, so much so I was unable to see the next step, let alone lurking danger. Lucky that, I was so intent, I didn't react when three gargoyles leapt out from behind the rocks and, screaming hairy curses, ran into the darkened village, disappearing down vertiginous alleyways. Incomprehensible curses now conjoined by cacophonous barking – wild echoes that persisted, long after we were through.

'Aaahooooo!' cried Jaime, winding up the opposition from a safe distance.

'Aaaaahhhoooooo!'' echoed a far crag – still wearing his turban, the mad Mullah of Mexico, doing his dervish dance, spinning closer and closer to the edge of the path.

'Aaaaahhhoooooo!' Nothing below, just total blackness and delayed action karma. Plenty of time to snort all that nose candy, numb to his brain when he finally hit base.

'*Oyé, hombre!*'

'*Qué?*' Startled, I looked up.

Out of the darkness, Jaime, advancing coyly, dangling a gold star from a striped ribbon. On tiptoes, like a pint-pot presidente awarding the *Croix de Guerra*.

'I take everything back, every bad thing I ever think or say to you,' he said, stepping back and saluting.

'From now you are el *generalísimo* en la revolution.'

'Really,' I gawped, baffled by his strange turn of behaviour.

'Yes,' he beamed. 'Think what we can do! No fok can stop such *fuerté*. Not even the *pinché* NSA.'

I didn't know any ASN, possessing as I did a dyslexic's disregard for acronyms, but they sounded really bad. Pinché suits from el norté, I guessed, glad I was in Mexico, and not in qué *loco gringo*-la-la-land, even if only on an icy mountain path, ascending ever upwards. By my watch, over a hour since the mad Mullah routine, add that to the cracking pace, maintained all the way, and it translated as at least four thousand feet. A long way without any sign of the town.

Perhaps we'd taken the wrong turn at the hollow tree? With my track record, the path probably an old prospector trail, leading to cul-de-sac canyon and a used-up mine deep in the *cordilleras* – some *generalísimo*, me. Better not tell Jaime, he'd be too disillusioned. Best take a breather and cadge something to smoke.

'Hey, Jaime!' I called. 'I don't suppose you have any grass?'

'*Cómo no?*' Stopping, he rooted in a bin liner.

'What kind of weed you want, man?' he said, looking up.

'I have choice?' I said disbelievingly.

'You are talking to *el número uno narcó tráficante*,' Jaime grinned proudly, pulling out a crocodile-leather case.

'Give it here,' I said, snatching the case. 'I have to check the goods for myself.'

'That is my *generalísimo*.' Jaime gave me the standard fist and forearm *macho* salute. 'Such *fuerté!*' Acapulco gold, Durango red, Mazatlán tops, Oaxaca black, Quintana Roo blue, all displayed in labelled pockets. The best Mexico could offer, and all mine, I considered greedily, amazed at such riches. So long since I had a smoke I couldn't remember, a poor state of affairs for someone who once prided himself on his connections. Still, I was back in the business. I was *el número uno narcó tráficante's generalísimo*, I thought proudly, sticking skins together, my first choice Mazatlán tops, pungent bearded heads, crackling between my fingers, as I rolled a huge joint.

'Xochipilli!'

'What you say, Jaime?'

'The god says to say he like you.'

'That's good,' I blurted breathlessly, neck follicles tingling with a rush of cannabinoids.

'He say you must look up,' Jaime said, in an awed tone. 'He send you a sign.'

'Whaa...' I mumbled. What was he on about?

'Now!' Jaime repeated insistently.

For the first time that night, there was light on the mountain facing us, at our backs the new-risen moon, casting its mantle on the far crag like a diaphanous gown slipping old shoulders. Suddenly blazing from the summit, an awesome conflagration, the light of Xochipilli wafting silently upwards, for the briefest of moments illuminating the whole mountainside, before dissipating into space.[1]

Struck dumb, we both just sat there, staring out over the precipice. And then I heard it, a faraway mournful tolling of the bells of the cathedral. We were on the right path.

'... *diez, once, docé, trecé!*' I counted. 'That's lucky,' I said, springing to my feet at the thirteenth chime.

'C'mon Jaime! The town's that-a-way.'

---

[1] An old tradition of prospectors in the *sierras*: concentrations of silver ore give of a gas that can be seen when the new moon shines at an oblique angle.

BOOK II

THE FATHER

1. WALPURGIS NIGHT AT THE CANTINA

Thirteen o'clock, and everything had changed. Come again? Since my departure certain facts had altered. Take that sign above the hotel door, now painted with a double-headed hawk and the legend, '𝔩𝔞 𝕳𝔬𝔲𝔣𝔣 𝔡𝔢𝔩 𝕳𝔞𝔩𝔠𝔬𝔫' – an unhappy marriage of German and Spanish – and below that, '𝔓𝔯𝔬𝔭. 𝕽. 𝖁𝔬𝔫 𝕳𝔞𝔭𝔰𝔟𝔲𝔯𝔤', in the same gothic script. A familiar name, though I couldn't quite place it. The new owner, behind the open door, absurd as only aristos can be, clad in britches and poncho, matching houndstooth tweed, bugger-lug sideburns almost meeting in a beard and a surfeit of pork pies in a rotund red face; native lads jumped to his barked commands, porting tottering stacks of cardboard boxes into the lit-up hotel.

At the street corner, on the left where a steep lane ran down one side of the old building, tethered to the wall, nine or ten burros, radiating animal heat, contentedly munching hay, steaming breaths comingling in the night air. Looked like the party had just arrived. Not a good moment, I thought gloomily, not a good moment at all.

'Mañana? And so soon? Hey, *gringo*, plenty room at this inn!' At least someone hadn't changed, I thought, looking around. Across the street, *cantina* Joe, all polished smiles and practised bonhomie, waving us over. His hole-in-the-wall bar heaving this Walpurgis Night.

'Not a good idea,' I whispered, grabbing Jaime's arm as he started forwards.

'Is my risk,' Jaime sniffed, taking the opportunity to freshen up his lipstick. 'I do not need protecting in this town, my generalísimo,' he said, hitching up his suspenders, smoothing down his dress and mincing forwards.

An ambuscade of wolf whistles as he pushed through half doors, reminding me of Jaime's recent change of sex. That was my friend the slime-balls were ogling, *borracho* fuckers! Ten *sombreros* camped around a keyboard player wearing improbable cactus headgear, playing *mariachi* tunes in the far corner. Rotating chairs, raising glasses, smacking lips like they already had the taste of her. Cherry kissers pouting back and Jaime returning the compliment to thunderous approval. This *cantina* was a men-only club. Dangerous territory for a *muchacha* on the run – more so if that *muchacha* was a transvestite.

'Easy *hombres*!' Joe boomed over the heel stamping din. 'Enough!' he yelled, manoeuvring his great belly behind the narrow bar, pushing up denim shirt sleeves over hairy arms leaning on the counter, grinning like a busted honky-tonk. 'My friend, you look like hell,' he rasped. 'What you been doing?' He tilted his chin, 'Climbing the robes de *las trés hermanitas*?'

'No. I mean, yes,' I muttered, slumping as exhaustion hit me.

'What you do then? Rescue this *muchacha* from a barrancha?' he grinned, rolling his 'r's like bowling balls in a back alley.

'A ravine is right!' I snapped out of my slump.

'Are you going to serve us or what? We're bloody freezing.'

'*Mescal*?'

'*Cómo no*?' Jaime leant an arm on my shoulder. 'I see you have my favourite.' Dangling a hand, she pointed a carmine nail. 'Up there, on the top shelf, *el gusano de diablo*.'

'So, you are not a total stranger,' Joe said, exposing a patch of perspiration on his shirt as he reached for an unlabelled brown bottle.

'My friend,' Jaime said, 'I am born in these mountains.'

'Where exactly?' Joe replied, sliding two brimming glasses, sans worm, along the polished bar.

'What's with all the questions, Joe?' I demanded, slopping *mescal* in my haste to drink up and get out.

'Is OK,' Jaime murmured. 'I can look after myself.'

'I am only being friendly,' Joe shrugged, reaching under the bar for a cloth.

'I tell you anyway, for I am feeling generous tonight,' Jaime said, watching Joe wiping up the spill. 'A little village, higher in the mountains. Maybe you even know it, Santa Domingo del Flores? I never forget, though it is a long time.'

'*Si*, I know it well. I have a brother in that village,' Joe nodded, mock serious. 'But never do I see such a bonita *muchacha* there.'

'That is because I am always wearing *pantalónes* the last time you visit.' Jaime leaned closer. 'Do not you recognise me Uncle?'

'Jaime!' Joe gasped. '*Qué pasa?* Why you dressed like this?'

'Not so loud,' Jaime hissed, eyeing the angle-on *sombreros*.

'Is this real?' I growled, turning to look at both in turn. 'Joe, are you everyone's uncle round here?'

'You are in Mexico, my friend,' Joe growled, hand on heart. 'Here big families *es* normal. I can count on a hundred and thirty-two in mine, brothers to second cousins. And all can count on me.' He hesitated. '*Es* why I have to talk with Jaime,' he shrugged apologetically, '*En privádo*.'

'Yea, sure,' I said, downing my drink, breaking out in a sweat as I stood up. 'Plenty of room at the inn, huh?'

'Sit down, my foolish young friend.' Joe flapped a hand at an empty barstool. 'I read all the reports in newspapers the Malinchés bring me.' he thumbed towards the lit-up hotel across the street. 'But only after she reads them first.' He gestured eloquently. 'Si, you can count on it, she knows about the reward. Whatever Helga has told you about Gomez,' he gestured with thumb and forefinger, 'They are this close.' He chuckled.

'I tell you, cross the street and you lead your friend straight into a trap.' Glancing round, he nodded at the *sombreros* in the corner, whispering amongst themselves.

'All Jaime's cousins,' he grinned, 'Even if he does not recognise them!' Drawing himself up, he thumped a fist on the counter. 'In my family *es* the same as brother. Blood so thick, *es* better than any superglue.'

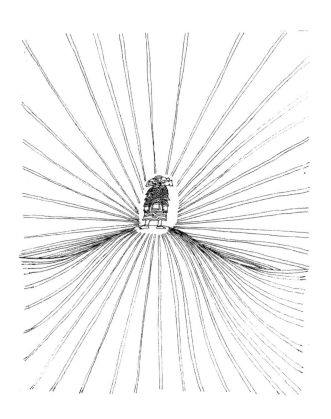

2. THE THIRD DAUGHTER OF NIGHT

So Jaime had a team. I was glad for him. A posse of cousins, good as brothers ... better even, since superglue had now entered the equation. So where did that leave his *generalísimo*? Out in the cold, watching the handshakes and backslapping from the street side of half doors - turning to face my mother, the only family I had. Incest, all she had to offer, by way of affection, and that a one-way ticket on the long slide. When I finally landed, 'hell' just another word for no return. No return?

I was returning. Not so much because I didn't have anywhere else to go; more like fate. Yea, I was living the life preordained. Every moment already entered in a book. Hell? I was half way there already, hurtling smoking rails. Way to go! But, perversely, maybe knowing that freed me? For if I was already doomed I was also ...

'Free, to do what the fuck I want.' Jauntily, I stepped across the street, back into the *bruja*'s lair.

But wasn't I forgetting someone? Herr Fucking Hapsburg, occupying the doorway. That was my light he was blocking. A palm upraised, a pork pie so presented.

'I'm afraid the hotel is closed.'

Same old song, same old story. I was about to launch and shoulder him aside, when Helga loomed at his back.

'Not to worry,' she breathed, her chin nuzzled on his shoulder, hands not quite meeting around his chest, rocking him back and forth. 'Peter, this is my old pal Rudy from Brussels, he buys the hotel for me, is not that *wunderba*?'

'Wonderbra!' I recycled, belatedly realising my trip to the plains had been a ploy all along. 'So,' I glared,

'Why'd you arrive by *burro* train,' I nodded at the donkeys, 'When it's so much easier to come by bus?'

'Excellent question,' Herr Rudy Fucking Hapsburg smiled patronisingly. 'That is because tomorrow, or rather later this morning, if all goes to plan,' ostentatiously, he glanced down at the luminous face of his Patek Philippe five-dials gold chronometer, 'At five o'clock sharp, we set off on an expedition into uncharted territory.'

'Better we continue this inside,' Helga whispered, glancing to either side. 'The street is so naked.'

Following the grossly disproportionately sized – her height and his girth – arm-in-arm lovers into the hotel lobby, I hung back as they turned the corridor, reassured to find the old retainer was still propped against the wall. Maybe the mummy inside the rusting suit of conquistador armour really was the corpse of my father, I reflected, adjusting the helmet, oddly comforted by the empty sockets staring blindly back. His continued presence a good sign, I thought, suggesting that, even this Walpurgis Night, some things were not subject to change.

The same couldn't be said of the salon, however, which was now decorated with bunting, as if for a homecoming. Pride of place on the mantelpiece above a blazing fire, a gold-framed daguerreotype of a certain Maximilian. Even I knew of the last emperor of Mexico, tragic archduke of Austria, but there was something familiar about the face, those absurd bugger-lugs, almost but not quite meeting in a beard. And then I made the connection – of course he was a Hapsburg, just like mine host, the baron.

'Excellent,' Rudy snorted, turning to smile at Helga, sitting pretty on the sofa beside him. 'What do I tell you?' He gripped her hand resting on his knee. 'Never I am wrong with first impressions.' Piggy eyes, swivelled my way. 'Peter, you must join our quest.'

'Quest?' I grinned. 'That implies a prize.'

'You will share the spoils, that I promise.' Rudy boomed.

'So what's it all about, this, um ... expedition?' Rudy waved at the portrait. 'The same purpose that brought my great-great uncle here,' he faltered, 'To his tragic death.'

'Really?' I said. 'If you don't mind me saying, I thought Maximilian was the dupe of Napoleon III and his ambitions for French global domination.'

'The historians have it wrong.' Rudy raised a fat finger. 'True, Napoleon ultimately put Maximilian on the eagle throne, but that was down to the plotting of Carlota and it gave Napoleon the excuse he needed to get rid of her. She hated sea voyages, you must understand, and wouldn't have come otherwise.'

'So,' I said, taking the seat opposite, 'What was your great uncle's true reason?'

'Ah!' Rudy let out a splendid sigh. 'Thereby hangs a tale. It all started when Maximilian opened the crypt of my ancestor Rudolph, the holy Roman emperor, and discovered a very strange cache of bones sharing his tomb.' He paused for effect. 'Rudolph was the first Hapsburg to win the purple robe, an honour, incidentally, that he shared with Julius Caesar. Hapsburg means "houff of the hawk".' His beady eyes twinkled. 'You may have noticed the little sign I put above the door?'

'Two heads are better than one eh?' I smiled.

'Beats having eyes at the back of your head.'

'Yes, of course,' Rudy said distractedly, patting Helga's hand on his knee.

'When one sleeps, the other wakes.' I nodded.

'As a logo for a hotel, I would have thought it's a bit schizo.' I paused. 'But perhaps that's the point?'

Rudy turned again to Helga, impassive at his side. 'Your friend may be perceptive.' He waggled a finger.

'But not perceptive enough.'

'So what am I missing then?' I pushed out a palm.

'Let me guess, the hawk isn't really a hawk.' Staring at a point above Rudy's left shoulder, I began, 'Yes, I can see it now, flapping leathery wings over *las trés hermanitas*, coming closer now, those two heads a trick of distance, merging into one great ugly head with a cranial bump of cartilage at the back, giving the impression it is looking both ways It's a pterodactyl! Yes, beyond doubt, not just a large *zopilóte*. That's a vulture, you understand,' I added, folding my arms.

I wasn't prepared for the stunned silence as they exchanged glances; denial in hers.

'Oh my friend,' at last Rudy said. 'You are my friend, you know. Until my monogram on the subject was privately circulated,' he raised a finger, 'But only, you understand, to the members of my club, no one else but Maximilian and myself fits the pieces of the puzzle together.' He sighed. 'With your insight, I probably don't have to tell you these the unmapped mountains are the last hiding place of the ancient pterodactyl.'

'Indubitably,' I nodded, keeping my face straight, wondering where this was all headed.

'Of course, in their ignorance, the local Indians call the flying dinosaur the *tzitzimime*. Why?'

Straining for an answer, I shook my head in an effort to clear it, but I needn't have bothered, for the baron's question was merely rhetorical.

'Yes,' he continued, oratorically, 'It most often seen in storms when lightning strikes the peaks. The Indians believe it is the double of thunder. And because it flies higher than any other bird, they also believe that the *tzitzimime* is the nagual of the highest god.' He paused ponderously. 'It is this aspect that makes the death of Maximilian more bearable.'

'Pardon me, baron,' I interjected, 'But surely Maximilian was executed by firing squad at Quertaro?'

'No,' Rudy shook his flaccid jowls, 'That was the story Presidenté Juarez put out to please Yankee public opinion.'

'Really?' I frowned.

'Yes,' he nodded. 'Juarez was an Indian and so understood the concept of honour, though as a republican, obviously he fought on the wrong side. Maximilian was accorded the same rights as the ancient Tolucan kings, who, by their custom, ruled for a year and a day. He was offered up to the sun with his many medals and staked out on a mountain ledge to wait for the nagual of the highest god. Despite the drugs they gave him, it was a terrible death. That is the reason for my quest. To rescue his precious bones.'

He raised that finger heavenwards. 'I have seen for myself the eyrie on the mountain they call *la Tercer Hija de la Noché* – the third daughter of night – on an inaccessible crag, close to the summit. He is there, I swear, along with all the lesser kings and their Indian treasure, gold enough to attract the nagual of the highest god, who, in the burning light of midday, confuses the gilded sacrifice for the glare of the sun. Enough, I promise to keep you in luxury for the rest of your life, if that is what you desire. For myself,' he sighed, laying a hand on his chest, 'The bones will be enough. Like Maximilian, I have no need for worldly wealth.'

Is that so, I thought, Herr Fucksburg, all right for you, with your ancestral crypt and hedge funds bordering rolling hectares and country piles, and your hereditary membership of the Brussels club of copraphiliacs, slurping golden shit till the cows come home. Some of us have to work for a living. Of course, I wasn't including myself, I'd never pay off the loans accrued in my student days, not without a degree or the inclination. But, though I flunked out, I had at least researched this shit about nagualism, naguals and doubles, and that was one subject in which the baron couldn't pull a blind on me.

3. SPERMICIDE

It was time - by the luminous dial of my fake Rolex - five in the morning, but still no sign of Herr Hapsburg. I'd awoken with a throbbing hard-on, perhaps brought about by all the bumping below my bed. When I looked down, two boys bolted for the door, giggling as they ran. Fully roused now, I wondered if somehow I had turned the wrong page and woken up in a Jean Austin novel, but no; this was no sassy Western, about lariats and lynching, this was seamy-side Mexico, those boys had been 'nekked', as Ms. Austin might have said, one hard on the heels of the other, not to mention he reddened buttocks. Rum goings-on obviously. I wondered what Herr Hapsburg's real purpose was for mounting his expedition? Those boys were barely into their teens. So why did he want me along? Perhaps he was afraid of the mountain Indians and discovery. Certainly a lot of cacti to hang his cojones on, out in purple sage badlands. And the worst of it was, even though I'd come up with it myself, I'd almost believed the story about the pterodactyl. Though my annoyance was chiefly at myself, I resolved to tell the Belgian shite-eater where to stuff it, but only after I had caught up on some sleep.

I hadn't counted on a Malinché sister which one? I didn't know disturbing my repose, slipping into the bedroom when my back was turned. No lock on the door you see, so easy to come and go in that renamed hotel.

Was this a test? Helga, I was sure, somewhere in the background, putting her up to it. Or perhaps this was my reward for stringing Herr Hapsburg along? In either case I didn't care. I was hard, rock hard, the blood all gone from my head to my dick and balls, which seemed to have sprouted wings. I was flying. But by *Jésu*, she was a hot *tortilla*, and I was the *salsa*. No sour looks from her pussy when I got up close. But then sheets wafted up again, letting in more than the draft and I was seeing double - no, triplicate, as though a third Malinché sister had come to join the show. Was this late entry her nagual, and the second one her double, I wondered absently. Lost in the moment, identical faces swimming out of velvet dark, hard to tell how many hands, bumps and curves. Native American skin, warm leatherette wrapping me in a multi-tentacular liposuction embrace, my half-baked whiteness and colonialist guilt expunged at last, my only worry when I rolled over the bed might not be big enough and, like the nursery rhyme, one of us might fall out. However, I need not have worried, for the three girls, obviously well used to working as a team, had everything under control, except the lead in my pencil, which I did, saving it up till I came with an enormous detonation that quite cleared my brain, and then we did it again, and again. Hey *cabrón*, I was riding high, until outside the shutters a cock crowed and it was time for the girls to go. Yes, I had it confirmed, triplets. Life would never be the same again. The strangest being ever I encountered. One face, with a multi-tentacular liposuction embrace. That was me; the weird sisters were stealing away with out the door, sperm enough to start a nation. Little half-casts with cheery grins. *Alto Anglo, from la nueva república de las sierras.* My contribution to the melting-pot of the Americas.

4. HEAD- START

Too late ... Never too late ... Always too late ... Way too late ... Conflicting voices in my head, and still I didn't get the message. What message? Thuds and bangs out there. Dragging sounds. Barked commands. Muffled giggling – a lot of that. Couldn't they stop? And then they did. All quiet on the Western Front. The big guns gone silent. Just the whoosh of leathery wings, swooping down on the cream of the crop, the dead and the dying stiffening in the mud. Flanders? No.

And there they were again, as I found upon entering the dining room, among food debris and plates, pterodactyls on menus I hadn't seen before, hand-drawn, swooping down on a cartoon expeditionary force, wending the three little sisters. The dishes on offer,

'Pterodactyl *tortillas*, con enchantas', surely that meant enchiladas? 'Pterodactyl tostadas, con queso del muerto ...' – the cheese of death? I had to be dreaming this. But no, that breakfast menu was real.

'*Houff del Halcon*,' in gothic script, underneath a two-faced hawk, its feathers stained red with *salsa* – wet red, like fresh blood, as I lifted the card, dripping onto the salutation printed below ... '*Adelante* Rudy!' Onwards and upwards, I supposed it meant, and, beside that, a passable caricature of Herr Hapsburg wearing a crown.

'You like?' Helga breathed, from above my head. Scary? I'll say! That mother just materialised. 'I makes that while you are screwing your sisters.'

'Sisters? My sisters?' I repeated, regarding her blankly.

'You know perfectly well,' she spat, grinning like a demented Cheshire cat. 'Las Malinchés!'

'What, me?' I frowned.

'Do not insult me with denials,' she scowled, towering like a column of black smoke. 'I know what it is you do with them in your room.

'You do?' I echoed stupidly.

'Yesss!' she hissed. 'And the worst of your lies is the one about the scissors.

'What do you mean?' I growled.

'Your wife is not at all like you paint her.'

'You know her?'

'Not personally, but we speak on the phone many times

'You have?' I gasped.

'Of course. I am your mother. Do you think I forget you, Quinton?'

'I don't know what to believe.'

'That poor woman. Why you tell so many wicked lies about her?'

'My dear, I can't help it!' I said, recovering. 'A congenital condition,' I smiled steely. 'It runs in the family.'

'Ach!' She clawed her brow. 'Why are so maddening? Do you think you are the apple pip in my eye? I must be out my skull to put ups with you. And you pay nothing for board! What exactly is it you wants?'

'Treasure!' I grinned, wondering what sort of mum would try to seduce her son and, when that failed, have his triplet half-sisters bed him. 'Or have you forgotten? We have a deal!' I waggled a finger.

'I am not so sure,' she snarled. 'Now I owns the hotel again, what is the hurry?'

'So Gomez was right,' I glared. 'You owned it before.'

'Yes, Quinton,' she said, implacable as a stone goddess.

'And now you've bought it back.'

'Wrong,' she smiled, breaking the spell. 'I get it as a present. Rudy signs the paper before he leave. What is a hotel to him,' she shrugged, 'When he has the treasures of an empire. You know he thinks he returns wearing the crown of Mexico.'

'You have got to be joking,' I said, sure she was putting me on. 'He is really that *loco?*'

'Yes, my son!' she leered, like a crocodile lazing on oozing mud banks, the growing gulf between us, a wide turgid river. 'Is in the blue blood, my son. All those European royals close related. Too much bumping about in stately carriages, that is why! Incest!' she said derisively.

'Makes you weak in the head.'

5. BACK AT THE CANTINA

Cantina Joe! In my hour of need, who else could I call on this siesta time? Jaime, wherever he was, I supposed, but Joe wasn't letting on, fingers patrolling the counter, marshalling sugar crystals spilled en route to my cup. The coffee, scalding hot, black and treacly, and 'on the *casa*!' Perhaps Joe was independently rich, he could even be the drugs cartel banker, this none-too-clean bar his preferred way of passing the time, luring ne'er-do-wells into idle conversation. No one else around, barring that dusty *caballero* who just walked in, from the Kalahari by the looks of him, dead to the world in the corner, presenting holed soles, boots propped on the cold stove, staring vacantly over half doors at the deserted street. Maybe he really was dead, I considered, watching a bar fly emerge from the gaping cavern of his mouth, stopping on sticky-tracks grubbing feet, before buzzing off to pastures new.

'You are saying?' Joe, prompted.

'Was I?' I frowned, wondering whether I had mentioned the second intimation and Helga's cancer.

'Sorry, I can't remember.'

'The new owner about the hotel,' Joe said, smiling indulgently.

'Oh yea. That crazy Herr Hapsburg. Packed up and offski early this morning.' I sighed, 'If I hadn't slept in, I might have tagged along.'

'I hear 'bout that,' Joe said absently, fingers doing the walking, intent on his sticky patrol.

'About what?' I demanded.

Joe looked up. 'About you sleeping in, my friend,' he smiled innocently. 'What else?'

'Yea, right!' I muttered, stricken by sudden guilt. What would he think if he knew I had been screwing my sisters? All three of them, bejesus.

'He goes after the treasure of the *tzitzimime*.'

'Pterodactyl, don't you mean?' I said dully, wondering how I failed to recognise my sisters from the start.

'No.' Joe shook his head emphatically. '*Es* not the same, my friend. The *tzitzimime* es. Pterodactyls *es* extincto.'

'And that is the difference?' I asked, grateful for the conversation and a distraction from black thoughts.

'Yes!' Joe said enigmatically.

'And this, uh, so-called *tzitzimime* treasure – was there ever one?'

'Sure, my friend,' Joe smiled beguilingly. 'Just like you have over there,' he inclined his head at the hotel.

I frowned. 'How many treasures?'

'Thirteen,' Joe said evenly, '*Es* a number sacred to the ancient Tolucans. The number of the sun and gold!'

'And the town?' I ventured, reminded of the wayward cathedral clock.

'Oh yes,' Joe nodded, 'We still follow the same system, thirteen hours in the day, and thirteen hours at night, just like the Aztecs have. If you look hard enough, always that lucky number turning up.' He glanced sideways. 'There, you see, in the sugar bowl, thirteen flies. Like the founding fathers of the town, thirteen *conquistadorés* after they find the mother lode, crawling on top of each other to get at the oro. Maybe *es* their spirits still trapped here, what do you think?'

Thirteen flies – Castillian knights in shiny armour, getting down to it, mining the mother lode. Yea sure, Joe. Pull the other one-armed bandit, mate. How many treasures? I guess I'd gotten the gist of one already. Mark that down to HRH Hapsburg. So that left twelve, fool's gold, I supposed, camouflage for whatever was real.

That longed-for payload? Just dirt, I guessed, unless you scored with Mictlán-te-cuh-tli, as I patently hadn't with my pathetic six intimations. Time for getting back to the hotel and facing up to whatever 'Mother' had planned. Probably my demise, I thought gloomily. But wasn't I forgetting someone?

Father! Imminent and transcendent, wherever I looked, guarding the gate to the sun ... Well, in the dusty corner by the stove actually – a beat-up corpse, revivifying, smoking mirrors blinking in time, focusing my way, snuffing my smell. How could that be? And yet there he was, boots clattering cinder-blackened boards, jerking upright, loping purposely towards me. Scary? I'll say, as if this was a messenger from the lord of death, stooping to lay a bony hand on my shoulder.

Surely I was getting confused, for the corpse of my poor father was that old retainer on sentry duty, in the lobby of the hotel. Before me was merely the latest manifestation of my projected need for a father figure. Whether chained in a chest and buried under the flagstones of my room in a mine, suited in armour in the hotel lobby or this half-dead vagrant, grinning vacantly – what was the difference really? He was only a lonely old *caballero* in need of company, just as I was, trapped in a self-pitying state, wondering just how long I had got, now that Mother had admitted she'd known me all along. And the worst of it was, she was in cahoots with my ex. That was one betrayal I couldn't forgive.

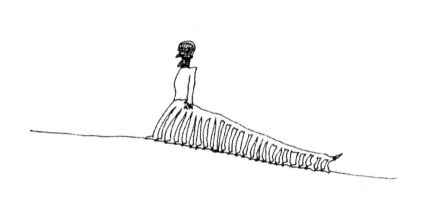

6. THE LONG MARCH

Hours since we set off. *¿De dondé eres?* This dusty *caballero* my guide, left behind by Jaime apparently – as Joe had explained – hiding out with the mountain 'injuns', somewhere beyond the dawn. Not even dusk yet and already the temperature was plunging below zero, our steaming breaths spaced behind like stepping stones suspended in the still air, the pale sun dipping towards a saw-tooth skyline marching with snow-dusted peaks, this burro trail swallowed in shadow, resonating to jitterbug hooves. Ahead, the Grim Reaper, bent backed over his big black mule, swaying in his saddle, leading the way. Father? Not exactly, but somehow. Just an old *gringo* panhandler, the last of his kind, living so long with the mountain injuns the cat had got his tongue, according to Joe.

A cat? More like a cougar, I considered, the old-timer responding to a distant howl echoing the canyons, standing stick steady in Spanish silver stirrups, cupping mittened hands to his mouth, chilling my blood with his animal rendition. A coyote, I guessed. So he was not entirely mute. Man-coyote, then. But which half was human? The beastly half, I guessed, thinking of the society left behind. My nymphomaniac sisters. Helga and her consuming lust. The gold that makes men mad. For why? Perhaps we were all aliens, prisoners of our own device, our much vaunted humanness just concealment from the awful truth that there is nothing beyond the stars but ourselves. The immortals, hiding out from eternity, blinkered in miserable lives.

Introspection, always a dangerous tendency – never more than then, my mule lurching beneath me, listening to pebbles scattering over an abyss. Just concentrate on the now. That distant glittering, a chance reflection on mica? But no, there was movement between fishtailing mountains gone scaly with mist. A burro train – donkeys and natives shouldering packs – a white man bearing his burden, leading the way, his burnished pate gleaming gold in a shaft of sunlight, penetrating the haze. That had to be the baron on his quest for *tzitzimime* treasure. Just as well he was headed in another direction, I thought, regarding cloud curtains closing in, sealing a Hapsburg's fate. For glory or bust? Bust, I guessed. Pushed from behind, dashed over rocks, a pterodactyl feasting on his brains. Perhaps that's what he really wanted. Expurgation of ancestor guilt and union with a living fossil. A dinosaur just like himself.

7. BEING TAILED

Premature night as we rode into a defile where a parliament was in session. Basalt outcrops fanged by ice, welcoming us with the engaging smile of a shark. Entering the picture, another black-backed hunter, rolling thunder over razor ridges – only those were rotors not fins, visored cyborgs occupying battle stations, black in beetle armour, behind the bubble eye.

The Mexican Army scouring the mountains for what? Bandits or pterodactyls? Perhaps bandits mounted on pterodactyls? That *would* pose a threat to the northern nation. A new superhero, to outflank stealth bombers. They wouldn't be interested in a couple of *sombreros* on mules. Or would they? I was certain of nothing, I might even be dreaming this, safe in my bed back in the hotel, wishing to god I was wrapped in blankets instead of a coarse woollen serape, one or more of the Malinchés nibbling my toes. That would explain the awful numbness, the untoward pelvic throbbing, this strange disembodied feeling like half of me was looking down on the other half – stringing along behind myself, wondering what the hell I was doing, entering Gehenna, first circle of hell, damned if you do and damned if you don't, flaming mists fired by the rolling red ball of the sun, huge below us as we crested the last ridge. A fanfare of trumpets wouldn't have been amiss, I thought, laying my head on steaming flanks gratefully.

'There, you see!' That biltong voice, an extension of an old-timer's grizzled mien – all cracked and crusty, just as I would have imagined. Yes, and real. No dream this. 'Look!' He pointed beyond the sun, dipping towards a fissured caldera crowded by three icy peaks, with us through our pilgrimage, only now the eminences were cloaked in royal purple, like a conclave of cardinals deciding which one would be pope. 'That's where we're headed, son, *los dédalo del diablo*, the devil's labyrinth,' he translated, chuckling.

'Fuck!' I cursed, rubbing saddle-sore joints. 'Why talk now and not before?'

'Because I'm dead back there, son,' he said, drawing on oxygen thin air. 'Only here am I ever really alive. Comes from living alto so long, I guess.' Twisting round in his saddle, he grinned lopsidedly, his deep-set eyes glittering in magenta sockets. 'The name's Coyote, son. It's a real privilege to help any friend of Jaime's.'

'So you *do* know him!'

'Of course, son. He is our *hope*.'

'What do you mean, hope?' I said, shivering, my euphoria of a moment before sinking with the sun.

'Plenty time later, son,' he said, gathering slack reigns in a mittened hand. 'Still a long way to go.' He pointed towards a track leading down through the rocks.

'That's our trail.'

'What?' I exclaimed, alarmed by this new development. 'It's almost dark already. We have to find shelter now, surely?'

'No,' he shook his head. 'Full moon on the rise.' He thumbed back the way we had come. 'Soon be bright enough to read a book, if you were that way inclined. Perfect conditions for a trek, son,' he chuckled.

'Yea, sure, Pops,' I muttered, maintaining my fantasy of hanging out with the dad I had never known.

'Whatever you say.'

Nothing else to do but follow my guide between hungry boulders, monuments marking the march of time and hapless travellers turned to stone, their features distended by the prevailing wind, whipping up as we rode on, numb to our saddles. Perfect conditions, huh. And this a mere trek, I considered dismally. Alright for him, 'ornery old mountain goat, in his leathery armour of hide and buckskins, acclimatised all these years. This was alien turf to me. Except there wasn't any turf, just pockets of snow concealing chasms and worse between the boulders. Plenty of aliens though – as the pink disc of the full moon slowly ascended, the petrified army encamped around, seeming to limber up and give voice in a chorus of subterranean noises, loud cracking echoing the fissured glacier, ghostly faces animating, leering in with ghastly grimaces and skeletal embraces, like this was a dance of death, and ahead that really was the reaper, leading me down, down into his kingdom of night. Dark fires burning down there, as if the sun was journeying ahead into an infinity of ice. An illusion, I reasoned, just a glacier reflecting stratospheric clouds joining bloody hands across glimmering dusk.

8. THE LOBOTOMY KID

Why ride when you can walk? Why indeed? A point of honour, my guide explained, our mules noble beasts deserving the last of our rations and, besides, both were exhausted. Etiquette of the mountains, or a test? I settled for the second possibility, trying to keep up. Meanwhile my mentor in trackless white wastes turning garrulous, the nearest corner of his mouth working overtime, keeping up a constant repartee. Well, he tried. Maybe he thought I needed distracting.

It seemed he'd come to the mountains to get away from the 'lectricity'.

'Come again?'

'Power lines, son. Can't abide 'em. Make ma brain *fizz*; what's left of it anyhow. Lobotomised y'know, they took the best part, leavin' me like Ah'm now, more dead than alive. Scraps for the thunder birds if the injuns hadn't gotten to me first.' He pulled back on the reigns and, stopping his mount for a moment, lifted his *sombrero*, revealing a circular scar on his temple.

'Who's they?' I managed, shouting into the wind.

'They'm,' he insisted, 'Southern 'lectric Power, if you believe in a name. The shit-eaters took me down to the third circle of hell, below Uncle Mo's office. Didn't matter Ah was family, not when I knew what I knew and was prepared to use it.' He pointed to his head. 'Ah still got the big picture, but Ah forgot all the detail, an', as every critter knows, the devil's always in that.' He spat.

'But that didn't stop them setting the cousins on ma tail, comin' in the middle of the night, whenever I got nice an' cosy with a *muchacha*, burning down more'n half a dozen shacks, men in black hounding me all the way through Texas into Mexico, 'till Ah lost 'em in these mountains. Thirty years ago, that was.'

'But why, for god's sake?'

'Punishment for leaking information 'bout the net they aimed to wrap around the world, just as the Spooky Tribe said they'm would.'

'Mobile phones?' I said, remembering a Hopi Indian prophesy about a net that would bring about the end of the world.

'Yea, that's one of the details. Of course, it's disaster for the bees.'

'How?'

'Ah forgot.' He tapped the scar on his head.

'Something to do with base stations complicating bee signals, ah seem to recall. Course, when bees stops pollinating, crops don't grow and everyone starves. But a smart fellow like you knows that.'

'Anything else coming through, Pops?'

'Nope.' He shook his head. 'I'm disconnected. Like Ah said, lobotomised. Ask again in a few minutes, son.'

'I will, Pops. If you didn't know more, I guess they wouldn't have harassed you all those years as they did. There's no profit in it.'

'Tell that to the cat that plays with the mouse. They'm wouldn't let me live, but wouldn't let me die, neither.' He sighed. 'That's the way it was in the company before they closed the circles. It's worse now that fortunes five hundred's running the show, even the mightiest nation on earth don't matter a darned thing. The good ol' USA, home of the brave an' free, takin' orders from they'm shit-eaters jest like the rest. They weren't goin' to let a squirt ruin their plans, blabbin' to hippie journals, or anythin' like that. Ah remember now,' he grinned, absently picking at ice pocketing cavernous cheeks. ''lectricity don't need wires and such like to get about. It's freely available, under our feet. The earth, spinnin' on the galactic turntable, a nine-track planet, symmetrically repeatin' orbital shells, tectonic plates in internal gridlock, with a wormhole bang in the centre. A point of collapsed matter, as small as small can be, accordin' to Uncle Mo,' he snorted disdainfully. 'But in mass, no more nor less than all they'm circles above, pumpin' out the buildin' blocks of onion-skin reality, photons an' 'lectrons, jest like the black heart of the sun only nearer. It's how to tap into it, that's what they don't want you to know. So they wired up this world, corrallin' every city, upsettin' the earth's nat'ral power lines, targetin' sensitives, siting transformers an' pylons an' God knows what else, right next to schools and anywhere ordinary folks

149

hang out, wrappin' whole communities in bad vibrations jest so no one cottons on.' He chuckled dryly.

'If they ever do, the cancer economy's finished. Free!' he spat. 'Corporations jest can't handle that word, cuts the market right from under them. That's why they hates the little Mexican injun so. In these mountains, corn is king, not dollars. The peso's useless thanks to all Uncle Sam's done, greenbacks only good for buying *gringo* cars and guns. Co-operation, that's how folk's gets on. Competition! All that's good for is runnin' rats in mazes.'

9. THE WORLD IN HIS HEAD

Flamingo dawn, or just under-lighted *tzitzimime* wings overhead, I couldn't tell, back in the saddle, high on altitude and *mescal* from the gourd my guide occasionally passed over. 'Unpleasant' was not adequate to describe the weather beyond the down-turned brim of my *sombrero*, the ranging wind bringing fresh flurries of snow with every gust.

Yes, but why the ominous rumbles always preceding rampaging cracks and accompanying detonations, and the distant plumes spied over a crystal landscape? According to my companion, the natives called this cloudy region the Well of the Worlds. There was even a crater, created by asteroid impact in the remote geological past. Under these unmapped mountains, he insisted, concealed from satellites by the glacier, was the greatest confluence of subterranean rivers – transcontinental amazons down there, some even navigable – the seven tenths of rainfall not run off the surface that has to go somewhere, wearing through the hardest rock. I'd have had to be mad not to believe him, after all he was my guide.

Los dedaldo del diablo, there it was, the devil's labyrinth, a fissured caldera of red entrails garnishing a crusty pizza base in a take-away of chilé canyons, packed tighter than the maze at Hampton Court Palace. A multiple-choice scenario obviously, with the added bonus of ice-rimed boulders precariously balanced above gloomy defiles.

One old coyote, reverted to muteness, leading the way on his hardy mule, standing on his silver stirrups, pointing up at rock overhangs, cautioning the need for silence. As if I needed reminding. After a few turns, the windswept snow gave way to drifting red sand, banked around large fallen stones, one boulder so big it almost blocked the narrow canyon, adding to the omnipresent sense of danger. Easy to defend this place, I thought, a few braves concealed behind the boulders looming the cliff tops could hold back the Mexican Army.

Then, at one branching of the canyons, old Coyote seemed to lose his bearings, but, after dismounting, on hands and knees he felt along the cliff base until his fingers found the ancient petroglyph of a feather pointing the way.

Wood smoke, acrid and welcome, indicating there was human life hereabouts. Coyote grinning back, his two remaining front teeth very white in the half-light, as if he was a phantom Indian guide, and we both had died. Maybe we had? Tiredness washing over me in waves; hanging in there by the pommel of my Spanish saddle. My exhaustion all but dispelled, however, when, rounding the next bend, we entered a half-moon canyon, the facing rock wall vivid red and deeply fissured. Old Coyote slowing his mule as I drew up alongside. 'D'you see anything particular, son?' he asked, at last breaking his rule of silence.

'Can't say I do, Pops,' I croaked, my throat dry.

'Look harder, son,' Coyote insisted, pointing out the striations of weatherworn cliffs, which, as I peered, became monumental Indian braves, close packed as teeth. No way was that the work of wind and rain. All of a sudden something flashed within a cleft. There was life beyond this canyon, I realised, that crack in fact a gap. We were almost home, a big word in that high country. Like finding a habitable planet in the vastness of space. All but impossible without a phantom *gringo* guide. That last thought, confirmed when I looked around – Coyote and his mule were nowhere to be seen. And no tracks neither. The only life about, one 'ornery old fly in shiny armour, weaving pieces of eight around my eyes. Nothing else to do but venture on, with questions in my mind and no father on hand to answer them. One of these days I would admit it – the world was my father – and leave it at that.

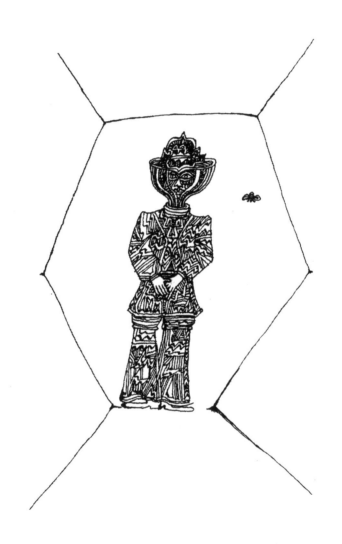

10. THE BEE KEEPER

'Jaime!' I gasped, looking up as I crawled a red stone passageway, smoothed by the touch of many hands, seeing him silhouetted at the end, back-lit by the ascendant sun.

Jaime must have known I was coming, for he was holding out a spliff. Weak and weary after the midnight crossing of the *cordilleras*, the last thing I needed was an enervating smoke.

'Take it!' Jaime insisted. 'Leave that *pinché* fok on the other side. Everyone who enters Happy Valley through that hole is reborn, my *generalísimo*. Take it, is the best my *sappatistas* grow yet!'

I was beginning to make sense of my surroundings. Encircling cliffs, slow-tumbling tertiary time, bleached by stratospheric sunlight, fissures and gullies acid scored, magenta shadowed where lower cliffs were buttressed by magma up crops, etched in ultra violet as I took my second toke. More colour changes as I downshifted, perceiving verdant white-washed stone-walled terraces, descending to emerald depths, where water sparkled amid stands of spindly trees. But I was more interested in what was growing in those stepped terraces, looping the flanks of the crater like fingerprints at the scene of a crime. Yes, I knew that shade of green, and I could smell it too, as a light updraft wafted the unmistakable odour my way. A redolent combination of BO and gruyere cheese matured in dirty socks. Sinsemilla, even at that distance, unmistakable.

Three tokes was all I managed. My machismo in question as knees buckled. My, that was superior gage. The best, Jaime had said. I wasn't in a position to demur, swaying metronomically, fighting a geyser rush of polyploids and cannabinoids to my abused and confused but ecstatic brain.

'We grow it for export to euroland. This year they have the best foking summer since '67. Peace and love in every neighbourhood. We think they need it even more than the *gringos*,' Jaime confided proudly, as we reached the topmost of the terraces spied from above. Bearded, sappy heads brushing my cheeks as we passed through the plantation. The heady scents of best bud only adding to my delirium as I sensed the animating force at the root of all growing things. I could even see it hazily – a magenta, electric aura, pulsing hairy stems. These plants were alive, haloed in energy fields. Despite the light breeze, precipitated pollen hanging over the bushes like clouds of unknowing.

The overgrown trail descended into a series of banked terraces before we came to a clearing filled with a melodic background hum, which I took to be an internal effect of the grass. But then Jaime proudly pointed out a line of conical beehives, buzzing with lazy activity. Workers in syncopated rhythm, communing in the sun, coming and going to the colonies.

'Bee heaven,' he said succinctly. 'Nectar to die for, *generalisimo!*' I was having trouble with the conversation. Everything Jaime said prompted a fit of the giggles, waves of laughter doubling me over, making walking difficult.

'Yea, sure, Jaime,' I guffawed, my jaws aching.

'Next you'll be telling me even the bees give you a buzz.'

'*Es* true, *generalisimo*,' Jaime said indignantly. 'For each harvest fiesta we deep fry and dip in chocolate just as the Aztecs cook them. You never taste the foking like!'

'I believe you,' I said placatingly, my attention distracted by sudden movement at the edge of the clearing. We were under observation, I realised with a jolt, glimpsing ghostly features and long silver hair before the watcher's pale face was concealed by the lowered brim of a scrappy straw *sombrero* as he resumed his task, steadily pruning sappy flowering heads from stout branches, dropping a steady cascade into a sack tied to his waistband.

'So it's true,' I breathed.

'What you say, *generalisimo?*' Jaime said, giving the native a lazy wave as we followed the path into more dense greenery.

'That was a Christos, right?' I rasped, my mouth dry. 'I had assumed the albino tribe was just another Mexican tall story?'

'You have it wrong, *generalísimo!*' Jaime chuckled. 'The story of a white tribe and the *Chicano Jesus* crucified by the *Españolos* is a rumour we put out to fool the satanistas at the cathedral. That *hombre* is *compañero* Manfred, the world's foking numero uno expert on permaculture. He brings a team from the Netherlands to learn us the ways of our Aztec ancestors, who give to the world,' he waved at the lower plantations, lush with variegated colours, 'chocolate, chilli, corn, tomatoes, peppers, squash,' he grinned proudly. 'With his help, now we get five crops a season.'

'That's just great, Jaime.' I gasped, stumbling on something brown snaking the undergrowth, 'I hope that's water?' I said, relieved the plastic pipe was not the anaconda I first took it to be.

'The purest you ever drink. But foking cold. We have to let it sit warming all morning in the sun, otherwise it chills the roots. Glacier floodwater we pump from down there,' he said, pointing at a group of huts, the long roofs shiny with solar photovoltaic cells in a tree-lined ravine where white water frothed in shady depths below red canyon walls. 'The *loco* Dutchmen like to skinny dip in whirlpools there, but is foking dangerous. Only the other week we lose one, so stoned he is laughing as he goes, swept into the tunnels, to where no one knows.'

'Way to go!' I giggled, imagining a laughing Dutchman bobbing away on a subterranean tide. 'At least he went happy.'

'Is no joke,' Jaime said, squaring his shoulders, hands to his sides, huffing like a bar-coded quetzal. 'He is a Sappatista, a true hero of *la revolucion*,' he proclaimed, a ridiculous bird, reciting the valedictory. 'We honour his memory.'

'Revolution! Come off it, ya wee bam,' I laughed, confident enough to risk the dialectic. 'All this is just business. Narco, admittedly, and while the hazards are high, the profits more than compensate. Stay in the game, play your cards right and one day this will all be legal and you'll be head honcho of a zillion-dollar corporation living in a glass mansion in the sun, instead of hiding out here in Happy Valley.'

'For the *pinché* NSA the shit that finances their black operations is legal already. But even you, *generalísimo*, can never call that crap grass, adulterated with foking toxic additives designed to bring on heart attacks, strokes and Alzheimer's in later life.' He bunched a fist, reminding me of an equestrian statue of Bolivar I saw once in Caracas. 'Quality organic bud like this makes you laugh so much you see through the curtain of lies. That is what the shit-eaters most fear.'

He was interrupted by a sudden roaring, downdraft from above, bending and breaking budding branches all around us.

'Ayee!' Jamie cried into the wind, reaching to his waistband for his pearl handled revolver, yelling to make himself heard over the din, 'Is the foking black thunder birds! Now we die!'

Black thunderbirds indeed. Next he would be telling me we were under attack by the *tzitzimime*. For all I knew, we were. A nightmare feeling of unreality, as we stood shoulder to shoulder, shocked by so many black-backed hunters, blocking out the blue. For Jaime this was the end, and he was determined on a hero's death, but not for me. I was his *generalísimo*, and *generalísimos* – as he reminded me, pushing me protesting into wooded depths where slender white oaks competed for the light – are supposed to lead from the back, live to fight another day. There would be future battles, and delicate flowers of Xochipilli, such as myself, should never engage in the hand-to-hand stuff. Bidding me adieu, he was so sweet, wrapping me in a warm but all-too-brief embrace, where white water foamed into a dark cavern. Before he turned away, heading up between the tall spindly trees towards a battle zone. Over the next ridge a creeping barrage of incendiaries and shell bursts back-lighting a bristling colossus massing over dense foliage – the deranged genii-loci of Happy Valley – billions of berserk bees rising towards combat-ready cyborgs dropping hand-lines, trailing a fleet of helicopters.

One disquieting sight, unmistakable through tinted Plexiglas, Herr Hapsburg behind the cyborg pilot, strapping on armaments as he prepared for the big drop. Yea, I should have known, his expedition had all along been a ploy, and the shit-eater was a NSA operative, using the hotel as a forward base in a battle plan to seize of the last redoubt of revolution in the cordilleras, and take control of this shifting Mexican reality, when aces are low and spades count as hearts, and kings double as knaves.

11. THE BLACK RIVER

Lost, I was lost in echoing passages, resounding with the impacts of successive explosions. The oppressive darkness, relieved only by stray shafts of light, penetrating voids in the rock above. Small stones and dust scattering about my head, cracks opening up in the walls as I ran, trusting more to luck than judgement. Narrowing confines forcing me ever closer to white-water rapids, throwing spray in my face as I stumbled over wet boulders.

A massacre was going on in Happy Valley, and all I had in my favour was a head start. Soon the battle would be over, then, when the baron discovered I was not among the dead, would come the pursuit.

They were professionals, armed and presumably equipped with night sight and the latest in tracking technology. My only chance was to put as much distance between myself and the hunters; I was a witness and couldn't be allowed to live.

Faced with branching passages I was undecided. Ahead, the rapids divided around a rocky pier, parting raging waters before a dark curtain – no light beyond, just the roar of monstrous falls somewhere further on. I had little doubt this was the Well of the World the old *gringo* spoke of. The two passages, just ahead, both sucking enigmas in a great skull socketed by blackness and my unruly fears. Some *generalísimo*, me. If only Jaime could see me now, I thought, shivering, but not from the cold. I saw that surging torrent running up the tunnel walls to either side of the rock pier, leaving no room for passage on foot; I was boxed in, unable to go forwards or back. And now, to add to my terrors, the passage was echoing with the sounds of my pursuers. Lights too, advancing beams, parturating the overhead rock in wavering slices. A black figure, silhouetted by the beam of a torch, suggested that the advance party was composed of cyborgs, who already had me in the night sights of their visors. I was doomed. Perhaps I was already dead. But there again, maybe not, I thought, making out a faint green glow emanating from behind the pillar.

That eldritch glow reminded me of another light, seen years before it seemed, but in reality only three days previously, when I received the second of my intimations from Lord Mictlántecuhtli. This, then, was my third intimation, his death light showing me the way. But did I have resolution enough to take the plunge? For I was out of time, as now the crisscrossing torch beams converged on the rocks where I crouched. It was do and die and the devil take the foremost. Yea, me, I thought, as my head cleaved black waters.

I was a spinning target in a maelstrom, flaring bullets zipping past, each time I came up for breath buoyed by bubbles and the feeling I was not alone. Death my constant companion as I swam, tacking against the current, praying that my running dive carried enough momentum to take me to the far side of the pillar. Then, as, the basalt pier loomed, it reshaped into a bristling colossus. The stone jigsaw of the column, anthropomorphising into the standing figure of Archeron, gate-keeper of Hades, bestriding breaking waters, where white spume slicked black rocks. His immense shins an arm's stretch away now, a surge of melt-water taking me round. Nothing to grab, blind luck and the suck of the undertow taking me just under the viscous prongs of a metal sluice, where the vastly bloated corpse of the laughing Dutchman was caught, his bulging eyes staring sightlessly ahead, one forearm trailing the rushing waters, his fingers brushing my head dangling the cross bar of the sluice just above, pinging with a final flurry of bullets as I was swept on.

On the far side, the crosscurrents seemed to cancel out, leaving the surface glassy with inky turbulences, enabling me to strike out for a stone quay, fifty feet off to the right, and a bronze ring hanging from a monstrous stone mouth that, in the stygian gloom, seemed more like a living beast, as, with a last desperate effort, I flailed a hand, knowing my fingers were too frozen to hold on, and pushed my arm through the ring. Treading water, hanging on by the crook of an elbow, staring at those heavy jowls, I realised I had seen the same stone lions on the embankments of the ports of great cities - London, to name but one -

making me wonder if I'd drowned in the crossing and been translated to the far shore of the River Styx.

Somehow I hauled myself up and over that enigmatic pier. Lying with water draining from my sodden clothes, my head resting on cold stone that vibrated with the thunder of the distant falls, I felt warm blood trickling from my shoulder and I was grateful. The chill in my bones confirming what I most needed to know. I was alive. But where, and for how long, were questions to which there were no answers, at least not for now. I was entombed more surely than if I was sealed in a sarcophagus. The weights of the rock above and the crepuscular death light of my demon lord oppressed me with the all-pervasive sense of being walled-up in a mortuary temple. A supposition that seemed corroborated, when at last raising my head, there on the pavement before me, in a clear plastic envelope was a sheet of yellow parchment. A certificate, I saw, blinking blearily. Diogenes was included along with a string of other names, some of which I recognised, others not, under the headline, 'Death Certificate', above an embossed seal of a grinning skull, ringed by the familiar inscription, 'memento mori', and below that the words,

'Do not hinder or obstruct the bearer'.

So it was confirmed. I had arrived on the far side of the Black River in Lord Mictlántecuhtli's shady realm. Still alive, somehow in corporeal form, yet numbered among the dead, with a certificate that was also a permit to prove it – suggesting in this shady realm I had a privileged status. Unlike those swaddled bundles, occupying countless regular-sized niches in the wall before me, which I knew could only be row upon row of ancient mummies.

A multitude of the dead that seemed to have no end. For even in this dim, crepuscular, green light I could make out that the wall of niches continued much farther than around the next corner. The broad causeway of the embankment, curving off into the distance, crenulated at intervals where elegant stone bridges that would have graced a Doge's palace spanned what I guessed were run-offs for more glacier melt-water – a network of deep channels that, with their architectural grace and style, oddly reminded me of the canals of Venice. Giving me, I supposed, more choice as to direction. Which was just as well, for around that next corner my way along the causeway was blocked by an impassable pile of irregularly shaped stones of smoky grey obsidian. A rockfall from above, I realised, looking upwards and into a jagged fault between grinding tectonic platelets, extending way into the black heart of the mountain above. The glassy fissure spilling more debris as I stared, a scattering of smaller stones raining down, filling gaps between the piled rocks. Some razor-edged splinters bounced the boulders at the base, stotting the pavement, before finally stopping at my feet.

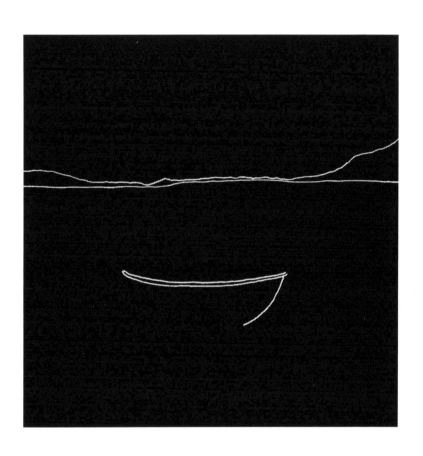

12. THE BOAT

Even before I looked over the dockside, I knew it would be there. The boat, more a skiff really, a long pole laying athwart the gunnels, bumping softly against the embankment wall where wet black steps, spectral in the green light and inset with strange fluorescent fossils, led down to the fast-flowing waters. That it was unmoored and yet stayed where it was should have alerted me to the strange nature of the craft, but I was so keen to secure it, I did not stop on the steps to consider the possible implications.

She was beautiful and slender, with room enough to lie out – why did I think that? I suppose because I already knew. But the knowledge, if indeed I had it, as yet was concealed from my consciousness. Then, as I hauled her broadside on and stepped within curved and caulked cedar planks, I noticed how steady and high she rode in the water. Already, I loved this bonny boat, which was just as well, as I was going to spend some time in her. But that was yet ahead of me. For now, all I knew was that I had a means of navigating this subterranean realm of my Lord Mictlántecuhtli.

'*Speed bonny boat like a bird on the waves, over the sea to Skye ...*'

Unbidden, words of a song from the old country springing to my lips as I punted along, standing balanced in the stern, careful not to stray into the fog bank to my left that obscured the other shore – if there was such – keeping close to the near embankment, for this method of propelling a boat by pole was new to me. One thing I soon observed was the ease with which the craft turned in the waters. Almost as if she anticipated my every move, poling this way and that, following the shore line, negotiating the tricky crosscurrents below narrow arched bridges, connecting regularly spaced wharfs where canals disgorged their contents into the Black River.

So far so good. I even felt cheered. Little did I suspect what was in store, but then all this was new to me and as such I was as an innocent abroad, making the most of exploring drear surroundings. Where even my way of thinking was weird to myself, as if I had taken on an another personality on this far shore, which, though light years from everything I knew, was somehow also deeply familiar, making me wonder whether I had passed through this domain of the dead before.

If only the corpse light of Lord Mictlántecuhtli had not been so dim, I would have been able to make out more detail of the cavernous walls towering above the deep canals. A compelling vista reminded me of pictures I had seen of Petra, a lost canyon city beyond the River Jordan, only here the scale was so much greater. Architraves, pillars, ornate entrances hewn into living rock. A compendium of architectural cultural styles – everything from Aztec to Zoroastrian. Classical, Gothic Revival, Fascist, Brutalist and Fin de siècle, and even Post-modern. Every window, doorway, grotto, as far as I could see, vacant except perhaps for further multitudes of mummies stored within. I hoped not, for already the sense of utter oppression, emanating from the endless niches lining the facing wharves, was almost more than I could bear. Little did I know, how much more oppressive they would become in time, which, I didn't need reminding, ground more slowly here than elsewhere.

It was useless to speculate for how long I had been punting when I saw the wandering light. As I have implied, time is ever in abeyance in that shady realm, except when the beacon shines from the left shore. My first sight made me feel that a pointing finger was ripping the very fabric of eternity and piercing the fog bank, before I was caught in its roseate brilliance and, quite unbidden by me, the prow of the boat turned into the beam.

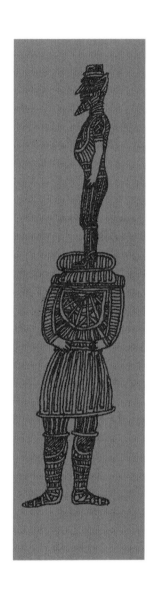

13. BOB

'Don't act stupid, like you don't know,' the hooded foreman said, leaning over the guard rail as, behind him, his saturnine work crew, glowing in their one-piece hooded orange overalls, trundled a covered trailer to the head of the jetty above. 'We've a full complement tonight.'

'Tonight?' I repeated dully, noticing over his shoulder a pale staircase in the distance, ascending cavernous walls towards the yawning entrance of an enormous tunnel, fitfully illuminated by a flickering red light.

'Sorry, mate,' he grinned, revealing a fine set of white gnashers. 'I forget it's always night your side of the Styx.'

'Styx?' I said, appalled to hear confirmation of what I had already suspected. 'Jesus ... fuck!' Next you'll be telling me I'm Charon the ferryman.'

'Too true blue,' the foreman nodded, 'Someone's got to do it. Now can we get a move on?'

'Hold on, I'm new to all this.' I pointed past the staircase, where a chain of similarly clad workers were passing down bandaged bundles. 'Where does that tunnel lead to?'

'Gehenna,' he replied succinctly, pushing back his orange hood to wipe away the sweat that trickled his forehead, revealing a neat pair of horns above his temples.

'Never heard of it,' I snapped, struggling to come to terms with what I was seeing.

'The dump of the damned, mate. The penultimate of the nine levels of Mictlán.' Peremptorily he turned, thumbing at the now uncovered trailer, which I saw was overloaded with bundled, bandaged bodies. Some, as I stared, appearing to shift slightly in the trailer, which I put down to settlement brought on by the bumpy ride.

'And those,' he laughed, 'Are the fucking rejects.'

'So who gets to go to heaven?'

'No one.' Shaking his head, he gave me the gladiatorial thumbs down. 'We're all damned.'

'Where's God in all this?'

'There is no God, only Lord Mictlántecuhtli.'

'You sound very sure about that.'

'I am mate. I am.' He grinned. 'Anything else you need to know?'

'Your name will do.'

'Bob,' he said, reaching down, extending a hand.

'Pleased to meet you, mate.'

A full complement, as my new mate Bob the devil had said, to be individually delivered to the other side before the next load was brought to the jetty tomorrow – whenever that was. At least I was to be compensated. Each of the stiffs came entirely swaddled, except for a gap over their eyes, which were closed by a pair of coins, which, with one notable exception – detailed later – were always twenty-four carat gold. The dates and countries of the variously named, aureus, bahts, bezants, crowns, cruzados, dollars, dinars, drachmas, ducats, escudos, francs, guineas, guldens, kaulas, kronas, lire, mohurs, obans, pistoles, pounds, pesos, rands, rubles, rupees, sovereigns, talers and other currencies too ancient and worn to decipher, offered no obvious correlation, other than the occasional coincidental correspondences, with either the apparent age or ethnicity of the deceased. Suggesting that the coins were allocated before transit below according to a formula known only by the devils of the relevant upper infernal region, where Bob informed me, judgement took place, before they were sealed in place by wax and set there as payment for the ferryman. Me, evidently.

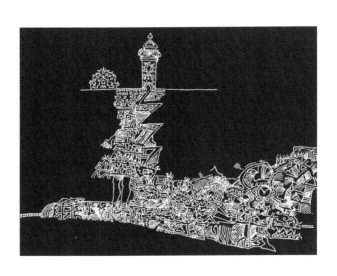

14. FOR WHO DOES THE BELL TOLL?

If only I'd had more room in the boat, I could have taken more. Correction: if only the boat had been willing, I would have taken more. Not the full complement of stiffs certainly, but given the available space, at least three at a time. However, every time I attempted to haul a second body from the lower staging where they had been heaped by the workforce higgledy-piggledy so untidily, the boat lost its characteristic steadiness and began rocking violently, the side-to-side motion threatening to tip the stiff already loaded – and myself – overboard into the fast-flowing waters. Not knowing the ramifications of losing Lord Mictlántecuhtli's precious cargo, and concerned that might mean forgoing his favour in the future, I resisted the impulse, though my urge to rebel against what I regarded as a monstrous imposition was surpassing strong.

At least I was clear as to what my duties were, which is always a help when starting a new job. I also liked the money – rationalising there would be some way to spend it later – though not the means of payment, which initially was distasteful. Even though taking my due, what Bob the devil called the 'ferryman's tokens', made me feel like a tomb robber, guilty of desecrating the dead as I cast the gold coins into the sump of the boat for want of somewhere better to keep my growing collection. But this, I reasoned, was Lord Mictlántecuhtli's realm, and beggars in his employ could not afford to be choosy. Be that as it may, I felt grateful, for it soon became obvious that the mummies I was so laboriously transporting in my little craft were not entirely insensible to their fate. As I manhandled them out of the boat, up the steps, across the causeway and, working my way along the wall of niches, finally shoved them in the next empty slot, little groans and moans told me what I most didn't want to know. Namely that, though catatonic, all were completely conscious of everything going on around them.

'Sleep, little one, sleep,' - a refrain I adopted while about my work. Did it help? Yes, I found it soothed my burden, delivering each to their final resting place on the far shore. Putting the lie to the age-old adage that, in the end, hell is other people.

It was a long time, in relative terms at least, before I learnt how to communicate with them. It might have been years, decades even, who knows? Certainly not Bob, my only friend, who, despite his assured manner, had but a thin grasp of subterranean reality as it was in Mictlán beyond the immediate exigencies of his blinkered existence. Something I learnt that was entirely in keeping with the nature of devils, who, just like middle-management in the higher realms, are task driven, never stray beyond proscribed boundaries and certainly not given to philosophising or indulging in abstract thought. Making them, as conversationalists, on par with drinking chums and casual acquaintances of the kind generally found in pubs and bars, which by then I only vaguely remembered.

But I liked Bob and, in my view, that made him important; not like the stiffs who came and went in ever-increasing numbers, personally delivered into their individual slots to await the end of eternity, when the planet plunges into the sun or is demolished by a giant meteor, which by the nature of things will have to be considerably bigger than the one that tore through the earth's crust and created all these subterranean levels of the damned.

How many levels? I only had Bob's word that there were nine, the first of which was Tláltipec, the surface world, where mortals live in denial of the direction in which they are all bound. For all I knew, there were more levels below, accessed by the Well of the World, into which the spiralling Black River and its many tributaries flowed - including the white-water rapids that had carried me to this far shore. The thundering sound of the falls an ever-present constant with the perhaps inevitable result that, with familiarity, it merged into background noises, just as the blood coursing the veins in the ears, so loud during infancy, recedes throughout childhood until it is heard no more. A slow change, marking the gradual transition into adulthood and decline. A sound that lies forgotten in the mind until dissolution, after which there is time to recall everything in the past, secure and swaddled in linen, separated from one's peers, in the wall that circumnavigates the Well of the World, in the ninth level of Mictlán. And that, just a skim on subterranean reality, below which there are more, many more, hidden depths to plumb.

How do I know this? What makes me so sure? More than anything, because of conversations with the dead, when, fog-bound in my boat, concealed from any watching eyes, out in the middle of the Styx, where thoughts can be shared when two coins are removed and the sealing wax is picked from eye sockets, allowing dusty lids to open. Once they accept their lot, the dead know everything; it's a simple fact. With nothing to gain or lose, all knowledge is open to them. Not that they usually want it. But that's the way of the condition.

The first time I talked with the dead, oddly enough, was with my mother. It was her size that gave her away. The first stiff I'd ever shipped whose head had to be propped up in the prow to accommodate her great length. There she was with the bandages fallen from her face, revealing her dues to the ferryman, the gold coins covering her eyes winking annoyingly in the sepulchral light as I poled the boat into the fog bank. Up 'till then I had waited until safely across the river to unpick the coins, but this time I took my payment when we were but half way. Kneeling in the prow, with my fingernails digging around the milled edges of the coins for the Mexican pieces – twenty pesos, Maximilians as it happened, circa 1866, in unusual mint condition, set in sockets head-side up. Worth an absolute packet, if I ever made it up through Mictlán's shady realms to the surface, where the sun shone gold. That's what I was thinking as her voice spoke clearly in my mind.

'Why do you think of monetary value, when it is your mother you are so roughly handling?'

I was astonished and, perhaps in an attempt to test whether she was still counted among the living, shook her violently by the shoulders.

'That's right, abuse me,' she laughed. 'You could screw me now. That's what you always wanted, isn't it, my dirty little boy?'

I tell you, even in death, she was a combative strumpet, my harpy mother.

Equally disgusted with us both, I left the coins where they were and, retreating to the stern, took up the pole again. I punted with all the energy I could muster, which wasn't much since, in Mictlán, I had to get by without food or sleep.

For the rest of the voyage, no further words were exchanged and, once on the far shore, to my regret, I laid her in a niche without removing those mint-condition Maximilian pesos, which were the best Mexican coins I ever came across in Mictlán. I could have gone back, of course, and asked her all sorts of questions relating to infancy, about my father and what happened after I left the mountain mining town, but I never did. An uneasy feeling made me suspect, despite her incapacitated condition, that she might get the better of me. Thereafter, I always found some excuse not to look for the niche, the exact whereabouts of which by then, perhaps conveniently, I had forgotten.

15. A DIRTY RASCAL

It was to be a quite a while before anyone else I recognised turned up. How long? A question difficult to answer exactly, as time was a subjective matter in Mictlán. However, by any reckoning, it must certainly have been years. In the meantime there were stiffs too numerous to mention. Conversations too, after adding their dues to my ever-growing pile in the sump and propping them up in the prow. Though I have to admit I soon became choosy, selecting only those with interesting faces or unusual coins. Once I had picked out the coins, how febrile the eyes of my chosen stiffs gleamed in the eldritch gloom, watching me leaning on my pole, punting the last six leagues of their journey, back across the Black River. All were scoundrels of some description or another. Elsewise none would have been relegated to the lowest level of Mictlán, as I had come to believe of the ninth. Included were all the usual suspects, swindlers, grifters, thugs of all kinds – rapists, muggers, murderers, serial killers and worse, I imagine, for not all were open concerning their crimes. But none came near, by degrees of latitude, longitude, turpitude or magnitude to even approaching, let alone matching, the mendacity of the leader who most unwisely claimed that only YHVH, the god of the Hebrews, who, as Jehovah, is also shared by Christians, had the right to judge him. That he'd traduced his country's formerly high reputation and that more wars had been launched on his say so, or mere scribbles on the backs of restaurant menus, than any predecessor had ordered was neither here nor there, as long casualty lists of civilians and combatants were meat and drink to Mictlántecuhtli. Instead, our beholden lord took grave exception to the spurious claim of divine protection according to Bob, who witnessed the judgement – taking a special interest because he knew that the politician in question was already in Lord M's employ.

But those matters did not intrude on our conversation, as much because the salient facts of the politician's rise and fall had faded from my mind, even though previously I was always hungry for the news.

No, what concerned me were the experiences we had in common as children, living within a few streets of each other - though my early years were spent in a Georgian rectory, whereas his a miserable fifties bungalow, a fact which never appeared in his biography - and then boarding at the school I have referred to earlier in my account. Elias Ashmole's. Yes, even in the infernal realm far below the surface level of Tláltipec, the name was burned on my mind, along with its satanic silhouette of three fretted spires that so dominated the north side of that capital city. Yes, we were both old boys, but there were enough years between us to ensure that our paths had never crossed 'till then, staring at each other across the length of a small boat crossing the Black River.

'I know you from somewhere,' I began, by way of initiating conversation.

'I expect that's because I was a player in the great game.'

'Chess?' I frowned, putting him on.

'Global politics, international relations, alliances between super powers, ending poverty - that sort of thing.'

'None of which means anything to me,' I said, ceasing punting and laying the pole athwart the gunnels, letting the boat drift into the descending fog.

'I can't believe that. Politics affects everyone's life.'

'Ah, but we're both dead,' I countered, reflexively patting the certificate kept in the breast pocket of my shirt.

'Yes, you're probably right,' his mental image sighed in my mind. 'But I still have my legacy.'

'Indeed, you do,' I grinned. 'Starting with the letters D.I.Y., together with a little symbol suspiciously like a prick with an eye at the tip of the glands.'

'How do you know about that?' he scowled.

'You were a few years ahead of me at school.'

'Elias Ashmole's?'

'Where else could a scholarship boy have picked up such a pukka accent?' I said, reverting to type, if not form.

'So you had a scholarship as well. My, my. And you, the ferryman. How we've both fallen. Only the right-hand angels, eh? But I still don't understand. D.I.Y. and Diehard Willy were my special secret.'

'Do you always advertise your secrets?'

'Wear them on your shirt sleeves, I say. That way you get noticed.'

'Does that include carving them on the lid of a desk?'

'You really were there, weren't you?' He grinned his famous grin. 'I did that while conjugating Latin verbs.'

'You also did it in the crapper.'

'Yes, I did it lots of times there. And the dorm, and the gym, and the science lab, and home economics. And, after I left, in barristers' chambers when studying the law. Of course there was that famous club in Brussels no one ever mentions ...'

'The shit-eaters?'

'Of course, and I even did it later in the White House when on the pan, though by that time I had no need to leave my mark.'

'Masturbation?'

'Naturally, every public school boy is a wanker. But I took it to a high art.'

'I still don't understand.'

'The bigger the lie, the straighter the face, the greater the thrill. Though the tension of maintaining an even expression does, I find, over a long period of time, strain the muscles of the eye sockets, especially on my left side. At school I had to do it with one hand in my pocket. But through practice, sheer, dogged, bloody minded perseverance, I eventually became so accomplished I developed special muscles in my groin so didn't have to use either hand. I got my rocks off doing TV interviews, answering questions in the House of Commons, at press conferences, giving speeches to Congress, the European parliament, during Cabinet meetings, banquets and receptions. Everyone knew and yet they couldn't tell. That was my secret of my attraction and the priapic source of my power. The way I cast my spell over millions.'

'And yet you say you had God on your side?'

'I do even now. He sent you, didn't He?'

I had no rejoinder to that and so I broke off eye contact, severing the mind link and shutting the diehard prick in delusory self-gratification forever and forever and forever. Amen.

Yes, just another posturing politician consigned to the dustbin of history, a reject relegated to the wall of niches in Lord Mictlántecuhtli's shady realm. Oh, and by the by, before I leave the subject, his fee for the crossing proved worthless; the two coins unpicked from his sockets were not gold as I originally believed and was customary, but gilt through and through – the same as his conscience, I suppose.

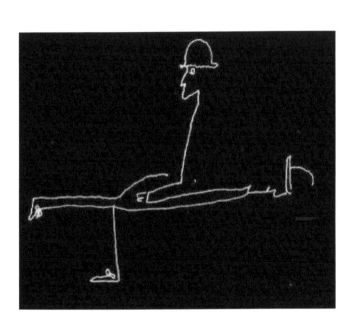

16. TURNED-UP

Before I go on, there's something I should explain. In Mictlántecuhtli's realm, I was in a translated state. Just the same as all those stiffs so laboriously transported shore to shore, to their final resting places in the wall of niches. Each bandaged bundle representing the immortal residue that cannot be destroyed, whether by fire, petrifaction or other processes. Of course, by the favour of my guardian demon, I was blessed with more substance, otherwise I could not endured the backbreaking toil, the endless tedium, the lack of sleep and food, the malicious gleam I beheld in the beams of many evil eyes – the price I had to pay for a bit of company and a few shared words, as wearily I poled my cargo across the Black River. Charon's lot was a bad bargain, I tell you, in the matter of Faustian pacts. But it was mine to endure and besides, bit by bit, coin by coin, my pile in the boat's sump was growing steadily. Translated gold, of course – that immortal residue sought by the alchemists, such as the great Paracelsus, otherwise the overloaded boat could not have ridden high in the waters. But gold none the less. All mine, yes, and recompense despite the fact I had nowhere to spend it.

Perhaps I had a fever – gold fever, the same as struck down the conquistadors, a malady from which there is only one relief, as Cortez explained to Moctezúma. Yes, you've got it, more gold. Which, in my case, came two coins at a time.

I was gouging out my next pair, scraping at the sealing wax filling the sockets, when I recognised some familiar features under the parted bandages. Who else, but my father? The prominent brow, praetorian nose and saturnine jowl; unmistakable. Kneeling astride his slumped form, propping his head and shoulders against the prow, I hesitated, unsure whether I could endure a conversation I had so desired for such an inordinate length of time.

My father, just the thought of him was enough to threaten my translated immortal state. Would he reject me all over again? If so, what would I do? Throw myself overboard? But then this was Mictlán, so therefore suicide, and consequently drowning, was not a possibility. I had to take the risk. After all, what did I have to loose, since I was dead anyway? Yea, with a certificate in my shirt pocket to prove it.

'My son! At last I've found you!'

Yes, that's what he said as bleary eyes focused on my face. I couldn't believe it. Of all the insults in the after world, that took the biscuit. This bastard was gagging on it, and so I did not reply, just staring back at the pupils in his sardonic hooded eyes. Yes, I knew him. That basilisk gaze was written on my mind. An acid stare, received drip by drip, from birth, cradle, through infancy, 'till the artful old dodger skedaddled so prematurely out of my life. Never mind my illegitimate status in a higher realm; he was the bastard.

'I've searched the realms of the dead high and low, and now, approaching the far shore, here you are. By Mictlántecuhtli's beard, it's a miracle.'

'I suppose I have to give you that,' I glowered.

'But couldn't you have found me earlier?'

'I tried, my son. But after the scandal, when I was stripped of my bishop's vestments and exposed as a philanderer in the newspapers, your mother and I separated, and thereafter her lawyer always denied me access. She had been my housekeeper you see.'

'Yes, I know about that. I looked her up in a hotel in a town, you might have heard of it, though it has no name.'

'Of course I know it. And the hotel, which I bought with the profits of several mines I owned in and around.'

'So how did you, a defrocked bishop, end up in the mining business?'

'It's long story, one that started shortly after your birth, when it was discovered I'd sired a son. I was forced to resign holy orders and so my travails began. Now that I've found you at last, that's all over.'

I smiled, thinking of the long search that had finally brought me to the Town With No Name. 'Yea, I can understand that. You might think it's funny, but I even thought I'd found you once.'

'Oh yes?' he beamed. 'And where was that?'

'In the hotel lobby, you might even know it, that mummy encased in conquistador armour. My mother said she bought it from the Black Friars up at the cathedral.'

'She did indeed, but that was no ordinary mummy. It was your forefather, the head of the Inkenhaton clan, an ancient Egyptian plundered from Mictlán by the Black Friars.'

'I don't believe that. We're all ghosts here in Mictlán. You stiffs are just the immortal residue of bodies, many of whom, I am sure, no longer exist in physical form.'

'Ah, but what has been lost in translation can be recovered and even, in some cases, resurrected. Never forget that the surface of the world is but Tláltipec, the first of Mictlántecuitli's nine realms, and populated not by the living, as the ghosts there imagine themselves to be, but by shades like you and me.'

'That's too difficult a concept, even for me, Father.'

Just accept it, my son. The body is only a manifestation of the aura. Don't forget that, here, in this the ninth realm, the immobile dead, "stiffs" as you describe us, know everything.'

'So how the fuck do I get back up to Tláltipec with all this gold?'

'Ah, now you're thinking like a true Inkenhaton, my son,' he said. In that dark place, his smile was like the setting sun, lighting my mind with golden rays.

My father was the last stiff I set into the wall of niches. But not before I resealed his eye sockets with the two gold eagle dollars he'd come arrayed with. Tears of true repentance, spilling my cheeks as, reverently, I stooped to kiss his forehead, begging forgiveness for all the curses and black thoughts I had sent his way. My emotion letting me know I was in transition – no longer a mere shade, but once again possessed of a soul, becoming corporeal, solid, flesh and bone again. Just as well, because his immortal residue was that heavy, I thought I would splinter under the load, bearing my filial burden, heaving him up the embankment steps, across the causeway and, finally, to his last resting place. After doing my duty, I stood for a long time, contemplating his still form, then, before I turned away, reciting a prayer, beginning with these words:

'My father, who art in Mictlán, hallowed be thy name ...'

But then a dream came back on me. My memory of the once-familiar world of Tláltipec returning with a dream of the life I might have had, sharing the same house with my aged father, sometimes hardly speaking for days on end, living like lodgers in the draughty presbytery, leaving our plates and dirty laundry for the only woman in our lonely lives – the cleaning lady whose name I can never remember – sometimes exchanging grunts as we pass on the stairs in the morning, shaving foam still adhering the bristles of his septuagenarian ears, in his red dressing gown briskly making his way down to breakfast, while wearily I ascend to my attic room, after working the late shift at the newspaper where I am employed. Only on Sundays do we eat together, an old family ritual by habit become Sephardic tradition, when we catch up on the news of the week, often talking late into the night. Reminiscing about happy days when the world was young, drawing draughts from the wellsprings of being, where our souls were once joined – when my glass gets empty, he winks and, half grinning, refills it with Arrak, his favourite tipple from his Egyptian days, the drink of sheikhs and common Bedouin, reserved for Sundays and the precious time we share. My father, missing always, but somehow not. Within me and without me, those parts somehow separated by a chasm, unbridgeable, and yet not. Waking into another dream in this life I never had, I sometimes feel such grief at my loss; anger too, like vitriol and water brimming my cup, and someone has just applied a match to my phosphorus brain, incandescent rage, rekindling a brush fire in my memory. My father at the western limits of the world, mourning his loss and mine. His after-image searing into my mind, as he stands back turned before an abyss, arms spread, a winged worm, black against the setting sun.

'My father, who art in Mictlán, hallowed be thy name ...'

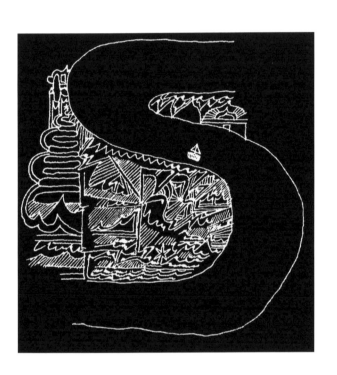

17. SAIL ON

It was the Day of the Dead and, technically, according to the regulations of the establishment, I was entitled to a day off. Trouble was, I needed the cooperation of a small boat. A very stubborn little boat, who *would* keep turning back towards the other shore where, I had little doubt, Bob the devil was already waiting on the jetty with another load of stiffs. But I was within my rights, and stronger now that I was transitioning back to flesh and bone. Moreover, in my Faustian pact with Lord Mictlántecuhtli, I'd never agreed to this posting. A detail, I knew I'd be unwise to mention to the little boat, who was riding lower in the water, suggesting that my cache of gold coins, stuffed in a collection of small sacks, artfully woven from bandages filched from the immobile dead, safe in the sump, was also in transition back to a base state. So, assuming a commanding position, standing in the stern, I produced the plastic envelope from my shirt pocket and, removing the parchment with a flourish, read out what I hoped was now a redundant death certificate, sternly reminding a contrary little boat that, on the express order of the lord of this realm, it was her beholden duty not to 'hinder or obstruct' my wishes, whether she approved of the new direction on which I was intent or not.

I did not mention my real purpose for wishing to head upriver, for acquainted as I was with the stubborn nature of the boat, I knew that would have been the end of the matter and the plan hatched after mulling over my father's account of his exploration of the lower reaches of the Black River and the country beyond. The old boy made the most of the interregnum before judgement, searching high and low for the son he had become convinced was also indentured in Mictlán's halls – a supposition that, though premature, proved ultimately correct as it turned out.

As the journey wore on, our pace steadily quickened, the current gaining in strength with the torrents out-flowing every passing canal, only adding more water into the Black River. I noted other changes too. Prior to our little jaunt, I'd been confined to working a stretch of the Black River lying within two wharves of the place where the wall of niches terminated in a rough protrusion of rock. This, as I later came to understand, was the last existing uncut section of natural cliff remaining anywhere along the entire length of that left bank, tumbling into the river close to the sluice gates marking my point of entry. Suggesting that in Mictlán everything had its limits, even eternity itself. For, if time wasn't measured by the wall of niches, I couldn't imagine what could be, except perhaps the ultimate span of humanity's tenure on earth. Not something I ever worried overly much about, especially not then, seated in the stern of the speeding boat, with nothing else to do but observe both shores of the river. To my right, regularly spaced jetties along the bank, steps behind leading up to dark tunnel entrances, all marked by a singular lack of activity. No devils anywhere to be seen. With the consequence my attention was drawn more to the opposite shore, where the architectural styles of the edifices lining the boulevards, bisected by canals, were in constant transition. On one street I observed, hoary old statues of Egyptian gods fronting ancient Greek amphitheatres on either side of the canal, while on another, Easter Island heads, glowered back, as though across the Pacific, at colonnades of giant figures with scowling Mesoamerican faces. The course of the river itself was changing too, every now and then the surging black waters, were divided by successions of islet promontories into widely separated channels, which merged only after diverging widely through low tunnels, worn through solid rock. But even then there were niches, lining the wall to my left. Every one occupied with a swaddled bundle. At such moments, the multitude of the dead seemed to press in with a claustrophobic, cloying intensity. Our passage was all the more uncomfortable until we re-joined the other branches and Black River broadened out again.

18. NO TURNING BACK

What did I say about the current strengthening? No turning back now, for we were caught on the dragnet of the ever-more deafening falls, concealed somewhere behind the drifting veils of spume, rising in billowing, back-lit cloud curtains, outlined by brilliant violet discharges flashing from electrical storms beyond. Coalescing, against the cavernous vault above, into cumulous thunder stacks, towering over the spectral lady of the mist, looming to our right in the middle distance. A natural spur of fluorescent white calcite, jutting the black headland, behind which, according to my father, lay the tributary we had to follow. But in this driving rain, we were shipping water from all angles, waves slopping the port side, forcing me to abandon punting, get down on my knees in the bilge and bail furiously, now utterly reliant on that bonny wee boat to steer a course to safety. The only one in prospect a stretch of calmer water in the lee of the white lady, meaning that the boat was having to tack up, down and back up again through the steeply furrowed foaming black torrents. A parting in the clouds off to the stern revealed the architecture of the falls, flash-lit by a jagged bolt of lightning striking way below. Just a glimpse, but enough to convince me; here were a multitude of black rivers, cascading an infinite-seeming series of cupcake gradations, stepping right down into what looked to be the sphincter of the world. A sucking, puckered, staring, black eye towards which we were surely headed. But no, at the last moment, when it seemed we were doomed to pitch over, the stubborn boat righted herself, turned, the prow dipping and then violently rearing – almost up-ending in the process – and suddenly we were suddenly flying, the keel clearing the crest of the ultimate black roller, before splashing down in the leading finger of that long stretch of calm water.

19. STARFISH

Incredibly, we were through, and I still had my gold half-submerged in the sump but safe, payment from a multitudes of stiffs – all but one of whom I wished to forget. The ardour of my time as the ferryman was already fading as, taking up my pole again, I resumed punting, knowing the boat had no other choice but to cooperate and steer a course up the tributary, aiming for a tiny point of white light that, in the darkness, looked just like a twinkling star, suggesting we were voyaging across the heavens, instead Lord Mictlántecuhtli's shady realm.

It seemed I had slept, for I found myself laying on a sandbar, the sacks of gold scattered about me, by a gushing spring – I guessed the source of the tributary. The bonny boat, however, was nowhere to be seen. My first thought was that it had voyaged on to that star, which was still shining strongly in the darkness yonder. Perhaps it had, for there was no sign of it anywhere along the winding tributary behind, in the corpse background glow a prussic-acid smear holding a pale mirror for the vaulting stone above, fading into the crepuscular green gloaming, in the opposite direction to which I was now headed, but this time by foot.

Was it a star? I wondered, again fixing my gaze on the distant luminary. Feeling my way forward into darkness, the crepuscular light fading with every forward step now I that was leaving Mictlántecuhtli's realm. After a while even the star seemed to dim, though the inky blackness about it appeared to have been replaced with a smudge of indigo blue. Like the sky as it sometimes appears in the twilight before dawn, I rationalised, remembering life before I joined the multitudes of the dead. But that was behind me, or so I fervently prayed, intent on a tiny patch of brightening blue, around which I could discern a shifting of mottled colour, reminding me of something I'd seen long years ago, before I fell into to that shadowy realm below.

20. RETURN TO ZENDA/ADDRESS UNKNOWN

L eft, left and right again - always followed by an immense sucking straight. All I had to do was remember the formula and I couldn't go wrong. But my father obviously had no inkling how life is for dyslexics - how even the simplest directions can overload the brain. Mine was steaming in this clammy subterranean heat. Perhaps I had misheard and it was the other way round? If so, I could have approached the Well of the Worlds the wrong way and be under Africa by now, that deafening roar the Limpopo, or maybe the cataracts of the White Nile disgorging by the mountains of the moon - and me with them, if the passage wall to my right gave way.

Maybe I was heading back in a circle, approaching the Well of the Worlds again, that oncoming clamour of lost souls cast overboard by Bob the devil, who I imagined to be the next stand-in ferryman, bumping the bottom, damned, damned and down. Down to Davey Jones' locker, not, as I pre-supposed, at the bottom of the ocean, but in Mexico, guarded by *las trés hermanitas*, concealed under the multiple stratum of voluminous stone petticoats.

Of two things I was sure, I was lost and my father's formula was redundant, with a massive cave-in blocking the ascending passage up ahead. Evidence of the continents cracking up, I supposed, taking a breather, setting down my sacks of gold, which had been growing heavier with each forward step, before scrambling up the baking rubble, intent on investigating whether there was a way through. Only, as I neared the top, the realisation finally dawning that this wasn't a cave-in, but a dump of desiccated body parts. Detritus of mummies, I presumed, plundered from the levels below, confirming what my father said about the Black Friars, suggesting that the cathedral was located somewhere beyond that circular opening in the passage roof directly above my head, through which I could make out another bull's eye in a vaulted ceiling, framing a circular patch of dawn sky, just the right shade of twilight blue, and some furtive streaks of wispy cloud signalling a fine day in prospect. Yes, the ultimate level of Mictlán, opening onto Tláltipec, the surface of the world I had left behind however many years before. Prompting the thought as I climbed that great midden of mummy parts, would anything be the same when I returned? Obviously not, I decided, because I was changed on the inside more than I could have imagined possible. Perhaps that was why, noticing a skull balanced on the summit, out of scale as a pea on the shoulders of a slumbering giant, I impulsively reached for it.

'Where to now, maestro?' I asked the skull, holding it out on the palm of my hand. I certainly didn't expect an answer.

'A *la luce*.'

After all the stiffs I'd individually manhandled into their personal niches, I should have been inured to hearing the dead speak, instead of reacting like I did then; losing my footing, all the funny bits in my face as I slid back down the pile - scapulae, tibias, humerus, carpalis, patella, metacarpals, tarsals, phalanges, even the dirt seemed composed of bone splinters, bound together by desiccated fibres - more fucking shrouds ...

Then, like a backing track for Dante's *Divine Comedy*, from all around, came rustling whispers, an innumerable host chanting repetitively, their massed voices getting louder and louder, 'A *la luce* ... A *la luce* ...' In other words, to the light, to the light ...

I didn't need any more encouragement. Unconcerned about my sacks of gold stashed at the base, I scrambled back up the damned assemblage, gagging on raining dust and rubble. Never a second thought as to who or what, or even on which relatives, I might be standing - panicking too much for that, fear of premature interment spurring me on.

I was through, standing in a high corbelled vault, constructed from stone blocks cut on the slant - a technique employed in ancient Egypt to disperse the shock of earthquakes - enclosing a workshop of sorts, set out with white marble tables, some occupied by mummies in a state of dismemberment - limbs separated at the joints, wizened heads from shoulders, bandages strewn. The other slabs occupied with cutting and grinding equipment, pestles and mortars, saws and chisels. Racks lining the walls behind, filled with canopic jars, variously labelled, 'fingers, toes, ears, eyes, sex organs, entrails', and a whole sub-section for brains, 'left hemisphere, right hemisphere, fore brain, reptilian brain', and so on, while others were just filled with grey powder. All that was of but passing interest, however, when compared to the facing stone staircase, lined up with the pavement at my heels, ascending steeply to that opening in the corbelled ceiling above, beyond which I could see dawn breaking through the branches of a bushy cactus swaying in the wind.

Freedom. The mere prospect was enough wipe from mind resurgent concerns regarding my precious sacks stashed in the darkness below. I only had a few more steps to go before I made it up to top. But then I saw what was moving those branches. Not the wind as I'd presumed, but an enormous stone-coloured bird, distinguished from any other I had seen by its total lack of feathers, with leathery scales and an ugly bump of cartilage at the back of its very large head. Perched, intent on prey, peering with livid-red intelligent eyes, trained on my face as I stood immobile on the staircase, in no-man's-land, half way up, or half way down, not knowing which way to move, but with no choice really, seeing as above was blocked, depending what way you looked at it. Not knowing, frozen, half way up the staircase. That was a tzitzmimime, I was sure. What else could it be? No other bird I knew of was so marked by scales instead of feathers. Obviously stationed there by Lord Mictlántecuhtli, guarding the entrance to Tláltipec – in other words, the surface world I'd left so long before. By the size of its great beak and sharp claws, and what had to have been at least a five-meter wingspan, the pterodactyl, chucamarra, call it what you will, was more than a match for this mere mortal; giving me no option but to retreat and look for another route out.

21. PRISONER OF CONSCIENCE

Of course, I remembered my cache of gold coins. How could I not when I was like Cortez, sick with gold fever? My mind, however, was rebelling at the thought of returning for the sacks through the circular opening at my feet into the unquiet darkness below. Stress, that's all it was, I reasoned. I'd been so long entombed, I'd developed a profound terror of being buried alive. I was even finding this mortuary workshop hard to endure, what with all these stiffs in bits lying all around. After I'd found another way out to the surface, I reasoned, I would return with a torch. My collection of coins would be safe enough 'till then, camouflaged as they were in the sacks I'd constructed from grey bandages of the same pale tone as that dusty pile, stashed at the base of the midden.

Life, I was rediscovering, is a marvellous thing, crammed full of fascinating distractions. Even the side passages where I found myself, after crawling out of that corbelled mortuary vault, via a stone portcullis, like the one leading into the king's chamber in the great pyramid in Giza, were full of surprises. Eerie sounds of cymbals and discordant chanting, that came and went as I explored the turns of what was proving to be a bit of a labyrinth. An overused word in this account, I know, but valid none the less in the context of those interminable echoing long corridors that led only to more of the same. Each, as far as I could make out, with identical proportioned blank doorways regularly spaced at intervals. An architectural style or actual blocked-up doorways, I couldn't tell. Feeling my way along, once more in darkness, wondering if I would ever again see the light. I shouldn't have worried for, around the next corner, half way up the corridor, ruby light was spilling frayed red curtaining. There was sound too, that of a religious service in progress in the room beyond.

I should have held back and stayed where I was, but fascination got the better of me. Would that I had not succumbed and instead tiptoed away from that baleful red light. But curiosity is a powerful urge hard to resist and, besides, that light was as oxygen is to a drowning diver, lost without an airline in the abyssal depths of the Humboldt Trench.

Seeing is believing, but still I couldn't credit what was going on. Through a hole in the red curtains, a view into a hoary past that I thought went out with the first dynasty of pharaohs and their pyramids. Those were ancient Egyptians in there - or at least their Mexican equivalent. Sons of Ra or - since I was looking over the gleaming, sweat-beaded, tonsured heads of Shemites - sons of Shem and grandsons of Noah, suitably robed in sackcloth and shod in sandals, some ringing cymbals others blowing on great horns shaped like griffins raised over their shoulders, all facing a dais directly opposite where a bigwig resplendent in purple robes was positioned between flaming torches on the wall behind, seated on an eagle-winged throne - or were those *tzitzimime* wings?

- a pyramidal gold mitre, ornamented by a lidded Horus eye, glittering on his dreadlock-wigged head, indulgently smiling and keeping time to the music with a metronome, the side-to-side swaying of his hand seemed to have them all hypnotised.

Not me, however, for I recognised that face, even though I'd only glimpsed it through a fretwork grill of the confessional. Who else but the Irish priest, Father O'Flaherty.

I thought nothing could possibly have topped that, but I was in for another surprise. Abruptly the snaking hand stopped its metronome back and forth as, simultaneously, the clashing cymbals, atonal horns and discordant chanting ceased. Everything was hushed, even the Shemite brothers seemed to collectively hold their breaths as Father O'Flaherty gestured to the side and, to the accompaniment of clanking chains, a manacled and hooded prisoner was brought forth, dragged on to the dais by a square-shouldered, blue-robed, cleric, with his back towards me.

'Sheriff-at-arms,' Father O'Flaherty commanded,
'Show the prisoner's face!'

That was my second surprise, for when the hood was removed I recognised the face beneath.

'Jaime!' I cried, unable to contain my astonishment and pleasure at seeing my friend alive, after believing him murdered by the baron's mercenaries in Happy Valley.

Then I became aware that the congregation of tonsured heads had as turned as one to stare fixatedly at the red curtain behind which I was hiding.

Although I had a running start, without a light or local knowledge or a floor plan as a guide, I was surely doomed, racing that damned labyrinth with sons of Shem and grandsons of Noah hot on my tail. Never more than then, with my pursuers' torches casting a slippery shine ahead to where I was caught in a dyslexic quandary, faced with a choice of right and left, or was that right or left? Both turns, as far as I could make out, dead ends.

Cul-de-sacs at the end of the rainbow? The other way around, surely? I discovered mine as I fell headlong. Did I trip? Or perhaps I had the demented idea of head-butting my way through. Certainly, I was crazed enough. A heavy stone door swinging onto saltpetre darkness. No time to wonder where or when as I swung back the hinged slab. Leaning with my full weight, fearing to breathe until the muffled sounds of pursuit beyond turned and finally faded.

This much was clear, I was in an old abandoned mine, light leaking a flagstone in the shored roof above, suggesting a way out. Conveniently there was even some furniture, an upturned chair and an old chest lying on its side with the lid open. Items that, when arranged with the chest placed below and the chair stacked on top, served as an impromptu ladder. Affording just enough stability to stand balanced with toes teetering on the seat, just long enough to shoulder up the heavy flagstone and at last push through to Tláltipec ...

Yes, somehow I was back home - the hotel the nearest approximation - in my old room, clutching a clear plastic envelope, which, curiously, when I got up from my knees after thanking divine providence for my deliverance, was laying on the floor before me. Inside was what looked like a certificate embossed with impressive looking seals and bearing my name. This, I had to check out.

First things first, however. I had to evict that sleeping stranger, snoring on my bed, laying with his boots on the sheets and his hat beside him. Bad luck, indicating a death in the house, but for who? I pondered, standing at the foot of the bed, unable to believe my eyes.

That was me I was staring at. That insouciant intruder was wearing my face. Parallel realities, I supposed. Somehow, somewhere, I'd blundered into one. For no way was I dreaming this doppelganger.

Congratulations, I thought, sitting down beside myself, a sudden lassitude creeping on. Death or transition? Mine to know and mine to find out – or the other way around? – my last thought as I keeled over.

P'SST SCRIPT

THE DOPPELGANGER'S DREAM

In the dream I'm awake in my bed beside my sleeping double, who's dreaming of a trial. Because he's my double and we necessarily share the same energy body, and with all that goes with that, I can see what is going on. However, although we have so much in common, my twin and I, we diverge where some experiences are concerned, and consequently many details of this dream, which is informed by his memories of a past he wishes to blot out, baffle me.

Take this Jaime, the manacled prisoner just delivered into the dock by an armed escort of monks from holding cells below. My twin hero-worships him, yet, from my point of view, the man's a real low-life, a narco tráficante with blood on his hands from his short but meteoric rise from *barrio* hustler to top pistolero, trading in death across the border. Perhaps that's a bit strong, for he does have some admirable qualities, not least his fashion sense and chutzpah, but when weighed against his many crimes, he certainly deserves to be arraigned. Although clearly not before an ecclesiastical court of shit-eaters, in the crypt of a cathedral where the repeating vaults of the elaborately carved groined ceiling are supported by splayed, tall pillars, rooting at the base. Giving the impression of a petrified forest clearing, shady with tenebrous presences, emanating the large lead coffins, stacked on stone shelves, recessed in the walls all around.

A detail that my twin finds disturbing, wishing, as he does, to expunge all memories of his time in Mictlán. But when faced with all those coffins, he can't, for with the scrying ability that is his special talent when dreaming, he knows they contain the predecessors of the master of proceedings, sitting in judgement on a dais before what is the stoutest pillar of that stone forest. Under his dreadlocked wig and gold-brocaded robes is the same Black Friar my twin spoke with in the confessional, under the mistaken belief that he was a Father' O'Flaharty. A title clearly false, for this is none other than the pope of Shemites, the church that predates all other monotheistic religions, even the ancient Jewish faith – sons of Shem, grandsons of Noah, by direct line, survivors of the first deluge, awaiting the second deluge on the sixth millennium since creation in the Town With No Name, in the last unmapped fastness of the *Sierra Madre*.

But since this is the ecclesiastical court of the Shemite shit-eaters, even though that is their pope on the dais, until the conclusion of the trial, his proper form of address is Worshipful Lord Horus.

Leaning forward, the pope addresses a tall and curious black-garbed figure, standing expectantly, back turned to the prisoner in the dock, behind him.

'Prosecutor, before we start, ahem ...' his croaky voice, ratcheted lower, 'By what calendar are we reckoning?'

'The Shemite calendar, Worshipful Lord Horus.'

'Long count, I assume?'

The Prosecutor nodded, 'Yes, my worshipful lord.'

'And the year?'

The prosecutor riffled his papers. 'Five thousand nine hundred and ninety-nine, Worshipful Lord Horus.'

'And, ah, what is that in the, ah, Tzendal calendar?' The prosecutor consulted a monk at his side.

After a moment he looked up. 'Five sun minus five snake, by Brother Valentine's calculation, worshipful lord.'

'No time to delay then,' the pope frowned, 'For the deluge will soon be upon us.' He paused, allowing the import of weighty words to sink in, before banging his gravel, silencing an outbreak of whispering from the Shemite Black Friars packed into pews at the back of the crypt. 'Order! Order!' I will have order,' he boomed.

'Sergeant-at-arms, is the accused fit to plead?'

'Yes, Worshipful Lord Horus,' boomed a voice my twin instantly recognised from behind the dock. Under those blue, ecclesiastical robes, the court officer was none other than Baron Hapsburg – revealed a secret Shemite all along.

'Sergeant-at-arms!' the pope ordered. 'Swear him in.'

'Worshipful Lord Horus,' the sergeant-at-arms replied, 'The prisoner declines to swear on the Pentateuch of Noah. He asks to be heard on his own recognisance.'

'So be it,' the pope intoned. 'Prosecutor, read the charges to the apostate.'

'Yes, Worshipful Lord Horus,' the black-cowled prosecutor responded, reminding my twin of a hooded crow as he hopped, more than stepped, up to the dais. 'Prisoner,' he began, turning to face the dock, 'You are charged with felonious acts; to wit, breaking covenant and peddling salacious lies injurious to the order. What plead you?'

'I am a *sappatista* of *la revolución*, I do not recognise this court!' the prisoner spat, his voice gaining strength and volume. 'I want nothing more to do with your filthy trade in body parts. I only went along because the mummies were useful for smuggling my *drogas*.'

'And where did you smuggle your, ah, drugs?' the prosecutor said, enunciating the last word as if the mere mention of '*drugs*' was a criminal act in itself, implying that the general context of trading in body parts was hardly relevant, if at all.

'You know perfectly well, through your foking tunnels.'

'Where exactly?'

'Below the foking borders, ass wipe.'

'Which borders?' the prosecutor interjected. 'You must be more specific.'

'Ok, I give you the foking list. Under the foking Rio Grandé, the foking River Jordan, the Red foking Sea, the foking Sea of Marmara, the English foking Channel, the Zuiderzee into foking Euroland, the ...'

'Enough!' the pope thundered, banging his gravel. 'I warn the accused, any further lewd outbursts and you will forfeit your right to a hearing. Furthermore,' he went on, 'It is not for you to question the supremacy of the court. You must answer the charges as given. What plead you?'

'Fok off, you foking worshipful foking ass foking wipe.'

'The accused has answered in the affirmative,' the pope ruled, again banging his gravel. 'Prosecutor, you may resume the interrogation.'

'Thank you, Worshipful Lord Horus,' the prosecutor replied. 'Prisoner, when you swore the sacred oaths, it was incumbent upon you to divulge neither the secrets nor the existence of the order. Do you remember this?'

'Sure,' the prisoner shrugged. 'So what the fok is this to do with the foking price of pistachio nuts?'

'The accused will answer all questions directly and without elaboration,' the pope interjected.

'*Vete la chingada!*' the prisoner cursed him. 'And fok you too!' he shouted, grinning up at the dais, receiving a blow to his back of his head from the mailed fist of the baron, in his capacity as the sergeant-at-arms, standing behind him.

'You will answer,' the prosecutor insisted.

'Prisoner, I put it to you that you passed on privileged information concerning the existence of the order to an outsider.'

'You mean the foking moron reporter from the Notional foking Enquirer.'

'Yes.' The prosecutor nodded. 'Tell the court where you met.'

'In Rome, after I finish our little business with brother Señor B of the Brussels Lodge,' Jaime laughed. '*Puta* foking *madre*, I fool the fok good, standing in the foking car park, in red robes with a gold foking crozier in my hand. The stupid fok even kneels and kisses the ring on my foking middle finger, after I introduce myself as "Cardinal Sin", *el ultimo* advisor on Latin American affairs to his holiness. Which would be true, only it is the wrong pope I am telling him about. For every word I say, he pays me in dollars, unlike you *pinché* pigs, who only ever come up with foking pesos. Meaning I always loose in the foking exchange.'

'So you admit the charge?'

'Why not?' Jaime shrugged, inspecting the broken state of his fingernails. 'Your foking Wor-shit-ful-foking-Lord-foking-Horus-foking goat-fok-ing-ass-foking-wipe is going to find me foking guilty anyway,' he added, looking up with a sly grin that seemed to imply he knew something the pope did not.

'The prisoner's guilt has been demonstrated beyond the shadow of a tzitizimime wing,' the prosecutor resumed. 'By his own admission

214

he has passed privy information beyond the circle, thereby breaking covenant. And in his latest testimony he has gone even further, denying the authority of our Worshipful Lord Horus, our pope and incarnate master, demonstrating complete disdain for the order. I have no alternative therefore but to demand the ultimate sentence.'

'I thank the venerable prosecutor,' the pope intoned ponderously, 'For his excellent summation of the salient points. I find the case so proved, that the accused, in his arrogance, did communicate secrets privy to the order, thereby imperilling his fellows, for if one is not true to all he cheats them, for they have loved him in all matters and are denied his love.' Again he banged his gravel, silencing a sudden expectant buzz from the back of the court.

'The prisoner will rise,' Lord Horus continued.

'You have been found guilty. Do you have anything to say before I pass sentence?'

'Fok you, do your foking worst, Don foking O'Flarty! ' Jaime cackled.

'Recorder,' the pope directed angrily. 'Strike his last response from the record.' He banged his gravel, silencing a sudden chatter from the tonsured Black Friars.

'Prisoner,' he said, setting an ill-fitting black cap in place of his papal mitre, askew on his wigged head, 'You will be taken from here to the tree of confinement, there to await your execution. Your end will be slow in coming, I promise, so that you may properly contemplate your many crimes against the order before your final judgement, by his most supreme majesty of the infernal realms below, whose name must never be mentioned within.'

'Viva Lord Mictlántecuhtli!' Jaime interjected with a joyous yell, shaking manacled fists up at the dais.

'He will fok you!'

'Bind and gag him,' the pope yelled, almost falling off the dais in his desperation to shut the prisoner up. But both knew it was too late, for the name of the great demon had been uttered within the sanctum. Now, as Jaime might have framed it, the *foking* destruction of the *foking* temple was *foking* assured.

BOOK III

THE GHOST WHO

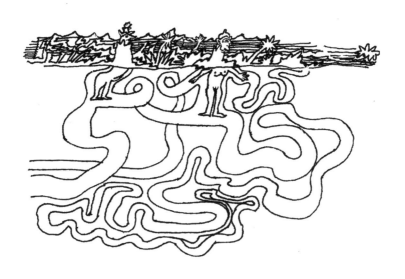

1. THE STRANGE HOMES
OF MR AND MRS CAMOUFLAGE

¡Desayuno! Para los muertos...

From the corridor beyond, a call to arms raising a renegade shade from Lord Mictlántecuhtli's penultimate realm, the promise of breakfast, wiping dreamlike recollections – hecatomb realities, gone as though they never were. The one jarring note, the clear plastic envelope on the bed beyond my double's out-flung hand. Inside, a document headed by his double-barrelled name in looping copperplate above an impressive gold seal, embossed with a skull and cross bones. 'Double' looked at it distractedly, putting off checking out the enclosure until later, food being the only thing on his mind just then.

'*Buenas días*, Helga!'

'And to you too, munchkins!' she said, offering up a heavily powdered cheek to kiss as he stomped into the salon like a matador on the case.

'Mmm! Chanel Número Venti Cinco!' Double wrinkled his nose at the cloying taste of face powder on his lips. 'And frying bacon! My favourite smell combination of a morning,' he trumpeted, taking the seat opposite, rubbing his palms with happy enthusiasm.

'I'm so hungry I could eat una ...'

'*Toro!*' Helga interjected. 'And what you get up to in the nacht,' she said, with an appraising look as she raised a denuded and pencilled eyebrow, 'To be having such an appetite?'

'I dun'no.' Double shrugged, wondering what she had against eyebrow hair, finding her voice more gruff, more Teutonic somehow. 'Dreaming, I guess,' he muttered, pondering her cosmetic changes, which though minor still seemed significant somehow. 'Who knows? Perhaps I've taken up walking in my sleep.'

'*Ja!*' Helga said, studying his face thoughtfully.

'The house can affect peoples in that way. It would not be the first time.'

She stopped as the kitchen door swung back on one of the Malinchés entering, bearing a weighty tray.

Food! Double couldn't take his eyes off the vision of a Hispanic *Nueva York*, rebuilt after the fall – tottering twin towers of *tortillas* slotting a red sun brimming a sauce boat, set down before a silver platter and a squidgy great morass of *frijoles*, crackling with bacon, overlaid by huevos rancheros, heaped sunny-side up, just how he liked them, not forgetting *zúmo de naranja* – freshly squeezed – and, glory of glories, strong black coffee steaming in an earthenware jug. A serious business, Mexican breakfast. He was so completely engrossed he failed to notice that Helga ate nothing and merely toyed with her helping.

'So, just the two of us,' Double smiled, leaning back in his chair, stretching arms expansively, cracking knuckles behind his neck. 'Tell me, did our friend get away all right?'

'And who is this you talk about?' Helga demanded with an asperity that was unusual, even for her.

'You know, Herr what's-it?' Double said, discombobulated by his sudden loss of recall. 'The Austrian chappie questing for ... turtles?' He frowned.

'No, that's not right.'

'You must have dreamed him,' Helga harrumphed.

'The only guest is you.'

That was his second jarring note of the morning. And he had such a clear recollection. A florid face framed by flaring sideburns. Silly bastard, really.

'Yea! A dream! That's it,' Double blustered.

'You're absolutely right about the hotel, Helga, weird vibes. Must be the emanations,' he grinned as a sudden vibration underfoot – transmitting, ankles, knees, thigh bones, hip bones, spine, and passing out his elbows – shook the table top. The cutlery rattled as if to emphasise his point. 'You know damned fine what I'm talking about,' he continued, rationalising the sudden tremor as a collapse of long-abandoned mine workings far below.

'And what is that?' Helga smiled, all wiles behind a powdered mask of face powder, applied as thick as icing on a sponge cake.

'Treasure, what else?' he snapped. 'You can't have forgotten our deal.'

'You surprise me!' she glowered, conflating, casting a shadow over the table like a rising thunder cloud late on a summer's day. 'Perhaps now your holiday it comes to an end?' she sneered.

'What the hell d'you mean, Helga?' Double frowned, sensing a new line of attack.

She sighed. 'Does your mummy never teach you? Sometimes you have to make effort to pluck the apples from the tree.'

Mummy? Double balked, as into his mind came an image of Helga swaddled in the sump of a narrow wooden boat, lying with her bandaged head propped against the prow, gold coins in her eye sockets, winking back at him where he stood in the stern, leaning on a pole, punting slowly across black waters into a fog bank delineating the limits of memory. What was that about? he shuddered, feeling as if the black dog of Mictlán had just walked over his grave. This morning he was even weird to himself, and the day was hardly yet begun. Emanations from below? Double doubted it. That bitch across the table? The split between the sexes, widening to an unbridgeable gulf? That time of the month come round again, the full moon bringing on the doomy feeling induced by proximity to blood tides. Periods, he reflected, give women the acuity to see beyond temporal limits, like the curtains of conditioning part a crack. Or crack *ajar*? Perhaps she knew something he was blocking out? Locked away in his brain, just like every other man, more uncharted regions than the dark side of Neptune, that was for sure.

'And what's apples got to do with it, Helga?' he countered, knowing attack is always the best defence.

'Maybe more than you know!' she snarled, taking the bait. 'The golden apples of the sun? You never hear tell?'

'Nope,' Double grinned, defying her with folded arms, leaning back in his chair.

'According to the ancient European legends, beyond the setting sun lies paradise and the orchards I speak of, guarded by the three daughters of nacht.' She thumbed towards the shuttered window. 'The same mountains closing in the town.'

'You mean *las trés hermanitas?*' he said, looking to the side and wondering why the window shutters to the street were still shut this late time of morning.

'What other mountains do you think I am talking of?'

'So!' he smiled, ignoring her last response,

'What's this, ah ... west-end Eden,' he said, slipping into sotto voce, feeling an odd unease creeping on, 'Got to do with the, um ... ah, treasure?'

'Maybe everything, maybe nothing,' she giggled gaily, switching moods and masks. 'In the stories there are fourteen, you know.' She frowned, the caked layer of face powder cracking as the skin of her forehead furrowed.

'Fourteen?' He reiterated, recalling *cantina* Joe's pronouncement on the subject. 'I thought there were thirteen?'

'Yes,' she nodded, 'Thirteen blinds, each without substance.' Her lips curled, cracking her powdered mask.

'Just like the empty promises of the church.'

'And the fourteenth?'

'Ah,' she smiled, the movement of her lips flaking the face powder at the corners of her mouth, '*La catorces*, the only one worth having, the legacy of *ventura*.'

'You mean "lucky"?' he said. Her face powder was now falling in tiny flakes onto the table cloth.

'That is what I say,' Helga scowled.

'And who was he, this "lucky fourteen"?' Double said, wondering if this somehow connected with the shot-out sign by the rail track in the desert and its bullet-riddled legend, '*Catorces*'.

'A black slave who won his freedom when he pointed out to his master the silver that would make all their fortunes, cooling in the ashes of the camp fire,' she said, suddenly unaccountably nervous, with both hands smoothing lustrous tied-back ... black hair, which Double suddenly remembered had been blonde before. 'But you distract me.'

'Eden, wasn't it?' he said, trying to regain a tight focus. Women, you never know them really, he thought. Certainly not this *bruja*, black to her roots and beyond. Dyed of course, he rationalised, otherwise her hair could not have changed colour overnight. Little did he suspect there was another, altogether more strange explanation.

'Ah yes,' she beamed, precipitating a further fall of face powder. 'The garden, of course, is long gone. The Spanish, they see to that!' she sneered. 'Those conquistadors and their descendants, slash and burn, turn the Virgin to desert. But the temple to her daughters remain,' she beamed.

'Where?' he groaned, certain the foregoing was all a canard.

'Here, you fool,' she said, knuckling the table top, tiny flakes dancing to her command.

'No,' Double shook his head, 'Credulous and a fool I may be, but you can't expect me to believe that.'

'Why not? Is the custom in Mexico,' she sniffed.

'Cathedrals on pyramid-es and always those on older structures, like the layers of a pavlova. Why not this house, la *Castilla de la Dinero*, on the temple the Egyptian colonists dedicate to the golden apples of the sun?'

'I've had enough,' he said, looking away – anywhere but at the cracking medusa mask of her over-powdered pale face. Stone, I'll turn to stone, he thought, unless I get the hell out now.

'Do as you like,' she said, catching on fast. 'But first,' she gestured towards the mess of plates on the table, 'You must clear these things away and wash up in the kitchen. Malinché has gone off for the day. It is time you earn your keep, do not you think?'

Returning, after a few minutes, Double sensed she was in a better mood, as he pushed through the salon door.

'You finish already?' she smiled down at him.

'Yup,' he nodded.

'The plates are clean?'

'Spotless,' he said entirely insincerely.

'And the ones from before?'

'With the others in the rack.'

'You do not put away?'

'I didn't think that's what you wanted.'

'Next time you polish and put away. Promise now.'

'Yes, absolutely,' he muttered, finding her overbearing as ever. 'Can I leave now?'

'You go to get drunk?'

'That depends,' he shrugged, shoulders angled on the door.

Helga sighed. 'I suppose if you must, you must. Come,' she said, standing up, 'I go with you, I have to make sure the sign is still up outside.'

'A sign for what?' Double said, as she pushed past him and led the way along the long corridor.

'To keep the perverts away,' she cast back over a shoulder broad as a sideboard.

'What perverts?' he called after her.

'Perverts?' she snorted. 'Pilgrims? What is the difference? You do not notice them swarming like flies in the street?'

'How could I when you keep the salon shutters closed,' he panted, forced to keep up as she set a fast pace.

'I do that so they cannot stare in the windows. So nosey the holy fools are, always judging,' she sniffed.

'What's the occasion?' he asked, following her into the little lobby, which became quite crowded when taking into account the old retainer in his dusty suit of conquistador armour on sentry duty behind the bolted door.

'Tomorrow begins the festival of Shem up at the cathedral,' Helga declared. 'Twenty thousand pilgrims in town tonight. Three days it lasts,' she whirled around,

'But this year I do not think it goes well.'

'Why not?'

'Because this time the Black Friars refuse to let the pilgrims kiss Shem's sacred shin bone.'

'Shin bone?' he laughed.

'That is what I say.' She scowled down at him.

'The friars use it for divination.'

'I thought the church authorities proscribed that, along with necromancy, black magic, voodoo and the rest.'

'The friars are Shemites not Catholics.'

'Of course,' Double nodded, puzzled he could have forgotten such a salient fact of the town. He stood back as she drew the long bolt and turned the large key in the old brass lock.

Holding the door ajar, she leaned around the jam. 'Good, still there,' she announced over a clamour of discordant chants, distant shrieks and wild hosannas coming from the street beyond.

'The sign?' he ventured, determined to stay on good terms before leaving.

'Ja, it say "*cerrado*",' she smiled, pulling open the heavy door. 'I keep the hotel closed for the whole festival.'

'Sounds a good idea,' he said, temporarily dazzled, squeezing past her into bright opaque light outside, swirling with dust raised by thousands of shuffling feet.

'Don't get too drunk, munchkins,' she laughed, slamming the door before he had a chance to step down onto the street.

2. JOE STICKS HIS NOSE IN

Shunted by the heavy door impacting his rear end, Double stumbled over a shaven-headed penitent, dragging himself along n bloodied hands and knees, lashing his back, between prostrations, with a flail of chorded rope knotted around little stones tied at the frayed ends of the strands.

'Jaime!' he blurted, coming face to face with the slavering flagellant. But he was mistaken, for, instead of smiling, as might have been expected, the self-abuser merely scowled and averted his bruised and bloodied face.

'Fuck you!' Double cursed to no effect, put in mind of a worm as he watched a pilgrim's painful progress, humping the cobbles, bumping his forehead in time to the handclaps of a troupe of sack-clothed choristers further on up the street, joyously singing what sounded like 'Gory Glory Angelitós,' under a banner of flapping canvas decorated with crude black crosses, interspersed with what he took to be representations of Shem's sacred shin bone, crudely rendered in blood-red paint.

For a moment Double felt like giving up the ghost and abasing himself to a god he couldn't comprehend, just like all the pilgrims, but his need for a drink in the *cantina* was too strong to join in the fun. Besides, he wanted to offload to Joe about his nephew. Jaime, last seen discounting a dream he only dimly remembered, leading the resistance back in Happy Valley.

What the fuck had happened after that? Double wondered, stopping in his tracks, oblivious of the happy-clappy throng, pushing past, such was his need to fill in the gaping void in his head. All he could recall was being deafened by a barrage of explosions; standing side by side with Jaime in the downdraft of descending black helicopters, before being pursued into some caverns, then nothing ... absolutely bloody *nada* ... Until, of course, he woke that morning with the most enormous appetite. As if by some incredible feat of somnambulism, overnight he had re-crossed the glacier and climbed back over the saw-toothed mountains and broken into the hotel. Impossible - but how else to explain wakening in his bed? Perhaps the caverns led into the lair of one those mythical birds of Joe's tall tales, and he'd been carried over the *cordilleras* in great claws. A ridiculous notion, but while he was on the subject, what were they called? Of course, the *tzitzimime*! Absurdly, Double felt a double-glow of satisfaction at remembering not only the local name of the giant birds the Austrian chappie had insisted were pterodactyls, but also the mad aristo's title, Von Hapsburg, last seen leading the helicopter attack against the Dutch dopers of Happy Valley.

Double sighed, sure all the *sappatistas* were dead now, including Jaime. Time to get that drink in the *cantina* and catch up with Joe, he reminded himself, body swerving an reliquary salesman rattling bones in his face, like every other god-struck mendicant in his way, dishevelled after the long walk up from the plains - the majority wearing ecstatic expressions lifted towards the sky, unlike the down-cast flagellants, on bloody hands and knees, their faces filthy, flat and drained. The procession flowing around the bandstand in the Plaza de la Revolución, where Gomez's victims were buried, and past the cathedral steps in the direction of a large purple tent with three tall pointed peaks like church spires, which he could see framed the slot at the end of the street to the limits of the town.

Feeling like he'd crossed a bloody Rubicon, rather than the width of a narrow cobbled street, he pushed through the half doors and stepped down into the hole-in-the-wall establishment. After the clamour and dust outside, the *cantina* seemed a place of peace and serenity. With not a pilgrim in sight, Double observed thankfully, his eyes adjusting to the dim light, noting that unusually Joe was not around. Instead, one of the Malinchés behind the bar, taking his order like he was a total stranger.

'Una doble, señor,' she smiled surgically, setting down a glass he wished was as clean as her gleaming teeth. '¡Nada mas?'

'Si,' Double pouted. 'Un pocito beso, por favour,' he said, surprised to see blind fury mounting her gold-irised eyes. He had only asked for a little kiss.

Feigning indifference, taking his drink, he sauntered over to the small table by the warm stove in the corner, pulling a chair away from the wall and sitting down with his back to the bar, wondering whether he'd fantasised the whole scene in the bed with her two sisters. Just like he'd dreamed up old bugger-lugs Baron Von Paedophile, he reflected, conjuring his fat face in the dirty glass cupped between his hands, pooled in oily *mescal*, sharing murky depths with a worm; silly bastard, really, with his ridiculous nineteenth-century sideburns, waving back from a precipice, unmindful of the native boy rearing up behind, curtain clouds closing on his view ... then a knee knocking into his elbow, drink and a worm slopping the table as he whirled around angrily.

'Holy shit!' Double gasped, finding himself face-on to a porky barrel-busting a belly button behind a denim shirt. 'Joe, it's you!'

'*Perdón*,' Cantina Joe salaamed, holding one hand to his forehead and a beer in the other, bowing in the manner of dipsomaniac Muslim mullahs. He called to Malinché behind the bar, 'Una doble *mescal* sin gusano, por el señor.' Grinning broadly he then gestured grandly towards the chair opposite, '*¿Con permisso?*'

'Of course,' Double growled, watching the worm drunkenly side-winding across the table in a desperate bid for freedom, reminded of Joe's dire warnings concerning imbibing the worm of the devil at the bottom of every bottle of local *mescal* – sure felt like he hadn't another friend in the world.

'It's been so long,' Joe beamed, 'But what is the matter, my friend?' He leaned closer. 'Looks like you bounce up on the *mala baja cuerda de la cama* this morning.'

'Yea, like a human cannonball out my bed, up an atom and in through the back door,' Double nodded, trying not to stare too pointedly at a delectable posterior – Malinché bent over the table, wet cloth in hand, closing on a saloon wriggler. 'That hotel has weird vibes, Joe,' he went on, as, avoiding his gaze, now studying her face, Malinché set down another *mescal* before him. 'I have these crazy dreams I can't remember for the life of me.'

'*Es importanté* you try. For the dreamer, losing recall is like forgetting his name.'

Double laughed, his bad humour at last evaporating. 'So that explains why I don't recognise myself this morning.'

'I know who you are,' Joe responded coolly, sipping his beer, bloodshot big eyes intent over a frothy rim.

'You do?'

'From the first moment, my friend.'

'*Por favor*,' Double pleaded, only half-jokingly,

'Enlighten me, *maestro*.'

Joe thumbed over his shoulder at the hotel. 'That first time, when I see you with Helga, I recognise the template.'

'Don't you mean my "basic type", Joe?'

'*Es* close, but template *es* better,' Joe chuckled.

'Template memories, or memory templates, that *es* the diddle.'

'The word is riddle,' Double interjected. 'One that is beyond me I'm afraid,' he sighed, 'Since those memories are buried just too deep.'

'*¿En serio?*' Joe lofted bushy eyebrows. 'You think I don't understand your connection to Helga?'

'You do?' Double blurted, feeling naked and exposed.

'Sure,' Joe said easily. 'There are many similarities. Not the height of course, but you have the same eyes as she had.'

'Had?' Double repeated, his stomach churning,

'What do you mean?' he said, suddenly afraid.

'My friend,' Joe said sadly, laying a broad hand on Double's shoulder. 'You must still be in shock. During the funeral, when it went dark, all through the hailstorm with only lightning to see by, I am looking everywhere for you.'

'Now you're kidding me,' Double said. 'I just had breakfast with Helga in the hotel. She was alive as ...'

'My friend,' Joe interjected firmly, 'Your mother is twice as dead as a doornail and buried one hundred times more deep. For months now the hotel has been closed, with only the Malinchés keeping it dusted. But you know all this.'

'I do?'

'Easy, my friend.' Joe's big hand squeezed a slumped shoulder. 'I believe you. Tell me, how did Helga seem when you left her in the hotel?'

'Same as ever. Well, maybe not,' Double hesitated, 'When I think about it she did seem a bit odd.'

'Describe her,' Joe insisted.

'One thing, she had black hair. Dyed obviously.'

'Are you sure it is not a wig?'

Double scratched his head uncertainly. 'I don't know.'

'Anything else?'

'I did notice her cheeks were heavily caked with face powder.' Double grinned, his humour returning.

'Perhaps she's got leprosy,' he added brightly.

'No, not, leprosy my friend,' Joe smiled sadly.

'Your mother wears make-up and a wig to cover the fact she is a ghost.'

'OK, she's a ghost?' Double said, suddenly dead calm, knowing with absolute certainty that Joe was right.

'But why has she returned to haunt me?'

'Could be something you have done. Or not done?' Joe shrugged.

'Like what?' Double said, as, unbidden, a memory of a pair of winking gold coins repeated on a Möbius loop in his mind's eye. That was a clue, he knew.

'Perhaps because you miss the funeral?'

'No,' Double shook his head, 'I don't think so.'

'Maybe something you forgot?'

'Like in a dream?'

'Maybe,' Joe nodded gravely, reaching for the bottle between them.

'I know it's something to do with tokens,' Double paused, knowing it was important to dissemble when it came to the subject of gold. 'I remember she's lying stretched out in a boat, with two tokens in her eye sockets, while we're crossing a black river.'

'*Es* the Black River of Mictlán, my friend,' Joe said, refilling Double's glass. 'You were together for her last journey.'

'Please don't say that,' Double shivered.

'*Es* true,' Joe insisted gently.

'I know,' Double said, staring fixatedly into his glass. 'I wanted to return for the tokens, but ...'

'*Es* because the tokens were your fee,' Joe interjected.

'But I never could find the place where I put her.' Double gazed upwards, anywhere but within, at memories of Mictlán. 'Joe, why has she come back?' He bunched fists, knuckled temples, squeezed cheeks out of shape, for a moment his face like a wolf looking at the moon, 'What is she after?' he howled.

'You,' Joe smiled, eyes twinkling. 'The essence of you.'

'I don't understand.'

'My friend,' Joe sighed, 'You have to take into account how it *es* with vampires.'

'She is a vampire now?' Double's voice went up in pitch.

'In a manner of speaking,' Joe held up a hand.

'Allow me to continue. Only by stealing from her first-born the essence which she lost giving birth can she become *flash* and guts again.'

'The phrase is "flesh" and blood,' Double snapped. 'Flesh and blood.'

'Thank you,' Joe nodded, imperturbable as ever.

'So what is this essence exactly?' Double asked after a beat.

'There are many names for it. Middleganger, Fetch, Ka. To the native peoples of Mexico it *es* the nagual. In a way, you could say it *es* like the soul Christians believe in, but so much more.'

'So,' Double sighed heavily, 'I have to protect my nagual.'

'Yes,' Joe said, staring at Double oddly. 'Yes, you, most of all.'

'Oh god,' Double blubbed into his hands. 'I still can't believe Helga's dead. She seemed so ... bloody permanent.'

'Don't remember, huh?' Joe said, his voice hard,

'Cabrón, the last time in my bar, you yourself are telling me she has cancer.'

'And when was that?' Double demanded though parted fingers; hating Joe at that moment, wanting, as he did, sympathy instead of plain, unvarnished truth.

'Before you take off with the old *gringo*.'

'And what the fuck was I doing taking off with an old *gringo*?' Double snapped as in his mind formed a grizzled face incised by the rays of a magenta sun, setting over a maze of snow-capped canyons like cracks in the world.

'Looking for Jaime, what else?' Joe frowned. 'My friend, I mean to ask, do you ever find him?'

'Oh god.' Double clapped his forehead. 'I meant to tell you, when I came in ... I keep seeing him in the street, in dreams. Everywhere I look. But he's dead, I'm certain of it.'

'You don't sound so sure, my friend.' Joe took Double's hand in his. 'You must explain.'

'There's not much to tell. He was showing me the sights of Happy Valley, then,' he gulped, 'The baron and his men descended from helicopters, there was fighting, explosions, and ... and then I found myself back in the hotel. I don't know how.'

'Start at the beginning,' Joe insisted. '*Es* always the best way.'

However, before Double could provide a clear account, he had first to disentangle the details of the battle from the memories of his time as a shade in Mictlán, which were somehow bound together with his t win's dream of Jamie's trial. Hearing him out, Joe was patience itself, every now and then topping up his troubled friend's drink from the bottle on the table between them, never once expressing incredulity as Double went on endless digressions of conversations with demons and of transporting stiffs to their last resting places on a far shore. But all the while, as Double continued talking, sorting his memories into sequential order, one thought kept pressing on the doubled hemispheres of his compressed and overloaded brain.

Coming to the end of his account, mindful of the death certificate in his room back at the hotel, at last Double was able to ask, 'Joe, do you think I am dead?'

'That depends on the way you see yourself, my friend.'

'How so?' Double frowned.

'Here in Tláltipec, the ultimate level of Mictlán, you, me,' he gestured grandiloquently, 'Those pilgrims out there, everyone here

233

are the living dead. All on our way,' a finger dipped to point to the floorboards between their feet, 'Down to the next level below, unless ...'

'Unless what?'

'That is up to you to find out, my friend. It is la catorces, the ultimate prize,' Joe smiled enigmatically. 'But for now I have to make plans to free Jaime from the *pinché* Black Friars.'

'But the trial was my twin's dream, nothing more,' Double protested.

'You are wrong, my friend,' Joe insisted, reaching out, squeezing Double's shoulder comfortingly. 'The messages of the dreaming twin are always true.'

3. LAND ESCAPES

What did he expect? Helga and *las Malinchés* haunting desolate corridors? A hunted feeling as he snuck in, sneaking backwards glances, 'till at last to his room, safe and with time to think.

'What the ...? Who the ...?' Double gasped, stepping inside, only then understanding that the tall stranger facing him across the room was in fact himself, reflected in a long mirror, fixed in his absence to the front of the wardrobe, giving it the appearance of an open door. Standing framed in the gap, Double's double, wearing an 'I know something you don't know expression,' to which Double took instant exception.

What was it about himself, he wondered? Why did he have to look so self-important and uptight, when in reality he was confused and in need of help? Even his own name escaped him, as he found himself fixated - a double in double trouble, unable to break eye contact with his reflection and look away. Until, with a superior smile, his mirror counterpart obliged, looking pointedly towards a clear plastic envelope interleaved in a paperback book laying on the bedside table.

Intrigued, putting aside the envelope for a moment, Double flicked through the yellowing pages of an early Penguin paperback edition of *The Lawless Roads*, a novel by Graham Green, which, he noted, was set in Mexico of the 1930s, during the Cristeros insurgency, when religious fanatics waged war against the state, which had banned public religious worship. All well and good, Double thought, but, in his present situation, not exactly relevant reading material. Perhaps something more pertinent was to be found in the envelope? But then, as he reached towards it, he glanced up, realising with a start there was no reflection in the mirror before him, that it was in fact a door, open to another room, identical in every respect but one. Namely that he was standing where he was and not there. Madness, taking him at that moment, for, without a second thought, overriding the protests of his rational mind, he stepped through the mirror to the other side, experiencing a flash of light from within or without – he couldn't tell – as he did so.

He was reaching for a similar plastic envelope interleaved in a paperback novel of the same title and author, laying on an identical bedside table, when a familiar 'Coo-ee,' not heard since he was a baby boy resounded from a distant quarter and demanded his immediate attention.

'Helga,' he exclaimed, reassured to see her hair was blond again, though not upon his second glance, noting, as she looked round from rummaging in an open cardboard box set on the polished dark oak of the old sideboard, that her hair was silver at the roots.

'Ah, there you are, munchkins,' she smiled, only then revealing her cheeks, which had become canyons in the craggy escarpments of her time-reconstructed face.

'Why do you not answer the first time I call?' she frowned.

'This box is heavy, you know.'

'What's in it?' he asked, keeping a safe distance in case her antique condition was contagious.

'Souvenirs,' she cackled, passing over something wrapped in tissue paper. 'I bring from my room to show you.'

'This is a souvenir?' he said disbelievingly, discarding the paper wrapping distractedly. 'Looks like ten-thousand-year-old biltong,' he muttered, turning it over in his open palm, regarding a blackened shrunken object, sheathed at one end in silver, the polished metal hallmarked with miniature symbols that he read to be an eye in a triangle, above what looked like an ink jar and below that a feather, which he suspected symbolised a writing quill.

'You are not far off,' she rasped, looming like the cracked shade of an antique standard lamp, standing looking over his shoulder, 'But not so old.'

'It looks … mummified,' he frowned in reaction to a word he had come to dislike for some obscure reason that eluded him. 'Shit, I know what this is,' he said, revolted,

'Ancient Egyptian, yes?' He scowled, holding it away.

'No, I mean for you to keep.'

238

'You mean it's a present?' he said, aghast, looking up, seeing her craggy face as a pockmarked cliff, undermined by time and tide.

'What a clever boy,' she said, clapping girlishly, disturbing the configurations of veins on the fly-blown parchment of the back of her gross hands.

'A fucking penis!'

'A *sacred* penis,' she insisted, every wrinkle of her collapsed face registering indignation and hurt. 'You should not be so disrespectful, that belonged to the founding father.'

'The founding father?' Double frowned. 'Of what? I need to know.'

'The Americas, of course, you silly boy.'

'Oh, come on!' he laughed.

'Be very careful,' she growled, 'That is a most powerful penis.'

'So who exactly was this founding father of the ... ah ... Americas?'

'A pharaoh of the Inkethaton dynasty. He founded a second empire in the lands of the west and retired there. Here, to this town, only then it was a temple. This is true, so don't shake your head. The father of history wrote this.'

'Herodotus?' Double snorted. 'I don't think so. And anyway, even if he did write that, Herodotus is also known as the father of lies.'

'I do not believe you!'

'Now *you* don't believe me!' Double laughed.

'OK, supposing I were to accept all that, what I still don't understand is why you would want to give me this,' he brandished the relic before the three ringed circlets of her hollowed eyes, 'I mean, why, for god's sake?'

'Because of your injury you are telling me of when your wife she ...'

'Enough of that,' Double shouted. 'I'm trying to forget my past.'

'But it will help. I promise.'

'Well, even if I did need help, what am I supposed to do with it?'

'As you like. Chew it, keep it in your pocket. Whatever way you use it,' she shrugged, threatening the structural integrity of her shoulders, 'A pharaoh's penis has restorative powers.'

'So why haven't you used it?'

'Because I wasn't born with one, silly boy.' Dismissed but not downhearted, Double decided against returning to his room, and instead, chose the path to redemption. The only place he knew, a hole-in- the-wall establishment just across the street. But first he had to return something to its former owner.

'Where do you want me to put it?' Double said rhetorically, only half-jokingly holding up the shrivelled relic, addressing his reflection in the dull shine of the breastplate of the retired old soldier, suited in conquistador armour, marking time, standing guard behind the lobby door.

'You need it more than me.'

'What?' Double gaped, glancing to either side, checking no one else was there.

'I said, you need it more than me.'

'This is the mummy speaking?'

'Yes, my son,' the mummy rattled. Despite his pharaonic status, his voice tinny and not at all impressive, Double considered, listening with an ear pressed to a dusty breastplate.

'You're not my father, by any chance?'

'No, my son,' the mummy replied with a dry chuckle. 'Though he is my son too.'

'Blood son?' Double interjected, keen to get this right.

'There is no measure other than ink.'

'I don't understand.'

'I was the scribe who wrote, I am pharaoh that I am. And lo, so it was.' Was that a sigh Double heard? 'Things were easier then.'

'And I am your son?'

'The last.'

'The last?'

'The end of the Inkethaton line.'

'So,' Double paused, 'If I'm the last, then you must be ...?'

'The first, my boy. The very first.'

'First and last? Then we're like book ends.'

'More than book ends, son. Mucho mas.'

Double was back in his usual corner of the *cantina*, sticking to his resolution of staying off the *mescal*, when Joe ambled over.

'Please,' Double said, gesturing to the chair opposite. 'Still no news of Jaime?'

'My friend, no news is good news where he is concerned,' Joe said, stooping to add two more beer bottles to Double's growing collection on the table.

'Really?' Double said, screwing off a bottle top and refilling his glass. He had been trying to decide whether it was half empty or half full. 'You are not worried?'

'No more than usual,' Joe said, sitting down. He nodded towards the hotel across the street. 'Everything OK with Helga?' he added, lowering his voice.

'Yes. No,' Double grimaced. 'You know, one minute, nice,' he shrugged, 'The next, ice.'

'Be careful, my friend, that *bruja*, she *es* full of surprises.'

'What should I watch out for?'

'Bait!' Joe smiled grimly. 'With hunters *es* always the way.' He glanced around the bar, 'The trap can be anything ...' He frowned. 'I know Helga and her stories, some I expect I even invent myself.'

'How so?'

'Once I call her my friend. That *es* before she takes over the hotel. Always she *es* asking questions about treasure.' Joe sighed. 'So many theories.'

'Like what, for instance?'

'Crazy *bruja*,' Joe looked up at the nicotine-stained plaster of the cracked ceiling, 'She *es* convinced civilisation *es* brought to Mexico by the Egyptians when *es* the other way round.'

'That's *macho* Mexican bullshit, Joe.'

'No *toro* involved, my friend,' Joe smiled mysteriously. 'Something the archaeologists can never take into account, the time distortions of Eden.'

'Eden?' Double balked at the second mention of the word that day.

'Yes, *es* how America *es* before the Spanish,' Joe grinned. 'The garden where once grow the golden tomatoes of the sun.'

'Tomatoes?' Double chuckled. 'Don't you mean apples?'

'The tomato it comes from Mexico, and originally *es* golden, like the sun.'

'So they were described as apples, I can see that, but a garden? Come on, Joe.'

'*Es* an old legend my friend. Paradise before the serpent.'

'Yes, America was Arcadia and very likely it was visited by ancient Greeks, and possibly other voyagers before them, hence the old story of the garden of the golden apples, I see that fits now, but time distortions?' Double frowned. 'How does that work?'

'Time flies when you are having fun, huh?'

'Always the way.'

'That *es* how it *es* in Eden,' Joe shrugged. 'A month there, a year any place else.'

'Uh, yea, right!' Double snorted.

'*Es* verdad!

'You are asking me to believe that Mexican pyramids are older than the pyramids of Egypt?'

'*Si*,' Joe nodded slowly. 'Mucho.'

'And Mexicans taught the Egyptians how to build them?'

'Those red-skins of the east have my esteemed ancestors, the master *borracho* builders, to thank for that,' Joe said with pride.

'What *borracho* builders?'

'*Es* a name we have for the pyramid builders,' Joe grinned. 'This tribe has a special liking for *mescal*, just the same as you.'

'And what about Moses, was he Mexican too?'

'By descent, yes.'

'And the pharaohs?'

'They are all Mexicanos up to the time of the Ptolemys, when the line is broken and the ancient secrets lost.'

'As I remember,' Double said, picking his words carefully, 'The Ptolemlys invented map making as we know it.'

'*Si professor*,' Joe nodded, with a hint of a smile.

'During that dynasty they were trying to recover the lost secrets from the Inkethatons, a dynasty very much into maps a long time before them, the most important of which *es* the location of the garden. Using a copy of one of these Inkethaton maps, Columbus sails to America, only in his map, the garden *es* called Atlantis.'

'My god.' Double slapped his head. 'Now I've heard it all,' he groaned.

'No, you have not.' Joe leaned closer. 'There is something more I must tell you.'

Menes, that was the pharaoh's name. The shrivelled daddy-mummy Helga had purchased from the Black Friars, recently reunited with his head, yet bereft of his penis, suited in conquistador armour back in the hotel, the source of all Double's sorrows apparently. Not his father exactly, save in a vague biblical sense, but his primogenitor nevertheless – multiply generations to the power of seven and you'll have the appropriate measure. Pull the other one, Joe, Double thought, wondering if the lost legacy from his father included his forefather's estate of the Americas. And, while you're at it, pour me another one, but this time make it a *mescal*, and have one on me too.

Siesta time, when even doppelganger dogs lie doggo, farting in stiff shadows. For once it was hot, no Englishmen about, nor Egyptians, or even pilgrims; only Double. One deranged survivor from a wreck of a life, staggering deserted streets, lost in a mangy dream.

This was himself, right? The one cardinal fact Double needed reminding of – shameless waster, for all that he was descended from a line of pharaohs and had a claim on the Americas, yea right, drunk in the afternoon, dragging his load past the soap-sud domed cathedral, bubble-brass doors barred against the sun and God and Jesus, cursed Shem-what's-its? This town in a state of perpetual denial, not even knowing its name. Like himself, Double reflected, taking a goat trail through scabby fields, gone hazy with heat, before reaching a high bluff commanding the desert plains thousands and thousands of feet below.

The world that existed elsewhere a riptide racing to the high heavens, the far mountains a bow aiming a quiver of arrows at the sky, so intensely blue his eyes hurt. Tears streaming as he stood bitten back by the savage *sierra* light, resisting what came next, delaying that moment, stretching it to infinity. Watching it winding a Möbius strip around the world, until, like a bat out of the blue, it hit him, shzam-bam, back of his head; that, if his existence as a thinking entity was measured by how he was always acted upon and rarely acted, he hardly measured up at all.

But like a glass that was half ... no, he corrected himself ... part empty, he was also part full. That elusive missing thought, notable by its absence, was therefore, in that sense, verifiable. Perhaps going towards explaining the gut feeling he had had ever since breakfast that morning, of being white bread with all the goodness taken out. The meat missing from his sandwich, the huff gone out his puff, the lead lost to his pencil when he was suckered into a game of blind man's bluff and misdirected by his reflection, nagual, essence, double's double, whatever it was, into swapping sides of a mirror simultaneously with a blinding flash – light from within and without, he realised, also experienced by his departing nagual – leaving him trapped here in Tláltipec, with all these dead ringers for characters he had known on the other side, inhabiting what he now thought of as the real world, instead of what it was, just another shadow play of old Lord Mictlántecuhtli in the Town With No Name, as he had come to call this place of ghosts, which he supposed he was numbered amongst. Scary thought, he was a spook like the rest, hanging on in Tláltipec.

The one exception being Joe, who, despite his evident and surprising lack of concern regarding Jaime, still seemed as substantial here as he was on the other side. However, even of Joe Double could not be sure, taking into account all the wormholes riddling the gorgonzola cheese of his memory. Starting with the mystery of what happened in the interregnum between escaping the fighting in Happy Valley and waking that morning back in his old room. His old room on the other side of a mirror, he reminded himself sternly, sure of nothing in Tláltipec any longer, and even whether he would find the hotel the same upon his return to face Helga; the harsh music of a counterpoint relationship in which he was not exactly sure who was haunting who.

4. DOG COLLAR

That had to be a different hotel, Double told himself, staring up at an unfamiliar pink stucco frontage below a watchtower that hadn't been there before. Unless, of course, this was the same hotel pictured in the old sepia photograph hanging in a reception room, taken during the Cristeros insurgency of the 1930s. A trying time in the town, according to Helga, because it was then briefly occupied by the Cristeros themselves, who used the building as their HQ.

Yes, and there they were below, gathered around the open door, alive as anyone could be considering this was Tláltipec – the upper level of Mictlán, for the uninitiated – Cristeros choristers dressed for a sack-race, manic brothers and sisters ash crosses, smudged on the raised foreheads of otherwise shining faces, bandoleras and rifles slung at cross purposes over shoulders, holding hands for holy joy, pogoing for Jesus, guns and revolution before barred Spanish windows under a flapping canvas banner proclaiming 'Vivo Cristo Rey' in big red letters, bleeding on the wind.

'What the ...?' Words wrung out, Double getting neglected thinking processes into gear, gawping as a broad-shouldered, imposing figure opposite – up to now with his back turned, conducting the heaven-facing choir, pocketing his baton in his Norfolk jacket and, turning, starting across the street towards Double, his jaw jutting under a thick head of tousled black hair, which brought to mind a typhoon on the loose.

'Who the ...? Double gasped.

'Who?' Reverend Who repeated, his flaring black eyebrows head-buttingly close, seizing Double's hand in a vice grip. 'Names are not as important as what is in here,' he roared, knuckling Double's chest, his iron fist beating time to every word.

'Yea, right!' Doubled sniffed, reacting to a guff of carbolic from the reverend's tweed jacket and matching britches. 'And they are?' he demanded, retreating a half-step, retrieving bruised fingers, nodding towards the choristers singing, '*Ay carramba, avé maria*, hark hark the *angelitos*,' or something like that. Straining to hear themselves over the snap and crack of canvas as, above, the banner stretched and slapped in the strengthening wind.

'*Los Cristeros*! Fighting for the soul of Mexico!'

Reverend Who replied, closing the gap. 'You should join us, my brother. Become a foot soldier in the army of the lord!'

'Sounds challenging,' Double said, smiling down the gnashing assault of decayed teeth and smoky black eyes, set in sooty sockets. 'Is there a war on?'

'Is there a war?' Reverend Who recycled. 'My God, do you not hear of the atheist hegemony? The communist plotters of Chapultepec?' he raved, peering psychotropically, his thick eye lashes, sluice gates on roiling tar pits, barred on a black tide.

'What the hell d'you think you're staring at?' Double snapped, taking another half-step back, wondering whether in his present white-bread, incorporeal, nagual-less state, he had anything left to protect.

'The mark of the beast, my brother. It is not yet upon you, but beware!' Reverend Who lofted a lightning-rod finger at the thunder clouds, stacking lead platters eight miles high over the gaunt buildings lining the narrow street. 'Lest it smite you unawares!'

'What beast might that be?' Double demanded, his back hard against cold stone.

'And it is written!' Again the Reverent lofted a finger, fairly sparking with messianic energy. '"Let him that hath understanding count the number of the beast! For it is the number of a man."'

'Yea, yea,' Double yawned deliberately, 'I know, *sex* and *sex* and *sex*. I've heard it all before, my man.' He thumbed towards the cathedral. 'I'm sure you have a lot in common with the Shemite Black Friars.'

'Shemites? Black Friars?' Reverend Who blinked.

'I think not, those apostates are ... the ... corpse-eating communists of the antichrist!' he choked, bunching five in Double's face. 'We come to smite them!'

'Good man,' Double grinned, immensely cheered for reasons that eluded him. 'Perhaps I'll join you later, who knows?' he said, sidling away along the wall. 'But now, if you'll excuse me, Reverend Who.' He gave a mock bow. 'I have things to do.'

Helga? Double wondered, doubting the evidence of his eyes, suspiciously regarding a reception room, which, in his absence, had been converted to a hospital ward. The nurse was certainly broad enough, but humped like a bison? And dressed like that? The dowager of spades then, all black taffeta and bustle, except for thin wisps of silver hair straying her calico bonnet and the white lace of her collar. Bent over the only patient in a delirium of agony, stretched out in the only occupied bed, in a far corner of the long room, where the upper walls and ceiling were striped black and tan by the swollen setting sun staring in through slatted shutters, reminding Double of the eye of a big cat, poised to pounce.

Helga the tigress? Or Grandma? he pondered. A far deadlier predator, if his father's one pronouncement on the subject was anything to go by. How had the old misogynist phrased it? Yes, the 'mother of harlots and abominations', somehow returned from the dead, posed as he always pictured her, furnishing his infant imagination with her scary stories at bedtime. When she said he had been greedy, about children buried alive in gingerbread mines. When she said he had been irreverent, about holy martyrs, boiled alive, burnt at the stake, eaten by lions, disembowelled, whatever. When she said he had been bad, about monstrous birds, usually the big black billed skuas that came swooping in the night and carried bad boys away, pinioned in their claws, to feed hungry chicks waiting in eyries high in witchy peaks above the clouds. Then, on rare days, when she said he'd been good, about treasure – all sorts: kings' ransoms, pirate hoards, Spanish bullion, sultans' gems, elfish silver, dwarfish gold, guarded by dragons, hidden deep within the mantled earth.

'There, there, that's better, isn't it?' she soothed in a crab-apple tone. Who else but Grandma, all bristles and barnacles, a face like the wreck of the Erebus, just as he remembered her through clearing mists of memory, bird billed and disdainful as ever, gimlet eyes fixed on his as, hesitantly, he approached her.

'Ah, there you are, señor,' she said appraisingly, looking him up and down as he came closer. 'Out walking again? Really,' she clucked, 'When a man in your condition should be resting.'

'And what condition is that?'

'Amnesia! You even forget your own name,' she sneered, ponderously turning her great bulk away as a piteous groan from the bed below drew her attention.

'Save me, sister,' the patient choked. 'They ... are coming!'

'And who the hell are they?' Double demanded angrily, wishing he had never gotten involved, looking down, wanting to look anywhere but the patient's horribly swollen face and one remaining eye, next to a bloody socket that looked as though it had been pecked out.

'He means the Black Friars,' she said, nodding towards the hulk of the cathedral, imminent and transcendent through slatted shutters. 'The foolish boy thinks to run away from his duties at the cathedral.'

'What's his name ... sister?' Double said, almost calling her 'Grandma' in his confusion.

'What's in a name?' she said. 'When we are all sinners in the eyes of the Lord.' Pausing, she licked wrinkled lips with a purple tongue speckled orange and brown at the tip. 'Perhaps if you would be so good as to keep the poor boy company while I attend to my other duties,' she added, with surprising agility spinning on a heel, rustling her bustle, walking off without another word.

'"Poor boy", did she say?' Double chuckled to himself, thinking the patient looked like more like a suffering Jesus on Nembutal, blood welling scratches on his forehead as if a crown of thorns had just been snatched from it, imploring him with black circlets, like coffee stains in a saucer ringing his one remaining eye, and the pain – the sweet, delirious pain – transmitted by tremulous fingers laid across the palm of Double's hand.

'What is that you say?' the patient rasped.

'So sorry,' Double said, his cheeks reddening with shame, realising he had been taking vicarious pleasure in the patient's pain. 'I was just mumbling to myself, honestly, that's all. Please don't worry, the nurse will be back soon.'

'The nurse! She is with them,' the patient croaked, flailing arms and rocking in the bed in a desperate bid to raise his wasted body. 'What, you mean the Cristeros?'

'Not them,' the patient mouthed, choking on phlegm and vomit. 'Though they are just as bad. I mean the apostates at the cathedral who deny the resurrection. To them, I am already dead,' he gasped, collapsing back on the bed. 'Is better you fuck me now. My superiors often use me that way. At least I will pleasure you with my dying breath, my brother.'

'You are perfectly safe with me,' Double said, wondering how to reassure him. 'I will protect you, I swear. No one will lay a hand on you.'

My brother,' the patient said, suddenly calm, settling back onto sweat soaked pillows. 'Mark my words,' he raised a finger, 'before the dawn, when the crow caws thrice, you will betray me.'

'That's just the way it seems at the moment, my friend,' Double insisted, thinking this was a case of too much Bible study and not enough buggery. 'You must rest now.'

'No ... no...' the patient protested, struggling to sit up again. 'I have to tell you before they come ...'

Hell all the way back, and again, with suitable black magic rituals thrown in for good measure. In a nutshell, that was his story. How could Double believe him? It was simply too incredible that God-fearing Christians, apostates or otherwise could do what the Black Friars had. Trying him in a hastily convened ecclesiastical court. Draining his blood, sharing it in a ceremony that was a perversion of Holy Communion, leaving his insensible body staked out for the evil birds of the mountains. That detail, with its gruesome overtones of ritual sacrifice, Double found particularly horrifying, reminding him as it did of Grandma's warning of the awful fate waiting bad boys in the night. But he was regressing, this wasn't the nursery of his childhood, purple banded with her favourite bedtime stories. Once more the swollen sun was slipping past slatted shutters, but another place, another time. Not Double's story, but his friend's, the patient who had miraculously broken his bonds after night descended in the form of a pair of enveloping black wings and had his eye pecked out, then been chased by a monstrous bird, possessed of outsized claws - which presumably accounted for the razor-like slashes about his shoulders - and driven over a precipice into a ravine, where he was found by the town's goat herder.

And that dread secret, kept so long? Behind the Black Friars existed another order, a Masonic 'conclave', its purported purpose to protect Catholicism from corrupt elements within the church itself, as well as from the seductions of heathen religions, but perversely borrowing from both.

Thus do the gods reward puny mortals, Double reflected, his head reeling with the patient's ravings about obscure medieval orders on two continents, the Teutonic Templars, a secret society of shit-eaters. At the time of the supposed Conquest, the society had for seventy years a toehold in the Americas. Its mission in the town, under the direct protection of the Aztec Eagle Knights, a cannibalistic martial cult, numbering among its initiates, a journeyman Teutonic Templar and Livonian knight. None other than the Hapsburg King of Spain, Carlos' protégé, Hernando Cortez, arch-kabbalist and co-conspirator, Wodenite and follower of Tezcatipoca, Lord of the Twenty Days, Shining Mirror of the Sun, still secretly worshipped in the mountains by the Black Friars.

Double would have learned more about this centuries-old corruption within the body of the church, had not Sister - Grandma - Helga, whoever she was, bustled in and shooed him out in a high-handed manner. His new-found friend's one eye followed Double accusingly as he slunk out the door, feeling he was betraying his trust somehow. But he was too weak to resist, or perhaps she was just too strong? Telling himself she couldn't remain at the bedside all night, Double resolved to return as soon as she left. But he failed to take into account her loud and wearisome prayers, addressed to the 'Lord of lords, in the highest of high' in shrill contralto hectometres that resonated the long corridors to his room, where he lay resting with one eye on the door, waiting for her to leave.

Cantina Joe, his face in a dream, looking in a door. No, not a dream. This was real, alright. Joe's real face then, looking in a real door. No, he thought, remembering he had gone through this before, not a door, a mirror that was a door! Come off it, Double groaned, reaching to the other side of the bed and pulling the other straw pillow over his head, just leave me alone and let me dream.

If only he could have admitted, at least to himself, he was just confused and needing help, lying there dozing, exhausted by all the goings-on.

'Wake up! Or you miss the moment, my friend!' No time to consider what moment, or even which continuum. Joe, huge above, his boozy hooter hanging massive as a warty trunk. OK, so that was an exaggeration, but such was his mammoth effect. Behind him, spied as if through the wrong end of a telescope, bullfighting memorabilia on a far *cantina* wall, as Joe slowly faded from view and Double finally prised open gummy eyelids. A dream, right. Yes, but in this town, Tláltipec was still the ongoing reality. Feeling chicken – and anything but brave – Double stumbled along the darkened corridor to the candlelit room, where Grandma de Farge was again on her knees, knitting wordy spells that, in his half-sleeping state, he perceived as ectoplasm entrapment crocheting a bed, and a substitute great-grandson who, as he was reminded by a line of song repeating his head, should have been him.

'I'm taking over,' Double announced with a determination contrary to the way he felt. 'You can go now, sister,' he said into her ear, kneeling down beside her. 'I'll take the next watch.'

No reply, unless he counted the low-brow Neanderthal frown he got in return. Perhaps she was weary and only just hanging on? No, not his great-grandma of the hump back, massive as a bison. How old? Around since that first cannibal feast. Cain her first son, and Able ... well, unable actually ... A strange conversation between the synapses of his brain while she recited prayers with an angry snarl.

'Great lord of days! We beseech thou, look down from thy smoking mirror amid thy astral armies of the stars. Yea, in thy infinite guiding wisdom, hear our humble prayer and accept the offering we bring, this poor repentant sinner, so weary of life, seeking succour and the shelter of thy encompassing wings ...'

'Sister!' Double interjected, sensing a rampant poltergeist of madness loose about the house, as the old sepia tinted picture of the hotel on the wall behind him crashed to the floor. 'You have to rest! Please allow me ...'

'And ... and ...' she gagged, dropping a stitch in time.

'Great spirit,' Double began mockingly, mimicking her pious tone, 'In your infinite mercy, look down on thy humble servant, so wracked and afflicted, a sinner, yes, but cheerful in the face of adversity, forthright in the defence of truth ...'

Now they were both going at it, her's the steel tongs and his the velvet hammer, their prayer marathon only just begun. No sense, apparently, making all the sense in the world to their patient, stirring into wraithlike life.

'My brother,' he managed, 'For fok's sake, shut the foking witch up!'

'I'm trying,' Double muttered, wondering what it was about the way the patient said 'foking' that chimed in his head.

But then the sister distracted him by redoubling her efforts, prayers flowing so fast the words blurred into one long gabble:

'And-consolation-in-your-bosom-in-accordance-   w
it h-t hy-inef feable-w ill-his -hear t- and-his -gonads -re
-deemed-in-your-   beninficense-salvation-his-sincere-desire-
that-he-may-be-united-   in-your-house-for-always-so-that-   the-
times-are-fulfilled-in-accordance-   with-the-prophesies-   of-
your-servants-who-have-gone-before-glory-   glory-faith-   hope-
and-glory-in-your-divine-malice-that-no-good-can-   out
wit-eternal-without-limit-sex-and-maximum-always-   this-our-
offering-o-great-one-   humbly-we-pray-that-in-the-   fullness-of-time-
you-reach-down-and-pluck-the-unleav- ened-bread-of-our-offering...'

'Stop this unholy cant, sister!' Double shouted, jumping to his feet. 'You must leave, or ...'

'Or what, impotent pedant?' she raged, pushing her vastly greater bulk into his.

That was a mistake, physical intimidation invariably easier to handle than overweening sanctity, whatever the provenance. Invariably, all that is required is a modicum of resolution and a preparedness to strike first. As demonstrated by a lightning countermove – Double surprising even himself as conditioned reflexes born of Master Wu's martial arts weekend course at the local community centre near where he then lived came into play. Hitting her, just once, low in the pelvic regions, his rigid fingers sinking deep into Bible-black taffeta, shining the same blue sheen as Grandma's bilious bustle, his last sight every night in the nursery, as she leaned over to turn off the bedside light. Engulfing him in busty black folds, buttoned with bone cameos carved by Sami reindeer herders -miniature portraiture a local industry in Lapland apparently – into likenesses of his female forbears on the matrilineal side. Eidetically imprinting his retinas, as the electric element in the fly-speckled bulb hanging from the ceiling slowly faded and night invaded the nursery, with a ma, pa and grandma portrait parade, the three banes of his young life, alternating ad infinitum down the generations, pouring like an avalanche of pyroclasmic lava, replete with sounds and selective matrilineal and patrilineal memories, death and victory revisited, mud huts and granite piles, burying him until the first light of morning, and the first bird, tapping the nursery window.

All the above passed through his mind, as he stood, knees knocking with ebbing adrenaline and delayed action fear, reminded of a hooded crow, watching her hobbling away, cawing with thwarted rage and pain. Not the end of it, Double realised, knowing she'd be back, and with reinforcements. But at least he'd bought a little time to prepare a refuge for his new friend. The only place he could think of ...

Double was just wheeling the hospital bed into his old room, when the wardrobe door burst open and out swept three Black Friars. With their charcoal-smudged faces and hooded cassocks bringing to mind a hooded IRA death squad, their knotted hands swooped in a parody of the skuas of Double's childish nightmares.

Only then did the patient cry out, 'Do not forsake me again, my brother!' But, taken from behind, Double was unable to intervene, as, from the street outside, came a raucous cawing, just he was stuck a massive blow on the back of the head. A familiar portrait parade overwhelmed him as he fell..

5. WALK ON GILDED SPLINTERS

To some universes there are no open doors, the only way in by vaulting the journeyman's stile of the Tectonic third degree. In other words, over high enclosing walls - and those walls were higher than high - that blow to Double's head had sprung him back-flipping over the ramparts and into a garden, where nature was the gardener and the flower beds were unsullied by the hand of man. There, the dullest weed exceeded the rambling rose when it came to estimation of beauty or the efflorescence of their perfumes, and gorgeous plumed *quetzalcoatls* sang sweeter than any lyrebird, from tree canopies shading sun-dappled meadows watered by tinkling cascades, issuing crystal springs in three snow-capped mountains sloping down to a wide river flowing out to a cerulean sea and worlds beyond.

Too good to be true, Double's first thought, looking out from the grassy knoll where he had landed, reasoning there had to be a darker side to his surroundings, since, in the essence of all things, always lurks the opposite.

But at least he was *home*. Recognition slowly dawning as he followed a winding path through hummocky meadows, every footfall raising butterflies iridescent with every hue and colour, leading him in an enchanted cavalcade towards a high privet hedge, harbouring the mystery of concealing what lay beyond.

A palace, perchance? Crystal-paned windows overlooking a zoological garden where all the exotic species of this world were gathered? Perhaps a dusky sultan arrayed in silken robes encrusted with jewels, waiting in welcome by the gate? Yes, the idle fancies of a dreamer, carefree as a lark in summer.

No gate, just a leafy arch, an orchard beyond, trees heavy with golden fruit gleaming in the sun. This, he guessed, the fabled garden, rumours of which, like tap roots, had reached down the ages, feeding the imaginations of *sappatistas* and questers alike. Was it a dream? Yes, such a dream that only myths are made of – in eidetic vividness, surpassing the highest moments of Double's myth-spent youth, making everything else seem dull by comparison.

Those golden apples, more than mere spheres, no less than solar orbs, radiant amid upper branches. Even to take bite would be sacrilege, Double thought, lost in wonderment, wandering leafy arbours, 'till at last he was called by a voice he remembered from before.

Recognising the cross-legged figure seated under a nearby tree, Double was overjoyed to see his one-eyed friend, cheeks round and rosy as pippins, glowing with inner light. Waving him over with an enthusiasm that seemed misplaced, considering the little assistance he had been when needed most.

'What is this place?' Double said, sitting down on the soft green sward of maidenhair grass beside him.

'It is the Eden under every sod. The sweetness at the heart of everything. It is everywhere, and at the same time nowhere, such is the parlous state of affairs between the foking worlds.'

'But what are you doing here?'

'I am the gardener.'

'Not the one-eyed king in the land of blind dreamers?'

'Just the gardener.'

'So this isn't just a dream?'

'My brother, why ask when you already know the answer?' The gardener shook his head reprovingly. 'What little time we have is too precious to waste on idle questions. Even paradise has its snares,' he warned.

'Don't you mean snakes?'

'No, that would be to add to a Biblical misunderstanding begun in the Pentateuch by Shem and the patriarchs. The snake represents the royal road to wisdom. It is the energy that some call the kundalini, which in you lies sleeping, coiled at the base of the spine.'

'And the worm?' Double said, distracted by a leafy rustling above.

'Yes,' the gardener paused, looking up at a heavy black cloud sweeping in from the west, 'There is corruption even here. Not where you think.' Lowering his eyes, again he scrutinised Double's face. 'It comes with every new arrival.'

'You mean me, don't you?' Double protested, hot with shame, his heart jumping a beat. He could have hated his friend then.

'Of course,' the gardener sighed. 'But yours is a particularly bad case, el gusano de diablo. Don't you remember you swallow one whole?'

'In that *mescal*, Helga, or was it Grandma, gave me?'

The gardener nodded. 'Those entities are the double and the nagual of the being behind you,' he said, staring fixedly over Double's shoulder, his sunny face suddenly eclipsed.

No cloud that, Double realised, turning around, but the scything wings of an enormous black crow, swooping out of a perfect blue sky, spreading scimitar talons like some grotesque creature sprung from the Thousand and One Nights.

'No!' Double gasped, rooted to the spot by panic. In that terrible first moment, his friend crying out, 'Help me, my brother, do not forsake me again.' His piteous plea, muffled as enormous black wings folded over.

What else could Double do, but turn and run – rent naked by abysmal fear, pursued by awful triumphalist cawing – into another dream?

No dream this, Double thought – would that it were – that old *bruja* spreading leviathan thighs, taking her time, and pleasure, lasciviously easing herself up and down, sucking his life force, her labia rough as sandpaper and dry as waterhole in a desert. A sudden flash of lightning outside, illuminating her face, leering ogerishly down over rustling black vestments, as the gasoline heat of her grindstone crotch transmitted a fever to his head.

'Get the fuck off and die!' Double spat, watching spittle splatter her nagual face, but there was no resisting the intense sensation washing over in waves, as, troll hands pressing on his, she held him down, pain and ecstasy like he'd never known, bursting an embolism in his brain.

But then, as her cardiovascular carpetbagger cunt contracted, he came and, simultaneously, an enormous detonation of thunder shattered roof tiles high above, a reflex action born of Master Wu's 'metal jacket' martial training came to his rescue, as he voided semen into his bladder, resultant kundalini energy surging to his aid, all the way from the chakra at the base of his spine to the crown of his head in that desperate moment as he made a desperate final bid to throw her off.

At last he was free, and Grandma Nagual was ... down, but not out, raising on hands and knees by the bed, and then she was up and running out the door, dragging her bustle, leaving a noxious odour as pervasive as rotten herring – a stain he knew would linger as long as the memory remained. Which, given his current condition, wasn't saying much, Double considered gloomily, staggering about, naked and disorientated by the stroboscopic flashes of lightning outside, fitfully illuminating the room as the storm passed over. He gathered up his clothes scattered about the floor, where his grandma had tossed them when he was out cold.

At last safe again in his room, Double was reaching out for a clear plastic envelope on the bedside table when, noticing movement at the corner of his eye, he looked round. Dead, I'm dead, he thought, on his first sight of the corpulent baron, obscenely dressed in body-hugging black battle fatigues. Standing where his reflection should have been, framed in the mirrored wardrobe door, stepping through, as Double stared, transfixed by shock, followed by three muscular monks in camouflage cassocks. The leading two, pointing semi-automatics at his chest, while the third, darting around, grabbed him by the arms and, cuffing his hands from behind, kneed him the small of his back, sending him stumbling into the open arms of the baron, greeting him like an old friend, planting slobbery kisses on his cheeks.

They were preparing to frog-march Double away when the baron, as if in afterthought, turned and booted the mirror through which they had just passed, smashing the glass into smithereens. Just one shard large enough remained for Double to make out a mirror version of the room with his insensible twin ... essence... nagual ... whatever, stretched out sleeping on the bed, before he was finally knocked out cold by a heavy blow to the back of his head.

6. THE NAGUAL

Remembering nothing of a dream he had been sharing with his now insensible Double, a nagual awoke in the energy body they cohabited, like a couple of tourists caught in a mix-up over a time-share apartment built for one, only vacating it entirely for the other when lost in dreamless sleep. He opened his eyes, noticed a clear plastic envelope on the bedside table. Curious, he saw it contained a certificate granting him access to all areas of Mictlán. Assuming it was a practical joke in poor taste and not wishing to read more, he placed it back on the small table. Only then did he become aware of the wind rattling the shutters by the bed, and a discordant choir wailing in the distance beyond. He could even make out some of the dirge they were so furiously singing: 'Ay carramba! Atender! Atender! Los heraldo angelitós cantar, Bless-ed be redeeming blood! Gory. (?) gory hal-le-lu-ja! Jésus es arrivé en Jerus-a-lem!'

This, a nagual had to see. Precariously balanced on a wobbly old chair, standing on tiptoes, he forced open the shutters, almost falling out onto the street as he let in the gale. Hanging out, holding on with one hand, peering into the middle distance, he was just able to discern his friend Jaime, last seen in the cantina, starring in the cameo role of Jesus in the passion play. Missing an eye, it looked like, but of course that was his penchant for stage paint and over-dramatisation, his 'broken' body born up on a big wooden cross at the head of the procession, passing through the Plaza de la Revolución about a quarter of a mile away. The wind bearing the stench of naphtha from a thousand flaring torches lighting the stone sides of the tumbledown medieval buildings lining the long street, dragging comet trails, lighting red the underbellies of monstrous clouds, scudding the sky above, reflecting on a many-headed beast below. The ecstatic faces of the crowd reminded him of gleaming scales on a side-winding snake, rippling with cohorts of red-crested helmets – Roman centurions 291 lofting spears to the rhythms of thunderous drumming, shouting 'Hail!' and 'Hosanna!' and 'Smite the Egyptian hierophants!'

– ascending the three hundred and sixty-five steps towards the cathedral and the Shemite soldiers of the antichrist preparing for Armageddon behind barred brass doors. Everyone playing the parts assigned them, in this que-*loco* version of the passion. Over the top as was usual for *fiestas* in Mexico, confirming what the nagual had read about such occasions; the whole local community involved and playing it for real, in a drama where mayhem was guaranteed and absolutely anything could happen.

Suddenly, out of nowhere, or so it seemed, an enormous ungainly bird, black against flaring lights, slowly flapped across his vision, almost close enough to touch, cawing raucously. A bad sign, whatever it was, the nagual thought, dejectedly turning away and only then noticing the wardrobe mirror, now smashed in pieces on the stone floor. Seven years bad luck, he thought, but for who exactly? He hunkered down, picking up a piece, seeing his face and and, over his shoulder, a figure standing close behind.

'Shit!' he exclaimed, twisting round. There was no one, however, just his paranoid sense something heavy was about to happen. He had to get the hell out. But how and where, he wondered, with the town taken over by religious zealots, and harpy Helga and the evil Malinchés prowling the corridors beyond, preparing to ambush him before he made it to the front door?

Then he noticed, at the back of the open wardrobe, a low gap in the wall. Just like in Grandma's stories of castles and dungeons, a secret passage, leading who knew where? Perhaps this was what was meant by the 'privileged access to all areas' written on the certificate? Was Lord Mictlántecuhtli was clearing a way? he thought, threading the eye of the needle and squeezing through.

There *was* a pitched battle going on up there, he realised, the cavities of this subterranean world resonating with the distant din of fighting, and he wasn't playing his part. Lost without a candle in a labyrinth of narrowing tunnels, belly down, wriggling like the worm he was, when the earth beneath his hands heaved and the tunnel ahead caved in.

The nagual's first thought was of *sappatistas* at work at deeper levels, undermining the dimensions. His second, he was entombed, just as the certificate back in his room implied, trapped for all eternity in Mictlán, realm of the dead. But no, he realised, becoming aware of a glimmer of light from above as the dust began to settle. He was reminded that hope springs eternal. Hoping hope for an end to all this questing. He only ever wanted a better life, but something always took over, forcing him on. When, finally, he reached his goal, he felt small satisfaction at a road run, a puzzle solved, an answer found. The relief only temporary before, like a rat in a laboratory experiment, he would be given another electric jolt and forced into an untrammelled section of the maze.

There must be a genus of god-scientists, he reflected, devoted to the study of dyslexic life forms. Left or right? What's the difference when you have no choice but to go on and explore every rattrap hole presented. All down to the mutant questing gene, without which we would never have ventured far beyond the *kraal*, he guessed.

At least he could breathe easier here, no more belly wriggling in these chiselled colonnades; commodious corridors reverberating with sounds shafting ventilation pipes in the ceilings, spaced at regular intervals. And always it seemed aimed at the same luminary, the north star, he guessed, judging by the trajectory, the faint starlight – clearly visible once his eyes had adjusted – falling in ethereal blue pools on polished black onyx, reflecting haphazardly on silver veining, suggesting fire creatures climbing the walls. Quetzalcoatls or salamanders? Quetzalcoatls, he guessed. The fabled birds of paradise, dragging comet tails. Firebirds for the journey, marking his path with their finery. Secret signs or just natural formations in the rock? Hard to draw conclusions in that minimal light transmitted from the other side of the universe – the shafts acting like telescopes, separating and magnifying that one star from countless billions in the galaxy. A strange feeling, walking in the light of another sun. Relief really, as if, trapped as he was deep within the earth, he had also escaped planetary confines. Stella major acting on his brain, just as the spirit passages of the pyramids must have acted on Egyptian initiates into the great arcana in which, as Elias Levi wrote, all history, past, present and future, was writ in stone by the Nile. The nagual's mind was wandering. What had Egyptian pyramids got to do with Mexico? Everything, his twelfth sense told him. Yea, sure. But when he rounded that particular corner, all he saw was a dead end. If he knew something pertinent, why then was the information so difficult to access? A function of his split-level brain, he guessed, those chiselled corridors, but one step up in the pyramid. And that was the connection, he realised. The cathedral above, like so many churches in Mexico, built on an ancient pyramid, and that only encasing an even older pyramid, just like the mid-brain is encased within the cerebellum, and that within the cerebrum. Each relating to a different age of man.

What walks on four feet, two feet, three, but the more feet, the weaker it be? The riddle of the Sphinx replaying in his mind, as he walked endless corridors that all seemed the same, threading the Cleopatra eye of that needle with the face of his mother – the eternal Helga – and the mummy of his ultimate forefather. Dead from thirst in the sands of Egypt. In a nagual, yet remembering. A cruel land. The unyielding sun, never setting, always stationary at high noon, until that final catastrophe when usurpers toppled his throne, casting him into the Well of the Worlds, leaving his son, the last of the line, walking deserted streets in a land with no name, towards his lawyer, for that final confession, when at last he would learn the terms of his father's will.

Thy will be done, thy kingdom come! But thy kingdom is blighted, the rivers run dry. And no fuel for fire. The forests all chopped down – just bitter cold of unyielding night, not even a star for company as he walked a hard road, questing ever westwards towards the setting sun, knowing his endless quest for a father's trust would soon be run. Love always denied, denied yet?

Then before him a great castle, flag-poled with towers to either side, a facade of pomp and misery, steps leading up to a rainforest atrium with mechanical cockatoos chirping and palm court musac playing – a commissionaire on hand to point him towards the offices across the steel and marble concourse – by glass doors, the partner's intagliate names illumined on a tablet of stone, Pagan, Crook and Crozier, waiting to take him down into the well of night, there to hear his sentence, he reflected, stopping by the reception desk, discovering he was early by a few minutes for an appointment he was unaware of having made, and the lawyer not at his post when the assistant rang through. Yea, he thought, take me down to the river, there to drink my fill of the black water. Piss and filth, swirling with blood of fatted calves. Yea, he resolved to drink his fill.

7. STEPS TO THE GOLDEN HANDSHAKE

How the minutes dragged, as the nagual looked for distractions in the sleek foyer that could have been any corporate office, had it not been for the scattered mementoes of a Pickwickian past? Even in the matter of finding the right word, his amnesia played tricks on his mind. A polished oak stick rack and hat stand, three bronze busts of the founding partners – the original Pagan, Crook and Crozier – looking down on an arrangement of lilies in a Lalique glass vase on a round table of grey granite set before a reproduction Georgian fireplace. The new world from an old perspective, under the same guiding precepts.

The law is the law is the law. There shall be no greater truth than this; the received wisdom of Shem and the patriarchs as laid down by Adam, in bound leather volumes, lining the book cases of a red-painted study that was the first circle of hell and the only warm room in the cold presbytery he knew as home, all of it coming back to the nagual now – amnesia no defence in Tláltipec any more – remembering the great man, pre-heating a son's young bottom before the roaring gas fire, bending him over his knee, announcing solemnly,

'This is going to hurt me far more than you. Never question my orders, and that is an order! Only after you have proved your obedience, submitting to my will in all matters, will you be allowed that privilege, young master.' Then the whacks raining down on his padded behind, his pants packed with pages torn from the encyclopaedia.

'Amen to artillery.' He was a sapper, even in that remote past, before he was boarded out to Elias Asshole's Reformatory for Wayward Boys, then cast out for undermining imposed reality and questioning orders. His father's image clouding over in the years that followed, moribund in memory banks, a grey headland socketed like a skull, looming over the fogs and a cold sea. As he imagined, alone in his school dorm, boarded out even in the summer holidays. Baffin Island, or somewhere like that beyond the Arctic Circle, unvisited since Frobisher's expedition seeking the fabled north-west passage to India, home to colonies of shrieking skuas and fulminating fulmars, his whetstone visage crumbling as a cliff undermined by time and tide - the changing mores of a tide-race century. But always in the roar of those breakers, the nagual could hear the pounding beat of his father's words - a coda more binding than the precepts of the elders of Zion and the Pentateuch, the first five books of the Old Testament, or, as the pedant preferred to call them, 'The 'Recension of the Babylonian Talmudists'. His stentorian ringing tones, carrying even through the door of the great study, closed on the regular Saturday matinee sessions, which always continued to the small hours of Sunday. When the conclave of elders convened to discuss the minutiae of the Bible, or so he once coldly informed him, after a sermon on minding his own business - lords of the cloth, monsignors, bishops, professors of moral logic, judges, historians and theologians - layman's opinion usually represented by his sometime shadow and advisor on temporal affairs, Mr Crook ...

Shuffling arthritically past, his father's loyal servant; could that really be him? Clutching a familiar-looking cracked black leather portmanteau to his preposterous pinstripe Saville Row front, myopically peering about over half-moon gold spectacles, across by the reception desk? Some things might have changed, such as these offices, but Mr Crook never, the nagual considered, inwardly flinching - expecting a knuckle-grinding crunch as the last time - but meeting no resistance as they shook hands.

'Ah, the young master,' he croaked, peering owlishly over thick lenses. 'Can it really be you?'

'Yes, in the flesh! Sprung out of a dream ... My father's dream of a son and successor, dashed on the black rocks of a north-western promontory,' the nagual wanted to say, but instead merely mumbled, 'Mr Crook, so good to see you. How long has it been?'

'More years than I'd care to count, young master,' the old lawyer said, joints creaking like rusty hinges, leading the nagual down red carpeted stairs to the basements, holding open the door to an anonymous office suite that smelt of cleaning chemicals, with dusty ledgers crowding metal shelves.

'Sit yourself down, young master,' he went on, indicating one of two plastic chairs and taking the other, setting the portmanteau on the table between them. 'An onerous duty, and not one I confess I have been looking forwards to over much.' Sighing, he reached into the portmanteau, setting a sheaf of documents on the table like Doc Watson spreading a hand of cards. 'Your father was certainly not the most receptive man in the world when it came to taking advice.' He paused meaningfully.

'And let me tell you, on more than one occasion, I tried to dissuade him against drafting this will. But, as you know, when he made his mind up on something, your father was impossible to budge.'

Even though such a detail measured the limits of his knowledge of his father, the nagual nodded – an old curmudgeon to friend and foe alike, this much he had already gleaned. 'Is there a problem with the will?' he asked after a judicious pause.

'Yes,' Mr Crook nodded slowly, 'I should say there is, young master. You see, your father employed an arcane legal device that went out of use in the eighteenth century.'

'That figures,' the nagual grinned. 'Behind the times as always, my antediluvian old man.'

Ignoring what he obviously considered a distasteful witticism, Mr Crook continued briskly, 'You needn't worry with the legal terminology, but, suffice to say, the effect was to create two back-to-back wills.'

'So there's two wills?' the nagual gasped.

'If you think of it that way, it will help you understand what control over the destiny of his children your father retains.'

'Retains?' the nagual reiterated. 'You talk as if my father is still alive.'

'Would that he were, young master. Would that he were,' Mr Crook said heavily, regarding his client gravely over half-moon spectacles, 'Then at least I would be spared this onerous task.'

'And who are these other children?' the nagual insisted, ignoring the lawyer's pained look. 'Did he marry a second time?'

'You *really* don't know?' Mr Crook's eyes narrowed. 'Even aware as I am of your father's capacity for secrecy, I find that incredible.' The lawyer sighed.

'After you were packed off to that school, the woman I always knew as the housekeeper, I am referring of course, to your mother,' he smiled opaquely, 'Had triplets. Three baby girls, identical in every respect. It was the sensation of the parish, the one dark blot, or perhaps I should say three,' he made a strange gurgling sound, 'In your father's forty years ministering to the needs of his flock.'

'And what do they look like, my sisters?'

Tugging his right ear, Mr Crook further distended a pendulous lobe. 'I was never very good at this but I will attempt a description,' he said, clearing his throat. 'Like your father, I would suppose, the same black hair and handsome dark eyes. But I have not seen them since they were babies, after the housekeeper... ah ...' He gave his secret smile again. 'Your mother left.'

'Do they know about the will?'

'I should say they do,' Mr Crook nodded. 'They have an appointment at the end of the week, and I don't consider it breaking a confidence to tell you, I shall probably be offering them the same advice as you.'

'Which is?' the nagual snapped, aware that the lawyer had just overstepped the bounds of probity into that no-man's-land under vulture-high command, where self-interest is the one pertinent law.

'You should think long and hard before submitting to the terms of your father's will,' Mr Crook said carefully. 'Quite apart from the first problem I mentioned, he has employed a number of other codicils to create a series of interlocking trusts, administering the component parts of his estate. Variously stocks and bonds, lands and other holdings, moveable assets and life assurance policies ...'

'And what is the point of all this?'

'I believe his intention was to place your mother in a position of absolute power, at the same time enmeshing her in an irreversible process not of her design. She is chief executrix, heading each of the trusts, and though your sisters are required to serve in a lesser capacity, collectively they can never muster enough votes to challenge her position.'

'And my role in his game plan?'

'Only that of powerless onlooker, I am afraid. For reasons known only to himself, your father chose to exclude you from serving in any capacity on the various trusts.' Mr Crook frowned. 'What was it your father said when we discussed all this? Ah yes,' he muttered, '"Fate or destiny? How will my boy decide?" I never did understand what he meant by that. Unless of course he was referring to the island of your mother's birth.'

'Do you know the name of it?'

'Unfortunately not,' Mr Crook inclined his head,

'However I do know it is one of three mountainous islands, located exactly on the Arctic Circle.'

'Yes, I heard that.'

'Your father said the fact was most significant.'

'Do you happen to know why?'

'I am sorry to say I do not, young master.' Mr Crook shook his head.

'Perhaps places, just like people, have their doubles, and those islands have their counterparts. Say, three mountains on the tropics? Do you think that is possible?'

'I am afraid you have lost me, young master,' Mr Crook said condescendingly.

'Never mind,' the Nagual snapped. 'What else do you know about the islands?'

'Only that they are near the, ah, Saltstraumen.'

'What's that exactly?'

'A whirlpool, the largest in the world, I believe, located somewhere off the north coast of Norway.'

'So it's confirmed, my mother's Norwegian, yes?'

'You may be correct young master, however your father never discussed her nationality, so I cannot say.' Mr Crook paused. 'As regards the island, all I am reasonably sure of, it is one of three within the tide race of said whirlpool on the Arctic Circle and there is a most curious phenomena associated with them, which of course your father was fascinated by.'

'Of course,' the nagual groaned, wondering how much more he could take.

'Your father was interested in anything that seemed to defy the normal bounds of time and space,' Mr Crook said.

'And these islands do that?'

'It would seem so, young master.' Mr Crook nodded, unperturbed. 'Your father mentioned that the Elizabethan explorers referred to them as floating islands, and I believe since time immemorial sailors in those parts have called the associated spectre the "Fata Morgana".'

'I think I heard of that,' the nagual sighed, wondering where and when. 'It's some sort of mirage, right?'

'A superior mirage, young master. Stretching and twisting the islands into fantastical forms that your father ascribed to the Möbius effect, as he called it.'

'I don't understand.'

'Frankly neither do I, young master. However, I did gather that, when the whirlpool appears in the mirages, some very strange effects can take place.'

'Such as?'

'I am afraid there I would be drawn into the realm of the purely speculative, something, as a lawyer, I cannot allow,' Mr Crook smiled lopsidedly. 'However I'd hazard a guess that your father told you about the spectre when you were a boy. It was one of his best stories. Perhaps you've forgotten?'

'No, I don't think so,' the nagual said firmly.

'Be that as it may, your father was quite illuminating on the subject. As I recall he said that the phenomena was caused by the interface between warm air resting on a layer of colder air immediately above the ocean, creating a refracting lens over which distant objects on the horizon appear to hover, projecting the apparition to diverse places.'

'Such as Mexico, I suppose.'

'Mexico?' Mr Crook said blankly.

'I was thinking of my mother's habit of appearing when not wanted.'

'Ah, I see,' Mr Crook gurgled. 'You were making a joke.'

'Correct,' the nagual grimaced. 'Look, all I want to know is what is the upshot of this ...' he paused, searching for an appropriate phrase, 'Bagatelle of shit.'

Mr Crook winced. 'You are referring to your father's estate?'

'Of course,' the nagual nodded.

Mr Crook sighed. 'I'll attempt to summarise. Your mother has a life-rent over all properties, land and holdings, moveable assets, stocks and investments, until she dies. And when that day comes, if there is anything left, which, knowing your mother and her spendthrift ways,' he coughed, discretely covering his mouth with a fly-blown parchment hand, 'I rather doubt, then the second will comes into operation, creating another tier of trusts and, at the head, a daughter of her choosing, the purpose of which will be to dispose of all remaining moneys to the surviving issue, including yourself should you live that long.'

'And you rate that an unlikely prospect?' the nagual glowered.

'Not at all, young master. Quite to the contrary in fact. From the little I learned from your dear father on the subject of his housekeeper, your, ah, mother, I understand she comes from an extremely long-lived line, and you can count at least one centenarian on the, ah, Lapland side of your family. So it is just that you may have to wait a rather long time for your inheritance.'

'I see,' the nagual said heavily. 'So you think I shouldn't have any part of it?'

'You should consult with another lawyer before you make up your mind, but, yes, that is my considered opinion.' He nodded sagely.

'But what's the point when I get nothing if I do?' Mr Crook shook his head. 'In that event your dear father left a locked box, which I have secure upstairs at reception, should you wish to make that choice.'

'And what's in this box?'

'That I cannot say, young master.'

'Can't or won't?'

'Your dear father did not see fit to tell me.'78

275

'Well, is it heavy, for example?'

'For a small box, I suppose you might say it is.'

'Heavy enough to contain gold, for example?' the nagual interjected hopefully.

'Possibly, but personally I rather doubt it.' Mr Crook shook his head. 'Your father always placed a greater faith in redeemable government bonds. Gold, he would say, is merely the stock in trade of pawnbrokers and jobbing jewellers.'

'Am I allowed to open this box before I decide?'

'No, I'm afraid not. Your dear father was most specific in his instructions, but knowing him as I did, and how often he spoke of his great love for you, I suspect it contains something of worth, perhaps even of inestimable value.'

'You are sure about that?'

'Your father would not leave you destitute, of that I am absolutely certain, young master.' Mr Crook smiled, exposing yellowed dentures. Death looked the nagual in the face at that moment. How could he have known his father's lawyer was numbered among the living dead. Not a legal eagle exactly, more a pin-striped vulture, grown rich from advising widows and orphans, picking over the spoils of victory in a no-man's-land on the dark side of Tláltipec.

Putting aside his paranoia of lawyers, the nagual took his time making up his nagual's mind. Left alone in that airless room, pouring over the poorly photostatted document that seemed an insult in itself, the print smudging under his fingers, the right margins borrowing a strip from each following page, grappling with arcane legal gobbledygook terms such as 'without prejudice, per stripes, the said residue' and 'residue of that residue, renunciation, forgoing purposes, parameter powers, hereunder, aforesaid, intestacy' and 'immunities' – Cronus' revenge implicit in every line – his father's will suborning him to submit and watch from the side-lines as his share was frittered away, and yet, his father's flunky assured him, the great man had greatly loved him. What to do with that pathetic love that could ignore him so resolutely? But perhaps his father was merely following a hallowed family tradition. So who then to blame? His father, or his father? A stain of Biblical proportions extending to the seventh generation? Seven to the power of seven more like, he considered, remembering a pyroclasmic portrait parade of simulacrum, simian ancestors, scrolling by. Overwhelming him, every night as he passed into sleep in the nursery – how many years ago? All the way back to the deluge and before, to that founding father who first pissed in his genetic soup, that proto-ancestor, the veritable worm at the roots of his family tree. Within him yet, an ancient Egyptian of some rank he had little doubt, given his father's predilection for pomposity and Pentateuch studies. But perhaps he was just inventing scapegoats. Maybe he'd rejected his father's love in a past too distant to remember, and this was all his fault. There is no refuge from guilt, even in infancy. From birth we are all answerable, he thought, and only behind the closed doors of death is judgement pronounced.

But at least he'd learned a few notable facts. According to Mr Crook, the housekeeper, his father's nemesis, came from an island associated with a mirage called the Fata Morgana, located near the largest whirlpool in the world, somewhere off the north coast of Norway. While just as weirdly, his father had been born to unnamed Coptic parents at the turn of the century and was fostered by Catholic nuns at the Sacred Heart Orphanage in Alexandria, Egypt; all this recorded in a legacy of seventeen thousand dollars to the order. A snip against the value of the estate, but, as off-shore accounts were still being uncovered by the diligent Mr Crook, and there was ongoing litigation with the Egyptian government for compensation for lands nationalised during the Suez crisis, that amount had yet to be determined.

Fate or destiny? The same riddle he'd posed his father, merely by existing, returned from beyond the grave via his chosen mouthpiece, Mr Crook. But didn't both words mean the same thing? A dictionary on hand on an upper shelf provided the answer. Fate, in the original sense, was the sentence pronounced over the birth of each individual by the original three weird sisters, known as the Norns, by his long-lived Laplander forebears on his mother's side, and accepting it meant accepting one's lot – in this case, he supposed, submitting to the provisions of his father's will, just as he supposed his father had all those years ago, when trouble arrived in his life in the form of Helga.

But destiny – implicit in the notion of the 'quest' and deriving from the Latin root *'destinatus'* – was subtly different, meaning the end or ultimate purpose for which an individual had been incarnated, and every life was a chance to achieve it. Knowing that, and notwithstanding his suspicions of Mr Crook, he really had no choice but to pick up the gauntlet, take the box and unlock the riddle destiny posed.

'*My father, wherever thou art, whether in heaven or hell, hallowed be thy name, thy kingdom come, thy will be done ...*'

Murmuring this as an incantation against any time-locked Jacks or Djinns, the nagual resisted the temptation to call his father 'shit-eater' and say, 'cursed be thy name, thy kingdom be undone', so much did he hate him then. His father, whose gold he lusted after as a desert hawk seeks the sun, Horus soaring on thermals flying into the face of Ra, in his quest for that eternal love, laying the cold metal box on reception desk, inserting the key, holding his breath for fear of the unknown. Telling himself what will be will be – wondering whether he'd regret his choice – turning the lock, lifting the lid, revealing a book bound in yellow hide, branded on the bottom left hand corner a portion of a circled cross, or perhaps a claw? The nagual wondered, imagining his father in Bedouin robes, like Abraham in the Bible, two hands raising a knife high, about to sacrifice the original fatted calf – his beloved son, Abel, bound and disabled, laid out on a stone altar at the behest of an angry God.

Dismissing the notion as too fantastical, even for him, the nagual turned the tanned skin cover, and the red and black marbled fly leaf to the Latin-dated title page, reading out loud:

'*The Book of Tell Tale Signs, Volume One*. Is this all I get?' The nagual's soaring hopes plunged to earth, hawk wings singed by the solar disc. 'Where are the other volumes?' he demanded, tasting bitter defeat at that the moment.

'There is only one volume, and you are holding it,' Mr Crook sighed over his shoulder. 'The great project to which he devoted more than half his life. Perhaps it was his wish you should complete it. Now that would be a worthy task.'

'Fuck that for an epitaph,' the nagual snorted, flicking the pages, watching a fly-past of hand-drawn signs, some of the images rudimentary

– almost childlike in conception, caricatures of animals and plants rendered like hieroglyphics, others exceedingly complicated, reminding him of computer circuitry and squiggly sequences of DNA. 'This is of no value whatsoever,' he declared.

'Perhaps not of financial value, young master,' Mr Crook murmured, 'But your father's scholarship was unequalled in his chosen field of study.'

'And what was that?' the nagual demanded, the rage he felt inside a molten riptide of lava.

'Why, I am astonished you do not know, young master! Your father was perhaps the greatest kabbalist of his age.'

'Kabbalist?' The nagual frowned, fearing his worst suspicions were about to be confirmed. 'Do you mean my father was into black magic? Is that how he made his money?'

'Not at all, young master, not at all,' Mr Crook said reassuringly. 'Your father was a reverend, a God-fearing man who made his money by scrupulous share dealings, I can assure you. If he did gain some small advantage from his knowledge of the Kabbala, which he once told me in Hebrew means "received love", it was no more than he deserved.'

'But what use is this to me?' the nagual moaned, noting, as he flicked over the remaining pages, a change to runic symbols. 'There's no text.' He made a fist. 'Not one damned word of explanation.'

'I really do not know, young master. Perhaps if you peruse the book closer you will find out,' the lawyer declared airily, pulling out a gold fob watch and chain from a pocket of his old-fashioned waistcoat. 'Good heavens,' he babbled, peering at the moon-phase enamelled face, 'I had no idea it was so blessed late. Please forgive me, I really must fly.'

8. CAST-A-WAY

More satanic transformations, the nagual considered sourly, regarding Beelzebub pinstripes of the parasitic variety, buzzing off and out the glass double doors. Drawn by the dung of another death, perhaps? The ordure of pastures new? Time to pack up and go, he thought, holding the book to his chest, but where? When he was stuck between the continuums, with no place to call home? But then, just as he turned back for the box, still open on the reception desk, his grip on the book loosened and something slipped out and fell to the floor. An old monochrome postcard, he saw, stooping to pick it up, presenting the pictorial map of an instantly familiar skyline of witchy peaks. Yes, the three sisters in jagged relief, from more or less the same perspective as he first remembered seeing from the bus, but somehow removed from bandit foothills and set down in a cold and comfortless sea. A prospect only somewhat softened by snow-capped summits, wreathed in spiralling mist, tall pines clinging to precipitous rock faces tumbling down to lower slopes, with meadows and patchwork fields dotted by hut settlements and grazing longhorn cattle, their shaggy brown coats rendered in exquisite detail. Boiling surf directly below, where running cliffs brimmed a monster whirlpool, named not Saltstraumen, as Mr Crook would have it, but, according to the card, the 'Cauldron of the Norns'. A scene, perhaps captured in a witch's eye, mirrored in a fish lens as she poured over her Norn's scrying glass. The monster whorls of that maelstrom rippled every which way, making it look as if the rugged islands that were all that prevented the ringing horizon and the world beyond from being sucked into the maw of the deep and torn to pieces by flotsam teeth, flossed by sails and rigging of all the sailing ships that had passed that way before.

Down the pughole, into the Well of the Worlds, that was for sure, the nagual reflected, a fleeting mental image replacing the panorama on the card, with thundering falls cascading in infinite cupcake gradations into a raging sphincter he knew he had once rimmed himself, chancing his way out of the abyss in Mictlán, the domain of the dead, he suddenly recalled.

Repressing a shudder, he turned the card over in his hand and smiled, a sudden flush suffusing his normally pallid features, as though his cheeks were brushed by an unseen hand. The nagual saw it was addressed in his father's characteristic crabby handwriting to the 'Young Master at the Presbytery'. His pleasure diminished, as he noted than it had obviously never been sent, for there was no stamp or postmark.

'My *dear son*,' it began,

'*This is a map of the Islands of the Elect, which you will not find in any atlas since they exist only in the minds of poets and dreamers. In the ancient myths they were always located at the very limits of the world. One day I hope to meet you there.*

Till then, when we renew old acquaintance, with very much love, your father xxx

P.S. Perhaps the other enclosure I have included will assist you on your quest.'

Did the nagual hear echoing laughter as he read this? Those 'Islands of the Elect' marking the place of his exile, in heaven or perhaps hell. A mirage, screened offstage in the abyssal black depths of a monster maelstrom that, on the flimsy evidence of the card, if it existed at all, was called the Cauldron of the Norns, sucking all the way to Mictlán for all he knew, out of sight but not out of mind behind the enclosing *tzitzimime* wings of the lord of death. And that enclosure mentioned so casually? Another map interleaved between pages of this fabulous inheritance, he thought bitterly, reflecting that it was all he had got in the way of 'received love' from his double-dealing kabbalistic father. Something about the map was familiar, yet unlike any he could recall. Desiccated by age, yet preserved in livid colour, the pigments unfaded by time, showing crudely drawn coastlines dotted by tracks and odd, symbolic-looking squiggles resembling cuneiform script, suggesting perhaps place names and significant points, described in code.

Perhaps the puzzle of the indexed landmarks had kick-started the old sod's interest in the Kabbala? the nagual pondered. A memory returning of a hobgoblin face, peeking in his bedroom door, seen prismatically through eyelashes as he lay snoring artfully in the way of kiddies feigning sleep. Watching his father tiptoeing in, then standing, staring down, breathing hard through his military moustache, before reaching towards the shelf behind the young master's head. What had he been up to so furtively? Was theft on his mind, or had he been clutching something when he leant over? Picturing his attic room as it then was, the legend 'Beware of Rufus the Dog' warning intruders in suitably toothy black lettering painted on knotty wood, the varnish stained and yellow with age; beyond the door, his sagging collections weighting chipboard shelves, treasure discovered during long country rambles that took him deep into the jungles of Chichen Itza, detouring with his penknife machete through the bramble thickets of Michoacán, before returning with pockets full of artefacts to record and catalogue in his museum of lost civilisations. The shiny dragon's tooth, found in the furrows after the spring planting, evidence of a former age of Titans, when giants ruled the earth; shards of pottery brought by travellers from far-off countries, the nagual could still see like enchanted islands in his mind's eye, empires and principalities once ruled by impressive names such as Prester John, Tamerlane and Montezúma; shells and bones of prehistoric fish – the skeleton of a coelacanth discovered outside the fishmonger's, confirming the Biblical story of the flood. Cast-off carapaces of crawlers yet unknown to botanists; rusty bottle tops left in the beech woods from bacchanalian orgies before the time of Christ; each item proving the world was far more incredible than the planet-wide prison of proscriptions his father, with all his strictures and pronouncements, had insisted it was, as he now seemed to recall.

Was he wrong? Did his memory lie? No! Twice no, the nagual told himself, suddenly becoming aware of an overhead CCTV camera monitoring his movements. Making that his cue, running out of claustrophobia-con- ditioned offices into the atrium past the commissionaire and his shiny row of medals, taking the steps to the street three at a time, hitting on smoggy rush-hour air, realising this was Manhattan on a wet Friday winter's evening, the lights all at red and the traffic backed up a zillion blocks, all the way over the Hudson to the new territories in China. Lost for direction – checking the map for curiosity's sake, finding a little symbol of a castle with scales placed to the side, a dotted line at a tangent, suggesting left, left, then dead ahead. Directions the nagual felt bound to follow. And, sure enough, after a couple of turns, arriving on a broad and empty highway, with easy walking on ample grass verges.

He had reached that border between one fiction and another, where suburbs give way to abandoned industrial estates, pylons leaking radon over dog kennel factories sitting not so pretty amid acres of cactus-cracked concrete, corrugated asbestos, sagging under the accumulations of loam and leaves. All this propped against the backdrop of the city. Shanghai? He guessed it could be. Pagoda high rises all lit up with dancing paper lanterns, brightening as darkness slowly fell …

And ahead? Like the lost enchanted islands of his childhood, featherbedded on murky patchwork depths, the purple hills of the Southern Uplands, rearing over scattered clumps of trees, marooned in mist, calling him from unfenced heather vastness to venture yet further into the rippling blue yonder where the world whorled away over the purple banded horizon, and into the high chaparral of his boyhood badland dreams, where three witchy peaks cowled in snow looked down on picture-book revolutionaries riding shotgun on hijacked trains, trailing steam across the tarbrush mesas dotted with the fires of bandit encampments, past *sombrero*'d Indians laying in ambush for passing *gringos*, hiding behind desert bluffs spiky with cactus.

Night, and no hayrick to lay his head, not even a rock to afford shelter from the bitter wind. Was this his sentence? To be a vagabond between the dimensions, a wraith glimpsed between blinks by commuters, sailing past on interstate flyovers, cruising en route home from the office or wherever they worked, orbiting the whorls of a witches eye. A scene caught in a fish lens, each one aloof behind the bubble-tinted glass of their bloated chariots puffed out with self-importance, secure with index-linked pensions, gazes fixed on geriatric condominium, glittering in the setting sun, dipping over cancerous city conurbations eating up the worlds. His lot, hunger and hopelessness, facing an uncertain destiny. Questing as long as there was life in these old bones. Old? Somehow age had crept on him unawares. His golden youth gone like so many golden coins scattering into the dark gully below, lost under heavy clouds when he turned to look. Nothing else to do but push on into the biting wind towards the rugged summits, at last to find a lookout point where he might contemplate all this.

But then a hole got in the way, a gusset parting in the heather and he was down – screw-balling zinc-shoed darkness, only just escaping the cut with another low score marked on his card. An eagle birdie at the ninth, actually a hole-in-one, since, from tee to green under the Town With No Name and taking in New York and Shanghai, was a par three. All detailed on a map with distances and dangers to avoid. Bunkers wide enough to lose the Sahara in, rough where it was advisable to go armed with something sharper than a no. 3 Panga iron, and one was in as much danger from stampeding elephants as from roaming bands of Masai speculators. Yes, the golf course of life, where the general aim is to extend your handicap and take as many shots as possible to get round. Just a few make it over the hundred.

Strangely, the hole only got deeper as the nagual descended, tumbling time into a new game – another life, he supposed, wondering what face would next be stitched onto his – as he was sucked into wormhole rapids stretching with chewing gum faces; cross-wielding Cristeros battering it out with bludgeon-battling Black Friars. This was the nagual's final sight as he was enveloped in the dust and hail, finally landing with a thud that clean knocked the breath out of him, back to the ground, staring up at black-brassiered ridges crosshatched by lightning striking out of a clear blue sky, and the lazy circle formed by three flail-winged raptors, gyring on a tornado twisting away in the distance, reminding him of that fateful glass of *mescal* and a *pocito* gut-wriggler – *el gusano de diablo* – doing the *sombrero samba* just the same.

But then a jackboot blocked his view, so highly polished he could see his face reflected – well, he guessed it had to be his – proximity to gloss brown leather making it a near certainty. Old? Yes, indeed, enough lines to map Antarctica, worm tracks charting a course almost run. Death sunny side up, clawed by crow's feet.

'We leave this *chingada* for the vultures!' announced a *castiliano*-accented voice over a distant fusillade of gunshots. 'What you say, *el capitán*?'

Now there were two pairs of jackboots blocking his view, razor-billed officers of the Cúerpo del Cuervo Négro, the 'black crow brigade', in stylish jodhpurs and belted battle fatigues. The officer who was rhythmically slapping a swagger stick against his palm, the nagual guessed was *el capitán*, shaking his capped head, the shiny brim resembling a gleaming black beak from that low angle.

'No, I think not! There is life in the old wretch yet. And who knows, maybe he is the one?' Raising a hand, he snapped fingers to a medical orderly, stepping up to his command. 'Gustavo,' he snarled, 'Strip and search the prisoner. Same drill as the others, an enema and a diuretic. After you have checked his vomit, take him away for interrogation.'

9. CHECKING IT OUT

Meat markets were like this, the nagual considered, taking in his surroundings in covert little glances, carcasses arranged for inspection, spreadeagled on slabs, hooked and racked like so many unbuttoned coats exposing what every medical student is required to know, the floors swilling with blood and puke. All around men screaming for mothers, Madonna and mercy; God and Jesus, fourth and fifth in the pecking order respectively. While black-hooded *torturadores* moved from table to rack and back again, using body concavities for ashtrays, applying bastinos, adjusting thumbscrews, garrottes, gouging gonads, scrying entrails for clues. From what he could gather, all because of a map someone was holding.

That someone was him.

'*Oye, campesino!*' a voice rang out over the hubbub, addressing him from the next table. 'I hear say you are the one?'

'*¿Estás loco?* An old man like me!' the nagual

laughed bitterly, making a pretence of struggling against his bindings – in any case so tight he could barely move his head, let alone arms and legs. 'Only young men have that sort of luck!'

'There is no luck in this place, just pain,' the anonymous voice insisted. 'I think you are lying, old man.'

'Yes, I am lying, lying on my back, owning nothing but my nakedness,' the nagual cackled, 'And soon to be dead, for which I thank the godness of good!'

'You are sure about that?'

'Of good no! His godness? Never! But of death, yes! Lord Mictlán is close you know, I saw him, with my own eyes, before they brought me here.'

'And what does Lord Mictlán look like, old man? the anonymous voice retorted scornfully.

'Like a black crow with the sky in his shiny beak, my son. The soldiers call him *el capitán*.'

'*El capitán del garra!*' the anonymous voice rejoindered tartly, his manner leading the nagual to suspect he was a schoolmaster. 'But only behind his back,' he added warningly.

'Why do they call him "the claw"?'

'Because he is the tool of the abomination that lives in Chapultepec!'

'Chapultepec?' the nagual croaked back. 'I know this name, but for the life of me yet remaining, I cannot remember from where.'

'Don't you know Chapultepec *es* el Castillo del Presidenté in México City?'

'Is it far *estas castillo?*' the nagual asked, knowing ignorance was his best cover.

'My god!' the voice moaned oratorically. 'We are fighting with our lives in the *revolución*, first against *Diez* and then *Huerta*, and this *pendéjo* does not even know of Mexico City?!''

'Even I understand that without *revoluçión* there can never be peace. It is just that sometimes I forget things. I am an old man, you know.'

'Yes, I can see that,' he said, straining against rawhide straps, a sudden note of suspicion entering his voice. 'A very strange, old man, I see that now. Your body is so weathered and wrinkled it almost looks like a ...'

He stopped as a tall shadowy figure loomed between them. *El capitán del garra*, the nagual realised, recognising the beaked silhouette instantly.

'You were saying, *maestrito del escuela?*' *El capitan* sneered, belittling the schoolmaster's professional status.

'Oh nothing, *capitán,*' the schoolmaster replied.

'He is just a pendéjo who does not even know there is a *revolución* in the country. I was just putting him right.'

'Are you sure you are not confiding where you hide the map?'

'If I had, he would not remember the next moment,' the schoolmaster chuckled, his chortles oddly juxtaposed against the background wails and curses.

'I am glad you find something amusing in all of this, *maestrito*. You will not be laughing when your turn comes, I assure you. And if I find you have lied, I promise you will void your *excramento* into your *pantalones* before I strangle you with your intestines.'

'Charming, isn't he?' my *compañero* said as el *capitán* swaggered away, continuing his round of the *camera de tortura*. 'Lucky he has no eyes to see what you are showing to all the world with your nakedness.'

'And what is that, my son?' the nagual said, already knowing the answer.

'The map, of course! Or do you take me for a *pendéjo*, too?'

'No! How could I when you are so learned and clever, with eyes to see what I, in my ignorance, cannot?'

'You mean you do not know?'' The schoolmaster was incredulous.

'My son, you may not believe this, but I am only just born into this world. All I have seen of myself is a face reflected in the shiny brown boots of el *capitán*.'

'*En serio?*'

'Yes, my son,' the nagual sighed. 'But tell me, what do you see in this map on me?'

'A way to escape the town,' he grunted, 'If only I can loosen these thongs ...'

Sappatistas at work, undermining the dimensions, a sudden detonation below announcing that fact, the resulting explosion lifting a slab – and the nagual – high over the room. Making him think he had been transformed into a dirigible and was floating free of his moorings, as dreamily he regarded the broad beams of the floors above, collapsing like a house of cards, before he was deposited with a thump that knocked all the wind out of his sails, for the second time that day.

'Old man! Are you still alive?' a voice said from a long way above.

Stupid question, the nagual thought, resenting the schoolmaster's hands rattling his cage, brushing the dirt from his face. Didn't the clumsy oaf realise he was only tissue paper stretched over straw stays. 'Yes, my son,' the nagual managed at last, with an audible click as his dislocated jaw snapped back into place.

'I thought you were dead.'

'What happened?'

'Sappers, I suppose,' the schoolmaster said, grunting as he eased the nagual out from under a tarred 327 wooden beam that had protected his body from the raining masonry.

'Now I remember,' the nagual winced, his ribs drawing black beads from the beam, as the schoolmaster hauled him out by the feet. 'The *sappatistas* below!'

'No, old man,' the schoolmaster grimaced, pausing to wipe the sweat from his smoke-blackened brow, 'You confusing "sappers" with the zapatistas in the south of the country, fighting under the leadership of *sub-commandante* Z.'

'This is true?'

'Yes, old man,' he answered tartly, ever the quintessential schoolmaster. 'Here in el norté, las brigadás de la *revolución* are commanded by one Doretero Arango, variously Pepe Gonzales and Francisco Villa, once a common bandit and now the talk of the country. You may even know him as Pancho.'

'Ah yes, *generalísimo* Pancho!' the nagual grinned, his pains dissipating in an instant. 'Even I have heard of him! Though where or when, I cannot recall,' he said, regarding the schoolmaster with amusement as he crouched down beside him, rubbing his emaciated legs to get his circulation going. 'So the sappers below work for him too?'

'Yes,' the schoolmaster said distractedly, hands blurring as they worked away, 'Though how they tunnel through the mountains is quite beyond me, old man.'

'The tunnels already exist, my son!'

'They do?' the schoolmaster blurted, ceasing rubbing and looking up. 'Is that how you arrive? But I forget, you are the map, so how would you not know?'

'The map is only what you see in me,' a nagual said, groaning with pain as the schoolmaster helped him to his feet. 'I know no more than you do, my son. Perhaps even less.'

'Stop right there! Move and I shoot to kill!'

No reward for guessing the owner of the voice, *el capitán*, stepping up with immaculately polished brown boots from concealment behind a ridge of rubble, aiming a long-barrelled Smith & Weston revolver with an unwavering hand.

'Oh no!' the schoolmaster groaned. 'How come you survived?'

'A charmed life, as you have already remarked,' *el capitán* grinned, his pressed khakis and fatigues reminding the nagual of a king cobra about to strike, as he advanced another few steps. 'I am protected by forces that you could not begin to grasp, even with your exalted intellect, *maestrito*.'

'Mere superstition!' the schoolmaster spat back.

'How the church and the state have pulled the *sombreros* over the eyes of the *campesenos* for centuries.'

'There are no *campesenos!*' *el capitán* declared, advancing a couple more steps. 'Just *locos* and leaders. And since you both fall into the first category, I am going to kill you.'

'And lose your only chance of finding the treasure?' the nagual interjected. 'Surely even you could not be that *loco, el Capitán?*'

'Who ... are you?' he demanded falteringly, as the nagual stepped out into a beam of sunlight shafting the stour of precipitated dust.

'I am the living map and gatekeeper of this reality, possessor of secrets undreamt of by your sceptical mind, *el capitán*. If I die, all this will cease to exist. Even you,' he said, feeling like the ancient of days, standing there pointing a withered finger. 'And the abomination you worship en el castillo del Chapultepec.'

Now he remembered the map anteceding all others: *la carta geográphica* of his years. Started when? Before the Pleistocene era certainly, sprung into consciousness, precociously aware – in a mammalian sense – of the need to survive the predators of Eden, dinosaur parents blundering the garden, hazarding hatchlings just crawled out diaper swamps. The primeval Miocene era, when he was hot-housed on Homer and Herodotus, his father dallying with the idea of emulating Phillip of Macedonia's achievement in rearing a world conqueror, declaiming whole passages from memory verbatim – as Aristotle once recited over fair Alexander's crib – pushing a pram along summer lanes, pointing out Ithaca in the blue yonder, citing the example of Penelope's constancy – unlike some others he knew – fulminating on the dangers of Cyclops and Sirens, the lures of the lotus-eaters, his voice faltering as always when bespeaking his admiration for Xenophon's battle tactics. Subverting the young boy's unconsciousness to his purposes, peopling an unformed mind with long-dead superheroes, dedicating a pantheon to the ancient gods in his son's imagination, turning young thoughts towards Conquest even before he was exiled from his attic room to boarding school at the age of seven, a *desperado* plotting escape and expeditions, all supplies of paper confiscated on account of his wilful disobedience, refusing to learn irregular Latin verbs, using the most readily available material to hand – his own hot-housed young skin, softest vellum, purest white as the first snowdrop in spring.

Dotted lines wrinkling antique parchment, still grist to his wrist after all these years, marking the way across slippery slates to the other attic skylight and the secret staircase below, not known even to the housekeeper. Peepholes strategically placed, eyes that peeled back on dusty ancestor portraits, the better to spy on his father come Saturday nights, when fraternal friends foregathered in a presbytery study – *los compañeros de la garra*, dressing up in black robes embroidered with ruby-clawed gold crosses. A right royal rookery of robbers, plotting coups wars and pestilence, unknowing there was a spy in the camp reporting on their activities to a higher command – the 'purple pimpernel', cloaked in invisibility, conferred by seven Talmudic seals tattooed to his breast in blue biro and, if the need for a quick exit interposed, seven league boots in felt-tip scribing on the soles of his feet, wings on his ankles allowing him to take whole mountain ranges in one bound or jump to Ursa Major to present his reports in person before the higher powers. All the stupendous events he had seen or would ever witness, his explorations through the snake-infested Hindu Kush to a remote valley where he witnessed the extraordinary excavations of gold digging ants written about by Herodotus, the snowy mountain passes above commanded by abominable red-haired giants with back-to-front feet, or the time he humped it across the waterless wastes of the Makrám on a camel. Every improbable adventure, painstakingly drawn in secret code on his body, *for eagle eyes only*. Indelible markings that were to outlast the nightly punishment scrubbings Helga administered in the tepid waters of the cast-iron bath, from which he would emerge, raw all over, only to be rubbed red, the tenderloin kid, smelling of rancid soap and mildewed towels, slinking off to hide by the only fire in the house, his wildly fluttering fledgling heart and steam giving him away, driven out the study by a bellicose bishop in flowing vestments and mitre, pursued with a venomousity to the attic door and no-man's-land. His father brandishing the crozier of his office at the foot of the attic stairs, yelling, 'Get up to your room like a ruddy angel!' And, if he was in one of his 'black dog' moods, 'Get thee to Gehenna! Be gone this instant, accursed imp of Moloch!' Standing arms akimbo, eyes bulging dangerously, watching his young son crying his way up the stairs, while complaining to the housekeeper down in the kitchen in loud and anguished tones, demanding to know how the hell could he even begin to think of sermons and proselytising, when his repose was disturbed in this way.

His Father, and his father, standing behind him, a succession of elders in conclave, pivoted on plinths, lined up the hall whenever the young master glanced back, holding spirit lamps to shining stone faces ... faces he would ambidextrously doodle between fingers and thumbs, giving simulacrums mobility and the power of speech ... conversations to run over the horrible howlings of Cyclops, who every night crept out of the wardrobe outside his door, and the siren calls of banshees and worse, which, come hell or high water, slithered up from the black rocks at the foot of the stairs to lay siege to the portcullis door of 'Rufus the Wolf ' – the reason he needed an escape route across the slates, and the map, in the first place.

Maps, sirens, quests; the Harijan housekeeper and her mother from the sugar-icicled north were in there too – Grandma and her tales of Woden and the Norns, subsumed by later stories from the classics, Greek heroes like Jason and his search for the Golden Fleece, the travails of Odysseus, Oedipus and the riddle of the Sphinx, setting down guide rails in the weirdness of a young master's mind.

10. MAN TREE

For a vast stretch of subjective time, Double felt nothing, except for an absence of sensation, as if the darkness without had invaded his body and mind. What body and mind? So now he was a *phantom* double, needing confirmation he existed at all. OK, he thought, so he did have a mind, perhaps even an energy body too, for he did seem to intuit a cutaneous tickling where his toes should have been.

But proof he had, for, following another interval almost infinite in duration, he noticed the faint tickling was back and, more than that, well on the way to conquering the distant lands of phantom feet and ankles he sensed yet could not feel. Was it bind weed, he wondered, so tenaciously spiralling phantom lower legs, camping out on the strategic positions of phantom knees, surreptitiously advancing knees and thighs, reconnoitring the hidden dips and rises of phantom lumbar regions, sallying the secret valleys of his phantom groin where undergrowth was coarse and tangled on lower slopes of the bare uplands of his phantom stomach? Defining him, over a period extending for weeks and possibly months, from without if not within, a hollowed, inside-out double, occupying a void where skin and all the rest should have been.

Only the crepuscular creep of columns of tendrils on the march to remind him that he ever had shape and form. A body he once thought of as his, but now understood had all along been only property. Not his to do with as he liked, but chattel – the plaything of a god. Not the god of the Cristeros, AKA sweet Jesus Jaime, hamming it up on the cross. Nor Shem, the demiurge the Black Friars prayed to in their cathedral. But a power far more ancient. None other than the lord of this land, with a remit extending eight levels below. Yes, his feudal master, the arch-demon Lord Mictlán, who, by the terms of their contract, if he remembered right, still owed him a favour or two. There was even a certificate back at the hotel, setting out terms and conditions.

But his phantom mind was wandering. What use was such a contract, without pockets to put it in. What he would have given for pockets and the clothes that went with them. Jacket, shirt and trousers. How many pockets? Breast pocket, hip pockets, inside pockets, back pockets. A lot of pockets, ten at least on his usual ensemble, when he thought about it. What was it about pockets? Maybe it was something kept in one of his pockets, back when he had a body and clothes. Which pocket? Perhaps a hip pocket, on his left ... no, his right side. Now he remembered. That revolting gift of Helga's, the wrinkled dick of his forefather mummy. For regeneration, she'd said. Had she anticipated his present situation, he wondered, for, if so, she must have meant his regeneration, which was thoughtful. Some chance without a body. But perhaps he was wrong and he was presently in cryonic suspension, floating in a vat such as he remembered seeing in the mortuary vault under the cathedral after escaping all those talkative stiffs in the lowest level of Mictlán. As he recalled, the stone shelves were set out with vats, containing mummy parts bobbing in bubbling amniotic fluid. However those vats had clear glass sides, whereas he was now encased in something through which no light could pass. But hold on, he thought, realising that the darkness without, if not within, was not absolute.

Before his phantom eyes, two shady chinks floating on brimming ink, blacker than night. Glimmers, hardly enough to register, but the nonetheless – proving he did have eyes; by default a head and body; perhaps clothes too. Which took him back to the subject of pockets, and that mummy-dick in his left, no, he remembered, in his right pocket. If, indeed, the dick was as sacred and powerful as Helga had claimed, then it surely followed that if he visualised hard enough, perhaps it would materialise along with his clothes. And lo, there it was, just as he focused on the thought, its shape defined against his non-apparent hip by imaginary creeping vines. So at least he had trousers and was one dick up. Which, though hardly solving the problem posed by his absent body, did offer some hope. Was it possible that the baron had shafted him with a suppository, poisoned with the pineal gland of a Haitian black toad, as employed by voodoo high priests to turn the fresh dead, dug-up and spreadeagled, butt naked as when they were born, on the high altar of Baron Cimitère, permanently into living zombies?

Perhaps that explained how he had re-joined the congregation of the living dead? He even thought he sensed some previously noted tenebrous presences watching from the side-lines, dead but very much there, recumbent within their lead coffins on stone ledges recessed in the walls of that ecclesiastical court. Farcical though the trial had been, the crypt was impressive. Certainly as dark and foreboding as any court in the Old Bailey, he was sure. More foreboding, since this was the Shemite court. How was it he could recall the detailing of the stone impedimenta better now than during the proceedings? His trance state, he guessed. Then he had scarcely noticed that the groined vaults were delicately carved with a latticework of leaves and branches, spreading upwards from stout pillars resembling a stand of trees. Differentiated, one from another, by girth if not height, and cunningly wrought arboreal details of bark, branch, bolus, nook and cranny. The one behind the dais where the Shemite pope sat was massive, he recalled. What if he was immolated within and those two chinks floating before his phantom eyes were peepholes in its hollow stone trunk? Deduction, deduction, deduction. What was it Sherlock Holmes had said? Once you had eliminated the impossible, whatever remained had to be true, no matter how improbable. Well, something like that. Even in his deepening trance state his amnesiac memory defaulting. But at least he had established the salient facts.

None of which, however, went towards explaining the strange case of the advancing tendrils, now tickling his absence of ribs. At the conclusion of the trial – in his dream that was not a dream – delivering his verdict, the pope had directed that the prisoner was to be executed in the tree of death, which seemed just another way of describing crucifixion. Not the sentence he would have expected from the prelate of the Shemites. A religion, which, like Judaism, originated in the Middle East, where, until the Roman Empire extended there, stoning was the preferred method of execution. Perhaps crucifixion derived from Roman or Teutonic contact in the dark forests of northern Europe, where the tribes sacrificed their captives in trees? Slitting the throats of Roman legionaries, taken in raids further south, hanging them head down from upper branches. Draining their blood to feed the roots of Yggdrasil, the great tree that connected the nine enfolded worlds of Nordic belief. Sometimes in spring, if the captive was important enough, when morning mists curled about and the forest floor was wet with the dew of more than one world, his body would be bound in budding withes, leaving him to die from asphyxiation as greening withes slowly tightened, bundled into hollowed trunk of a standalone white oak such as were sometimes found in forest clearings, where lightning strikes were most frequent. The same trees that grew tall sheltered from the frequent lightning storms that struck the high *sierras*, safe in the shadowed depths of Happy Valley. Not like the blasted ancient white oak, standing at the forking of the path, on the bare lower slopes of three witchy peaks encountered during the long hike with Jaime.

Which brought to mind the black baron and what he knew of the lightning-struck family tree of the Hapsburgs – yes, yet more strange facts, made accessible only by a deepening trance state, first gleaned on long afternoons when it was raining on the lawns outside the windows of the presbytery study, and a lonely child had to content himself with pouring over the leather-bound books of a bishop's voluminous library – the British Royal family, themselves Hapsburgs, claimed descent from Woden. A wanderer from parts unknown, who, like another wandering sage of the middle Bronze Age, Confucius, had a penchant for dressing in black and communing with crows. Woden assumed the powers of a god after hanging head-down for nine days from the upper branches of a rowan tree, when he plucked out one eye and, casting it into a nearby cauldron as an offering, read the runes of life, the universe and everything with the other. Revealed in the spatter marks of his dripping blood congealing on red berries and brachiated leaves below that, with their usual thirteen divisions, symbolised time and were considered by the Teutons a charm against witches. Which was just as well, for the Norns, three mad sisters who lived at the base of the mightiest white oak of them all, were always skulking somewhere about.

Worshipped by the Teutonic tribes, who went on to conquer the Roman Empire, Woden gave birth to the saying about the one-eyed king in the land of the blind, and was known to successive generations as the man who measured the world. The same epithet accorded Voden, the red-haired giant wanderer from the east, who was welcomed as a living god and built Palenque before departing for mountains to the north. Where, according to one Mayan legend, his treasure was guarded by an ogress and her three identical daughters. Similarly, in the ancient European stories of the garden in the land where the sun went down, the three daughters of night, or the 'great ink' as he was referred to by the eponymous scribe of Samos in his famous scroll, guarded the golden apples of the sun. In Nordic legend, Woden is described wearing a long black cloak and wide-brimmed black hat. Just as Voden is pictured in a Mayan codex. Was it then a coincidence that Malinché, the captive Aztec *bruja*, gifted by the Mayans to Cortez, persuaded the conquistadors to dress in black cloaks and matching hats and to delay their disembarkation to coincide with the date of the great god's return? A most special day, heralded for millennia in the Mayan long-count calendar, when the founding father would reclaim his Eden of Meso-America, lately held in trust by the Aztecs, who inherited the obligation from their predecessors, the Toltecs – a pyramid-building tribe with a liking for *mescal* ...

His penis promised physical regeneration to a phantom double, the last of the line of Inkethaton and, by default, the rightful claimant of the Inkethaton empire of the Americas, which once extended from Hudson Bay in the north to regions in the south where the Incas once ruled in his name. But only if with phantom teeth and jaws, he could masticate and then somehow ingest the horrible relic, after first removing it from his phantom pocket, which of course was impossible, not least because he was bound in the budding withes of a white oak tree from a sacred garden that, in the centuries following the Conquest, had retreated the *sierras* to Happy Valley. Its wooded slopes finally reduced to cinders in the attack led by the mad Baron Hapsburg. The same who had interred him in this stone tree. Why? Because when it comes to pedigree, an Inkethaton always trumps a Hapsburg in the depth and reach of a family tree. The baron was just jealous of his roots, that was all. And besides, the bastard needed him out the way in order to pursue his bogus claim for the throne of Mexico.

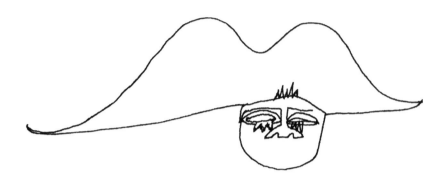

11. LOST HIS BODY IN MEXICO

Movement behind two scratchy chinks cut out of pen and ink darkness, describing a pair of dolorous eyes. Peeking in at him, peeking out at a beam of moonlight, painting silver a threesome of sylvan nymphs entering a petrified forest glade in slow limbic glides from an offstage door. As, from beyond, a distant horn piped a slow lament that seemed to Double bound and stuffed in the hollow trunk of a stone tree, the opening bars of a funereal fugue marking his imminent demise. A dirge, beat by beat, step by step, in the worrying interweave of a dance, taking him down. Down to a time before, when he and his sisters played charades in the pillared attic of the old presbytery, that one Yuletide they were together, dressing up in theatrical costumes found in a wooden chest discovered among the possessions left behind by a disgraced bishop, lately departed for lands unknown. But that was then and this was now, Double reflected, reading cuneiform runes in the contrails of their hot breaths, hanging hoary in the still-chill air of the otherwise-deserted crypt. Ethereal eddies that, instead of dissipating, to his considerable surprise, only intensified in luminosity as three Norns circled closer, scuttling the carved roots of a stone trunk. The spectral trails of their coy advance, foxfire coursing arboreal pillars to pendentive vaults suspended above, silvering the impedimenta of stone leaf and branch, transforming a twilight crypt into the orchard of a garden that came back to him as if from a dream. A dream when he talked with his friend below dappled branches, boughed low by golden apples like the sun going down. Whereas the offerings above seemed more like crab apples, pale as the harvest moon, round as pearls and ready to drop. Like himself, he thought, dimly aware that, with every forward step, the damp chill of a threesome of silhouettes was further invading his bones. While, without a hollow stone trunk, spectral contrails snapped at three pairs of heels shuffling beyond, putting him in mind of a pack of weasels, jostling for space in the crepuscular half-light behind piercing eyes, glinting in the same butterfly winged masks his sisters always picked out when playing the game. The game when they were the Norns of Yggdrasil and he was the sacrifice - a captured Roman proconsul stripped of his toga, wearing nothing but a circlet of laurel leaves on the crown of his head, bound and tied to an attic pillar while owls hooted from rafters high above, waiting for their share of the spoils and bloody entrails when all was said and done.

Once again he remembered a pinking scissors attack in the dead of night, and his horror at his first sight of the bloody mess revealed below Amish covers, then, after the divorce, setting off on a coitus interruptus - finished before it started - journey. Getting it on, never getting it up, with strangers met in bars and dives who could never match him in desperation no matter how hard they tried. Doglegging it widdershins twice around the world, 'till at last he reached the town where the answers have no name. And now this, his sisters weaving their Norn spells around the base of a stone tree. A hornpipe fugue, taking him down ... down to that night in a hotel bed with three identical kitchen maids, and the question he now needed answering: how come they got it on when his rebuilt soldier never could with anyone else, his mother not excepted?

Cuneiform runes that was how, he realised, Lapland spells learned at Grandma's knees, whispered in his ears by an unholy threesome, conceived by a Catholic bishop and his harpy housekeeper when Saturn was ascendant and six planets were retrograde. Tricking him into believing he was at last successfully getting it up, and not only that, keeping it up all night - a performance even the *bruja* of the north, with all her evil wiles, hadn't managed to coax out of him - when in fact he was bound and tied to bed post. A he transformed into a she, shafted from behind by the stiff little dick of his forefather, while below a truncated root was sucked and blown. His sisters working as a team, taking turns to give him head, 'till he came so copiously they needed cups to collect the gummy stuff.

All this, spelled out in the cuneiform runes of contrary contrails hanging hoary in the chill air of the crypt, as the Norns wove one more spell. A rebuilt soldier-man at last budding into life and standing to attention as they danced around the swollen base of an old tree. This their parting gift in a relationship that, with the exception of two torturous episodes, had been one long goodbye. His final humiliation in a lifetime of humiliation and hurt that, by the regenerative power of a pharaoh's penis in his pocket, his little man should be made a working whole again, ironically just as he died, suffocated by evanescent green shoots coiled in a stranglehold around his neck.

All was quiet in the dark crypt, the sisters long gone, taking their foxfire with them. Yet, within a swollen stone trunk, where a bulging bolus was fuzzy with green sprouting shoots, something of Double persisted. Not so much a breath, but more than a last exhalation. A vaporous contrariness retaining enough of a fractured self to have thoughts. Yes, a true Inkethaten, persisting right to the very end, which duly unfolded when, engraven on the dark before him, appeared a face such as he remembered from before. The obsidian mask of a founding father, inlaid in a hollow within a stone trunk, incised with peepholes that now described the black eyes of Lord Mictlán.

'Father?'

'Yes, my son.' The voice was resonant and deep, not at all as a vaporous Double remembered, when, to an ear pressed against a breastplate, it was tinny and small.

'You have come?'

'Yes, my son.'

'But it's too late.'

'Not too late to return a favour.'

'But I'm dead.'

'Yes, definitely, my son.'

'So it's over.'

'That is for me to judge.'

'But how when my body is plant food?'

A vaporous Double in conversation with a mask in a crypt gestured to a tall trunk, fuzzy green with new growth from a bundled husk rooting in a stone hollow.

'Immaculate plant food, as more than one family member is involved,' Lord Mictlán chuckled.

'But how?' a vaporous Double insisted.

'*In Tláltipec, as elsewhere in Mictlán, there are always ways and means, besides which you still have memories to recover.*'

'What, more memories?' a vaporous Double said suspiciously.

'*Yes my son.*'

'What of particularly?'

'*It started with a book.*'

'What book?'

'*A forbidden book.*'

'Forbidden by whom?'

'The last usurper to challenge my rule.'

'Who exactly?'

'*Your predecessor on the fork behind you on the family branch of a great tree.*'

'I don't understand.'

'*How would you, when you are only a leaf?*'

'A leaf?'

'*The last leaf my son. Parched and blotched, but a true Inkethaton to the end, still holding on after the winter's gales.*'

'How come?'

'*Because you my son are the ghost who wouldn't give up!*'

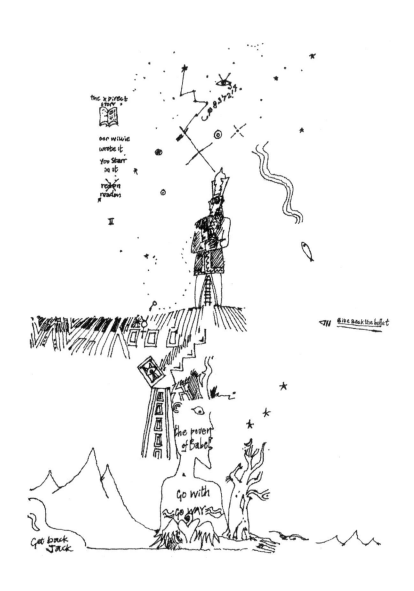

12. THE PICTURE BOOK OF MEXICAN HISTORY

Revolutions take planning. But then comes the time for action, when all plans have to be chucked out the window. In Pancho's case - we are discussing the Mexican master bandit here - out the *railway* train window. But *ferrocarril* train window sounds so much better. *Ferro* meaning iron, forever associated in a young master's mind with Fiero, Villa's fearsome accomplice from the old days. Pictured in a forbidden book filched from a bishop's library, stepping down from his private freight car, branding a youthful imagination with his searing stare, standing second only to Pancho in a pantheon of revolutionary heroes. How a young boy wanted to be that man, stand next to the sun, the most loyal of Pancho's *generalísimos*, his doppelganger forever defending his back against sneak astral attacks - stars and bars, Yankee legions mostly.

Once, just to settle a barroom bet, Fiero gunned down a complete stranger across the street, merely to prove his point that men dying on their feet always fall forwards. Another revolutionary excess, also illustrated in the book, the killing of three hundred mercenaries; so called colorados in the employ of crillo cattle ranchers involved in a land grab of northern Mexico, some of their holdings bigger than mid-sized European states. Fiero going about his business like a fox lose in a chicken coup, famously complaining to his adjutant, relaying reloaded pistols through the open shed door, that his trigger finger was tiring.

How such fierceness appealed to a young master, again and again returning to his favourite image of Fiero, wishing he could do the same to his elders, who, no matter how much they insisted, were not his betters. Starting with a bishop he now called *el capitán*. His disengaged father on battle manoeuvres again in his study below an attic bedroom. The old curmudgeon, pacing back and forth on creaking boards, rhythmically slapping his officer's swagger stick against his palm. A small boy's heart pounding in time with the sure knowledge that soon it would be his hide *el capitán* would be tanning. Time to pad out his pants with *The Picture Book of Mexican History*, those moustachioed heroes, his last defence against the tyranny of one patriarchs in particular.

But back to a slow train, incendiary of course, *el salamandra del sol* segmented as a worm, clanking across a blood red sky, trailing sparks to torch the tarbrush *mesas*. A string of fires under-lighting the haggard faces of ragged bands huddled atop the black hulks of freight cars. Divisions del Norté warming hands behind sandbagged gun emplacements, the revolutionaries sharing *mescal* and *muchachas*. Pretty girls with black hair tied up in red bandannas, swaying to revolutionary carillos played by revolutionary *mariachis*, while out front more villaistas rode the cow catcher, hanging over the rails on the look-out for mines left by the retreating federal army, sharing the cramped metal platform with a blanketed squaw clutching a baby to her breast and cooking *tortillas* over a flaming brazier.

'Where are you going?' came a shout from the darkness beyond. A peyote hunter, tall and lanky as a praying mantis crossed with bean pole, standing stock still, holding his white *sombrero* to his bare chest, arrested by that monstrous iron horse, snorting steam from a multitude of pipes and valves. Stopped before a busted section of track, where, under handheld flares, villaistas were laying out shining lengths of steel, levering pins and prising twisted rails from slatted sleepers.

'To the Town With No Name,' said the engine stoker, leaning on his shovel, presenting a coal-smudged face gashed by the whites of his eyes and teeth. 'Why don't you join us, *compadré?*'

'*En serio?*'

'*Cómo no?*' the stoker shrugged, 'When this civil war is your fiesta too!'

'You will then give me a poor peon with no place to call a home, a gun to kill the *gringo crillo* who has stolen the sacred lands of my Hutcholi ancestors?'

'*Si!*' came a deeper voice, as a bulky man in a rumpled tweed suit, topped by a dusty bowler hat tipped at a jaunty angle, stepped out into the light of phosphorous flares. 'I, Pancho Villa, not a foking hidalgo son of a someone, as maybe you think, but the son of a *mulata* abandoned by a *barquino* wineskin off the boat from Barcelona, who foking calls me "Doretero",[2] meaning my whole life I have to fight every *chingada* who insults my name, present you this pearl-handled pistol presented to me by General Scott of the US Army. And I promise you plenty bullets to kill the *Españolos* when we take that town. For four hundred years they have been stealing your treasure. The *oro* and the *plata* that are the sweat of the sun and the tears of the moon for the long-suffering sons of Lord Mictlán.'

Revolutions require planning, and action too. But revolutions also need financing, certainly more pocket money certainly than a young master ever dreamed of. But money, in a land with a history of economic troubles such as Mexico, does not have the same intrinsic worth as elsewhere. Especially then, when the peso was in free-fall, foreign capital had taken flight and the federal government only controlled about a third of the country – and even less of the people.

All this was somewhat pedantically explained in *The Picture Book of Mexican History*. A footnote providing further information about the currency then in circulation – Austrian shillings, French francs and Mexican pesos from the days of Maximilian, dollars, deutchmarks and sterling to name but a few.

In this paper-chase of symbols and signatures, the problem was to determine which script had value and which had none. At least until Generalísimo Villa made his famous 'Counterfeit Decree', giving notice of an imminent change in banking practice. Presently, only bills personally signed by himself or one of his commanders would be accepted as legal tender. A deadline was set providing ample opportunity to exchange old and soon-to-be-defunct moneys for the new notarised bonds. Predictably, when the deadline duly passed, revolutionary coffers were overflowing with sheaves of hoarded dollars and other denominations so essential to purchase arms and munitions across the border.

By this means, the illiterate maestro of economic planning achieved what Marx and Engels had only dreamt of – if only within the six northern states controlled by the Divisions del Norte. Their beloved generalísimo at a stroke demolishing a reality construct imposed on successive generations,

---

[2] Was Doretero Arango (Villa) the inspiration for the Johnny Cash song 'A Boy Named Sue' – different names, same story.

since King Croesus first coined it in Lydea. Yes, that fiction some people base their whole lives on, namely money. But even so oro and plata, those metals of the sun and moon, were as yet untarnished in the minds of the many celestial majesties retaining the power to promote new growth and breed worms in the hardened hearts of the criminal master classes.

There was one place where any amount of gold and silver counted for less than a mine of beans. The Town With No Name, under siege these past months by an advance contingent of *villaistas*. All supplies having long since run out, its defenders reduced to a diet of the scorpions then plaguing the town. Even each other, after cannibalism became a privilege of rank, by edict of *el capitán* of the black crow brigade. With his clipped moustache, permanent scowl and fixed stare, bearing an uncanny resemblance to the master of the presbytery and as mean a *hombre* as you could ever wish to meet. Transplanted by the dreams of a young master to the cauldron of revolution, defending the federal government treasury, the *Castillo de la Dinero*, its vaults stacked to bursting with ingots of useless oro and plata.

El capitán of the claw was fascinated with all things yellow, pus, bile, snot, diarrhoea, especially when it turned liquid and dribbled the inside of his legs, scaly with worm casts, as happened every full moon when the *gusano de diablo* sheds its skin. *El capitán* never missing the opportunity to commune with the golden-clawed monster transmitting electrical impulses to his brain. In the privacy of his personal latrine, on his knees, stirring body wastes in porcelain pan with a swagger stick. Before belting up his pressed khaki trousers and stepping out into the sun – the only yellow he didn't much like, since it burnt his sensitive skin.

Gold was another yellow he liked. Oh yes, he liked that very much, especially in 'bricks', the way the guards in the *Castillo de la Dinero*'s basements called ingots. Now that was something to build a house with. Sometimes sitting alone in his vaulted latrine, he would imagine his dream *castillo*. A gold edifice, of perhaps ten thousand bricks, topped by twenty-four carat towers that would never tarnish nor require any maintenance or cleaning, as they were made out of the precious metal.

The rooms inside, much the same, no decoration, just gold bricks, course on course, of course.

Yellow hair on busty bitches jackbooted up to lardy thighs, he also liked, especially the thatch he was forced to look up to. Well, perhaps that wasn't quite accurate, he was uncontrollably attracted to blondes, the bigger and more bossy the better, but their hair had to be the exact right straw shade, too light or dark a tone and his feelings turned to revulsion. Once he had found himself on a flea infested mattress in a brothel in the port of Veracruz with a most gorgeous jackbooted *fräulien* with the biggest boobs ever, just off a banana boat from Hamburg, but then, he just as he was about to press home his golden rod, he had noticed her flax was black at the roots.

Before leaving the establishment he was obliged to pay a hefty surcharge for the stripes the whore would bear for the rest of her days. A beating well worth the pesos and one he often thought about with pleasure afterwards.

The yellow he loved and, but for a golden-clawed worm pulling on his gut-strings, would have reigned supreme in his firmament, was the *amarillo* of the auricula primrose. His first sighting each time *primavera* came around never failing to induce a profound, if temporary, change of mood. A memory of how life could have been and yet might be, if only the *sierras* of the world would bloom primrose.

Scryed in wavering shadows on the sloping walls of an attic bedroom, the Grim Reaper scuttling desert sands. Or perhaps that scythe was really a claw dripping with venom? Hard to make out, those shadows doubling on deeper shadows. *Los cardinales*, a coven in conclave? A rookery of hooded crows crowded on a *caldera*? Centre circle, *las trés hermanitas*, no doubt about the identity of those three *brujas* stirring up seismic change in magma-mantled depths.

Slips of yew, tongue of *chihuaha*, liver of kabbalistic Jew, *gringo*'s nose, *tzitzimime* wing, *mescal* worm's sting ... yes, all that and more into a *caldera* went, while, far below, *el salamandra del sol* clanked ever-closer across desert plains.

Over the years Fiero had served Villa well. Husband and spouse were never as close, except perhaps in the original meaning of wife, the distaff mate who weaves the bed sheet. Bedfellows then? No. But accomplices, yes. Drawn together by the weird of their lives, the weft and woof holding together a great tapestry that was to set the design of the century. All the revolutions that followed patterned on theirs. Lenin and Trotsky, taking their cue from the Mexican triumvirate, Villa, Fiero and Zapata. As they in turn had been inspired by Prince Falling Eagle, executed after he refused to reveal the whereabouts of the Aztec treasure smuggled out of Tenochtitlán. And Cuauhtémoc's heroes? Surely, included among them, Votan, raised by the Tzendal tribe to the status of a god – the man who measured the world and gave meaning where before there was none. Indivisible with Wotan, master of the wode and primogenitor of revolution, who unchained the 'fury' and brought down the Roman Empire – Spartacus, Wallace, El Cid, Robespierre, Toussaint, Washington, Garibaldi, Paine, Muir, Urrea and countless unnamed heroes ... even a young master ... his avatars.

Stepping down from his box car, dripping warm blood onto cold rails below, Fiero scooped a handful of dirt and stood up, watching as a gust of warm wind scattered the sand slipping his blood-stained fingers towards the emerald light glittering on the distant *cordilleras*, heralding dawn over the eastern horizon. It was the time he called the hour of the dog, neither day nor night, when his mind was sharpest and only coyotes were about. A fine time for contemplating those three northern-facing peaks, hiding from the world the town where he had been born. The snow-capped summits of three little sisters, darkening as massive thunder heads reared from the south.

'Even the mountain gods are with us!' a nearby voice declared as, simultaneously, a distant clap of thunder rent the thin *sierra* air.

Fiero recognised that rich baritone. Just as well, for he had shot men for creeping up on him unawares. Interrupting those precious private moments, usually before the dawn, when he cast out the demons perpetually hitching rides on his shirt tails. Demons he saw skulking in long shadows at the end of day, lurking in the eyes of friends and strangers. Most especially in ejaculations his victims often voided, spurting their souls at the moment of death. Sperm stains he studied, just as Woden did aeons before. Killing was a dangerous business, and the worst of it was the voices others rationalised as conscience but Fiero knew were just ghosts with which the world was thickly populated. Legions he would one day join, but before that he meant to have himself a time adding to their numbers, something he thought of as pre-posthumous revenge for the horrible threat of life eternal promised by the priests who raised him in the Town With No Name.

'Pancho!' Fiero said, without turning round, a grin splitting his tombstone face as it always did when he spoke that name – the *cabrón* was a living legend, even if he was an asshole who would not take a drink. Despite that, there was still more fun in him than a *cantina* of *locos* with firecrackers exploding in their *pantalonés*.

'You are through talking to *puta gringos*?' Fiero demanded. 'At last we can get to the action?'

'Already the telegraph wires are singing, Fiero,' Villa said softly. 'Today their newspapers will be full of our victory in Zacatecas. The *gringos* like winners, not losers. Huh?'

'That side I leave to you, Pancho,' Fiero grinned fiercely, his love for his *companero* a black bird clawing at his breast. 'I am thinking of what I just learn from a federal army *padre* before he dies.'

Pausing, Fiero reached for his pack of *cigarillos* and lit a lucifer with a practised flick of a thumbnail, cupping hands, shielding the match from the dry Sonora wind, drawing deep on smoke while Pancho waited patiently, standing with hands clasped behind his long back, looking across the desert at the emerald light of dawn, spreading on the eastern horizon.

'There is a second tunnel into the town. Up to now only known only to the priests of the worm,' Fiero said, hoicking a great gob of spit just as a yellow-hooked scorpion scuttled across the sand by his boots, drowning the insect in a phlegm of a far deadlier predator, reminding the young master scrying the scene in wavering shadows on a bedroom wall that, in the armoury of arachnids and storytellers, hooks invariably count as claws, whereas the claw, in essence, is a multitude of things, pain mostly, but the torment of pleasure too.

13. PANCHITO

It takes claws to get a grip on reality - any reality - and in the casino of the cosmos, realities come in packs and are constantly shuffling. That's where blind hope comes in. The hope that springs eternal. The steady hope of young minds, dreaming a way out of penal regimes imposed by beastly parents. Like this tunnel undermining the defences of the Town With No Name in one direction and, in the other, signposting the fortress of a foreign god that, to Pancho Villa, was ultimate enemy, since on that rock lived the procurer of the suffering of his people over centuries. Presented with that choice, what other course did he have but to turn towards that citadel,[3] taking with him Rudolfo Fiero and the Divisions del Norté, leaving only a squad of *sappatistas* under the command of the young master Panchito, who, with his ferocity in combat, tantrums and transformations, more than made up for what he lacked in stature and experience. A pint-pot *generalísimo* in overlarge pantalones, it was true, but one for whom he had high hopes.

Over the centuries the tunnel had served the priests well, its worn passages worm-smoothed and beaten by the traffic of countless sandaled feet. Papal nuncios among the delegations passing unseen in and out of the Town With No Name, spiriting away native treasures to gather dust in the vaults of the Vatican. Heretical manuscripts, such as the famous Codex of Uxmal, which included a catalogue of secret names of god

---

[3] In the annals of warfare perhaps the most daring unrecorded chapter was Pancho Villa's underground assault on the Vatican, culminating in the capture of a sacred gourd stolen from his people. Pancho finally died in 1922, his last words: 'Tell them I said something clever.' Three years after he was buried, his body was dug up and his skull removed to a private ossuary in Boston, which houses a vast collection of stolen bones of people who, over the ages, earned the enmity of an ancient secret society, which numbers many US presidents, living and dead, among its members. Pancho Villa's skull is displayed in a case on a shelf alongside the skulls of Cromwell, Thomas Paine, Eva Peron, Geronimo and Charlie Chaplain to name but a few.

known only to the Tzendals, supposedly burnt in the sixteenth century by Bishop Landa. Relics like the sacred Gourd of Coatlicue, containing the sacred seed of Quetzalcoatl, which must be rattled at the end of every epoch of the sun, to summon the new world.

A new world Panchito longed for, this worm passage tunnelled under ditch-dull realities, where rules were undeviating as rails set on beds of stone, to a door fixed by blind hope in the sacristy of a cathedral that was perhaps the best least-known wonder of Christendom. Its towers and transepts, flying buttresses, fluted vaults of the thousand polished porphyry pillars purloined from the temple of Amun-Ra on the banks of the Nile; the vast echoing basilica, its pilasters, pediments and niches crowded by gargoyles and gilded statuary; the rock crystal rose transept window representing untold generations of indentured native labour, every pane painstakingly ground by hand; the interior of the great dome painted with an enormous trompe l'oeil picturing Shem descending in a blaze of glory to rescue his 'chosen' people; while the exterior of the dome was sheathed in Aztec gold, smelted, it was whispered, from the great disc of the sun and the girdle of Coatlicue, plundered from the temples of Tenochitlán – all of it shaped out of the magma of creation by a questing young mind ...

Questing. That was the ticket, but where? Into the dark continent located between his none-too-clean ears ... largely unexplored, with only a few scattered settlements at the confluences of turgid rivers and strategic high places, such as the Town With No Name. Nameless because ... because names were power, marking the awesome finality of things. The world might end if he let slip that secret. Better to forget, buffeted as he was by so many strictures from without ... contradictory admonitions from father and housekeeper, acting like leaden clouds, piling up to obscure the sun, causing thunderstorms, hail and dyslexia ... double-double trouble in later years, when exiled from home and hearth, let down by all but a few of those he had counted as friends, he wandered far and wide, confused by countless correspondences internal and external, searching for himself in a looking-glass world. All of it shaped out of the magma of creation by an amnesiac god, gone walkabout these past billion years, searching for his maker beyond the stars, Chronos, the father of time, who ate his children, as good a name as any other for the bungling architect of creation, imposing strictures, where there had been none before ... prescriptions and admonitions ... rules made to be broken by those who followed. Questers and jokers, shuffled out of the pack, cast aside by the cosmic croupier, going their own way, shaping reality out of torments imposed by others, the unknown soldiers of the future, living unrecognised by their fellows. Moving the dead weights of the masses with the power of their dreams.

The captain (mentioned twice in dispatches) was not amused, to put it mildly. Pipsqueaks, like that demon spawn of his loins, should be seen and not heard, obey orders without question and, like good little mice, should only squeak when squoken to. He wasn't a monster, as his son seemed to believe, nor was he a philandering bishop, as the young master had once accused him, nor a kabbalist in league with the nine lords of Xibalba (wherever that was), plotting coups and pestilence, destabilising perfectly legitimate regimes the world over, a notion so completely irrational it spoke volumes for the state of the boy's mind, either that or it had been implanted by his mother, a woman much subject to delusional fancies, who once claimed she was a sword swallower run away from the circus and would keep insisting her wedding vows only obligated her to keep the former presbytery clean, serve three hot meals a day (never once in all the years served on time), in return for the housekeeping expenses – and certainly not conjugal rights.

Not that the captain was too bothered in that regard, the fires of passion having cooled to an arctic frigidity since that fateful first meeting when, taking a shortcut over the moors after West Wickham Cross, he had stumbled upon her bathed in golden sunshine, spreadeagled in the heather, performing her devotional rituals to Helios, as she explained later, putting him in a compromising position, from which he sometimes doubted if he would ever recover.

The hastily arranged marriage, another of her mad notions, a midnight wedding in a deconsecrated church operating as a furniture repository, the ceremony performed by a part-time pastor, apparently some Lapland relation from north of the Arctic Circle, an imbecile reindeer herder hardly able to recite the matrimonial vows, bringing a curtain down on his bachelorhood. That perfect state every man is born to, and every man despises until it is too late. Alas, he had fallen prey to the most immoral and unscrupulous women it had been his misfortune to meet.

That first meeting so precisely matching his masturbatory fantasies of amatory assignations with amazons in lofty public places, he sometimes suspected she was a harpy sent by the Norns to punish him for wasted seed. A suspicion that would lead one to suspect the retired captain was a wanker and of a paranoiac turn of mind, as indeed he was, a tendency induced by the strange events that that regularly befell him. Happenings invariably anticipated in dreams, both nocturnal and waking, and all the more puzzling for that reason. An idle fancy, a name or a face would take root in his mind and, before too long, something akin or approximating would take place, leading him to suspect either that time followed a circular direction and was forever coiling back on itself, crossing and re-crossing arbitrary but nodal points – worm singularities, as some modern scientists called them – or that there was some supernatural agency at work.

His Helga, despite her harpy origins, was just a fact of life he had to get along with. But relations with his son were a different matter. Badly brought up and boorish as the lad was, knowing only the headlong charge, all was not lost yet. Perhaps the best thing would be to remove the boy from his mother's malign influence. A regime of boarding school and summer camps, and hang the expense. A course suggested by his confidant Mr Crook, as good a friend as a man could hope to have. The lawyer never interrupting a captain's interminable discourses, which always had the same end in view, the erection of a monument of might and majesty, casting a suitably long and eclipsing shadow. Testifying for all time one mortal's life and achievements. That last entry a blank space in his scheme of things for, though he had always known he was destined for greatness, indeed that the Norns themselves had decreed it should be so, chanting over their fabled cauldron that doubled as a whirlpool, never seen until it was too late by sailing ships plying the icy waters in search of the Isles of the Blessed at the very limits of the world, he could never quite decode that pre-determining primordial sentence. Even though there still resounded within the wyrd that was the warp and woof of him, Clotho, the blind sister, singing as she span, announced a life of worth and grace that would raise a star in the firmament to light the footsteps of those that followed. Yes, something like that, he was sure. But what the star? Where the constellation? His firmament had been obscured by clouds rolling up from the west ever since he'd taken that shortcut across the heath and over Wickham Moor. Unbeknownst crossing into one of those nodal singularities when time worms back on itself. Too preoccupied to see the danger presaged by dreams and omens over the years, until it was too late. Yes, he could not blame himself for falling, knowing as he did, no man of mettle could have withstood her siren lure.

Her ample charms, acting upon him as the sticky secretions of a Venus fly trap, as drawn into that clawed embrace, he fell, his futile struggles, only ensnaring him further. His bachelor idyll fast fading to an arcadia in memory, golden days when winged thoughts were as clear and far ranging as the beam of the Pharos Lighthouse, seventh Wonder of the World, calling to ships over stormy seas, warning of submerged reefs, the Fata Morgana and sundry other dangers, lighting triremes and barques to harbour and safety, bearing exotic cargo from every quarter of the known world, and some from beyond, fabulous feathers of birds of paradise from the garden of the west, 'Quecha' cocaine for the sons of pharaohs and their courtesans, silk and sandalwood from Cathay, unicorn horns and giant ostrich eggs from the court of Prester John, the despotic but benevolent Christian emperor of sub-Saharan Africa, where men were blue and grew nine foot tall, possessed two heads and lived more than five hundred years.

All this recorded in the scrolls and manuscripts of the Alexandria Library, like that city's lighthouse, the greatest in the world, containing the totality of knowledge then known to man, most of its four hundred thousand volumes consumed by the great fire in AD 391 bringing the curtain down on the Heroic Age, ushering in the Dark Age that was to last a thousand years, when all Europe, with the exception of its western fringes, reverted to savagery and men became as brutish as swine. All this predicted by Erasmus of Phillipa, patriarchal philosopher, kabbalist and cosmologist, founder of Alexandria Alternative School of Anatomy, and propounder of the 'Grand Central Theory,' also known as the 'Junction Box Theory'. The first attempt to explain nature of the world and everything, rubbished by his great contemporary Aristophanes – who also dismissed the writings of Anaxarchus[4] – and later rejected by Copernicus, but, despite this, in the opinion of a captain, was a profound contribution to the sum of all that is known, even though there was no monument nor mausoleum dedicated to his name.

A matter the captain meant to put to rights, just as soon as he published his magnus opus, intriguingly entitled The Book of Tell Tale Signs and Other Portents and, including among the essays, treaties on Erasmus' great works lost in that calamitous fire, reconstructed by proven kabbalistic method from the sole surviving text, a charred papyrus, inherited from his unknown mother, according to the Coptic nuns who first raised him, a blonde giantess run away from the harem of the last Caliph of Cairo, who was known to favour big women.

How big is big? Big is big, it goes without saying. But big is bigger than small, and small is bigger than wee. Using a well-tried kabbalistic formula, 4.5 counts as 1.25 when comparing big titties to big willies. Unfortunately, given his predilection for oversized broads the captain was not over endowed in that department, at least in his own estimation, downsizing his own while over estimating his rivals', usually glimpsed in stolen sideways glances and always in underground urinals. One penis in particular – a close encounter in the Bakerloo Station toilets on the Piccadilly Line, wartime London – providing the inspiration for his damascene conversion, when scales fell from his eyes, as belatedly he realised even a weenie cannon can fire a mighty shot, and the phallic

---

[4] When Alexander learned from Anaxarchus of the infinite number number of worlds, he wept, but then he laughed with joy when Anaxarchus told him of the openings into these worlds, and how he might seek them. Asked by Anaxarchus what prize could justify so perilous a journey, Alexander replied, 'That for which I sacked the cities of Asia, and searched near enough a world, the treasure with no name.'

symbolism of Erasmus' speculations on the origins of the universe at last became clear.

As it says in the good book, knock and you will be answered – well, eventually. But what if nothing happens? Kick heartily, and again if needs must. But what if there is still no answer, and that door has been reinforced by gold plates inches thick, as was recently ordered by *el capitán*, barred, bolted and barricaded from without? When all else fails, and authority in its citadels, in this case a cathedral, proves deaf to the clamour below, take the revolutionary option, blow away that door and some of the foundations too, as happened after the young *generalísimo* directed his *sappatistas* to lay charges, pressing the plunger himself, fulfilling an ambition nursed since nursery years, ever since he first learnt about dynamite and its creative potential for change.

KA-BOOOOM!! Surely they used kryptonite, thought the young *generalísimo*, for the blast seemed out of all proportion to the tiny amount of sticky stuff impressed into hinges and locks.

KA-BOOOM-BOOOOM!! Roll that one again, considered the pint-pot generalisimo, as came a series of answering echoes from lower depths, the blast reverberating cavernous walls below the catacombs, where hunter's bones lay strewn with the skeletal remains, sabre-toothed tigers, long-toed lemurs, ground sloths, giant hominids, hairy mammoths, long-horned bison, even a few creatures of legend, basilisks, chimeras, among the predators and prey, entombed a hundred thousand years, ever since the violent cataclysm that ended the world known as '4 Sun' by the Maya, fire descending from the sky, as a comet crashed into the earth.

KA-BOOM-BOOM-BOOM!! Now there were counter echoes, even louder, from above, peeling detonations that sounded exactly like rolling thunder, which of course they were. The thunder storm arrived right on cue, blanking out the explosions, even to the Brethren of the Worm, celebrating vespers in the basilica a few levels above. The subject of the evening sermon, a brief summation of the events that led to the great schism with the mother church in 1859, coinciding with the publication of the Origin of the Species by Natural Selection by the false prophet Charles Darwin (also the author of the lesser-known Vegetable

Mould and Earthworms). Father O'Flaherty giving the lowdown on the dramatic discovery of the fossilised hulk of a boat in an icy cave near the summit of the highest of three little sisters, which could only have been Noah's Ark. Ten emerald tablets found inside, giving the ultimate truth that this world is a lie, all walking, crawling, grunting, talking, living forms, with the exception of the progeny of the one worm, were but incubuses dreamed up by a childish god, petulant in his tantrums and transformations, given to destroying his creations in fits of pique, using any ready means; piss, vomit, fire and asteroid impact. This revelation causing the brethren to reinterpret holy writ and discard all but one of the books of the Bible after the story of Noah, that exception being the Epistle of John, since it dwelt on the wickedness of man, retribution and coming calamity when the world of '5 Sun' would finally end by wormquake, as the golden-clawed denizen of the deeps roused from slumber at last.

Although all but one of Erasmus' works perished by fire – and even that of doubtful provenance, since the papyrus in the captain's possession had never been authenticated by any accredited expert in the field – the pedant is not a complete cipher. Aristophanes described him as a big man with an ugly red nose, covered in bumps and gristle, which was his most readily recognisable feature, 'marking him out from other mortals, as a cracked pot stands out on the potter's shelves'.

Simeon of Tarsus, with whom Erasmus was personally acquainted, said he was 'much given to making jokes' and was an excellent storyteller, though his stories generally erred on the 'fantastical side, dwelling as they did on the junctures and dislocations between the worlds of gods, men, and lesser creatures'.

Another source, the blind poet Hecatitus the Simple, insisted he was a 'down to earth salt of serious aspect, who invariably rose a'fore the cock crow, and was always diligently occupied in one study or other'.

What all the commentators did agree on, however, was that Erasmus disappeared during a lightning storm in the Sinai Desert in 63 BC.

According to one apocryphal account, 'the wrath of Amon descended upon the braggart in a great whirling fog. And when the black cloud finally lifted? Erasmus of Phillipae was no more to be seen'.

A singular occurrence that has passed into history without much examination.

'Poor old Erasmus of Phillipa passed away.'

'Oh yes? And how did he go?'

'In a thunder storm. A black whirling cloud descended and bore him away!'

'You don't say! Happens all the time to these new philosophers, an occupational hazard, I suppose. But what do you expect when you go round impugning the gods as he did. Why only last week in the market I heard him ...'

Just so. Always plenty scoffers about with ready opinions, yes, too many around in old Alexandria to include here. What mattered to the captain was the manner of his hero's death. Uninformed historians, passing over the remarkable occurrence with scarce a backwards glance, unknowing or unmindful of Erasmus' words on the subject, as quoted by Hecatitus the Simple:

'Since death is the apogee of life, the moment is a study in itself. Great warriors seek glorious death in battle, miserable misers seek miserable ends, while seekers groping for answers all their lives, find truth at last.'

Trawling back from that moment, decoding the 'Alexandria Papyrus', the captain found it appropriate that Erasmus had been uplifted to heaven on a tornado, since so many of his speculations had concerned the forces set into motion by whirling twisting things, the 'wormholes' that were the windows and doorways into unseen worlds, 'through which gods and demons flitted at will'.

Time, Erasmus maintained, was a collective conspiracy; a story driven mass fabrication, born of blinkered lives, and a need to delude ourselves into believing events proceed in a sequential pattern. Life is chaos, and any sense of continuity a complete illusion. Reality, as he explained it, was a spherical envelope existing in a void, perhaps populated by countless such envelopes, maintained by the thoughts of the resident sentient creatures - certain individuals, whether by intention or unconscious attribute, in dreams or waking, possessing the ability to rupture the skein holding back the void, causing a temporary or even terminal collapse of that reality, as happens at the end of every 'age'.

The foregoing being the cause of many otherwise unexplained events, such as the sense of knowing a place before one has visited it, or foretelling the day and manner of one's death, as Erasmus did. Predicting the day a wormhole would spirit him back to a far country, where friends were waiting. This distant land none other than the fabled garden of the golden apples,[5] sought by questers and *sappatistas* alike, seeking escape from ditch-dull replicant realities, each simulacrum a paler copy than the last, the wish fulfilment of bureaucrats and legislators dreaming of open-prison societies staffed by sadists, graveyard worlds where hope lay long buried, patrolled by police and padres, where rules ruled, disorder reigned and crime paid only those in the know.

Those in the know, including the captain, transposed to a revolutionary reality that was anything but dull, at the behest of his worm master ... his son and heir, though *el capitán* would hardly have recognised him, disguised as the lad was in thigh-high buckskin boots, improbably droopy moustaches under an overlarge *sombrero*, putting his best foot forwards, determined to roust occupying vermin from the Town With No Name ... This was his reality and he wouldn't share it.

Never mind those armed guards, sheltering from torrential hailstones, crack federal troops huddled over in the entrances to those mines or that the hook-nosed *capitán*, mumbling under his breath, looking out from under a striped awning, anxiously checking for signs the thunderstorm was abating, was his father. No, that was a louse, parking his behind where he wasn't welcome, touring the plaza in his palanquin in the style of an Indian raj, supported on the stout shoulders of four brawny soldiers, circling a great erection rising wraithlike above the Town With No name, its upper reaches lost in plumes of mist ...

What was *el capitán* so rabidly mumbling?

'Money. Money. Money. Money. Money. Money. Heheh. Money. Money. Money. Money. Money. Heheh. Money. Money. Money. Money.

---

[5] In most accounts the garden is guarded by a giant worm or dragon, this perhaps a clue as to the means of getting there.

Money. Heheh. Money. Money. Money. Money. Money. Heheh. Money. Money. Money. Heheh. Money. Money. Money. Heheh. Money. Money. Money. Heheh. Money. Money. Money. Money. Money. Money. Heheh. Money. Money. Money. Money. Heheh. Money. Money. Money. Money. Heheh . Money. Money. Money. Heheh. Money.'

The word is so real, so central to so many realities, so rooted in shit, it did not distort or lose its meaning, despite the occasional snigger, even after the foregoing repetitions. Most words begin to defray after three or four, while some words, carry little if any meaning – at least in this bubble reality – like god, for instance ...

God. God. God. God. God. God. God. Cod.[6]

God. God. God.

The word just refuses to stand up and bark, unlike its reverse, the word 'dog', which is ready to wag a tail with just one saying.

God, give me some money! A prayer that never works. One has to apply a different appellation if one wants the sky to shit gold. Such as, 'Panchito, give me some money!' The pint-pot *generalisimo* on the case, with his personally notarised revolutionary bills illustrated by his smiling countenance on one side, and on the other a hand drawn map giving the location of a crock of gold, at the ready. Just in case *el capitán*, with his machinations succeeded in rupturing the envelope, and punching through to the void, bringing an end to all this. The last chapter ... the last page ... and all because one word was done to death. A word no amount of repetitions could unstitch. A word that moved men's lips, more than any other, whether waking, in sleep or in prayer. That word was money, defraying because of the extraordinary conditions prevalent in that Mexican reality, the cumulative effects of hyper-inflation and so many devaluations, the collapse of the banking system, the bandit insurgency, the corruption, the worm ...

Money might have lost much of its value, but oro, that metal so beloved of Croesus, and all the worm masters that followed, still reigned supreme in the firmament; as long as it did, the grand central reality

---

[6] The Noviet, an Eskimo people, living on the island of Novia Sibir in the Laptev Sea, believe they are descended from the which is the Milky Way, still lighting the sky at night.

through which all wormholes were routed would hold. But remove that pillar - that mighty trunk of Yggdrasil, the world tree - and reality collapses, or so reasoned *el capitán*. He was no worm master, with the forces of the multiverse at his command. The appellation of common jobbing torturer will do, he thought, looking up at the Babel of wooden scaffolding, pit props plundered from below, causing the collapse of mines and catacombs as far afield as Rome itself, every tree from a hundred miles around, supporting the great bronze barrel aligned on the sun. A thousand feet high already and, with each casing added, mounting ever higher.

Like a salamander, segmented of course, *el capitán* thought, wiping away a tear, temporarily blinded, as at last the sun emerged from a silver-scrolled cumulus that promised an end to the storm. Just as well, for that was the moment Panchito chose to descend from the cathedral, taking the steps three at a time, running towards concealment behind the great pile of ingots, stacked high as a house ramparted with battlements and towers. Golden bullets, piled in the shadow of the great barrel, ready to fire at the sun, when *el capitán* judged the moment was right.

That moment was fast approaching. High noon, thirteen o'clock by local time. Denouement for the reality maintained since the Conquest by the thoughts of its indigenous population, the vast majority living in fear and trepidation, the value of the pesos in their pockets shrinking in proportion to the rising paranoia, terrified as to what might come next, the approaching Shemite millennium, brought on by the prophesies of a local, supposedly native, seer, el espíritu, who no one knew, but everyone knew of - actually *el capitán*'s mouthpiece, Father O' Flaharty.

Mr Crook by another name, disseminating rumours through the confessional, sometimes disguised as a *borracho* in the local *cantinas*, telling of the approaching end, when six thousand years after creation, the sun of the fifth millennium would crash to earth and worms would breed in the gathering darkness, eating everything from within, multiplying exponentially until at last there was nothing left to eat and they consumed themselves. The new world[7] that followed, sterile and dead as the moon

---

[7] New world order: see any US dollar bill for details, under Nuit's eye in the pyramidion.

itself, where nothing moved except long shadows, tracking over a vast desolation caused by the greed of man.

It was done. Even as the derrickmen up on the scaffolding slotted the last bolts into place, a squadron of troops stepped back from the breech, more than a thousand feet below. Saluting smartly at *el capitán*, looking on from the palanquin, signalling that their job was complete, the house of gold successfully dismantled and ten thousand bricks tamped down in the barrel, bedded on a kiloton of explosives, and the fuse at last laid.

A long blue twist of paper extending perhaps ten feet from the breech, reminiscent of home fireworks, catherine wheels, roman candles and the like – and, for scholars of Erasmus, the twisters that arrived unheralded, spiriting away worm masters to regions beyond our ken, leaving only mystery in their wake. Worm masters despised by *el capitán*, belatedly realising after a lifetime of struggle, he would never join that elect band, now bent on revenge and bringing the whole edifice of fiction down upon himself, firing the greatest store of gold ever assembled in Mexico, oro amassed since the Conquest, the sweat of the sun and tears of more than a million slaves toiling their whole lives in absolute darkness. An appalling act of annihilation about to be witnessed by the federal troops assembled around the plaza, all the captives who had survived up to now, along with perhaps a thousand miners brought up from below, bringing down the sun on the world and ending a young master's dreams.

But not if a *generalísimo* had something to do with it. Panchito, at that moment hunched up in darkness, atop a great pile of gold, his chin resting on tremulous knees, hands clamped to his ears, eyes screwed shut, biting his lip as *el capitán*, a sardonic smile breaking out on his face, lit the long blue twist of paper and stepped back to admire his handiwork ...

There is no point even attempting to describe the awesome power of that detonation, the magnitude of the explosion, the force of the blast, sending the young master rocketing upwards in a shower of gold.

El capitán was no more. That evil genius intent on wiping the whole programme of fictions – crashing reality central – had been erased himself. Backfire from the breech, combined with the thunderous detonation reverberating the surrounding mountains brought half a little sister down on the town. The landslide, burying it deeper than Pompeii or even Herculaneum, preserving it for future archaeologists to mull over: the mystery of the giant bronze tubes with their odd serpentine stippling scattered around the plaza; the native miners and their oppressors, federales and crillos, all hostilities forgotten, cowering and defiant, huddled in groups, in attitudes of terror or acceptance. Perhaps the most poignant of the stifled lives, a mestizo trying to shelter his woman, in turn shielding their child, clutching a puppy to her chest, clenching in one fist a perfectly preserved revolutionary bill featuring the smiling face of a *generalísimo* on one side and a curious map on the other. All these wonders as nothing compared to the treasures of the cathedral, the great altar preserved completely intact, with its antependium of the flayed skin of the golden calf, with mummified Brethren of the Worm abasing themselves before it, their prayers unheard by the absconding young rascal who had dreamed up this world. But nowhere in the rubble was there found any trace of *el capitán*, annihilated by the wrath of a worm master, the back-blast from the breech, consuming him as if he had never been.

All this experienced by a retired captain, holed up in his book-lined study, hiding from Helga the harpy housekeeper in the presbytery of prescriptions, as a worrisome worm perturbation, a sudden shifting deep within his being, as if all the kabbalistic ciphers encrypting his mainframe programmes had in a flash been rewritten. Confused, he retired early to bed, not realising 'till morning he had suffered a stroke, when he became aware of a paralysis affecting his organs of speech. This perhaps the ultimate reason the young master was cast out to Elias Ashmole's Reformatory for Wayward Boys. Only once to see his father again, a shared loss made greater by their lack of communication, the hectoring pedant, transformed to a mumbler overnight. Hoarding words as misers hoard gold. Only by dint of enormous effort marshalling his forces, that one visit to the boarding school, very much the martinet, sitting upright with his black fedora shading his eyes in the back of his hired chauffeur driven car, ticking the lad off, telling him to mind his Ps and Qs, unable to conceal his irritation when the boy asked after his mother, the housekeeper having absconded with most of his stocks and shares – more than a lifetime's accumulations – since he had inherited the portfolio. The bitterness of the lengthy divorce case, settling like fallout, shrouding any happiness they'd shared in the past. Obliterating a far country as if it had never been, accessible only to a worm master, in his childish dreams of the orchards of the sun, playing with the three sisters he always wished he had ... Las Malinchés, sharing the same face, as only identical sisters can, waiting ... that next world, a worm away in Uncle Joe's *cantina* in the Town With No Name.

EPILOGUE

'Uncle?' That's what I said, the familial word, unbidden, spilling parched and gummy lips, as, prising sweat-sodden cheeks from the sticky tabletop, blurrily I made out a greying turkey buzzard, an ugly hooter, lumps and bumps breaking out all over, foreshortened and massive, pushing up to mine.

'At last you begin to guess at the truth of our relationship and my responsibilities towards you!' Joe beamed, clapping a spatula hand on my shoulder, setting another *mescal* on the table before me. 'Si, I am your father's brother and, by the terms of the pact we made so long ago, his keeper also. Though I have to tell you I have been failing in that department recently.' Pausing, he laid a hand on heart. 'Not through any fault of my own,' he added gravely, 'But because Helga the hotelkeeper refuses to hand over his immortal remains.'

'Hold on a minute,' I gasped, gulping the contents of the tumbler, slopping *mescal* down my shirt front in my desperation to clear the fogs of a monumental hangover. 'When did you make this pact? And why?'

'It was after he rescued me from the only wadi in the whole of the Sinai Desert deep enough to drown a rat in. Even though your father was then serving as a captain in the British Eighth Army, at first took me for an Egyptian spy, with the generosity that was the mark of his nature, gave me el beso de la vida.'

'You mean mouth to mouth?' I interjected, feeling the fogs clearing at last.

'*Es* the same,' Joe said, 'But I prefer *beso de la vida*, since it sounds so much better than mano a mano.' He lofted bushy eyebrows. 'How you say – resuscitation? It put me his debt and made us brothers, even though I hated his guts for the worm he had in there.'

'But what the hell were you doing? Drowning in the only wadi in the Sinai?'

'*Es* where blind chance dropped me.' Joe shrugged. 'I am surprised you have to ask, a worm master like you, knowing as you do of the holes between the worlds from all the adventures you have while snoring in my *cantina*.'

'Now I'm confused again,' I said, shaking my head, only partially clearing reforming fogs. 'You mean I've been here all the time?'

'All the time?' Joe tut-tutted just like a turkey.

'What sort of *loco* question is that for a worm master to ask?' Languidly raising a hand, he snapped fingers.

'Malinché,' he called without even bothering to turn round, 'Come and join us, and bring another *mescal, sans el gusano del diablo*, for my dear nephew here, and a cervesa for me.' Smiling steely, he leaned closer 'till our heads were almost touching. 'While we wait for the girls to do some work for a change, lees'en hard, and lees'en well,' he rasped. 'I have a message from your father.'

How many Mexicans does it take to pour a *mescal?*

In the Town With No Name, at least three, on the evidence of my own eyes. Or perhaps I was seeing in triplicate, except there was only one bottle in view. The same impassive face, however, looming over – las dos equis and always looking for a 'Y', as Helga called them. The weird sisters. Las Malinchés, for the want of a better name.

'Allow me to introduce you,' Joe announced.

'Clotho, Atropos and Lachesis,' he chuckled wryly. 'Your sisters and everyone else's sisters.'

'Everyone's?' I reiterated. 'How is that possible?' Joe shrugged. '*Cómo no*, dear nephew? When es the three fates stood before you.'

'Now I know I'm dreaming,' I said, giving each an enquiring look in turn, reciting names and assigning duties – just as my father declaimed Hesiod over my pram all those years before – 'Clotho, the spinner of the thread of life; Lachesis, blind chance, who determines the lot of every man; Atro ... po,' I stammered, noticing for the first time, the third sister was holding a pair of shears to her side, 'Who at the end cuts the thread ...'

Joe wasn't winding me up, or anything like that. Nor had my time arrived. The girls, or should I say Norns, were just being sociable, though at first it didn't seem that way. Their uniform expressions unchanging as they sat across the table, sipping iced Tia Maria in long glasses, staring into the middle distance dolefully. Sisters? Yes. Peas from the same pod. But confess I was distracted. That message Joe had passed on earlier preying on my mind.

'The crook at the end of the rainbow, *es* Meester Crook!'

'Come again Joe? Don't you mean crock?'

'No, crock *es* good, but Crook *es* better.'

'Are you trying to tell me my father's trusted advisor and most loyal friend has been up to no good?' Snarling, Joe slammed a fist on the table. 'Now you begin to get the picture, dear nephew. All your problems trace back to that *cabrón*. The cause of your estrangement with your father, and your father's troubles with Helga.' He sighed mournfully. 'You know they murdered him, exactly as he predicted they would.'

'How?' I demanded.

'A leetle snake they slip into his bed.'

'Was it an asp by any chance?'

'So you do know something?' Joe's eyes narrowed.

'No,'. I shook my head, 'Just a remark my father once made about my mother. "Crocodile emotions with the bite of an asp".'

'Perhaps at last you understand, it was to protect you he sent you away to boarding school,' Joe said, placing a finger to his lips as *las Malinchés* loomed into view with our drinks.

Another *mescal* and another *mescal*, and I was beginning to get the picture. Time and their separate characters had wrought subtle changes on their physiognomy.

Clotho, despite her haughty mien – the mask she presented to the world – was the most remote of the sisters. Atropos, the coldest, possessing an icy radiance, chilling even at a distance. But in Laechelis I detected, or thought I did, a glimmer of interest behind her blind stare.

The all-knowing sisters. Blind to their brother before them, yet missing nothing. This the triumvirate of *brujas* who had overthrown my father. One little snip from Atropos' shears and his life was over. Even though I never knew, I knew. His passing preceded by portents diverse and multifarious, one of which was a dream, where he appeared at my door, and in abject tones, pleaded with me ...

'To do what?'

'Die for me, young master, that I may live.'

'Fuck off!' I told him, appalled at what he was asking. 'After all you told me about the sisters, and you try to trick them in this way.'

It never did occur to me to complain that he hadn't been in touch for years.

But yet he pleaded, like Nebuchadnezzar, chewing the cud of his wasted days, on hands and knees, weeping saline tears, until I cast him out, into the teeth of that howling black gale. Damned but not quite out, my life hanging by a thread as, behind the scenes, *el capitán* attempted to renegotiate the deal.

Snip, snip. Even though I never knew, I knew. Those shears were closing and a male of the ancient Inkethaton line had to pay, Atropos would not be denied her quota.

Night-time-real-time, but dream-time yet, and I was walking across a city park, about to cross a path seemingly rolled over the sod, when suddenly I became aware of two tall and immensely thin men in black with beak noses approaching rapidly from either side - no sound accompanying their certain gait, their long steps equidistant and hypnotically matched as I approached the nexus, wanting to turn round and flee, but somehow unable. At the last moment, by enormous effort quickening my pace, passing through the closing gap, just before their trajectories crossed, feeling as I did so a thread shear away at my back, knowing then I had lost someone very dear. My father? How could that be? I hated the old bastard.

Another dream. A rolling verdant tapestry as wide as my life - at strategic intervals, playmates, playthings and a centrally placed clock, with the same scene racing across the dials, the sun and the waxing and waning moon alternating across the face. Along with a cavalcade of castles, hovels, milkmaids-a-milking and soldiers-a-drumming under passing clouds and pursuing stars. While above in a broader, bigger sky, my anguished father - *el capitán* no longer - looked up to the blue heavens with tears rolling his cheeks. Tears that were his last bequest and parting gift, as his imploring face faded from view, becoming pearls of the finest blue water, strung across the sky. And then I knew who had died, knowledge I retained on waking, even though I couldn't quite believe the colossus had fallen. The same day as I left New York for Mexico, on a mission to find the rest of my family, lost all these years.

Mexico, for Christ's sake, I'd never been there - except in my *loco* imagination perusing *The Picture Book of Mexican History*, yet at every turn of the trail, it all seemed so familiar - until I arrived in the town, encountered that murderous mother and swallowed the worm, ever after searching a maze of rooms and passages for a way out, desperate to escape my family - what was left of them - dead and alive, those that had been there at the beginning, there at the end, as the once-great tree withered, beset by *tzitzimimes*, harpies and conquistador dreams ... whole again, my little man *and* my nagual restored by the sacrifice of a double in a stone tree - a fair exchange in the circumstances. Writing this account for the want of something better to do.

Waiting for the day when the tunnel to the outside world would re-open and I could finally escape into the greater reality of Tláltipec.

One more thing about *el capitán*, my father in his altered worm state. What the fuck was he doing, you may ask, hanging out in *las tres hermanitas*? It's a good question. One day I suppose I'll find out, when at last I run out of thread and find myself under his command again - perish the thought - serving time in some theatre of combat or another. Who knows? Perhaps with the vanguard of sacrifices, doing battle against the astral armies of the stars and protecting the sun on its perilous journey through eternal night. Perhaps that's where I'll find him.

FIN

POSTDATA

How much of the above is true? In the tradition of storytellers I'm tempted to say the lot, but I guess no one, no matter how credulous, could swallow that worm whole even if it happened to be the case. I am prepared to swear, however, on the bones of my beloved father, that the town, as represented, is accurate to the facts as I have been able to assemble. The precise name is another question, as is the treasure, or treasures – including a cache of gold coins stashed below a cathedral vault, all of which I wholeheartedly bequeath to that perspicacious reader who picks up on the clues and gets there first. As far as I am concerned you're welcome, just so long as you don't mention my name to that mother, still managing that renamed hotel.

Before I depart ... There's one loose end that needs rolling. Remember the barrel-chested *borracho* with the most annoying nasal snicker sharing my seat, swapping sneers for cigarettes as the little bus ascended the cobbled road towards the tunnel, that first journey into town? I met him again, oddly enough, the same day I completed the first draft of the foregoing account, near to the summit of the highest of *las tres hermanitas*. Did I say near? I was yet a long way off, about to give up, with another few hours of hard slog before me, when he jumped out, from where I don't know – since there was a complete absence of cover in that vast plateau – and, sniggering madly in his idiosyncratic way, ran, shoved and dragged me to the top, where I promptly collapsed, the closest I've come to expiring, at least that's the way it felt. When I finally stood up, I could see neither hide nor hair of him for a hundred miles around. One thing I can report, however, is that, within a few feet of where he'd delivered me, was a solitary rose bush with the sweetest, most mellifluent perfume. Just one sniff enough to convince me that the divine is yet among us, and the arcadia of the Americas, known to the ancients as the garden of the golden apples of the sun, is much closer than I had thought.

LAST WORD

Oh, and one more thing, unlike the mother described in this novel, mine is a sweet, rather elderly lady much given to charitable works. To the best of my knowledge she never worked in the circus, is not a serial killer – except perhaps of bugs in her garden, and is far too small to be a troll ...

Printed in Great Britain
by Amazon